HOW WE
DISAPPEARED

Jing-Jing Lee

ONEWORLD

A Oneworld Book

First published in Great Britain, the Irish Republic and
Australia by Oneworld Publications, 2019

This paperback edition published 2020
Reprinted 2020, 2021, 2022

Copyright © Jing-Jing Lee, 2019

The moral right of Jing-Jing Lee to be identified as the Author of this work has been
asserted by her in accordance with the Copyright, Designs and Patents Act 1988

ISBN 978-1-78607-595-6
ISBN 978-1-78607-413-3 (eBook)

Text designed and typeset by Tetragon, London
Printed and bound in Great Britain by Clays Ltd, Elcograf S.p.A.

This is a work of fiction. Names, characters, places, and incidents are either the product
of the author's imagination or are used fictitiously, and any resemblance to actual persons,
living or dead, businesses, companies, events or locales is entirely coincidental.

Excerpt from *The Blind Assassin* by Margaret Atwood, copyright © 2000 by O. W. Toad,
Ltd. Used by permission of Doubleday, an imprint of the Knopf Doubleday Publishing
Group, a division of Penguin Random House LLC. All rights reserved. Li-Young
Lee, excerpt from 'Furious Versions' from *The City In Which I Love You*. Copyright
© 1990 by Li-Young Lee. Reprinted with the permission of The Permissions
Company, Inc., on behalf of BOA Editions, Ltd., www.boaeditions.org.

Oneworld Publications
10 Bloomsbury Street
London WC1B 3SR
United Kingdom

For the grandmas (halmonies, lolas and amas)
who told their stories, so that I could tell this one

For Marco, always

'The best way of keeping a secret is to pretend there isn't one.'

MARGARET ATWOOD
The Blind Assassin

'I'll tell my human
tale, tell it against
the current of that vaster, that
inhuman telling.'

LI-YOUNG LEE
'Furious Versions'

Part One

Wang Di

She began in the first month of the lunar year. They said she was born at night, the worst time to arrive – used up all the oil in the lamp so that her father had to go next door for candles. It took hours, and it was only after muddying up swathes of moth-eaten sheets the neighbours had given in the last few weeks of her mother's pregnancy that she emerged. As her first wails cracked through the hot air in the attap hut, he went into the bedroom to look at her, a worm of a thing freshly pulled out of the earth. When he saw the gap between the baby's legs, the first-time father spat, then slumped in a chair at the kitchen table, eyeing his wife as she nursed, already thinking about the next child.

That is one story.

Or, she began when her mother found her in a rubbish skip. She was walking to the market with four eggs her hens laid that morning, was passing by the public bins when it started to whimper. The woman looked in and there it was – a child, scraps of leftover dinner on top of it. She took the baby home and brushed the dirt off her face. Waited for a week to see if anyone would come and claim her. They kept her when no one did.

The third and last story, told to the child by her aunt, was that she was born and her father took her to the pond; the one where water spinach grew. Villagers went to collect it in armfuls when they could afford nothing else for dinner, and it was by this vegetable, completely hollow in the middle of their stems so as to warrant the name *kong sin*, empty heart, that her father put her. The aunt told this story each time she went to visit, and each time, as she got to this point in the story of her niece's birth, she would stop, smack her lips and lean in close, adding that her father had tried to push her under with the tip of his sandalled foot. She explained that it wasn't easy, what he was doing, because the water was shallow and the weeds were holding her up.

'You were bobbing in and out of the water,' she said, 'and the whole business was almost finished with when you stopped crying from the feeling of damp on your body and simply looked at him. Your eyes opened up a crack and you just stared into his face.'

The aunt couldn't say why but it made the new father take the child back home again. He put the bundle on the table like a packet of biscuits and told his wife that she could keep her if she gave birth to a baby boy next year. They didn't bother naming the girl for a few weeks, but when they did, they named her Wang Di – to hope for a brother.

This morning, as with most mornings these days, Wang Di woke to the ghost of a voice, a voice not unlike her aunt's, calling out her name. As she lay in bed she remembered how her aunt once asked if Wang Di wanted to live with her; she could adopt her and take her away since her parents thought so little of girl children. She wouldn't be like them, she told her, casting an eye at Wang Di's father, but would make sure she went to school, got two sets of uniforms and books. An education.

'What do you think, Wang Di?' She'd smiled, a hopeful, shuddering smile.

4

Each time she remembered this, Wang Di wondered how her life would have been different had she said yes (in her mind her parents would have said *go, good riddance*), if she had gone to live with her aunt on the other end of Singapore, ten miles south in Chinatown, with its narrow alleys and smoky shophouses. Or if she had grown up and been approached by the matchmaker at the right time, and the war hadn't torn through the island as it had: in the manner of an enraged sea, one wave after another sweeping everything away.

What she remembered most though, what she liked best, was the way it felt to hear her name, softly spoken.

Because the only time her parents used her name was when someone important was at the door, someone life-changing, or rich. The matchmaker was both. Auntie Tin had appeared at the door one Sunday and snaked inside past her mother before she had been invited to. A few months later, war would arrive on the island. Auntie Tin visited a second time during the occupation and then again – the third and last time – after the war, when Wang Di had little choice but to say yes. She had been the one to tell Wang Di what the words in her name meant and she had been the one who plucked her away from her anguished parents, away from the stolid silence of their home four years after they first met.

When Wang Di sat up and opened her eyes, the faint hum of her name was still in her ears, a song she couldn't stop hearing. Her hand fluttered to the faint scar on her neck, right where her pulse lay, then went down to the line on her lower stomach, the raised welt of it smooth beneath her fingers. Eyes closed, she already knew what kind of day this was going to be – dread was pooling in her chest but she put her legs over the side of the bed and stood. Shuffled the narrow path to the altar. Eleven steps and she was there lighting up joss sticks for everyone she remembered, saying, 'Here I am, here I am,' as if they'd been the ones calling out for her: The Old One, of course; her parents, her aunt and her two friends, one who died earlier than everyone else, and the other, whom she hopes is still alive. She was walking away from the altar when she turned back and lit up three more, planting them in among the fallen ash. Then she clicked the radio on before the memory of a child's face, a memory as clear and smooth as a polished stone, could wash over her.

'Breakfast, Old One,' she said. Out of habit. Muscle memory. Her mouth hanging open in the quiet after her words. She knew there was going to be no answer and why, instead of the brown damp of newspapers, she was now surrounded by the scent of clay. Brick. A new-house smell that made her feel sorry for having woken up. It was still dark out when she walked into her (new) kitchen and saw herself in the (new) windows: an old lady with a curved upper back that made her look more and more like a human question mark; grey-and-white hair cut mid-neck – a style the kindly neighbourhood hairdresser called a 'bop'.

As the water boiled, Wang Di ripped off yesterday's date on the tearaway calendar in the kitchen.

There it was: May 24. To make sure she wouldn't forget, she had written '100' above the date. One hundred, as in 'It's been one hundred days since my husband passed away'. One hundred days spent regretting the fact that she hadn't said and done all she could for him. She touched the black square of cloth on her sleeve – the black badge that told everyone that she had just lost someone close; the black badge that she wore even in bed on the arm of her blouse – and unpinned it. She fixed her eyes on the calendar again, for so long that the print started to squirm. Like ants on the march. Weaving left and right. The way her mind did these days, moving from past to present, mixing everything up in the process. She could be watching the news or doing the wash when everything blurred in front of her eyes and she would be reminded of something that happened years ago.

More and more, bits and pieces of her childhood came back to her, especially this: the many mornings she had watched as her mother stirred congee in a pot. Neither of them saying anything as she did what girl children were supposed to and laid out the cutlery. Five porcelain bowls. Five porcelain spoons. All chipped somewhere, the smooth glaze giving way to a roughness, like used sandpaper. Her mother would remind her to give the one perfect spoon to her youngest brother – Meng had a habit of biting down on cutlery as he ate from them. 'He's going to swallow a bit of china one day,' her mother used to say.

For the last hundred days, it was the Old One who came back to her. How she had left him that evening. The way he looked – she should have known; was trying not to think it while she combed his hair, telling herself how little he had changed. His hair was a little thinner, like a toothbrush that had lost some of its bristles. Thinner, and more white than black now, she thought as she combed it back. Lines around his eyes that stretched to his temples. She wanted to say it then, how he hadn't changed much. Instead she said, 'You look good today. Colour in your face,' and wondered if he could tell she was lying, wondered if by saying it, she could will it into being. He smiled while she rubbed a damp cloth over his face, his neck, his hands, cracking his joints as she wiped from palm to nail. She saw how blue his fingertips were and knew it was a bad thing even though she didn't know why.

Chia Soon Wei had said nothing as his wife fed him his evening meal and cleaned him. Every single word drew much-needed breath out of him, made his heart flutter and race. His voice used to ring through people, through walls, like a gong being struck. Now, it flitted out of him like a dark moth, barely visible. He nodded to thank her as she sat down and held the sidebar on the bed, and wanted to start talking before she got up again to do something else, like pour another tumbler of water or tuck the sheet under his feet. Wanted to urge her to finish her story before it was too late, before both of them ran out of time. He knew what the unsaid did to people. Ate away at them from the inside. He had told Wang Di nothing. Not until a few years into their marriage, following a rare day at the beach. After that, all he wanted to do was talk about the war. What he had done. Not done. He'd brought it up one day at home, was beginning to tell Wang Di what happened during the invasion but stopped when he saw that she was drawing back from him as he spoke, as if she were an animal, netted in the wild; and her face, how wide her eyes had become, how very still. The point was made even clearer when she woke that night, kicking and thrashing, cracking the dark with her cries. He had watched her until the sun came up, in case she had another nightmare, afraid that he might fall asleep and have his own. His usual, recurring one. One that he woke quietly from in the morning and carried around with him. One he had been carrying around with him for more than fifty years.

That day, at the hospital, he wanted to tell her that he understood, that it took time, gathering courage, finding the right words. But what a pity it was that they hadn't started earlier. What came out instead was this: flutter flutter. A whisper that crumpled in the air half heard.

'What did you say, Old One?'

'I said you should finish your story. From yesterday.'

She nodded to mean yes, yes I really should, but her hands were shaking. She had told him everything. Everything but.

He beckoned to her. Closer. Come closer. Wang Di went to him, leaning towards his mouth.

'There's nothing to be ashamed about. You did nothing –' he looked at her now, so fiercely that she had to force herself to hold his gaze '– nothing wrong.'

'I know. I know.' But she was shaking her head, her body betraying what she thought. What she wanted to say was: You might change your mind. You might change your mind after I tell you the rest of it. So she hemmed and hawed, then started talking about the various neighbours who had come over to say goodbye over the last few days, about the trash heaps that people were leaving behind, piled up along the corridor.

One of the last things she said to her husband was, 'You should see the state of the building! Rubbish everywhere – old textbooks, a mini fridge – as if it doesn't matter anymore, now that the building is going to be demolished.'

This was another thing she regretted. How she had rattled on instead of asking him if there was anything he wanted to tell her, to unburden himself of. And this one question in particular: where he had been every 12th of February (until his legs started to fail him) and *who* with. All questions that had looped over and over in her head the first time he had left and come back again at the end of the day. All questions that she'd practised saying out loud every year after that while he was gone. That she pushed away the moment he returned home. And all because of that little voice, not unlike her mother's, which hissed at her, warning that he might want answers of his own, out of her.

And then what would happen? Would she stay silent? Would she lie?

This is how it became their part of their life. Wang Di turning away when he said he would be gone for the entire day. How she would say goodbye to him over her shoulder as if it meant nothing to her; how she laid out the dinner things in silence when he arrived home later that day smelling of smoke and dirt and sweat. All of this, they repeated. A play of sorts, an act, that they would repeat year after year for almost half a century.

Even then, at the last, she let it lie. A sore point left untouched for so long that it would be too painful, too ludicrous to bring up at the eleventh hour.

She skirted the topic. Started complaining about other people's rubbish.

At eight that evening the nurse came in, and in the quiet way of hers, signalled the end of visiting hours. A tap of her white ortho-paedic shoes on the floor. A low cough. Wang Di stood. She and her husband had never hugged in public. Not once in fifty-four years. Instead she gripped his hands, then his feet on the way out. Cold. As if he were dying from the bottom up.

The old lady batted away the thought by waving her hand. 'Bye-bye, I'll see you tomorrow.' Her words sounded strange, like an off-key note in an orchestra but she kept smiling. Nodding. Squeezing his foot.

He waved without lifting his elbow off the bed.

Wang Di waved back, turned the corner and left.

The next day, she had woken with the resolve to try harder, reminded herself not to hold back later on. She had made him his favourite soup: pork with pickled cabbage and peppercorns and she left it to warm in the slow cooker while she did the day's collection. Returned home when it got too humid, the heat like a hot damp blanket around her body, and opened the front door to the salty perfume of bone broth. It was almost noon when she arrived at the hospital with the sense of something gone wrong. If she could she would have run. For a moment, when she got to his ward and found him gone, she half expected a nurse to come and touch her arm and say that he was just in the shower, he was strong enough now. Or that he had been wheeled away for an X-ray or scan. But no. She was there for a few minutes, the red thermos like a weight in her arm before anyone took notice of her.

The bed had already been stripped. What they would never tell her was the way he had died. How his heart had stopped beating and the doctor on duty and two nurses had hurried in. How the young doctor had leaped on top of the bed, knees on either side of the patient, and started doing chest compressions. How, finally, the head nurse – the same one who went into the ward to tell Wang Di that her husband had passed away – had laid a hand on the doctor's arm to get him to stop. He climbed off the bed, straightened his clothes and looked at his watch, noting the time of death. 10:18.

'We called you at home but there was no answer.' The image of the doctor and Mr Chia, dead or dying, bounding up from the mattress again and again from the force of each compression was still playing behind the nurse's eyes. On and off and on, like a film projector on the blink. She pinched the top of her nose to make it go away. 'He went peacefully...like falling asleep,' she said, her voice cracking at the effort of the small, merciful lie, her cloying words. Like talking to a child. When in fact what happened was the man's heart had failed. He had been lucky the first time. Not the second.

Wang Di couldn't fathom the possibility that the Old One was dead, couldn't even begin to think about it so she started apologizing to the nurse instead. 'I'm sorry. You called? I'm sorry I was out.' She had been picking up cardboard and newspapers, getting her collection weighed at the recycling truck when the Old One had died. $9.10. That was how much she had been paid that morning. She tried to recall how it had come to this, how quickly it had happened – in little more than a month. First a cold. Then this. How could a cold kill you? she thought, reaching forward to put a hand on the bed. The sheets on it were cool, fresh from a cupboard. It was then, while the nurse was giving her the pale, sanitized version of what had happened, telling her that his death had something to do with his age and an infection and his heart – that the words 'I should have asked him, I should have asked him,' thrummed in her head.

So that when the nurse asked if there was anyone they could call for her, perhaps a child or another family member, all Wang Di could say was, 'I don't know. I don't know anything about my husband.'

Afterwards, she had sat in a white-walled room as they brought her papers to sign. When she told them she couldn't write (or read), someone ran out for an ink pad and helped her press her thumb into it, as if she hadn't done it before, couldn't manage it herself. And the way they kept saying his name. 'Chia Soon Wei,' over and over again, she forgot why, could only think about the fact that she had never called him Soon Wei. Not once. It was a week after the wedding ceremony before she could look him full in the face. A whole month before she started to call him Old One, a joke (another first with her new husband) because he was eighteen years her senior.

At his wake, the guests – mostly neighbours – kept saying the same thing to her: 'Uncle Chia had a long life.' Each time, she had nodded and replied, 'Ninety-three,' as if to reassure them and herself that they were right, that ninety-three was good enough. It made her wonder how long she might last after him. Later on, lying alone in the dark after his cremation, she had decided that ninety-three was nothing at all. He had promised more.

A month after that, she had moved from Block 204 to this apartment. As was planned before the Old One's death. Everything went on the way things did after someone died. The housing officer came by to give her three sets of keys. The volunteers at the community centre packed everything up and installed her in the new place. While all this was happening, Wang Di spoke and walked and slept with a Soon Wei-sized absence right next to her. The illogicality of it. Both of them were supposed to move to the new place. Just as both of them had looked at the buildings offered by the housing board and picked out the one closest to the home they'd lived in for forty years. The housing agent had rolled out a map of Singapore – a shape that always reminded Wang Di of the meat of an oyster – and drew dots to show them where the buildings were. 'Here,' he'd said, 'here's where you live now.' He drew a red dot. 'And there, there, there – those are the buildings that are available.' Three more red dots. They chose the one closest by, a thumb's length away on the map. It turned out to be thirty minutes away on foot. It might as well have been another country, another continent.

Moving had meant losing him again. Losing everything: the neighbours with whom he would play chess for two hours every evening before coming back up to help with dinner. The stall from which he would buy a single packet of chicken rice every Sunday afternoon, him taking most of the gizzard, her taking most of the tender, white meat. The medicine hall's musty waiting room where she'd sat, staring at illustrated charts pointing to body parts both inside and out, while the *sinseh* took his pulse and stuck needles into him. Each of these things, person, each place, holding a part of her husband like an old shirt that still retained the smell of his skin.

After the movers left, she had busied herself unpacking, opening box after box until she tore open the one filled with Soon Wei's belongings. She had disposed of nothing, given nothing away even at the volunteers' quiet urging. There they were: his walking cane, four shirts, three pairs of trousers, and two pairs of shoes. His sewing kit. A plain wooden box containing his Chinese chess pieces, the words on top worn smooth from touch. A biscuit tin packed with newspaper clippings and letters. She had sat down then, on top of the box, and wept.

The box was now next to the bed. The surface of it clean, bare except for an alarm clock. Once a week, Wang Di peeled back one cardboard flap so she could inhale the scent of his clothes and papers, then shut it again, as if the memory of him could waft away if she left it open for too long. She looked at it now, her fingers furling and unfurling. No, too soon, she decided, then got up to open the front door. This was what she used to do – leave the front door open to let the neighbours know she was home – the gesture like a smile or a wave. But it seemed they spoke a different tongue here. Her new neighbours didn't even leave their shoes outside because they thought they might get stolen. Two months living here and she had only exchanged a hello and goodbye with someone's live-in domestic. Now and again she heard voices, soft and companionable, passing her door. The shuffle of well-worn soles. But they were gone before she could unstick her tongue from the roof of her mouth quickly enough to call out a greeting. She wondered if she might be able to do it again, hold a proper conversation. All she said nowadays was 'Good morning, how much does this cost?' 'Too much!' 'Too little!' 'Thank you.' Maybe she would be found one day wandering the streets, able to say little else. To make sure she wouldn't end up like that, she sometimes repeated the news as she heard it on the radio, saying the words aloud, aware that the Old One might have said these words to her had he been alive; he liked to read the thick Sunday paper to her while they sat on a tree-shaded bench.

As she listened to the news radio that morning, she recited:

'Household income. Grim view of bottom earners. Top percentile richer.'

'Schoolboys arrested for throwing water bombs.'

'National University of Singapore revamping its courses to produce more leaders for the country.'

'And now we have the hourly traffic updates. Major incident on the A.Y.E.'

A quarter of an hour later she had said all she was going to say for the rest of that day. She made coffee. Halved a mangosteen – his favourite fruit – and placed both halves in a bowl, white flesh facing up. A hundred days. At the altar, she stuck three joss sticks in the tin can and cleared her throat. The thought that she'd had months ago, at the hospital, blooming to the surface. I never let you talk. I should have let you. Here she paused, picturing how she had stopped him each time he brought up the war. How she froze, or left the room, or cried. How his need to talk about what happened during the war had given way to her fear of it, so that she was left now with the half history of a man she had known for most of her life. 'I'm going to fix it. I am,' she said, a little below her breath. She wasn't sure how. Not yet. But she would find out, had to find out, all that she could about what happened to him during those lost years. 'I'm going to fix it,' she repeated. Here her voice gave, and she had to force herself to smile and change the subject. 'I might need your help but you don't mind, do you? Staying around?'

Because aside from Soon Wei's photo on the altar, there was a stark absence of anything else that might hint at a wider family. An absence as real as a wall, so solid you would have to be blind to miss it. No cluster of toys for visiting grandchildren, no extra chairs around the kitchen table for large weekend dinners. Nothing on the walls except for the pages cut out of *Zao Bao*, the Chinese morning paper, and the English paper (which the Old One couldn't read but had clipped out anyway for their accompanying photos). He had collected them for years, and the collection had grown over time into a patchwork of paper tacked up on the wall of their home. On the day of the move, she had made sure to remove the articles herself. One of the things she did that first evening in the new apartment was to put them up on the wall along the kitchen table, a fine approximation of where they had been before. There was one picture of Senior Minister Lee Kwan Yew shaking hands with the Japanese prime minister, a short column of words right underneath it. Another was a photo of two women in traditional Korean dress; one of them held a handkerchief to her face, the other stared straight into the camera, lower jaw hard, daring the viewer to blink.

The Old One had watched her face as she looked at the two Korean women. His voice was soft, cautious when he said, 'People are still talking about it… People who remember what happened during the war.' And he had read the column aloud, which he did when there was something in the paper that he thought might interest her. She had listened and not said a word. The quiet afterwards was so thick she felt that someone had wrapped a bale of wool around her head. Later that evening, when the Old One was taking a shower, she got up to peer at the woman whose face was half obscured. That could be her – Jeomsun, she thought. Wang Di remembered how, decades ago, they had talked about her going to visit one day. Jeomsun had laughed and promised to take her on a long walk into the mountains; it was one of her favourite things to do. Wang Di had told her it would be her first time then, seeing a mountain, climbing one. There were no real mountains in Singapore, she'd told her, only hills. Jeomsun had said, 'You know, it sounds strange but I feel the absence of it. Like I've lost a limb, or an ear, almost. You live in a strange country, little sister, the wet heat, the land all flat and small.' It was then that Wang Di realized how little her world was, how strange and cloistered everyone else must think of her place of birth – all the soldiers and tradesmen, the captives brought over by ship. A cramped little prison island.

The memory had landed like a hot slap across her face. She couldn't stop hearing their voices – not just Jeomsun's, Huay's as well. After decades of muffling their voices in her head. Of trying not to see them when she closed her eyes at night.

Later that evening, she had asked, 'Those women that you read about, who are protesting… Do they live in Korea?'

'Yes, yes. But there are others too. In China, Indonesia, the Philippines…' He had stopped there, nodding slowly. Eyes on her the entire time.

He had given her that same weighted nod earlier this year as he waited for her to speak. The week before he caught a cold. *The* cold that made him ill for close to a month before he toppled over with a heart attack. But even before all that, before the visits to the Western doctor who dispensed antibiotics like giving candy to children, before Wang Di's long wait for the ambulance which seemed to take the entire afternoon to arrive, before all that, he seemed to know it was coming. The approaching, ultimate silence. And he had behaved accordingly, Wang Di realized afterwards, and insisted on having a Lunar New Year meal. A proper reunion dinner, not sitting in bed in front of the TV but at the table. She had returned home from collecting cardboard one afternoon to the smell of roast duck procured from Lai Chee Roast Chicken and Duck at the market. There was soup stock bubbling away in an electric steamboat on the table. And fishcake, raw stuffed okra, silky tofu and straw mushrooms, all plated on the side, ready to be plunged into the boiling soup. Sweet *tang yuan* to round off the meal. Cutlery already in place. She had smiled and combed her hair while he scooped rice into two bowls. It had been years since they had shared a reunion dinner like that and they started off much too polite, sitting straight up in their chairs as if they were meeting for the first time. It took them a while to stop watching each other over the tops of their bowls and begin talking about their day. The sweet dumplings they ate to the sound of the eight o'clock news on the radio, settling back into their easy silence.

Later, she went to bed and found him sitting up with his eyes shut. Wang Di had to resist the urge to wake him – she had never liked watching him as he slept. His face was meant to be lively. He had dark, bristling eyebrows meant for wiggling above his eyes, a sturdy nose that he wrinkled as he worked. A mouth full of square teeth that he ate and grinned and tore off threads with. At rest now, it was as if he were only a fraction of himself. Wang Di could see what he might look like if he were never to move again.

So she put her hand on the top of his shoulder and shook. 'Old One, are you awake?'

He flared his nostrils wide but said nothing, nor did he slide down into his usual sleeping position, flat on his back with one arm above his head. She sank into the mattress, close to his feet, trying to find the firmest spot in their sat-upon, laid-upon, age-old bed, and waited for him to speak.

'Tell me a story.'

It was then that she knew he had been waiting to say this. Waiting decades for the right moment. And now he couldn't wait anymore. 'What – what story?'

'Any story.'

She stayed silent for a while until he put his hand on hers; she had been tapping her nails on the bed frame without meaning to.

'Just talk about something from your childhood, where you went with your mother on market day, for example, what you saw there.'

The clock ticked its thin, plastic tick. Minutes passed. The first thing that came to her was this: 'There used to be a man who sold his songs near the city.'

She stopped to look at him and he nodded slowly, telling her to go on. 'He would be outside one of the coffee shops whenever it was not raining, sitting on a bamboo stool, a well-worn walking stick gripped in his left hand. His face looked like it was made of ragged sackcloth and he hardly moved while he waited for the right moment to begin. Then he sang. And the sound of feet around him hushed for their owners to hear better. The market with its stalls selling vegetables and home-grown poultry, the noodle stall with its sweaty cook pouring pork-based soup into bowls. The chatter of the market never stopped, but the sound of his voice, his songs about home, about missing the old country, about love and its ills, lulled everything around him into a different rhythm. Even the noodle man, with a cloth wrung around his neck to catch drops of sweat, could be seen using the same cloth to dab at his eyes whenever he thought no one was looking. People clustered around the old man, going close, listening with hands behind their backs or clasped at their chests and at the end of it, some of the people who had gathered around to listen threw coins into a tin mug.

'I always stood at the edge of the crowd, out of sight, peeping now and then to look at the expression on his face. It pained me that I had nothing to give him and I made myself walk away before the end so that he wouldn't see me – never with a coin but always there, long after my vegetables and eggs were sold, listening.'

When she stopped, she could hear the last of her words clinging to the warm air in the room. He opened his eyes and nodded once more. *Go on.* She took a deep breath as if she were about to plunge her head into water, ignoring her mother's voice in her head. What she had said to Wang Di the night before her wedding: 'Remember. Don't tell anyone what happened. No one. Especially not your husband.'

When Wang Di spoke again, it was about home. About the year it all began – her almost-marriage to someone else, her too-short childhood, the war. For a week, they sat like this in the night, in the dark, the Old One leaning towards the sound of her voice. This was how she started.

October – December 1941

If Auntie Tin had arrived at our door an hour earlier, I might have found myself married off right before the turn of the year. As it was, her rickshaw driver was new to the island and kept taking one wrong turn after the other.

'Honestly, they should know where they're going, don't you think?' she whispered as she dabbed her temples with a handkerchief, trying to explain her fluster. I didn't yet know who she was, or what she was there for, but I was already on her side. Anyone who had to meet my father's steely silence that day deserved to be pitied. I wanted to tell her that it was not her fault, that she had simply come at the wrong time.

My parents had been having the same fight every few months for over a year now. This evening, it had begun as it always did, with my mother brandishing a letter.

I heard my father curse under his breath, promising that he would take her earnings away to stop her from bringing any more letters to the letter reader in town. My mother was the only woman in our village who kept the money she made, hiding coins under floorboards and within the hems of her clothes. My father closed one eye to it, and to the fact that the other men in the village mocked him for being soft.

'They're starving,' she cried, 'the people in my old town. My *home*.'

It was only when the Japanese captured Shantou that my mother started calling it 'home'. Until then, she only mentioned her birthplace occasionally, each time with a voice steeped in relief and guilt. Relief at having escaped the oppressive poverty and the natural disasters that swept through much too often. Guilt, of course, at having left her family behind, and how easily she had done it. When news came through about the Japanese navy's arrival on the Southern Chinese coast via motorboats, then of the city's quick capitulation in mid-1939, my mother wept openly and called out for her *da ge* and *er ge*, her *nainai* – her two older brothers and her grandmother. I could only stand by and watch, my stomach heavy, churning. Later that day, I went to the outhouse and almost tipped into the hole at the sight of fresh, red blood in my underwear. When I told my mother that I just had my first bleed, her face lifted in a half-smile and cracked again into sobs. For many nights after that, I dreamed about ships and blood. All of it silent, backdropped by the sound of my mother's weeping. I was fourteen.

For the next two years, she'd continued talking about her large extended family and the crumbling, grey-tiled building that they shared with a number of other households. The inner courtyard where they would gather to share a pot of tea on a clear day. Her pet geese. How she used to take dips in the river in the peak of summer. Her parents had betrothed her to my father as soon as she was born, and when she was fourteen (and he, eighteen), they got married. My mother moved out of her parents' home and into my father's ancestral home in the next village up, only to wave farewell to him a few days later. It was a full day's journey before he got to the port of Guangzhou and almost two weeks in a junk before it docked in the promised land – Singapore. There, amidst the babel of languages (other Chinese dialects he could just about comprehend; plus Malay, Tamil and English, which he could not) and a quay teeming with bobbing sampans, he stopped, breathing in the hot air, smoky from the exhaust of idling trucks and the long pipes of foremen directing their labourers between boats and warehouses. Even then, through the lingering vestiges of seasickness, my father could smell opportunity in the air, a riotous mixture of rice and chilli and tobacco, and realized that he would never again see his family's roaming tracts of barren farmland. Never again see his mother, though he had promised to return once he had made his fortune. Out of the depths of the ship's hull and away from its sweating, sickly masses, this simple act of walking across land almost made him break down in regret and gratitude. By the time he arrived at the address he had been given – a Hokkien clan house – he was so euphoric from the bustle and colour and temple music coming from every lane and corner of Chinatown that he said yes to the first job he was offered. The next day, he bussed up north to a part of Singapore dense and dark with rubber trees. A different world, he marvelled, though he soon realized that he had exchanged the onerous farm work back home for similar work that paid him only a few cents more and required him to rise at two in the morning instead of five.

By the end of his first day, his face and arms were mosquito-stung and his hands scored from multiple accidents with his tapping knife. His fellow workers quietly laughed as he stumbled over tree roots. Rubber tapping paid badly but it doesn't break your back, they reminded him. In a few weeks, his skin had stopped reacting to insect bites and his eyes had grown used to the gloom and depth of the rubber grove. He sent money home every month. Along with the money, my father included a letter enquiring after his parents' health, and then his young wife's, in that order. They wrote back, his eldest brother's slashing script seeping through the paper in spots, telling him that his parents' health was good but for the usual aches that came and went with the rain; that his wife was readying herself for married life learning to sew and cook; that his six siblings were busy trying to coax something out of the leached soil.

It took my father years of scoring veins into the trunks of trees and years of living in an eight-to-a-room dormitory before he could afford a house. A little wooden house in Hougang, a village notorious for the stench of its pig farms, but a house all the same. It was several months before he could send for his wife. By the time she set foot in her new country, they had been apart for four years. My mother was the one who recognized my father. Went up to him and tapped him on the shoulder. For in the space between their first and second meeting, she had changed – child to woman – the milk fat on her cheeks had vanished, tapering down to a pointed chin. She was all but unrecognizable. To her blank and unwavering gaze, all my father could say was, '*Lao Po*, you have changed!'

'*Lao Po*,' my father now said. Wife, old woman. He only called her this during the height of an argument, or when he was trying to plead with her. 'We already send money home every Lunar New Year. We can't afford boat fares for anyone, much less the entire family. Look around us. Do you think we have anything to spare?' I followed the sweep of his arm as he directed it around our attap hut, pointing at the one rattan chair that no one ever sat in because they were afraid to wear it out; at the one bedroom where all of us slept, my brothers and I sharing a single bed, sleeping head to foot to head; at me. I was standing at the dining table, chopping up kong sin vegetables and making sure there were no snails hidden among the deep green stalks when he nodded in my direction. 'We can't even afford to send her to school.'

'Are you telling me you're going to let them starve? Is that what you're saying?'

'I'm saying we are barely making ends meet. I'm saying that the boys can't read or do their homework after sunset because we're rationing the candles, I'm saying we have nothing to give. Look,

look.' He turned out his empty pockets, flapped the hem of his shirt to show how thin the cotton had become from years of washing.

'One of my brothers is thinking about coming over.'

'What are you talking about? You think the boats are running? There are Japanese ships in their harbour. The whole of Guangdong province has been under Japanese rule for two years. What do you think they're going to do if anyone goes to the port looking to leave? This is madness, this is –'

'If no one is allowed to leave, how did this letter get to me? Maybe there is a way, if they travel inland.'

'And what then? Even if they manage to cross the South China Sea without getting captured by the Japs. What then? Who's going to give them jobs?' My father was almost heaving. His back curled like a cat's backed into a corner. The rubber industry had collapsed a few years ago. With it went the plantation and my father's job. Now he did what work he could: poorly paid odd jobs for a furniture store in town, and manual labour in the pig farms in our village sometimes, only to make ends meet. 'What, do you want to sell one of the children to pay for the upkeep of your family? Maybe the girl?'

That was the moment Auntie Tin rapped on the door. I smelled her perfume before I saw her, a floral note amidst the deep musk of farm animals and earth around us.

'Hello, hello, Mr Ng, Mrs Ng. I'm Mrs Tin,' said the visitor, smiling.

My parents, caught mid-quarrel, folded their arms across their chests.

The visitor continued smiling and held out a paper bag with both hands. 'Pastries. Tangerines.'

My mother passed the paper bag to me and said, 'Go. Finish making dinner out the back.'

Out of sight, I tried to eavesdrop on their conversation but they were whispering, their voices drowned out by the cries of children playing outside and the chatter of our neighbours relaxing before their evening meal. The smell of tangerines filled the kitchen as I finished washing the vegetables and I was trying to start the fire underneath the wok when my mother called for me.

'Wang Di! Bring us some tea.' Her voice like a crack of a whip, making me wonder what I had done this time.

When I brought them the tea, my parents were sitting on the kitchen stools and the woman was deep in our one good rattan chair, making the wicker stretch and creak as she looked me over from top to bottom and up again. The curls in her hair were freshly set and there was gold on her arms and on her earlobes, little yellow hoops that she rubbed every now and then between finger and thumb as if to make sure that they were still there.

She nodded as I handed her a cup. 'Good girl. Call me Auntie Tin.' Then to Ma, 'You have just one daughter, yes?'

'Yes, just one.'

'And did I hear you say "Wang Di"? Is that her official name?'

My mother nodded and Auntie Tin turned to me, the perm wobbling on her head as she did so. 'Girl, do you want to know what your name means? Would you like a husband? I have just the man for you in mind.'

It was only then that I realized that I didn't know what my name meant. The realization dropped like a stone down my throat, into my belly. Confused, I nodded, then shook my head. Yes. No.

My father said nothing but started agitating the spoon in his cup, as if he were ringing a bell.

'*Wang*, meaning "hope" or "to look forward to". *Di*, "little brother".' She turned and gestured outside with her hand, as if she knew that my brothers were out playing and might step through the doorway any moment. 'Wise name. And good girl'– she nodded at me –'for bringing your parents good luck. Two brothers, this is something I can tell potential suitors about.'

My father dropped the spoon with a clatter. 'She's too young.'

'Oh, it doesn't have to be today. I'll just put her name down and you can let me know whenever you're ready.' She drew out a palm-sized notebook from her bosom, blood-red and pulsing with all the names and potential it held within its pages. 'Ng. Wang. Di,' she said as she wrote, the fortune mole above her lip leaping with anticipation. I had never heard my name spoken so many times in one day and I hadn't seen it written before. I leaned forward to watch the characters appear on paper, admiring the way she did it, as easily as brushing crumbs off a table.

伍望弟

'You are, what, seventeen this year?' she continued, pencil hovering above a line.

'Sixteen,' my mother corrected.

'Ah, good. Just right.'

'She's too young.'

'Lots of girls get married at this age.'

'We'll need time to talk about this.' My mother turned towards my father, who looked away, out of the door, as if he were expecting someone else to arrive.

'Of course, of course. But don't take too long *ah*… People get nervous during times like these – they start to think about families, babies, making a home of their own. A lot of women back in China got married before the start of the occupation, you know, just to make sure that they don't get taken away to be dancing girls, or worse…'

I heard my father muttering below his breath in dialect. 'Another one. Another woman who cannot let go.'

'Mr Ng?'

My father cleared his throat and switched to speak in Mandarin. 'That has nothing to do with us. That war is all the way across the sea.'

'You may think that but I've heard differently.'

My mother was nearly in tears. The letter, I knew, was still tucked up into her sleeve. 'What? What have you heard?'

The woman now lowered her voice and leaned towards my mother. 'Oh, that they're getting close, spreading out. You know that they're planning to attack Malaya, right? And once they have Malaya, they will come down south. And then it will only be a matter of weeks, if not days –'

'*Hu shuo ba dao,*' my father muttered. Nonsense. 'The British are here. They have ships and planes and cannons protecting our island. A few Japanese soldiers aren't going to defeat the British.

'Then why do they keep sending soldiers here? Why do they tell us to dig air-raid shelters? To go to the hospitals and donate blood?' Auntie Tin's voice was low, her matchmaker's charm put on hold for a moment.

She had walked past the bomb shelters, of course. The one my father had dug one morning along with four other men as the village elder gave instructions from outside the trench, his hands behind his back. For a few hours, the air had been filled with the chink of metal hitting earth and dry rustles as earth landed back on the ground. When the village elder retreated into the shade, the men started to talk, laughing at a joke I couldn't hear. My father was back before lunch, the shovel tipped carelessly over his shoulder. He didn't know why they bothered at all since no one was going to use it – it was going to fill up with rainwater, he said as he took a drink of water. The bomb shelters didn't look fortuitous. They looked like trenches. Like rectangles of carved-out ground, waiting for coffins to be lowered into them.

Auntie Tin opened her mouth again, caught herself, and turned her unspoken words into a wide smile. I saw a silver tooth in the back of her mouth.

'All I'm saying is, Mr and Mrs Ng, all the good matches might get snapped up if you wait too long.' There was something in her eyes that hinted she was prepared for anything that might happen, almost; that it was this ease of adapting, her flexibility, that had given her all she had. Her jewellery, her cotton samfu with its silky knotted buttons. 'So yes, discuss this among yourselves. I will visit again after the new year.' Then she beamed, eyes crinkling, patient, like a snake that has just swallowed a fat brown hen. She had got what she had come for: tea, a friendly exchange, the beginnings of a guanxi – a connection – to another young woman in the village.

'That woman didn't know what she was talking about.' My father had been bristling all day ever since the visit from the matchmaker, but my mother ignored him as she gave everyone except him a bit of the salty radish omelette. 'We're not going to get her'– he pointed his chopsticks at me – 'married off just because of some silly rumour. Anyway, we need her at home.'

He had said the same thing when I was ten and a teacher from the neighbourhood school came to ask if I was going to be enrolled that following term.

'It's brand new and only half an hour away. Ten minutes, if she has a bike,' she had added, looking around to see if there was one. Her eyes went left and right, right and left, to the open door and the windows until she saw the one my father used for work, the front and back carriage rusted over and strewn with metal parts, a spare bicycle tyre. She cleared her throat and sipped the tea my mother had given her. Even the sounds she made drinking were delicate. Her hands were pale, almost white; small and as perfect as a doll's. 'Uncle, please think about it. Times are different. We might still live in the kampong but everyone sends their children to school now –'

But my father had simply waved his hands in front of her. 'She has two brothers; one is in the third year of primary school, the other will go when he's older. That's already two sets of uniforms. Plus the books. The shoes. We can't afford to –'

'Oh, please don't worry about that. People donate things all the time, I can help you with –'

'No. No help. We don't accept charity.'

'Nearly everyone receives an education nowadays, even the girls. She's already a few years late but we can –'

'She's a girl. What can she gain from going to school that her mother can't teach her? We need her at home.' He pointed into the front yard, where the chickens were, and then into the wild, open back yard that extended into the trees. While my father cycled around the city doing odd jobs for a furniture store (deliveries, mostly, and bits of light carpentry) and my mother went around the village collecting laundry, I went to the market every morning with a basket of eggs and sweet potatoes. Once there, I would lay out sheets of newspapers and spread out what I had. Sometimes all the produce went in an hour, sometimes I had to take everything home again with me; and the weight of it slowed me down so that I arrived home later than normal. I would see my mother watching from the window, knowing that I had made no money that day but she would say nothing and I would say nothing. The feeling of it would pervade all throughout dinner so that my throat closed up and I would have to swallow again and again to keep my food from rising from my stomach.

I nodded. When the woman looked at me, it was with a look that made me feel watched – the way an animal might feel watched. She was cautious with my father like that, as if he were a large dog, tame enough, but which could still pounce.

'I don't want to go to school,' I said, even though no one had asked me. My father nodded as I hoisted Meng onto my hip. Look at this, I wanted to say, to shame her, to remind her that there were needful things – and then there were things that people wanted, that anyone could want, but could live without. Meat and fish for dinner more than just twice a year. New clothes. An education. I had stared back at her, unblinking, wanting to sound older than I was, wanting to be on the side of my family because they were the only thing I knew. 'I don't need it,' I'd added, revelling in a sour satisfaction as the teacher got up to leave.

My mother, still sore about my father's refusal to send money to her family, refused to speak to him throughout dinner. Every now and then, as she moved to pick up morsels of food to put into her bowl, I heard the crinkle of paper under her blouse. A few days later, I saw her wrap her jade pendant, a pale green stone that she had always worn on a loop of string around her neck, in cotton and slide it into an envelope. I imagine that the jade was still warm when she brought it to the post office. For the next few months, I would catch her in the middle of reaching for it, her hand going to the dip in her throat, and find nothing. My father never noticed.

I imagine, too, that she was already thinking about sending her family the pendant that evening. The matchmaker's warning about the war was ringing in my ears but the only thing I could think about then was my future husband – what he might look like, where we would live, whether he would be kind.

Yan Ling came by the following day as I was feeding the chickens and collecting their eggs. I felt her watching me and knew what was on her mind before she'd said it.

'Did she visit you as well? The matchmaker?'

'Yes.' I rolled one egg, still warm, in my hand. Who would collect them, I thought, if I weren't around?

'She wanted to talk to my sister, not me.' Yan Ling bit her top lip, then released it so that her cleft reappeared, bruised and shining, like a fresh scar. 'What did your parents say?'

I shook my head and set the five eggs in my basket, nestling them in a circle, pointy ends up. When I turned back, she was chewing on the end of her plait, looking relieved.

We set off for the market together, trading details about the matchmaker's visit as we went down the lane. Yan Ling's parents had taken one look at Auntie Tin, the precious metals adorning her neck and wrist, the gifts of fruit and biscuits and said yes. They had brought out her younger sister after pinching her cheeks red and pink, and forced her to smile for the audience of one. 'Do this for us,' they had told her. She was barely sixteen.

'They made me sit in the bedroom, in the dark, until she was gone,' Yan Ling said.

I made useless, empathetic sounds as we went down the lane, past the other attap huts that were waking up, not knowing who to feel worse for: Yan Ling, because she had been passed over as if she weren't there, or her sister, for having been bartered for some food and the possibility of a bride price. I kicked at the *lalang*, their white, feathery tails. My skin would itch that evening and I would have to prise the weeds' sharp teeth from my cloth shoes and my trousers. Neither of us said anything until we were outside the boundaries of the kampong, far enough to have left behind the heavy stench of pig pens and chicken coops, far enough so I could breathe in the smell of green and dew.

'Do you think I'll ever get married?' she asked.

I didn't want to hurt her but I didn't wish to lie to her either so I said, 'Do you want to?'

'I want three children, not seven like my mother. And all girls. I would hate to wash dishes all my life and end up with someone like my pa.' There, between us, was the unspoken knowledge of her father's quick temper. The way he disappeared for days on gambling binges, only to return when he was clean out of money. In the days after his homecoming, Mrs Yap would visit and cry over cups of tea while my mother rolled a hard-boiled egg over her fresh bruises to take the sting and colour of them away. 'What about you?'

There was a pause as she smiled. The look on her face struck me as strangely knowing, as if she was privy to something I wasn't. It only became apparent to me what it was much later. This knowing had nothing to do with experience, but a conviction of her own desires. While I bargained with housewives and maids during the day, she was in the thick of downtown, working in a bustling kitchen next to cooks and waiters and delivery boys. From that, she seemed to have secreted away a kernel of private knowledge: the kind of men she liked, and the kind she didn't. I was only a year younger than her but still a child by comparison, unburdened by longing.

'No. Not yet. I want to leave the kampong and go into the city. Maybe I could do that first.'

'How?' Her eyes were round, incredulous.

'I could get a job. A proper one. Where they pay you a salary at the end of every month. I don't mind being a tea girl for a while and sharing a room with other women. And maybe… Maybe I could go to night school.' I stopped there, hearing how foolish I sounded.

Some people, treated poorly, grabbed any chance they could to lash out at anyone within touching distance. Yan Ling wasn't one of them. She waited a little before replying and her words were soft, hesitant, an effort to cushion my hopes. 'You will be so good at school. You're clever. Not like me. I'm going to be stuck washing cups and dishes at the eating house all my life.'

'*Aiya*, don't be silly.' I said, wanting to change the subject.

'You'll learn so much. Then you'll find a job you like and meet a nice man and marry him. Don't forget me then. I'll still be a village girl who knows nothing. The only gift I have is knowing if my mother's carrying a boy or a girl. It's a boy this time. Again. You can tell from how high her belly is.' She stopped and looked at me. 'Promise me you'll come back and visit.'

We hooked pinkie fingers. The way we had done the first time we met. My family and I had just moved in and I had spotted her walking past our new place several times, looking in as I swept dirt out of the front door. She was always next to her mother or carrying a brother in her arms. A week later, I ran into her behind the public outhouse. She was crouching with her back pressed into the wooden wall, a finger pressed to her mouth. I only saw the cleft carved deep into her top lip when she took her finger away.

'Yan Ling!' someone was shouting, a woman. 'Come here this instant!'

'Why are you hiding?'

'*Shh*... I spilled my brothers' milk.'

'Oh,' I said. 'I have to go.'

'Wait. You won't tell?'

'No... I don't even know you.'

'My name is Yan Ling. Now you know me. Don't tell.' She had extended a hand, then stuck out her pinkie.

'Wang Di,' I said, and we shook hands like that, with our little fingers. I waved at her before running home, past the woman, who was holding a bamboo whipping cane in her hand.

That was more than ten years ago. We walked to market together most days, and most days we slowed down as we passed the neighbourhood school, a single wooden building, low and twice as long as it was wide, with a signboard over the front door. We did that now, watching as teachers and children from our kampong and beyond walked in. The students walking in were wearing khaki bottoms and white cotton shirts – dusty and rumpled because it was a Friday and most of them owned no more than one of each. I watched the boys walk in, a circle of pale yellow on the backs of their shirts from sweat and play.

Yan Ling stopped walking and put the end of her plait in her mouth again. 'What do you think they do all day?'

'I don't know.' I didn't tell her about the time I had crept in close after the bell had rung and crouched under a window, listening as the roll was called. Everyone was speaking in crisp Mandarin, not the dialect that we used at home. After all the names had been shouted out, the teacher read out a poem:

> *Before my bed, the moon is shining bright,*
> *I think that it is frost upon the ground.*
> *I raise my head and look at the bright moon,*
> *I lower my head and think of home.*

I didn't tell Yan Ling that I recited the poem to myself sometimes as I was walking back from market and that I could only guess how much I was missing out, that I thought it must be like being blind and not knowing how much I wasn't able to see, all the colours and shapes of things that I could poorly imagine.

We were about to leave when a neighbour waved at me from the doorway of the school building. I waved back, a little too late – she had already turned away to talk to one of her classmates. I tried to recall her name but what came to me were my mother's words, ringing loud in my ears. *They adopted her from another family – couldn't have their own, you see.* My only thought then had been, why not me? before a thin acid of betrayal flooded my stomach, shaming me into pinching myself. Still, I couldn't help thinking of her as the younger, luckier sister I'd never had, and watched out for her every time I passed the school. There were books in her bag, books in the crook of her arm. Her school shirt was fresh, so white it was blue. I heard her laugh before she went inside. If I'd been her, I thought.

At the start of December, Yan Ling's mother came over with a box of kueh and announced that her daughter ('No, not the older one, no. Yue Qing, the pretty one') was getting married. Her smile was triumphant. This time, she didn't stay for tea but lapped up my mother's good wishes and my brothers' excitement over the pastry box.

'So? When is it happening?' I asked Yan Ling that Sunday.

'In February, right before Lunar New Year.' She tried to look unconcerned, gazing from me to the palm trees that stuck up twice as high as the tallest houses. Pedlars passed with their wares, balancing aluminium canisters filled with soup across their shoulders. The weekends meant little to me, except the possibility that the produce would go quicker. For Yan Ling it meant nothing but more work. She washed dishes for a row of stalls along the street and on weekends they piled up all day until evening fell. Often she only got home after dark with her shoulders fallen in from hours hunched over the public tap, her hands red from scouring bowls and plates.

'Do you think I'll end up a spinster? Like a Samsui woman?'

I thought about the women, new migrants, who stuck close to each other, as if they were still back in Samsui. The way they kept their hair brushed into one rigid pigtail. I often saw them working at construction sites with their scarlet headdresses, their faces smudged grey with dirt, the flesh on their bones scant and darkened by the sun.

'No, of course not.'

'You know, there are rumours about them – taking blood oaths never to marry. My mother says there's something wrong with women like them. That they're unnatural.'

'You'll find someone, don't worry.'

She made a sound of disbelief and touched her lip. I'd asked her once if the cleft hurt and she shook her head. A minute later, she changed her mind, saying, yes, whenever she saw her reflection.

My tongue went dry, gritty. I chewed the inside of my mouth to make it water. 'Follow me,' I said, and ran ahead until I got to a fenced-in orchard. I spotted a tree close to the perimeter and sniffed the air. There they were: yellow globes dotting the green canopy. A breeze shifted the branches and they bobbed, nodding to me, *yes, yes,*

yes. I handed Yan Ling the eggs and vegetables and went to the tree. It was a young one and would be easy work. I grabbed one branch with my right hand, pushed my foot into a hollow and hoisted myself up. I grabbed a higher branch with my left hand and pulled upwards again until I was wedged between trunk and limb, and reached, plucking the one closest to me, fat and yellow as a monk's robe. As I slipped down the trunk, I heard a man shout. 'AY! What do you think you're doing? Stop!'

'Quick,' Yan Ling said, 'Let's go!'

We ran past the orchard, past empty fields, until we reached the first noodle hawkers already serving their first customers, their faces hidden in bowls steaming with broth, stopping only when we got to the heart of the market, tight with hawkers jostling their pushcarts against their neighbours'. We went past servants with their starched white blouses, and mothers with babies strapped to their backs, and said good morning to the garlic and ginger man with his baskets full of ginger roots large as hands and the fruit seller with his piles of tangerines and melons waiting to be picked. Everyone was calling out for customers with croaky morning voices. The itch of dried shrimp and chilli in my nose. I pulled Yan Ling into an alley behind a row of shophouses and she watched as I pierced the skin of the mango with my fingernail, pulled back the soft leather and held it out to her.

'No, no, you're the one who plucked it. You should start.'

The sharp sweetness of the mango made my teeth hurt. I held it away from my clothes so that juices dotted the floor.

'*Na.*' I passed the fruit to her. She took a cautious bite, and a second, larger one. Then looked up and grinned at me, revealing all of her front teeth up to the gums. For the next few minutes, we crouched, passing the fruit back and forth until all that was left was the pit, a white heart.

I slept soundly that night and woke only when my mother shook me. When she did I forgot who I was for a second and reached out with my arms, like a child. I had dreamed about the wail of sirens. It sounded so real, I wanted to tell her. The words were in my mouth, were almost spilling out when I sat up and realized it was still in my ears, the siren's howl circling above like an enraged animal. Then a thrumming in the clouds and then a sound like too-near thunder, the ground shifting.

'Ma?'

'Get up, get up. We have to go to the shelter.'

It was four in the morning. War had begun.

Kevin

An endless *whoosh-whoosh* in the depths of my pocket, and some more when you think you've heard enough. Then when you've gotten used to the whooshes, the sound almost becoming a sea-sound, a wash of noise you can fall asleep to, you hear the voices.

Sometimes it's Albert and his friends, calling out for me, except instead of shouting my name, they shout words like, '*chao ah gua*' and 'retard' and 'sissy'. The first time I turned around to see who it was, Albert nearly went purple laughing. Most of it, most of what they do, cannot be captured on tape. Things like standing behind me at morning assembly and spitting in my hair when we are all reciting the pledge, yelling, 'We, the citizens of SingaPORE, PLEdge ourselves as one united PEOPLE,' so that the Ps land wet on my neck. Things like stepping on the backs of my shoes so that I lose one and they start kicking it to each other, making a game of it. Things like that. Once, they kicked a soccer ball at me. When I play the tape back, I can hear the smack of it against my head. But mostly there's the *whoosh-whoosh* of me going to the little garden near the school's back gate, then a hush when I sit down and eat my lunch. The shush of the afternoon rain against the ground or a window, which I recorded hours of, trying to get the rumble of thunder on tape, except it's usually so low and far away that it never gets captured (although I think I can hear it if I strain hard enough – a ghost of a sound). You can hear the school bell ringing but you can't feel the hurt of it on my ears through my pocket, all the way from that little tape. The sour little pinch of being quickly forgotten by David, my best friend from primary school. Forgotten because my grades were too crap for me to get an Elite Secondary Education (not that my parents would have the money to pay for it even if I did) like he is getting. Of our phone calls getting shorter and shorter because David is too busy hanging out with his new friends, while my only companions during lunchtime are the koi in the fish pond. This would be something he would have liked – the tape recorder. I can imagine how we would have messed about saying stupid things into it just to hear how our voices sounded – exactly like us and nothing like us at the same time. But it is no fun when there is no one else to listen to your own crazy words with you so I put the recorder on when I need to, when there's something that needs remembering. People say things all the time without thinking and then they forget about it (like David, when he said we would keep on going to the arcade every Friday afternoon, like we used to). Then when it comes up again I can play it back to them and say 'Remember? this is what you said,' and 'See, I told you,' and 'Hear that, you were raising your voice after all,' because sometimes people (my parents) don't realize they are shouting and I have to put my hands over my ears, which only makes them louder still. It's like their ears are switched off to their own voices. Other times, I put the recorder on when there are important things I need to remember. Like what my parents talk about in the van when they think I'm asleep in the back ('I think we had him too late.' 'What? No, *lah*.' 'I'm just worried. You know, sometimes I don't understand half his homework.'); the thing Ah Ma – my grandmother – said to me just before she died ('I found you! Pease don't baneme… Ifoundyou and tookyouawaay').

39

I started recording things partly because of Ah Ma and partly because the optician told me last week that I was going to go blind. He said it when I finished reading the letters on the chart. It didn't take long. I climbed up onto the big chair and covered first my left, then my right eye with a piece of cardboard. With each eye, I got as far as the first letter at the top, E, and only because I remembered it from the times before. In fact, I couldn't see any of the letters. I couldn't even see the edge of the poster where it met the wall.

The optician said it again in front of my mother, when we were out in the bright business part of the shop, with the rows and rows of glasses looking out at us, all of them winking in the light. 'Keep it up and you'll go blind, little boy,' he said and smiled; he wasn't even going to try to hide the dollar signs in his eyes.

I wanted to ask 'keep what up' but my mother was already saying how could it be possible, I had my prescription changed just last year.

'Less than a year ago, wasn't it, Kevin?'

I lifted my shoulders up the way my father did whenever she asked him what he wanted for dinner.

'What is it now? Minus what? Seven?'

'Seven point five. Both eyes.'

'At least they're the same. Balanced.' I said.

My mother looked at me and then back at the man. She leaned forward and whispered, as if sitting further away from me and lowering her voice meant that I wouldn't hear her.

'But he's only twelve! He's not really going blind... Is he?'

'I'm almost thirteen!' I corrected her. Twelve years and seven months, to be precise. But both of them ignored me.

'No, *lah*, miss,' said the glasses man, trying to flatter my mother. 'Joking only, joking only.' He was still smiling.

My mother did not smile back. She looked exactly the way she did when she had to go to school to talk to my form teacher, after the school nurse saw the bruises on my legs – blots of black and purple and yellow – and pointed out the one on my back during the annual check-up.

I was only eight years old then, and my form teacher was one of those who felt that she had to bend down to talk to her students. The lower she bent the sorrier she felt for them, I realized. The teacher was almost squatting when she said, 'How did you get them?'

'I don't remember except for that one.' I pointed to the one near the hilly bumps of my spine. 'That one is from when I walked backwards into a table.'

'Hmm.' She chewed the end of her Bic pen and asked again. Her voice was pillow soft and I could smell the cough drop she was hiding in her cheek. 'How did you get these bruises really? Don't worry. You can tell me.' She put a hand on my shoulder. I could feel the sweatiness of her palm even through my shirt sleeve.

I told her what I'd said before.

'Hmm,' she said again, and left to get Miss Tan.

After school, I had to wait outside the nurse's office while both of them asked my mother questions.

They talked for a few minutes before Miss Tan opened the door. 'Kevin, tell me how many fingers I'm holding up.'

'Okay.'

'Okay what?'

'Okay, I'm ready. Hold up your fingers.'

'I am already –'

'Already what?'

When we were in the bus, my mother shook her head and said, 'I thought you were just really clumsy.'

We went straight to the opticians. Afterwards, she brought me to the mini-mart close to home and told me I could pick out three items. I was so surprised when she brought me to the mamak shop below our flat and said, 'You can pick any three' – meaning I could pick out no-use-things (like balloons and ice-pops and Polo sweets that I ate only because I could whistle through the hole in the middle) – that it had taken me twenty minutes to decide on a Hiro cake and two erasers, one with the English flag on it, one with the French.

That was five years ago, a lifetime. In the space of five years, I had finished primary school (though I hoped I wouldn't have to – hoped and hoped that the millennium bug would crash all the computers so I wouldn't have to go to my new secondary school), lost my only friend, and become an outcast in my new class. The erasers are now thumbnail-sized, and only the blue bit is left of the French flag.

Back then I could still see what faces people were making even when they weren't sitting right next to me. Now, unless I press my face right up to whatever I'm supposed to see, everything is a smudge of cloud and colour.

While I read the posters on the optician's wall – TAKE AN EYE BREAK EVERY 40 MINUTES & LOOK AT A TREE – my mother picked out my new frames from the hundreds, thousands, lined up under the glass-top counter.

'How much is this?'

The man took out a calculator and started tapping on it. 'That one, with student discount…hunnerd-twenty.'

'That one?'

Tap-tap-tap. 'Hunnerd-seventy-five.'

'Anything below a hundred?'

'Oh, that one *lor.*'

'Come, Kevin, try these on.'

She handed me a pair with plastic rims, thick, black. I removed my own glasses, then put them on. I could just make out a me-shaped blur in the mirror – a beige-yellow circle, black on top. 'How does it look?' I asked, turning to face my mother.

There was a pause before she said, 'We'll take them.'

The optician coughed and rustled some papers. 'And the lenses? You want high index? Better get them for strong prescriptions like his, so the lenses are not so thick.'

'How much?'

The calculator went tap-tap-tap-tap and my mother sucked in her breath. 'The normal one is okay.'

When my father came home that evening, I told him that I was going blind.

He pulled his right ear and said, 'Makes your ear sharp.'

At school, I'd hoped no one would notice my new glasses but of course Albert did. I had known him ever since we moved into the block but we had never been in the same class. The moment I stepped into the classroom on the first day of secondary school and saw how he had been watching me walk in, how his lip had gone up a little on one side, my stomach started to hurt.

It hurt that morning, when I looked in the mirror and saw that the glasses covered half my face. At least the bowl cut which my mother had given me was growing out. I spent ten minutes combing my hair forward to see if it would cover up the glasses, the thickness of the lenses and frames, until my mother started screaming about me missing my ride. It didn't help that the new glasses kept sliding down my nose. Or that she'd thrust the red thermos at me in front of Albert, and in full sight of everyone on the bus, or that my breakfast congee had extra fried onions on top, stinking up the school bus when I opened up the thermos. I tried to ignore Albert when he shoved me at the steps of the bus so that he could get off first. Pretended not to hear him and his friends calling out to me, 'Oi, gay boy' – '*ah gua*' – 'retard!' But some things are harder to ignore. All of that was fine (at least that was what I tried telling myself). What was not fine was finding the cover of my maths and English workbooks scrawled with the same words, alongside cartoon mounds of shit inked in black marker. On the pages within – both blank and those filled with my own handwriting – were more drawings: a face, with giant specs and rabbity teeth, which was supposed to be me, and a crude sketching of a cock and balls next to an exercise where I'd filled in all the missing verbs in a sentence.

After that, I brought my lunch (always the same: char siu rice, no cucumbers, extra chilli) to the garden even though no one was supposed to. When the school janitor was there, pulling up weeds and tending to the rabbit hutch, I had to go somewhere else. Not the canteen, where they were sure to see me, so I skipped lunch and just went to the library. Once, when the library was closed for inventory, I made the food-stall auntie put my lunch in a takeaway bag and brought it to the boys' bathroom, locked myself in a cubicle and ate sitting down on the toilet seat. It was March, during one of those too-hot afternoons that made the back of my uniform stick to my chair, when Ms Pereira told us to bring in our workbooks for the quarterly check. This is it, I thought, this is the end. I could already see it: Ms Pereira's nose flaring when she saw the lewd drawings, then calling my mother to talk about my 'problematic behaviour'. Or worse, Ms Pereira getting the discipline master to cane me in front of the entire school at assembly. I wondered which would be worse, throwing my books into a bin and saying that I'd lost them, or getting new workbooks for all my classes and copying everything I had done so far into them. Except I couldn't afford new ones, even skipping lunch to save up for them wouldn't be quick enough. I did the only thing I could think of: go to my grandmother.

'Ah Ma, I need some money.'

'For what?'

'I need workbooks.'

'There's a whole stack under the coffee table,' she said and went to look for them. My stomach started to hurt when she bent down and the knobbly bits of her spine poked through her shirt. 'If not, you can go down to the convenience store. Ah Beng's shop sells them cheap.'

'Not exercise books, Ah Ma. Workbooks. I need the one for English class. The expensive ones you can only get at the bookstore.'

'*Har*? Why? What do you mean? Don't you have one already?'

That was when I told her what Albert had done. Before I had finished, she'd gotten up and hobbled over to his flat a few doors down. I heard her high voice even from the living room, snapping in my ear like a rubber band. Later that evening, I heard Albert crying as his mother whipped him with her bamboo cane. My mother had looked at Ah Ma as if to say 'look what you did'.

'He drew in my workbook,' I said, showing my mother the pages. She flinched when I got to the page with the cock and balls on it before looking away.

'Just ignore him. Sticks and stones may break your bones but words can never hurt you.'

That was when everything else came out, I couldn't help it, about Albert calling me names, putting out a leg to trip me whenever I went past.

'I can't even have lunch in the canteen because they make fun of my water bottle.'

'What's wrong with your water bottle?'

'IT HAS THOMAS THE TANK ENGINE ON IT.'

'Boy, don't shout at your mother,' my mother said. She breathed loudly, in and out of her nose several times before she continued. 'Ignore them. They're just jealous.'

'Jealous of what?'

'Be the mature one. You know, there are two types of heroes? The flashy ones and the quiet ones. The quiet ones grow up to become doctors and pilots and policemen.'

'I don't think I can become a pilot,' I said, squinting at her.

'They become teachers and civil servants and vets.'

I thought about the time I had two white mice, Harry and Jane. How Jane had got pregnant. We separated them but in the end, when she had finished giving birth, I got there in time to see her pushing one baby after another – plump, raspberry pink – into her tiny mouth. My mother had screamed but Ah Ma had simply brought the mouse back to the pet-store owner at the market. Harry died a few weeks later in his food bowl, round as a tennis ball and just as firm, after overeating from heartbreak.

A year ago, when I was in the last year of primary school, my teacher had written in my report card: 'Kevin is well-behaved but rather lackadaisical.' My mother had made me go to my room to get the dictionary and look up the last word.

'Lak-uh-dey-zi-kul,' I'd read. 'Without interest, vigour or deter-mination; listless; lethargic.'

'What? What's that mean?' Ah Ma said and made my mother translate it for her. 'Well, who's this? Is this that *keling* teacher? They don't know anything.'

'Ma!' my mother said.

'What is she, Wei Han? This teacher? Is she *ang moh*? Or *keling*? Her name sounds Indian.'

'MA, don't use those words in front of the boy. You're supposed to say "Indian". *Keling* is a bad word.' But she was looking at me, not at Ah Ma. She does this every time my grandmother says anything like that, ever since I embarrassed my mother in front of her boss, Mr Truman, during a company dinner when I asked if he was the ang moh my mother worked for. He had laughed and said yes but my mother turned red and piled food onto my plate to stop me from talking.

'Mrs Singh is Indian,' I said. 'She brought homemade *murukku* to class for Deepavali.'

'I hope you didn't eat them. Don't know what these people put in their food. They are all the same. The Malays steal, the Indians just drink beer all day...'

'And what do the Chinese do? They just say ugly things about other people all day,' my mother muttered before turning her attention back to me and narrowing her eyes to let me know if I were to repeat any of these things to anyone, I would be in trouble.

I saw my father dart his eyes at my mother, then at Ah Ma and dart them away again and I knew he was thinking about the Tiger beers he had after they went to bed. He had one every night, and usually many (many) more than that on Friday and Saturday nights. I didn't have to go to bed early so I would sit and shell peanuts for him. If he was in a good mood, he would help me with my maths homework as he drank and let me tip the empty cans so that I caught the last drops with my tongue. They didn't taste like anything, just fizz and metal. Sometimes he drank and watched TV until he fell asleep, snoring and waking everyone (except Ah Ma, who is hard of hearing). Once, next door even came to complain about the noise.

'I don't think I can be a vet and I don't think I want to become a teacher,' I said.

'It doesn't matter. Stop complaining about Albert. And besides, you have no proof that he drew in your book.'

'Proof?' Ah Ma said, 'You want proof? Just look at that neighbour boy, you think he's a nice child? Fat as a pig, mean as one too.' Then she went on to tell the story about how a sow had taken the hand off a child when she was living in the kampong. 'We let our pigs run around the village the way people now let their dogs run around their garden. Pigs are like people; half are nice, half are devils.'

All of this, I remembered as BEFORE THE STROKE, because AFTER THE STROKE was when Everything happened. Ah Ma had her first stroke that evening just as the Chinese ten o'clock news was finishing. The newscasters were saying goodnight when Ah Ma announced that she had a headache and tried to get up from the sofa. Then she fell over and couldn't get up on her own again. While my parents lifted her onto the sofa – my father at her head and my mother at her feet – I looked on and couldn't move, not even when my mother screamed at me to get the phone. All I could do was stare at the bottoms of my grandmother's feet, child-sized, a callus near her right pinkie toe.

I was following them out of the door when my mother shooed me back in. 'You have school tomorrow. Stay here and I'll call with the news.' I sat on the sofa by the phone until I fell asleep. It was one in the morning when my mother shook me awake to say that my grandmother was okay – that she'd had a stroke and was all right but my father would stay with her just to make sure. The following day I took the bus to the hospital after school. When I got there, my father was fidgeting in his seat next to the bed. I could tell from the way he was tapping his fingers on his knees that he had been there for some time and had been waiting for me to arrive. Ah Ma was sitting up in bed; one corner of her lip was glistening with saliva and I was torn between wanting to give her a handkerchief and running out of the room.

Then my father got up to go to the bathroom and left me alone with my grandmother. It was in those five minutes that Ah Ma said it. The thing that was going to come true later that week. As soon as we were alone, she turned to me and said, 'Wei Han, listen. I'm going to die soon and when I die, you can have everything in our room.'

'Ah Ma!'

'There is money in my underwear drawer, in a biscuit tin.'

'Ah Ma!'

'Maybe you should write that down, in case you forget.'

'Ah Ma, stop!'

'And the cassette player and my tapes, you can have those as well. Go and get it from my overnight bag over there. I want to show you how to use it so you don't break it.'

She spoke slowly, putting effort into making each sound. I looked at her for the first time since the previous night and saw that one side of her face was not like the other, as if she had been tilted and left like that, leaning at an angle. I couldn't figure out which side was the wrong one, the bad side, until I brought her the cassette player and she reached out with her left arm. Ah Ma, a righty all her life. She put it in her lap and pointed with her left index finger.

'Look. Press here to play, there to record. Remember to rewind the tapes when you're finished listening. Always rewind them. Don't forget.' The earphones unspooled and dangled from her lap, swinging in the air.

'But those are your tapes.' I knew there were about twenty of them on her bedside table, all filled with hours and hours of Hokkien and Teochew opera. She would sit in front of the radio and when one of her favourite operas came on, she would call out '*Aiya*!' and walk-run into the bedroom, arms swinging at her sides to propel her forward, and I would hear the crack of a new cassette shell being opened for the first time, the snap of the cassette deck being shut. Then she would come back out again and put the recorder next to the radio, push Record, and wave for everyone to keep quiet, a crooked finger to her mouth. At night, she slept with it on her chest as if that would make the sound of the people and instruments travel through her person and into her head. Most of the time she fell asleep with the music still whining out of the speaker and I would have to get up, feel my way over to her bed in the dark and click it off.

'It sounds like stray cats in the alley,' I had protested one morning. I had held my face above my pork congee so that my glasses steamed up and I wouldn't have to look at my grandma while I complained about her. I said it twice, first in English, then in Mandarin. '*Hao xiang mao jiao.*'

My father laughed and I knew I had won. The next day, he'd got Ah Ma earphones for her music and she went to sleep that night with the earbuds in, the black cord of it twisted around her hand. The funny thing is, after that, it took me longer to fall asleep.

Remembering this, trying to stop Ah Ma from listening to her music like that, made me want to hit myself in the face.

'But it's yours.' My cheeks were burning from the memory of having complained about her and I couldn't look at her in the eye.

'And it's still mine. Until I'm dead. And don't let it get rusty while I'm in here. I might be gone for a while.'

'Ah Ma…'

My father came out of the bathroom. 'Boy, are you ready to leave?'

I stood up and waved goodbye to Ah Ma.

A few hours later, while we were having dinner, Ah Ma had her second stroke.

That night, as we waited once more in the same pink-and-white corridor, outside the same room, I asked my father when Ah Ma would be able to go home and he just looked away. That was when the doctor came out to say that we should probably prepare ourselves; it was unlikely that Ah Ma was going to improve. Then he pressed his lips together and scribbled something on his chart. His shoes made squeaking noises as he walked away from us. Instead of thinking about Ah Ma, I scrabbled around in my brain for other things to think about and came up with two. One: that I wasn't going to be a doctor. Two: Ah Ma's cassette player.

It was strange that night without Ah Ma hobbling around in our two-bedroom flat – the absence was solid, something we tiptoed around, pretending not to notice. I closed my eyes and tried to imagine what it would be like going to sleep with an empty bed on the other side of the room but the thought of it made the dark behind my eyelids darker than black. So I stopped. Instead, I got up. The cassette player was still in my school bag from earlier that afternoon, when she'd forced it into my hands. I took it out, pressed Play, and left it on her pillow so that I could just about hear the tinny faraway sound of her music sneaking out of her earphones at the loud bits, the exciting bits, when the gongs and cymbals really got going. Then I closed my eyes again and pretended that she was there, listening to her opera, her head propped up on her wooden pillow.

The rest of the week that Ah Ma was in hospital, my parents and I talked about everything else but about her. Even when we were there, next to the bed, with the tubes going in and out of her and the machines making little beeping noises, everyone pretended that we were at home sitting around after dinner. Except there was no TV to look at, and Ah Ma was lying down instead of sitting in her usual spot in the armchair. She looked even worse than before, even less like herself. That one side of her face wasn't just slightly crooked now, it seemed frozen, as if it didn't belong to her.

My mother used her Hospital Voice the second we were in the ward. It was soft and an octave higher than usual; it sounded wrong, like lullabies sung outside, under the afternoon sun. It made me think something bad was going to happen (it was, it did).

'Hello Ma,' she whispered, 'how are you feeling?'

My grandmother was lying down and had to press a button to make the top of the bed fold up with a 'zzzng'. While we watched it inch up, all I could think was I didn't understand how she could be comfortable on the hospital pillow the way it is, soft and almost flat and covered in plasticky cotton. I felt like asking if it might be better to bring her her wooden pillow from home.

'*O-gay*,' my grandmother nodded. 'Eden?'

'Yes, yes, we've eaten. *Na*, soup – peanut and pig's tail.'

My father stood by while my mother tucked a handful of paper towels down the front of Ah Ma's hospital gown and spoon-fed her, his eyes far away.

I tried to guess what it was he might be thinking about instead. His clients? Their swimming pools? Worrying if he smelled too much of chlorine? The plants that he was growing in pots in the corridor outside our door? I stopped there. I realized I knew very little else about my own father. Then a little black thought crawled in. Maybe he was thinking about how expensive it was, a bed in a hospital. Almost a week. Maybe he was thinking it was better if –

He looked up. I stopped myself, squashing the thought dead. Like an ant under my finger.

'Kevin,' he began, 'what do you want to be when you grow up?'

'Huh?'

'You know. A job, a profession. You're twelve years old. In secondary school. Time to start planning what you want to do.'

'I want to become a journalist.' The thought had fallen out of my mouth as if it had been there all along, waiting and waiting for someone to ask the right question.

My mother looked up as if someone had just pinched her. She looked at my father while he rubbed his head, the way he does when he's confused. 'Oh. That's funny… That's what I wanted to be when I was young.'

'What happened?' I said, and wanted to take it back at once, it was as if I had just asked THEN WHY ARE YOU A POOL CLEANER. 'I mean…'

'Oh. No money to go to university. What to do…' He shrugged.

My mother was still looking at us in the way that meant *like father like son* and feeding Ah Ma soup at the same time.

'Like it?' my mother asked.

Ah Ma nodded and the movement spilled soup out of the not-working side of her mouth.

'Tissue paper, tissue paper!' my mother yelled, not using her Hospital Voice.

My father and I just stood there, gaping. By the time we unfroze, a nurse was at her bedside, dabbing at her face and gown. Tissues flew.

The minute the nurse went away, Ah Ma started to cry.

*   *   *

'What's going to happen to Ah Ma?' I asked the question again over dinner. Rice, sambal *kang kong*, the soup that Ah Ma had drunk and spilled.

My parents continued eating, but a bit noisier, as if wanting to drown me out.

I asked again, 'What's going to happen to Ah Ma?'

Clink, clink, clink, slurp.

I set my chopsticks across my bowl.

'What's wrong with you? Finish your food.'

'I just want to know…'

'A little too salty, this,' my father said, poking his chopsticks in the stir-fried greens.

'It's the sambal – the prawn paste I used in it must have been extra salty. Boy,' she turned to me. 'Eat your vegetables.' She gave me a heap of kang kong, enough to bury the rice in my bowl.

My father snipped off a bit of omelette and reached across the table to drop it on top of the greens. '*Na.*'

That was when I realized that this was something else I wasn't allowed to talk about. Along with 'Why does Albert not have a father?' and 'Does Pa not have a father? I've never heard you talk about him,' and 'Why did you have me so late?' (This last one I found out just last year, when second aunt drank herself silly on one glass of champagne at her daughter's wedding and rambled on about my parents having tried and tried for years to no avail, and were ready to give up when 'pop!' I came into the picture.) And these were only a number of the many things I wasn't supposed to bring up. The problem was nobody had given me a list detailing all the forbidden topics. Lists helped to make things clear, to line up the thousand and one thoughts that I had in my head. I needed one to show me what it was I wasn't supposed to say. The heading would go OUT OF BOUNDS or WHAT NOT TO SAY. Under that, I had my fourth entry: 'The maybe-possibility that Ah Ma might die.'

Number five would be 'Death, in general.'

'Boy, what are you doing? Your food's getting cold.'

It was as if nothing was different. As if her chair wasn't there, empty and pushed in against the table.

Finally, I said, 'Do your hands feel more, after you go blind?' Because this was an okay thing to talk about and I wanted something (anything) to fill in the quiet. After I asked the question, I could hear the chairs creaking, my parents wriggling their bums as they relaxed again into their seats.

My father chewed on the end of his chopsticks for a moment before replying, 'I don't know. I guess so.'

'But doesn't that mean that your skin feels more, and if your skin feels more maybe things hurt more? Or is it a superpower you can turn off and on?'

'I can see you pushing your food around, you know,' my mother said. 'And you're not going blind.'

That was all they talked about the rest of the dinner. I even forgot about my grandmother and the hospital, for a minute.

I decided then that this was what I should do as well. Not thinking. Not talking. I could start tonight. I would pretend that it was normal that Ah Ma wasn't around. But I needed something to distract me. That was when I remembered what she had said and decided to pick up her cassette recorder. It was just lying on top of her bedside table, gathering dust. There were more empty cassette tapes in the drawer beneath, my father had gotten her a whole box of them because she didn't want to or didn't know how to rewind and record over things.

I figured I had to collect sounds to remember by if I was going to be blind. That night, I punched little holes in a piece of paper with one of my mother's sewing needles. Then I closed my eyes and put my fingers over them. I tried and tried for minutes and felt nothing. Just maybe-bumps here and there. Maybe-bumps because I wasn't sure if I made up feeling them or if they were really there. When that didn't work anymore, when Ah Ma started tiptoeing around the edges of my thoughts again; the tubes stuck into the top of her wiry hand, the smell of the hospital – a kind of clean that was scarier than comforting, I reached for the recorder and spoke with my Inside Voice:

THINGS I DON'T HAVE TO SEE ANYMORE IF I GO BLIND

Ah Ma's half-frozen face
The other sick people in her hospital room
The way Pa walks, with one hand on his back, after cleaning extra dirty pools to pay off the hospital bills
Ma, when she eats dinner with her eyes closed after doing overtime at the shipping company
Public toilets
The way the boys in my class smile all crooked when I walk past them
Lao Shi's scary hair when she doesn't tie it up

I felt better. Just for a few minutes. I played the tape over and over again to drown out the noise of my own thoughts about Ah Ma. About what I should have said to Albert when he called me all the different things that he called me, until I fell asleep.

Chinese class is four times a week, Mondays, Tuesdays, Thursdays and Fridays. Monday to Thursday is when Lao Shi puts her hair up. On Fridays, she lets it loose and the black, thick curls fall around her face and down her back. They make her thin face look even thinner. Fridays are when she shouts about the homework she corrected during the week. The black cloud around her head shakes and trembles. White flecks of spit form at the sides of her mouth when she starts to tell us off.

'*Ni zhen de shi bai chi*,' she says, shouting the last two words. 'Oh, you really are an idiot.' This is what she says when someone does their homework badly. Or, '*Ni mei you yong tou nao* – You're not using your brain.'

She said it to me once and I was quite glad. I took it to mean she believed there was something in my head that could be put to good use, if I wanted. When there are assignments missing, she starts in on all of us even though it might be just one or two who didn't hand in their work.

'You think I get a bonus for marking more work? Ungrateful, lazy, inconsiderate, all of you!'

She says this in English to make sure that the really weak students, the ones whose parents speak Mandarin only during Lunar New Year with distant relatives and even then just the few stock phrases wishing good luck and prosperity, understand her as well. Sometimes, after Lao Shi is done shouting, she leaves the classroom, slamming the door shut behind her, and I can breathe again. No one talks or moves when she is gone because she can be back quicker than we hear her (she moves like a cat for someone so tall; she's the tallest woman I know). Sometimes she comes back and her face is changed, the way someone's face can be changed after they've been to the sink and washed the day away. Other times she comes back with her long, wooden ruler and puts it to use, not on the girls though, that isn't allowed. Just the boys and recently, just Albert. I try not to look when the ruler makes a fat *thwack* on his palm because she calls you out and gives you one for looking happy as well – 'What are you smiling about? Get over here.' Once or twice, she didn't come back. The entire class simply waited in silence until the bell went and then we put our things in our backpacks, everyone moving in slow motion, in case she returned and we looked too happy to be leaving.

*   *   *

I was in that class on a Friday when it happened; the last day of school before the June holidays. She was telling us about her office hours during the break, saying that she would be around all morning from Monday to Wednesday and to come with questions if we had any when someone knocked and put her head around the door. Lao Shi went outside and there was a lot of whispering for a moment before she came back in, wearing a different sort of face. The face she had when I saw her giving a stack of textbooks to a girl who couldn't afford them (the only one in class who was poorer than Albert and me). For a few seconds I could see what she might look like as a next-door neighbour or a friend of my mother's. She had that face on now. Instead of feeling comforted, I felt my bladder being squeezed like a water balloon.

I knew what was coming but I still jumped when she looked at me and said, 'Wei Han, pack your bag. Your parents are coming to pick you up.'

Her voice was polite and even. The way she had spoken to the other teacher, but even softer. I felt everyone watching as I put my stationery and books in my backpack and I knew that Albert's eyes were on me, hoping and hoping that I was in trouble. I would have chosen to stay if I'd known what was coming. I would have chosen to get on the school bus at the end of the day and have Albert lob paper bullets at me, or stomp on my feet, or seize whatever he took a fancy to – a packet of chocolate Hiro cake that my mother had dropped into my bag, or my pencil case. I would have happily taken the bus and then got off with him at the foot of our apartment block; have him push past me to get into the lift on his own while I waited for the next one or simply walked up six floors, all the while wishing I were taller, broader, or at least had perfect sight. I would have chosen to go through all of that each day for the rest of my time in this school, because I knew what it meant to be gently called out of class like this. I didn't want to leave.

Wang Di

'You know what the problem is? It's too late for us.' The baker snapped the two halves of his metal tongs together as he waited for the old lady to decide. 'Too late for change. Too late for moving from one building to another. They think that people our age – sixty, seventy years old, can still adapt to a new building, a new neighbourhood.'

Wang Di had told the baker about her morning – half of it spent trapped in her new bathroom with its fancy, folding door. She had struggled with it for ten minutes before sitting on top of the toilet, debating whether or not to pull the red pull-for-help cord. She was about to do it when she kicked at the door out of desperation. The thump echoed through the flat and the folding door folded, creaked open. She stepped out of the bathroom. Sat down on the closest chair she could collapse onto.

'Isn't this easier?' The housing officer had said a year ago as he brought Wang Di and the Old One to the new flat – the flat that was 'in the same neighbourhood, still Ang Sua, Red Hill', or so he kept saying. Wang Di had asked if the distance was walkable, she wanted to be able to visit the shops while they still stood but he had said, 'better not, especially with uncle's bad leg' and suggested they take the bus instead. She had asked how much the bus fare would be but he didn't know. After that, they had lapsed into a strained quiet during the fifteen-minute drive, most of it spent in thick traffic. The new building, 6A – cough-syrup orange – had lifts that stopped on every floor in the building. Except the housing officer called it a *studio*. She had tried saying it but had got stuck on the first syllable: *Suh-tu-dio*. The *suh-tu-dio* was a one-roomer as well, and the elderly couple trailed behind the man as he showed them the apartment, making the most of the only two doors in the narrow space (one that led to the storeroom, the other to the bathroom) by opening and closing them and touching everything – the light switches, the taps, all the windows.

It would take her time to unlearn decades of memory. This was not how she thought the end of her life would be like: on her own, in a flat that was stark white and much too quiet, stripped of the things she'd been used to for most of her life. I will get used to this, she thought. I've got used to worse. It was this last thought that made her get up and leave her strange apartment. Once she was out, she kept on walking. Her knees still felt weak and she had the feeling that if she stopped, she would fall and never get up again. So she walked past the coffee shop next to the building filled with food stalls she had never eaten at, manned by people she didn't know, and started on the long stretch of road that was Jalan Bukit Merah. Wang Di kept to the shade of the wide-branched trees, her feet crunching on their fallen leaves as she passed pairs of Filipino maids pulling market trolleys behind them, passed uniformed children camel-backed with school bags, passed yawning house-dressed women and elderly Indian men in lungis walking their dogs, and armies of white-shirted men and women heading for bus stops or the train station. Walked for half an hour, at least. When she was nearly there she stopped for just a second to look up at her old pink-and-yellow building, then crossed the street to get to the bakery on the ground floor. Her feet were aching and it felt like the sun had scorched a hole on the top of her head but she knew why she was there. What she had to do.

'I've only lived in the new flat for three days. Time,' she told the baker, 'just needs time.'

'But that is precisely the problem. Time. We have none! Ah, except you, Mrs Chia. You are what...only?'

'Seventy-five.'

'Ah, see? You're a *gin na* compared to me. Just a child.'

She said nothing but waited to catch his eye before she continued. 'Since I'm here, I just wanted to ask... You've known us, the Old One and me, for a long time. Did he ever tell you about his life before we moved here? You know...during the war.'

'The war?' The baker's face expanded in surprise, then he snapped the metal tongs again as he frowned. 'No, I don't think so. He didn't really – oh, but he did tell me where he used to live before: Bukit Timah.'

'Yes, but was there anything else? Did he ever mention anything to do with February?'

'February? You mean like a birthday or something? No, nothing like that. But I know he worked for years in town. Told me he moved because it got too crowded and dirty.'

Wang Di straightened up. 'Do you know where? Which street, I mean?'

'Sorry,' he shook his head. 'Only so much this head can hold.' He looked away, kindly rearranging the pastries on the counter before him as she flushed and dabbed at her forehead with a cotton handkerchief. When she was done, he asked, 'Are you okay? How are you coping with the move?'

How am I coping? Wang Di thought. Then a flash of memory. The trees in front of her window, almost as tall as the buildings around them. *Her* trees. The dark-green scent of their leaves mixed with the sting of exhaust. She turned around to look at them now. Soon they would be gone. Torn out of the ground like weeds. But to the baker, she said, 'I'm okay. Same, same. Going back to my rounds tomorrow.'

'Maybe you should stop. Not good to keep on walking around like that in the heat. You know, the island is getting hotter, with all the buildings. All concrete and steel and glass. How not to get hot?'

Here she brought out the little speech she always gave everyone when they asked. A face-saving speech. Little lies that made up a big lie. 'Oh, I wouldn't be able to do that. Nothing to do. I'll get bored sitting at home.'

He nodded and made sympathetic noises. 'Oh, I know, I know.'

But when Wang Di tried to pay, Teo held out the bag and waved his hands at her. 'No need, no need.'

It was in the last few years living in their grey and broken down flat in Block 204 that Wang Di became Cardboard Auntie. She had just been dismissed from her cleaning job at the hawker centre for being too slow and had put off going to the bank for some time. She waited two weeks, until what remained in her purse were a few silver coins and a safety pin that pricked her finger each time she reached in to scrabble around, hoping for a lost cent, or a dollar note, folded and wedged into a corner. When she got her bank passbook back from the cold, smiling teller, she pinched it tight in her hands until she arrived home. Then she went into the kitchen and opened it to the last printed page.

$92.77.

This was how much they had left, the two of them together. She at seventy-two years of age and the Old One at ninety. Wang Di stared at the page until the numbers started to shift and bloom into different shapes. She pushed a fingernail into the paper, scoring a slight curve into the blank space beneath the digits.

On her first day, as the red-eyed koel sang its woeful *koo-wooo koo-wooo* from a treetop, Wang Di reached her arm into the bins around her neighbourhood, called through quiet storefronts or knocked on back doors to ask if they had any used cans and unwanted boxes. It took getting used to, took learning, like everything else. On good days, she received up to ten dollars from the collector. If it was raining, she considered herself lucky if she got two.

It wasn't long before she started to bring her gleanings home. The Old One looked away every time she returned with one more item: a small glass bottle, a collection of bottle caps. Stuffed them into the kitchen cupboards and drawers, underneath the bed, on top of their slanting wardrobe. As if to fill up the empty corners of their lives, the quiet between them, to leave no room for thought.

It was to this quiet that Wang Di returned that afternoon. This same quiet and lack of questioning that she now regretted.

She could recall the first time her husband had told her he wasn't going to work that morning – was leaving home that day to take care of something. They were still strangers, muddling through their first week of marriage, of knowing each other. She had felt watched as he waited for her to ask where he was going. 'Okay, of course,' she'd replied instead.

He did the same thing the following year on the same day, 12 February, and every year after that. After he left his boss's shop to set up his own tailoring stall, he would ask Wang Di for permission to leave, just for a few hours, as if she were in charge. She had the idea that he was doing something shameful – the way she was doing something shameful, going to the *sinseh* for herbs that turned out not to work – so she didn't ask.

The yearly ritual only stopped when his leg became so bad that even a walking stick was of little help. The first time 12 February came and passed without his half day away, Wang Di almost wanted to ask if he had forgotten but let it rest. It was much too late to talk about this, she decided, it would only bring up the question of why she hadn't wanted to know all these years.

'I should have asked,' Wang Di said, as she looked at his photo on the altar. Then she did the only thing she could to feel at home again: she went to bed. Even though it was thirty degrees outside and her flat was lit with the afternoon sun. Even though Baker Teo's words were still buzzing between her ears. The look on his face when she started asking him about the Old One, a look that said, 'Why talk about what happened during the war?' and 'Why now?' She lifted the thin blanket over her head and closed her eyes. As she lay on her mattress, she tried to weigh her two fears against each other. Her fear of his past and her own, swathes of it still untold, and her fear of the future – one that was absent of her husband. The only other time she had lain in bed like this was the day after she began telling the Old One about what had happened to her when she was young, just on the cusp of adulthood. How it had felt, all that history like a large, wriggling fish she was trying to wrestle to shore, how she had to fight not to get pulled under. She remembered how she had told him all she could until a familiar dread stoppered her throat. That night, the nightmares returned (her first in years) and he had to hold her hand while she slept, as if trying to prevent her from being swept away by a swift current.

She thought about the way people stayed on afterwards in the very places they had died, wondered if the Old One would be able to find her new place or if he would linger in the building, even as construction workers took it apart and grew something new in its place. If he were still here, she told herself, she would ask him instead. None of this creeping-around-and-asking-the-baker business, as if she were doing something she was not supposed to do. She would ask him and hope that he would forget about all the times she made him hold his tongue, hope that it wasn't too late.

'Is it true? Have I run out of time, Old One?' The answer, when she sat up and looked around her, was clear. It echoed in the things she had accumulated over the years, brought over from the old flat (much to the chagrin of the movers) to fill this chalk-white, new apartment. The cardboard boxes bricking a half-wall that led from the entryway into the living room. The plastic bags hanging from doorknobs or left gaping on the floor, all of them filled with inconsequential objects – rubber bands, jam-jar lids, disposable plates and bowls. The kitchen table covered with piles of junk mail and letters that she couldn't read, that she'd left unopened since the Old One died. His things, lifted out of the box and put back in their respective places: his clothes, in his side of the thin plywood wardrobe, clean and folded. His sewing kit on top of the TV, expectant, like a plant waiting to blossom. It echoed in her ears – too late, too late.

December 1941 – March 1942

When we emerged from the ground on the morning of 8 December, we were almost surprised to find everything still there. For much of the night we'd crouched in the bomb shelter, breathing in the smell of mud and fear, listening to the thunder of planes overhead; I expected to see evidence of the night's terror as my father pulled me out of the bomb shelter, but nothing in our village, nothing on the surface at least, had changed. When we were back home, my mother set about making coffee and laying out the breakfast things while my father told my brothers to get ready for school; a stoicism that they had picked up from having spent their youths living from one disaster, economic or natural, to another. My brothers and I were shaky from lack of sleep but instead of snatching a few moments of quiet indoors, Yang and Meng stood outside watching thick plumes of smoke rise from the city centre and waft over like dark clouds.

Later that day, a few of the neighbours came with news that the island's airfields had been destroyed, that people in the city centre had lost their homes, but my father insisted that this was hearsay. 'Rumours. Nothing but rumours. We have the British on our side. More likely that the sky will fall.'

A lull seemed to confirm this. Then a second air raid occurred, and a third.

After that, for the next six weeks, we knew little else but the sound of air-raid warnings and planes and bombs. My father led the short dash to the shelter each time, a few hundred yards beyond the attap huts, all the while looking overhead as if we would have been able to outrun a plane or a bomb if one had been heading towards us. I was in charge of keeping Yang and Meng close while my mother carried two wooden buckets, one from which we would sip during the night and one in which we took turns to relieve ourselves – there was no knowing how long we had to wait.

Throughout the six weeks, even as we felt the tremor of bombs sinking into the ground just over a mile away, my father held on to the belief that the war would be over soon. It was this stern optimism and the fact that our village had, so far, escaped the air raids, that allowed Yan Ling and me to continue going to the market every day. As we walked, she relayed bits of news that she had overheard on the radio at work.

'The newscasters keep talking about how hard the soldiers are fighting the Japs and how they won't give up. No one's worried. Not my boss. Not my parents. Especially not my parents. All they talk about is the wedding.' It was early February and her sister was set to be married in little more than a week. 'My mother was so upset when they announced the curfew last week. All day she complained, "What about the wedding dinner?" Yan Ling imitated her mother, her eyebrows going up and down in dismay. "The restaurant has already been paid" – she's praying for the war to be over so that they can have the wedding party.'

'But the ceremony will go on? The dinner's not that important.'

'Not to my mother. She wants to show everyone how well my sister married – the meat, the fish, the mountains of noodles and sweets.'

'What does she think about it?' Yue Qing was only sixteen, my age, and I could not imagine leaving my family to live with someone else – a man, a stranger – that I had met just once for a half an hour.

'I heard her telling her friends that she can't wait to leave home. I don't blame her. *I* want to leave as well.' We reached the market just then and she waved goodbye before weaving her way through the morning crowd.

Even with the bombings, the market lost none of its colour. Business went on, punctuated now and again by air-raid sirens, which everyone seemed determined to ignore. Behind the noise and bustle were gradual signs that things were changing: the constant buzz from the neighbours' radios; the curfew, which meant that we had to sit in the dark for most of the night, listening to my father tell ghost stories until my brothers and I fell into fitful sleep.

As the Japanese troops swept through Malaya, more and more people fled south. I didn't realize the full extent of the exodus to Singapore until I accompanied my mother to Chinatown one weekend. There, under the arch of the five-foot-way where the letter writer usually set up his table, were whole families sitting on the floor. Mothers nursing infants, grandfathers perched on discarded wooden crates. Outside, on the street, I saw lone figures separated from spouses or parents or siblings. There was one boy about Meng's age – not older than ten at most – begging for coins from passers-by, and scraps from a whole line of food hawkers – only to be shooed away each time. As he got closer, I saw that he had a layer of dirt on his face and neck, save for the clear track lines his tears or sweat had made along the side of his face. He seemed abandoned, had the skittish manner of a kicked puppy. As he neared, I looked down, hoping he wouldn't come to me. When I raised my eyes again, he was gone.

There were also soldiers, mostly Indians, and ang moh from Britain and Australia, sitting on kerbs. Their bandages mottled scarlet as they smoked their cigarettes down to the nub. All of them – both the soldiers and the homeless – seemed to be waiting for something. Food or help or a hospital bed, and I never found out if they got any of those things. Or if they would disappear in the air raids, with no one to claim them.

'Have you noticed people in town? The new people, I mean?' I asked my father at dinner one day.

'What? Oh, you mean the refugees. Terrible. But don't worry. Once the war is over, the police will take care of things again. It will all go back to normal, you'll see.'

It was days away from mid-February when Yan Ling's mother sent her on a trip to Chinatown, a monthly errand – part duty, part treat – that I accompanied her on, usually to procure things we couldn't get from our neighbourhood market: herbs from the medicine hall or scrap cloth from a tailor they were friendly with. This time, her orders were all for the wedding. While she bought a packet of fragrant Oolong for the tea ceremony, then a box of rouge for her sister from the beauty store, I wandered the narrow aisles, picking up one glass bottle then another and looking through the amber bottles to try and see how the world might look like with different eyes. We were leaving the store when Yan Ling showed me the two coins in her palm. 'My mother said I could keep the change.' Two cents could buy us a bag of iced gems that could last us a few days or two shaved ices that would last minutes.

'First, I have to sell these,' I said, lifting my basket to show her how heavy it was with produce.

It was while we were in Trengganu Street, pushing through the sweaty market crowd that the sirens wound up, wailing higher and louder than I had ever heard them. All around us, stall owners packed up and their customers abandoned their half-finished meals to get to their feet. Mothers picked up their children while housekeepers with bunned and netted hair scattered into the alleyways. Neither Yan Ling nor I were familiar enough with Chinatown to know where to go – not in a snap; so we stood, watching to see who went where. As we did, a plane crossed overhead and I looked up. It was flying so low that the pilot's face was starkly visible. He was a young Japanese man, little older than I was, and his face was so serene he could have been someone, anyone, driving his new car down a freshly laid road. I was thinking this, face tilted skyward, when Yan Ling took my arm and shook me, making me drop my basket. Five eggs rolled out and cracked on the tarmac, spilling their yellow insides.

'What are you doing? Run!'

Yan Ling pulled me along, through a crush of people coming our way, trying to avoid rickshaws and cars recklessly tearing down the street. We saw a crowd surging towards the entrance of a shelter, barred by the linked arms of two white men, their pin-striped shirts drenched through, ties askew.

A voice rang out, high-pitched, despairing. 'They're not letting us in!'

'It's only for the ang moh,' someone else cried. 'It's no use.'

The next air-raid shelter was full, the way leading down into it choking with civilians and the stench of sweat. So was the next. The streets were starting to empty. As we retreated into the five-foot-way pressing close to the shuttered shops, I heard someone singing, 'the bombs are coming, the bombs are coming.' The singer, mad or drunk, zigzagged into view before wandering ahead, his voice sailing up, cracking through the scream of the siren.

'Should we turn back and run home?' I asked. But Yan Ling only held on to my wrist, squeezing it tight, then tighter still.

'Here, in here!' There was a woman waving at us from half-way behind a shutter, just a few shops down. I thanked her as we squeezed past, into pitch black and quiet, and settled down onto the concrete floor. Someone struck a match and lit candles, passing the light from hand to hand until all four corners of the room were lit. There were tables all around, and chairs pushed back from them. Underneath the table tops crouched men, women, and children. I counted about fifty. After some minutes, we heard a long, ghostly whistle, then the thunder of something like God striking ground close by. The building shuddered. Pots and pans clattered onto the kitchen floor in the back and the jars of chopsticks on each table crashed to the floor, dispensing all of their contents. Throughout all of this, no one made a sound, not even the infants nestled in the crooks of arms.

'Are you okay?' Yan Ling whispered. I looked at her for the first time since we stopped running and noticed that there was a bloodied gash across her forearm.

'You're hurt,' I said.

Without a word, an elderly man closest to the kitchen slipped away and came out again, tiptoeing between groups of people to hand her a dampened tea towel. 'Here, you should clean it. We don't have any iodine in here or I would have given it to you.'

'Thank you,' she said, wincing as she applied the towel to the cut.

All around us, people were starting to whisper.

'I should have left the island when I got the chance.'

'And go where? It's not safe off the island. The British care about what happens to Singapore. We're not some far-flung little kampong up in the north, we're actually important. I heard they're going to deploy more ships. And not just the English, the Australians –'

'You should all wake up. They're losing. *We* are losing.' Everyone turned to stare at a man sitting in the middle of the room. His face was thin, pale and he had a pair of wire-rimmed glasses tucked into his shirt pocket. 'Why would they bother protecting this island anyway? They have their own country to defend. Most of them, the ang moh who used to live here, have gone back. They started leaving the minute the Japanese landed in Malaya.' His face reddened as he finished speaking, as if he had not meant to; was astonished at the sound of his voice in the enclosed space. He looked down, took his glasses out of his pocket and started polishing the lenses with a handkerchief.

The people in the room murmured, some nodding, some turning away to whisper sharply to their neighbours. More planes overhead. Then another round of bombing, this time further away.

By the time it felt safe to leave, it was late in the afternoon. It was only when I stepped out that I saw the caved-in building to the left of us, just a street away. There was still smoke rising from within the rubble and as we approached, I saw people sitting among the piles of rock, like wildlife caught in traps. An ambulance waited, the red cross on it shiny, as if painted on minutes ago, while three first-aid workers pointed at different spots in the debris and argued about where to begin digging. Close to them, a row of civilians looked on with white handkerchiefs pressed over their mouths and noses, and I wondered if this was their home, if it used to belong to them, the stone and soot of it, spilling out into the road. We passed a few more shophouses that had been hit, all of their insides exposed, bricks spat out like poison.

A little further up, on Temple Street, rickshaws had been scattered, as if swept around by a giant hand. There was a sound like a constant wail, a smaller siren that had continued sounding its alarm. Then I saw it, a woman my mother's age, squatting in the middle of the road. Her mouth was open in a howl and she had her arms extended towards a doll. I blinked. Not a doll; it was a boy of about five, on the ground. He was wearing a short sarong around his waist, had his arms spread out as if in sleep. There was nothing, no sign of injury except around his mouth, a splash of blood like a dark strawberry birthmark. His hair was swept back off his face, as if combed and set lovingly by an adult hand. I waited and waited for him to stir and crawl to his feet but he didn't.

'Don't look,' Yan Ling said, pulling me away, turning my head with her hands. 'Don't look.'

Against all common sense, our neighbours went ahead with the wedding despite the daily air raids. Only a small cluster of people gathered outside Yan Ling's home to watch Yue Qing leave her childhood home. She was dressed entirely in red; her veil was so heavily embroidered that she stumbled a couple of times even with Auntie Tin's help. I held my breath until she was seated inside the waiting rickshaw. As she was led away, Meng turned to me. 'Jie-jie,' sister, he said. 'Are you going to get married like this one day?' I laughed and nudged him towards the direction of home.

The wedding dinner had to be cancelled because of the curfew. The day after the ceremony, Mrs Yap went from house to house, distributing cuts of meat and noodles that the restaurant had divided into takeaway boxes. It was the best meal that we'd had in years and would be the best meal that I was to have for years to come.

That day, as Mrs Yap gushed about the ceremony to my mother, I went outside to join Yang, who was leaning against the wall of the hut. He was watching the sky for planes, something that he'd started doing ever since the first air raid. We stood side by side for a few minutes in silence until he said, 'I haven't seen any of the ang moh's planes for days. Only the Japanese ones.'

I shook my head, uncomprehending.

He made an impatient click with his tongue. 'Ever since the war started, I've seen mainly Allied planes flying overhead; Brewsters – barrel-shaped with short wings – and Hurricanes, fighter planes that look sleeker. But lately my friends and I have only spotted Japanese planes. You can pick them out easily, not that you have much time to – you'd be in trouble if you stayed still instead of running – but they have red circles under their wings and on the sides of their bodies, the same red circle that's on the Japanese flag.' He looked up again. 'I've only seen their planes in the past few days. No others.'

They took the city quickly. Overnight, it seemed. The way it went reminded me of the time stray dogs broke into our chicken coop and I lay in bed, blinking awake, knowing something had changed while we were all asleep. The rooster hadn't woken us up that morning and the air was still, unpunctuated by soft bird sound. When I entered the yard to collect the eggs, I found just one hen, half dead, its wings torn into a new shape, and called for my father. There was nothing left to do but watch as he picked it up gently in both hands and snapped its neck. That night, my mother put the cheapest parts of the chicken – its throat and back – into a soup. The rest she sold, then bought three chicks to replace the ones we lost.

This time, again, it was the quiet that hinted at what was to come. It was the first morning of the Lunar New Year but the only thing that came to mind as I woke was that we had slept through the night – an entire night uninterrupted by the wail of sirens or the whirl of planes above us. It was the quietest New Year I had ever known. No firecrackers or the distant music of dancers visiting the wealthier neighbourhoods with their white and gold lion costumes. No children going from door to door wishing their neighbours a happy New Year, smiling wide in anticipation of an *ang bao* filled with a coin or two. The night before, we had dressed ourselves in our cleanest, newest clothes, eaten reunion dinner without much comment, and wished my parents happy New Year at midnight. My mother had given each of us an *ang bao* and I had pressed my fingers around the edge of the coin within until the red envelope tore.

The quiet persisted throughout breakfast. As soon as my father had finished, he got up and headed for the door.

'I think I'll go and see if I can get some news,' he said, jerking his chin towards the direction of the village elder's home. 'Maybe it's over. Maybe the ang moh got rid of them.' He tried to sound hopeful but the cords of muscle in each side of his jaw twitched as he clenched and unclenched his teeth. 'Why don't you make some *tang yuan*? I'll be back in time for lunch.'

As we waited, my brothers and I rolled uneven, marble-sized globes of glutinous rice dough and lined them up on the table as a pot of sweet ginger syrup simmered above the charcoal fire. We worked silently, letting our hands move along to their own spell, all the while keeping an ear and eye out for my father.

He returned an hour later, just as we finished washing our hands and wiping off the table. My father pressed the top of his head with a flat hand, smoothing his grey hair forward. I knew what was coming but strained to hear it anyway. His voice was so soft the bubbling from the pot almost drowned him out.

'They've surrendered. The Japanese have taken over.'

They renamed the island Syonan-to and pushed the clock forward an hour so that we were on the same time zone as Tokyo. For us, the people living away from the city centre, there was little change. A different currency. A different flag. Superficial things.

That first week, a neighbour stopped by to talk to my father. '*Aiya* – first we had the British, now we have the Japanese. This is just a handing over of power. Nothing more.' The man shook his head.

My father's face was turned away from me but as he responded with a tight, wry laugh, I could picture his eyes – cold, unconvinced.

'At least the bombings have stopped,' the neighbour said as he left.

At the end of February, we were all at home when we heard a voice, tinny and faint at first, that grew louder over the course of minutes. From the window, I saw a man in plain clothes, walking up the street with a loudspeaker held to his mouth. 'All men aged eighteen to fifty must report to the police station at nine in the morning. Failure to show up will result in heavy punishment.' He said this in Mandarin first, then repeated it in various dialects, passing the houses in an easy stroll, as if he were the rag-and-bone man drawing attention to his trade.

My father left just after dawn the next day, saying he couldn't bear to sit around and wait and that it was a long walk anyway. My mother made him take a change of clothing and some boiled rice wrapped in banana leaf, all bundled up in a square of cloth, and wept as he left.

She wept again when he came home that evening, his face dark and lined, as if he had aged years in the course of a single day. The first thing he did was to take his shirt off and lay it on the dresser. There were marks on the left sleeve, slightly smudged but it was evident that they were characters in Japanese.

'Don't wash this,' he told my mother, looking at me to ensure that I heard him as well. 'Make sure the stamp remains on the sleeve.' Then he went to the large basin and washed his face, letting the water drench his arms and undervest, yellowed from age.

The only thing my father said at dinner was this: 'It's a good thing Yang and Meng are still children.' Yang was fifteen and looked it, while Meng, at ten, was small for his age.

For the next few months, my father would wear the shirt every time he left home, even if only to go to the public tap for water. When it became unbearably soiled, he took a pair of scissors to the sleeve, cut out a square of cloth with the Japanese symbol on it and wore it pinned to his chest whenever he stepped out of the house. After the war, my mother found it tucked into the pocket of one of his trousers. She put it into the bucket we used for burning offerings to the dead and watched as the fire slowly took it.

That night, I listened to my parents talk when they believed that we had all fallen asleep. It was the first time I'd heard my father whisper and I only caught slivers of conversation through the curtain that separated their sleeping area from mine and the boys'. His words merged with my half-formed dreams so that I woke in the morning heavy with dread.

'I had the strangest nightmare, Ma,' I began when I sat down at the kitchen table.

My mother pinched her lips together as I described it to her – soldiers, hooded figures with pointing fingers, lines of men being led onto trucks.

'No dream,' she said, when I was finished. 'They took half the men at the reporting station. Half of them. Put them onto trucks and now they're God-knows-where. A number of our neighbours were taken. The Tiongs, both father and son; and the Tans; and that man who owns the pig farm. They're going after the business owners, and those who work for the British… At least that's what your father said.'

'The Tiongs? You mean Mr Tiong next door? But they're not business owners. They're like us.' I gestured around our home the way my father had a few weeks ago, pointing out the dignified squalor surrounding us – the hand-sewn curtains, the one, seldom-used candle that lit up the hut when dusk fell.

'I know, that's what I said to your father. He told me they were picked out from the line by someone wearing a hood. Holes cut out for the eyes…like an executioner. *Choy choy choy*,' my mother spat. 'I shouldn't have said that. Anyway, no one knows where they are. Anything can happen.'

She turned away to light the fire under the pot of congee. 'Don't let your father know that I told you this. He already left for work because he couldn't sleep.'

At 10:00 a.m., my father returned home. 'The store is closed. I waited for an hour and asked the other shop owners in the street but no one knows anything.'

He tried again that afternoon, then every single day for the next two weeks until one morning he arrived to find all the stock – chairs and tables and cabinets that he had lovingly sanded and oiled – thrown outside in a heap and the shop shuttered and chained. There was talk that his boss had been taken away during the round-ups (the *sook ching*, or purge, as it came to be called years later) for donating to China's resistance efforts. There was no notice, no one to go to with his questions, so he gave up and started looking for a new job. My father never found out what had happened to him.

It was this need to put rice in our bowls again that pushed our family routine back to what it was before the invasion. My mother resumed her laundry rounds, and I went to market with my eggs and vegetables for the first time in a month. The night before, my father instructed both of us to keep our heads down and bow to each and every soldier we came across. He repeated this again as we left home early next morning but it seemed little had changed until we approached town. There were barricades at every turn. At each one, sentries rifled through my basket, then waved me away. The closer we got to the centre, the more I saw of them. Soldiers, passing in their cars. Soldiers, inside jewellery shops and tailors' getting measured for suits. Walking in pairs, making sure everyone – especially the men – looked compliant enough. I kept my head down and stared at their boots, only looking up once I was clear of them. My first day back in town made me feel like I'd entered another country. Out of almost every window hung makeshift Japanese flags cut from white dust cloths. The red and white of the flags, the sound of cloth flapping in the breeze, all of this gave the street the outward appearance of a parade, and it only served to make the unnatural hush seem even sharper, more malevolent.

I was never there for long. An hour in and all of my produce would be bought up. The eggs were always the first to go. I didn't know it but the other market stalls and grocery shops, the ones that relied on deliveries from the shipyard along the Singapore river, were suffering, their stock thinning as the warehouses in the city emptied.

It was in March that the first of the soldiers came. There had been murmurs, talk about them going from village to village, taking whatever they wanted – mostly food and supplies. I had heard enough from passing neighbours and the nervous whispers between my parents late at night to know that it was a near certainty. I didn't know, not then, that they had sacked an entire village during the invasion. That they had stormed Alexandra Hospital the day before the British surrender, had raged through the buildings, going from room to room, drunk on bloodlust, shooting and bayoneting doctors, nurses and patients. Even those lying on the operating tables had not been spared.

I didn't know it that morning so I was fearful but darkly curious when I saw their vehicles approach, telling myself that my over-wild imagination created scenarios far worse than what could happen in reality. I soon learned that I was wrong, of course.

The entire kampong fell silent as the trucks came up the road. Even the dogs – wild ones that roamed the village, scrappy things that barked and howled at anything, a falling branch, a shout – even the dogs fell silent at the approach of the trucks. No one spoke until a mechanical whine cracked through the air. A loudspeaker being turned on. There was the sound of a throat being cleared, then a male voice. This time, the man spoke Chinese and Hokkien, and interpreted now and again for the Japanese. 'Everyone – men, women, children – gather outside right away!'

'Stay behind me,' my father said as the truck stopped close to our hut. 'And bow. Bow deeply. Don't look up. Whatever you do.'

My father unlocked the door and made us trail behind him. 'Keep bowing,' he reminded us.

I did as I was told. From that angle, I saw their boots, laces fraying at the ends, daubed with mud.

'Get into a single line! Closer, closer!'

While most of the soldiers went into our homes, two of them kept guard, pacing in front of us. I stayed bowed the entire time but the shine of wood caught my eye – it was the wooden end of a rifle and it had a delicate inscription carved into the grain. I watched it as it moved from left to right, and back again. Then the soldier halted, spinning the rifle around so that the knife that stuck out of the barrel caught the sun, flicking light into my face.

Everyone stood still as the men worked, moving back and forth between the attap huts and the two trucks. Twenty minutes was all they needed. For twenty minutes, the air was filled with the clatter and thud of objects being thrown into the back of the trucks, the squawk of chickens being startled. There were a few shouts then the motor sputtered to life again. We waited until the sound of the engine had faded away before straightening up and going back inside.

We returned to find boot marks trailing across the floor, all over our hut. The kitchen ransacked.

'They took everything,' my mother said, her mouth an 'O' of shock.

All the sugar in our cupboards, all our long-grained rice. Even the flour that we had recently used for the tang yuan. All three of our hens, although they had missed one egg, hidden beneath a pile of dried grass dotted with fresh droppings. Our mosquito nets had been ripped out of the ceiling. Even the rattan mats that we slept on were gone.

To replace what we had lost, my mother accompanied me to the market the following day. While I laid out my paltry wares on sheets of newspaper, she went from shop to shop, looking increasingly anxious as she came out of each one empty-handed. Eventually, she crouched down next to me. 'No one has any rice or noodles,' she said, 'not even flour. Or salt.'

My mother took a deep breath and looked up and down the street. 'Stay here. I'm going to talk to Mrs Chang over there. Find out if she knows anything,' she said, and left for Auntie Chang's porridge stall, a pushcart that I often passed.

Ten minutes later, when I had almost finished the day's selling, I heard shouts. Someone saying please, please. Another voice barking an unfamiliar language.

The crowd moved away from the source of the noise, in my direction, and I stepped up onto the sheltered walkway to get a better look. From where I was, I could see a group of soldiers two bus lengths away, descending upon a young man, yelling and slapping his face.

'*Aiyo*, someone forgot to bow again. Happens every day,' said a woman next to me, almost dismissively.

But the soldiers didn't stop. One of them took out a pistol and aimed it at the man, making everyone around them step back. The crowd started to disperse. Shoppers, sellers with their carts all moved away, wanting to be elsewhere. Someone trampled on the few stalks of vegetables that remained on the newspaper I'd spread out on the ground. I stayed for as long as I could, waiting for my mother to reappear until I was shoved back along with the tide of people. I would go around the block and double back to look for her, I decided.

I turned a corner. That was when I saw the wooden poles in the ground. At first I thought it was a strange Japanese custom, a totem symbol or a marker of sorts until I got closer. And then I saw the heads of the men. Three of them, each spiked onto the top of a pole.

I fell backwards, dropping everything, then I got up and ran, not thinking about where I was going. I ran, only slowing down when I was out of the city.

My mother was home when I arrived.

'What happened? I was looking for you.'

'I – I was looking for you too. Ended up walking another way home. My basket. I lost my basket,' I said, reaching into my pockets to check for the coins I'd earned that morning. Still there.

'I'm just glad you got home safe. Are you okay?' She made a movement as if to take my arm, but stopped and showed me what she had in her shopping basket instead: a bag of flour that would make enough noodles for one meal and little more, and a packet of salt that fit in the palm of her hand. 'Hardly anything left in the shops. No rice or sugar. I got this bit of flour for five times the usual price.'

Soon after, we found out that deliveries had been dwindling ever since the Japanese raised their flag over Singapore. The limited farmland on the island could only yield so much – most of what was produced went to the Japanese army, who had, in the three weeks since the takeover, laid claim to everything. Rice, the most precious edible commodity, was being diverted from our warehouses to their army kitchens and stores. What was left – broken grains, mostly – they dealt out to the rest of us. My father would receive a ration card that week and with it we would be able to buy rice, flour, sugar and salt once a month. All of which would dwindle until my father was bringing home mere fractions of what we needed, and my mother had to make do with drawing salt from dried shrimp and old jars of pickled mustard greens, and substituting the bulk of our food with tapioca, which flourished even in the hard ground behind our home.

Over dinner, my mother talked about what she had seen at the market. 'I heard the man was trying to get some rice. He tried to steal some when he found that they had raised the price in all the shops.'

My father looked at Meng and Yang, pointing his chopsticks at them. 'You boys be careful. The Japanese police caught looters this week, punished them. And as if that wasn't enough, I heard they displayed the looters in town.'

I looked up then and the sudden movement made my father turn to me. 'What? Did you see something?'

Much later on, I often thought about what would have happened if I had told them what I'd seen that day. How the heads had still looked like they belonged to someone, and the blood had attracted swarms of flies so thick their hum seemed to breathe life back into the men. How there had been mud in one man's hair, as if it had been kicked about in the dirt for fun. And the littlest of mercies: their shut eyes. I wondered if it would have made a difference, if my telling them about this horror, witnessed up close, would have propelled my family into exercising more caution. But I didn't say anything. Not that day.

Kevin

'Come here,' she said.

I could hear the squeak and stretch of the foam mattress as she tried to push herself up with one arm, her good arm, but I didn't want to turn around, not yet. I stayed facing the window, counting until I was ready. Then I smiled and turned around.

'Ah Ma, you're awake!' I looked at everything in the hospital ward: the beige equipment, the beige tables on wheels, the beige bed frames, anything but my grandmother's face as I helped her sit up. Saw her birdlike shoulder as I circled her arm with one hand, my fingers almost meeting my thumb. Kept on not looking at her as I helped her sit up. Then I did – and I was sorry. Her thin hair needed combing and I knew she would be ashamed if she saw her own reflection; the white and grey strands sticking up and out to the left, unravelled from the bun she usually kept it in. I hoped she didn't see it in my face, how bad she looked. Her eyes were hard and fever-bright, her skin now tighter than ever around her cheeks and forehead so that I could almost see right through to the flesh under her face; the veins running up into her head, the eggshell white of her bones. She smelled of old skin covered up with the floral scent of talcum powder, which someone, probably my mother, had dusted over Ah Ma's neck, down into her back and front, so that the top half of her torso looked ghostly, like it belonged to someone else. I wanted to look away again but she craned her neck towards me, her mouth puckered leftward into a beak.

'Are you thirsty?' I filled a plastic cup and put a straw to her mouth like I'd seen my mother do before. Ah Ma took a few sips, clamped her mouth shut and pushed my hand away.

'Enough, enough.'

She puckered her mouth again, crumpled the end of the blanket in her hands and swept her hand over the cloth, making staticky tic-tic-tic sounds – so many that I thought I might see sparks flying from her. When the blanket was finally smooth, she pulled at it again so that the smoothing was undone. I was watching her hands, thinking how much they looked like pigeon's feet, lined and raw and gnarled with bumps where there shouldn't be, when she said, 'Son…'

I looked around, thinking that my father must be in the doorway, back from getting tea and sandwiches in the canteen, but there was nobody else in the ward except for the five other patients in their beds. One of them, a man around Ah Ma's age, was looking at a basket of fruit on the table in front of him and talking to it in a voice loud enough for me to know that it was Cantonese, but too soft for me to make out the words. Once or twice he paused and nodded, the way my mother nodded when the neighbour complained to her about the problems her children were having at school, then continued talking.

'Son,' Ah Ma repeated.

'Pa went to the canteen. If you want him now I can go and get him.' I said, stepping back so quickly the plastic folding chair almost tipped over. But my grandmother had already shot out one arm and wrapped her fingers around my wrist, so tight that it reminded me of how she used to do the laundry, wringing water out of all the clothes and towels and things until they were almost dry.

84

'Ah Ma?' I heard myself, the way my voice started on high and went up at the end, higher still. 'Ah Ma,' I tried again, trying not to sound scared this time.

'Son,' she said, slow and clear so the words could come out properly. 'I have sumding impordant to say before I... I... Budd you have to promise. You can't blame me.'

'AH MA, I AM WEI HAN,' I said, sounding out each letter and opening my mouth so wide I could feel the corners of my lips crack. When she didn't respond, I put my head down and whispered, 'I'm boy-boy.' I could feel my cheeks getting warm when I said this. Boy-boy, *mam-mam*, *shee-shee*, this is why my classmates ignore me, I thought.

'I'm boy-boy,' I repeated, bending over to whisper this into the curved seashell of her ear.

But Ah Ma didn't seem to be listening. Didn't seem to hear anything other than the rush of words coming out of her own mouth.

'Slow down, Ah Ma. I don't understand you. SLOW DOWN.' When she didn't, I did the only thing that I could think of. I took out the tape recorder and pressed the record button.

'I found you! Pease don't baneme... Ifoundyou and tookyouawaay. They were dead ormowheregobemouuuuund...I...dinnnnow... Eerbuddyelsewasgoooh...and...waadoondydyingdohell. I wannded-dosaveyou. Youwerejusababy, soniddle. I wannded to look forem, I did, but ondmund begamedoendend idbegame dooyears tree. EndnafterdatI just cuddent. I couldn't.'

She stopped and breathed in through her mouth, the effort of it making a deep hollow in her throat. She seemed to be waiting for something, something from me, but I didn't know what.

'Dooyouvergeefmee? I tried to look forem. Ayr reelly did. Eyydunwanyada blammee weenyfindoud. Pease forgeef me.'

While my grandmother begged, the patient who had been talking with his fruit basket sat up and watched, holding a peeled banana in one hand. Another patient got out of bed and slowly, carefully drew shut the curtains around her cubicle. When the clink and drag of the curtain hooks came to a stop, I repeated, 'Ah Ma…' I pulled at the arm she was holding on to and felt, with each tug, the tightening of her grip.

Then I asked, because I felt I had to, because I could taste the words, thick and bitter, rising up my throat. I needed to spit them out.

'Who? Who were you looking for?'

She took a big gulp, like a fish on land fighting for air. 'Your parents.' Then she closed her eyes, turning her face away as if she couldn't bear to see. 'Doyoublamemeee? I'm still your mother, righhh? Do you blame me?' There was a long pause. Her eyes were still closed and I thought for a moment that she was gone. Then she turned back to look at me, eyes wet but clear as I'd ever seen them. 'Do you blame me? Pease,' she said and then in Chinese, '*qiu qiu ni.*'

I shook my head and realized my tongue was stuck to the roof of my mouth. I swallowed and said, 'No.' I wasn't thinking when the rest of it came out. 'No, Ma. I don't blame you.'

When she finally let go of my wrist and closed her eyes, I knew that there would be no waking her up this time. The bright-red call button was pulsing in front of my eyes so I reached out, jammed my thumb into it and braced myself for the wail of a siren, something loud and alarming and appropriate, but nothing happened. Ah Ma still had her eyes closed. The too-slow pips coming from the heart monitor machine were slowing down even more. The man in the corner had gone back to chatting with his fruit basket. I pressed the stop button on the recorder and put it back in my pocket. Finally, I heard the soft clip of someone brisk-walking along the corridor.

When my parents came back into the room a few minutes later smelling of coffee and sweetener from the hospital cafeteria, the doctor was already there.

'What's going on?'

'It seems she had another stroke.' The doctor stopped talking and looked at me, then looked back at my mother again. She nodded. My father nodded. I wanted everyone to stop nodding and just say the obvious but no one did. The doctor signed his name on the bottom of a chart, clicked the pen and put it back in his breast pocket. He stood there with his hands folded behind his back. Everyone except me seemed to be waiting for something.

'Boy, are you hungry? Let's go outside, to the canteen,' she said.

I nodded but I stood where I was and watched as my father sat down in the chair next to the bed, picked up Ah Ma's limp hand and stroked it. He held on to it with both hands, as if he were trying to warm her. It was the first and only time I had ever seen them touch.

'Let's go.' My mother took my wrist, the one that still had the sharp bone-feel of my grandmother's fingers on my skin, and led me out.

All the way back home, I thought about telling my father what Ah Ma had said before she closed her eyes. I could repeat to him the few words that I'd understood, poor Ah Ma, struggling to get the words out of her crooked, half-frozen mouth; the few words that were now in my chest (*I found you*) and were growing in the secret dark (*I took you away*). Growing and growing into a feeling (*They were dead. I found you. Please forgive me*). I felt like when I was little again and taking my first bus ride. We were on the bus for only ten minutes before we had to alight for me to throw up at the bus stop. The words churned around in my stomach until we were almost home; once or twice, my fingers hovered over the rewind and play buttons on the recorder and I wished I had my earphones with me so I could listen to it right there in the back seat and try to make out what my grandmother had tried so hard to articulate.

That evening, the phone rang just as my mother was plating the dishes for dinner. I waited for my father to get it but he was in the bedroom so I picked it up.

'Hello, can I speak to Kevin Lim?' went a badly muffled voice.

'Yes? Who's this?'

'I want to make sure I'm speaking to the correct Kevin Lim. What is your full name?'

'Kevin Lim Wei Han. Who –'

'Wrong! Your name is Kevin *Chao Ah Gua*.'

I heard laughter, several different voices, on the other end of the line.

'*Chao Ah Gua*, I know you still sleep with your grandmother. Too sissy to have your own bed, right?'

'I'm going to hang up.'

'Why? Because you need to get your Pampers changed, retard? Why don't you go to a special school? No one likes you here.'

I could feel my mother standing not four feet away so I kept my face down and said nothing.

'Boy,' my mother said, fake whispering. 'Tell your friend it's dinner time. Food's getting cold.'

'Bye, Albert.' I hung up the phone.

I spent some time washing and drying my hands extensively, making sure that my face was normal again before I left the bathroom. My father was sitting at the table and staring into space with his chopsticks in his hand. My mother pushed the bowl of soup towards him but he didn't react.

'Was that Albert? The boy next door? Good. Good to see you making friends at last.'

I went to sleep that night in the room I used to share with my grandmother. The room was now all mine. I wondered if they would move the other single bed out and when. And when they would put away the things in her chest of drawers. I was about to fall asleep when my father came into the room. I put on the lamp, which was a mistake. It lit up the shadows under his eyes and around his mouth. The lines that had been hiding on his forehead. It made his face white-yellow and I thought about my grandmother's bloodless face on that stiff, plastic, hospital pillow, and all the other faces that had been on it, had dreamed and drooled and cried into it.

My father swayed left and right on his feet but stayed where he was, in between the writing desk and my bed. 'Are you okay?'

I said yes but it came out more as a question. 'Yes,' I repeated, to make sure he wasn't going to ask again. 'I'm okay.'

'Do you still have classes next week?'

'No. It's midterm now. Today was the last day of school.' I sat up straighter and rubbed my eyes. How strange it was, to remember that I had been in class today, sitting next to Victor and adding item after item to the list of holiday homework at the end of each class. If I flipped to the last page of my notebook now, I would see a red circle around the words 'show-and-tell', with exclamation marks all around it, each one signalling my alarm as the teacher talked about the assignment; how it was supposed to be an essay, as well as a five-minute presentation. Next to me, Victor started talking about his trip to Canberra and how he was going to go snorkelling and bring back a coral reef to show the rest of us who were never going to see one. I would have told Victor that he was going to the wrong city, if his plan was to go snorkelling, but my tongue was leaden with the fact that I was going nowhere and doing nothing. Nothing then, to show or tell. There was talk about Penang, Kuala Lumpur, and Hong Kong until I noticed Albert – his face stony and dull in the sea of excitement. He wasn't going anywhere either. Below 'show-and-tell' I had scribbled down 'Zoo? Underwater world? Ikea?'– the last barely readable because the thought of going to Ikea (my mother had drawn a circle around a dining table in the magazine and told me that we were saving up for it; we were going one weekend during the June holidays, she said) and then talking about it in front of everyone had made me want to laugh and cry at the same time. I thought about the map tacked up on the wall right above my head. It was old and faded but the mark I had made, right below Malaya, was still red. 'Little red dot, see there?' My father had showed me, pointing it out. Then he went on to explain that we were right on the equator and that was why it was hot all the time and rained every day at three in the afternoon. I had looked at the speck he had pointed at and coloured it in with a red marker pen so I wouldn't have to squint to find it anymore. My father had driven us across the island once, west to east. It took forty-five minutes. Tiny. And I would have to find something worthy of a show-and-tell on this tiny, tiny island.

This was what I had worried about most of the day, about the holidays and the zoo, about the show-and-tell. And then I was in hospital watching my grandmother die.

'Because if there're classes, I can write a note so you don't have to go. With the funeral and cremation, you'll have to miss them.'

'Okay, Pa. But there's no more school... Only remedial classes during the last week of June.' I spoke slowly to make sure he understood. This heavy-faced man with his faraway eyes.

'Chinese?'

I nodded. 'And maths.' I wanted him to say something. To reprimand me again for having done badly enough during the midterm exams to need extra classes but he just nodded.

'Okay. Alright.' He turned to go, then stopped. 'With Ah Ma gone, you're going to be on your own during the day. Once your mother and I go back to work. You're old enough, aren't you, to be on your own?'

I nodded.

He nodded back, then shut the door behind him. I waited a little before getting up and opening it again just an inch. There was the smell of my grandmother in the room – a combination of jasmine and talcum powder and old cotton – and the imagined sound of her music in my ears, and I didn't want it to be the last thing I was aware of before I fell asleep. Outside, in the flats on our left and right, the night went on: reruns on television, the metallic tinkle of kitchen utensils being put away, someone shouting at someone else who didn't or couldn't shout back. I could separate our own noises from the others: my mother's bedroom slippers across the floor, the steady whirl of the fan in my parents' room. I heard the bed creak as my father's weight descended upon it, I heard the light go off and the rustle of their blanket as they each settled into their side of the bed, and I waited for my father to start snoring. Waited for him to start off suspicious and soft, and wind his way up into sounding like my mother's blender if you put a stone into it. The familiar sound of it sent me to sleep the way opera music sent my grandmother to sleep. Used to send. I waited and waited but it never came.

Wang Di

There were just two people left who'd known the Old One and she had two hours that evening to find them. Two hours between five and dinner time, during which the cooler temperatures made it pleasant enough to be outside. She knew them simply as Leong and Ah Ren. At the Old One's funeral, Leong had shaken her hand and said how sorry he was while his brother – younger but greying before him – stood aside and looked on. She hadn't asked that day, but was aware, from talk, that they had chosen to stay in the same neighbourhood. She remembered how the housing agent had told her it was 'just down the road', and how endless the trek of that morning had been, and armed herself with a plastic bottle and her pushcart.

As she walked she had the discomfiting sense of having stepped, unwittingly, into another country. Her new building was sickly orange, and each one in the cluster was violently coloured, not sun-bleached and streaked with pigeon and mynah droppings. There were more flowering plants around the new estate, another riot of colours, green and pink and purple, to make up for the shut-in feeling people get from living in shoebox apartments. For more than an hour, she weaved in and out of the clusters of buildings, taking note of lift landings and large public bins, the back of shops and food courts where people left out boxes and tins emptied of beans, meat or fruit in syrup. Made a map of the neighbourhood in her head and tucked it away for later. The Old One had often marvelled at her memory, at the ease with which she rattled off telephone numbers, recipes she got from the cooking show on TV, and led the way to places that she had visited just once. 'That's what happens when you can't write things down, I have no choice but to know it all by heart,' she'd explained. And stopped. Wishing she didn't remember everything. Soon Wei had noticed the look on her face and changed the subject, talking about how forgetful he was getting, how lucky he was to have a young wife. 'Silly old fool,' she had laughed, shaking her head.

It was only after dark that Wang Di decided to call it a day. She wondered how long it would take her to find the brothers and what she would do if she never found them. She didn't even know their last names, couldn't call directory services to ask. Both thoughts were enough to make her want to lie down and never get up again, so she kept walking until she couldn't anymore, until she was out of the fold of buildings and in front of a newly built shopping mall. Glossy as a beetle. The cool air within it like a blast from a fridge every time someone entered or left the building through its sliding glass doors. Next to it was the train station, which the housing officer had boasted about. They could hop on and off public transport if they wanted to, it was practically at their doorstep. Made things easy for visiting children and grand-children, he'd added.

Except we don't have children, she had wanted to shout, and my legs are no longer what they used to be. This neighbourhood and all that it contained, from its cheery Welcome! sign to the wet market, smelling of sea and flesh and earth. It was all she had known for years. This neighbourhood contains all of my life, our lives, and we're going to die within it.

She had delivered this speech in her head that night as she tried to fall sleep, wishing all the while that she had got up the courage to say all this to the housing officer who hadn't bothered to look at either of them in the face the entire time.

This is what growing old is like, she thought now, staring at the hordes of people streaming in and out of the mall. Being surrounded by more and more alien objects, small, sharp-edged and shiny all at once, until one day it simply becomes too uncomfortable to sit among all this strangeness. This was how the Old One looked in his last few weeks – uncomfortable. He had no intention of moving into Block 6A, bright orange and built just for the elderly.

'No one is going to make me move,' he kept saying. 'I'm staying right here, where my home is. Elderly people living with other useless elderly people, what a foolish idea. At least where we live now, the next-door neighbours would come and help if we were in trouble, if one of us fell down. What if something happened to us in that Old People's Housing Estate? Who would come and help? No one would hear us. And if we were lucky, someone with arthritic knees.'

Eventually, the housing officer got him to sign by hinting at the possibility of a court case. 'It will be very inconvenient for everyone involved,' the man had added, flapping the end of his tie and looking at the tips of his too-shiny leather shoes. When he left, Soon Wei had sunk into himself, as if someone had let all the air out of him.

To cheer him up, Wang Di had gone to the market that afternoon for chicken wings, coconut milk, and freshly ground curry paste for his favourite meal. She arrived home to see him seated at the kitchen table with his sewing box in front of him, lid off, spools of white, blue and grey thread rolling away from him.

'Look,' he said, happy as a child in a sandpit. 'Look what I found.'

The table was spread with photos, ID cards, letters and newspaper clippings that she couldn't read. There was more underneath the bric-a-brac, but he took one photo from the pile and handed it to her. 'See who it is.'

The paper was thin, its four corners bent soft. A young woman, dressed and made up in clothes and make-up that clearly belonged to someone else. She was perched on the edge of a wooden chair, looking just off-camera, in a way that suggested that she was about to ask if it was done and could she move or get up now. Her mother had spent the entire morning coaxing the tapered ends of her hair on both sides of her face so that they curled around her jawline. Her fringe, normally pinned back from her face, had been combed forward, as if to assure the looker that she had plenty of hair, really. Wang Di hadn't seen the photo in more than half a century but she remembered why her hair had been cropped. Two decades later, in the sixties, the length would be fashionable, but that day it had taken the photographer more than a moment to recover from his shock at seeing her.

'How old were you?'

'Seventeen. My mother had to save up for weeks to be able to afford it.'

What she did not say: that Auntie Tin had given out copies the year the picture was taken and not had much luck. That she had reused the same photo, which Wang Di's mother had kept in her dresser drawer for almost four years, when Wang Di was twenty. A little old, in those days. It was something her mother had worried about until Auntie Tin told them that she had found the perfect man. Thirty-eight years old. Recently widowed. Not Hokkien. Teochew. But still heaven-sent.

'This was taken a few months after the occupation.'

'You weren't the only one. I remember my neighbours were hurrying to get husbands for their daughters. People getting married after curfew, in the dark. Strange times.'

'You were still married then, weren't you?'

He nodded, a faraway sadness settling around his shoulders. 'And then years later, I met you.'

'Years later.'

'Almost a lifetime.'

March – August 1942

After what happened at the market, my father decided that my mother and I had to stay within the kampong for our own safety. I still had my makeshift stall, though it was now confined to the heart of the village, close to a little huddle of shops. Sales were slow and whatever I sold went at a cutthroat rate in the afternoon, when the villagers knew I was close to packing up and going home; unlike the city dwellers, they had the space to grow their own vegetables and the knack for foraging in the fields. Vegetables were easy enough to get. What we all lacked was eggs, meat, fresh fish and staples, like rice and flour and salt, which my mother knew would remain scarce until after the war. It was with this intuition that she cleared out a plot of earth in the back between the trees and got me to help plant the cuttings of cassava, potato and tapioca plants. When rice rationing was at its worst, forcing entire households to live on a single bowl of rice a day, it would be these cuttings that kept my family alive through the next four years.

While I busied myself with the stall and the kitchen garden, Yan Ling continued going into the city. Instead of walking with her, I waved from the garden as she passed the house. Sometimes she stopped to chat but more and more I only caught brief glimpses of her as she left for work, braiding her hair as she ran up the lane. I had finished doing my chores one evening when I decided to visit her. Instead of Yan Ling, it was her mother who answered the door.

'Are you looking for Yan Ling? She's still at the eating house.'

'Oh, I thought she would be home by now. What time will she be back?'

'I don't know. Late, I think. The eating house is even busier now with the Japanese soldiers. They've had to put in more tables.' She paused and looked me up and down as if seeing me for the first time. 'Listen, do you want to make some money? Yan Ling said that they are looking for more waitresses. I heard there was even an advertisement in the *Syonan Times*. They want girls aged seventeen to twenty-eight. You're seventeen, right? I would get Yan Ling to do it if she could, but you know...' She tutted, brushing a finger over her top lip. 'They only want her working in the back of the house.'

The possibility of bringing in money interested me almost as much as the chance of seeing my friend again. 'I'll ask my parents.'

'I heard they pay well. You get tips.'

'Tips?'

'If they like you.'

My next word would have been, 'Who?' but I heard my mother calling out for me and had to go. 'I'll ask my parents,' I repeated.

I did it over dinner. The rations weren't enough, as my mother had predicted but she made do with what we did have, spreading the essentials thinly across the weeks so that we wouldn't run out before the end of the month. To achieve this, she supplemented our meals with the root vegetables that we had planted – adding them to every dish – and used pickled vegetables and anchovies and chilli to impart flavour in place of salt. That night, we had watered down congee, bulked up and tinged purple with tapioca, and topped with pickled radish.

'Ba, Ma, they're looking for new waitresses where Yan Ling works. At the eating house.'

'When did you see her?' my father asked.

'I didn't. Her mother told me. They need more people to help out…and you get tips.'

'Tips?' my father spat. 'You know who gets tips? Tell that woman to keep her suggestions to herself. She can get her daughters to do whatever she wants but I don't want to hear –'

'No need to get angry, *la*. She was only trying to help,' my mother said. She shot a warning look in my direction.

'Help? There's enough for you to do at home. Once it calms down, you can go to the market again with your mother. Maybe we can make some money selling sweet potato plants.'

There was a moment's silence before my mother spoke again, her voice strained, a little too high. 'Children, your father found a job today. Did you know?'

'Ba, you found a job?' said Yang, looking up.

'Just for a while. Carrying stones at the construction site. The shophouses and shipyards need to be rebuilt.' I knew what this meant – taking away rubble from caved-in shophouses, back-breaking work that only *xin ke* – fresh immigrants – were willing to take on, work that he was lucky to get now. I knew, too, how much my father hated it.

My brother flinched. 'You mean… You mean you work for the Japanese now?'

'Yang, finish your food.'

In April, Yang and Meng went back to school to find that most of their teachers had been replaced. All the Chinese instructors were gone; some of them, the husbands of women in our neighbour-hood, had never made it back from the reporting stations. They simply vanished, as if they'd never existed. No one asked questions; the wives they left behind adjusted by taking on odd jobs in the city, all the while hoping that their husbands might return home one day.

'I don't want to go anymore,' Yang said after his first day back. 'All they do is play the Japanese broadcasts and make us learn their national anthem.'

There were no more Chinese language classes, he informed us. Instead, there were new teachers at school. Students spent most of their time learning Japanese. 'Even mathematics is taught in Japanese now,' Yang went on. It was his favourite subject and I remembered how he said he wanted to teach it one day, perhaps at the same school, perhaps in the city, he didn't yet know.

'I don't want to go anymore,' he repeated over dinner. It was then that I looked up and realized that his face had changed in the last few months. He used to look like my mother, with the same softness in his cheeks and mouth. Now, when I looked at him, all I could see was my father. The swarthiness of his skin, the angles in his jaw.

Both Yang and Meng grumbled for a few weeks but they got used to it, the way children their age got used to things. Before long, they were coming home from school with dirt on their shoes from playing football in the bare field as if nothing had changed. Meng, in particular, took to practising his Japanese around the house. '*Konnichiwa*, good afternoon. *Ohayou gozaimasu*, good morning. *Arigatou gozaimasu*, thank you,' he would chant, repeating his vocabulary list until Yang shouted at him to stop.

Nothing had changed except everything had.

The island was small, smaller than my parents' ancestral town in China, and news spread the old way, with people whispering to each other as they went about their work and grocery shopping. Each Sunday a neighbour would drop by our hut and sit down for a half hour of gossip over coffee; they would tell the boys to go outside if they weren't already playing in the fields. I was usually in the back, quiet and forgotten. This was what I heard: a whole kampong set ablaze because the families, all of them Chinese, were among those who sent money back to the old country so they could buy weapons to defend themselves against the Japanese. The way the occupiers simply took what they saw and wanted, bales of expensive silk from the tailors, bicycles from people on the street, pushing them off and riding away, laughing. From the travelling noodle hawker, we heard stories about women and girls as young as ten being assaulted in their own homes by bands of soldiers, their children and husbands bayoneted if the soldiers met any resistance.

I listened to these stories, always the same stories in a slightly different form, gorging myself on each little detail. At night, I turned them over and over in my head as I went to sleep in an effort to guard myself against similar horrors. As if by thinking about them, dreaming about them, and keeping them close, they would be kept away from us in real, waking life.

It was around this time that the women in our kampong began turning into boys overnight. Oversized shirts and trousers replaced floral blouses. Some wore caps to shield their faces and bound their chests to hide their curves. A few went a little further and shed their braids and ponytails to take on short crops – dark, jagged ends cut close to their necks. The rest got married. Month after month, I watched as rickshaws rode up to our neighbours' houses. There were no fireworks, no music at any of the weddings, little else but the sound of light chatter as the bride got into the rickshaw, and the others followed. One of these women was a cousin of Yan Ling's. For the occasion, Yan Ling had been coiffed and made-up. Normally she would have enjoyed it but now she looked uncomfortable and her eyes were far away. It was the first time in months that I had seen her and I tried to wave from where I was standing, within a crowd a little away from her family, but she did not look. Not once.

'Lucky girl, she'll be safe from the Japanese,' said my mother to a neighbour.

'Oh, it's no guarantee. Those people, they don't care…' The neighbour lowered her voice, her words drowned out by the sound of more clapping.

When Auntie Tin came by a few weeks after that, she received tea and a bit of kueh that my mother had made from the previous bit of flour and sugar we had. This time, my parents were the ones who wanted something out of the visit.

'It might take a while. So many girls want to find a husband.'

'I know, I know. It's the way things are. But please, her father wants it to happen as soon as possible.'

'I'll try my best. I always do. Wang Di will need to get a photo taken. And tell her to smile, she looks so nice when she smiles.' The matchmaker looked naked and lost without her earrings, her bracelets. All that remained was one jade bangle around her left wrist. The bangle slid down her arm as she waved goodbye and I wondered what she had sold the rest for and if it was enough to keep her family from starving.

'I wouldn't ask you to come with me if your mother wasn't ill,' my father said. I wanted to say of course she was ill, she ate scraps so that Meng and Yang would have enough, but I shut up and listened as he handed me one of his shirts and told me to rub coal dust onto my face.

We had to get rice, flour and noodles, each from a different distribution centre. Throughout the journey, he reminded me time and again to lower my head and keep my eyes to the ground. The queue at the distribution centre went all the way down the street and it inched along for an hour until a fight broke out.

'What's going on, Ba?'

'Ah, the usual. Somebody's trying to cut in. A young couple.'

I stepped out of the line for a better look, just in time to see an open-top vehicle pull up. Two uniformed men jumped out, shouting in Japanese. One of them started waving his rifle around and the line shifted, moving away from the men in a wave. A sharp scream, and then, 'No, please. She's my wife!'

There was a dull whack of wood against flesh. Then another scream. I moved my face into a gap above my father's shoulder just in time to see the woman being hauled out of the line and dragged into the vehicle. Her screams didn't stop but simply faded away as the car started up again and drove off.

The line murmured and surged, spitting the man out. He got up and stumbled in the direction the car had taken.

'Oh, poor thing,' someone behind us tutted.

'Stupid. Making trouble and attracting attention. He shouldn't have done it. Cutting in like that.' My father turned away. Even with his arms folded, I could see that his hands were trembling. It took half an hour before we got to the front of the line.

The sky broke on our way back and only stopped when we were in our kampong. It was three in the afternoon and by the time we reached home, we were both soaked. My father put his bags on the kitchen table and hurried towards the door. 'I'm going to get the salt. You can stay home.'

'Oh, you're going to fall ill like that,' my mother said when I went in, dripping. She was thin, paler than I ever saw her and looking fifty instead of her thirty-odd years. 'Come here, there's fresh water in the bucket.' She made me follow her into the backyard, told me to squat and tip my head forward as she poured warm water over my head. The rationed soap was black and bit into my skin but I kept quiet. Later, whenever anyone mentioned my mother, I would remember this. The smell of wartime soap, the rasp of her fingernails along my scalp.

My hair had grown waist-length from neglect, and I was at the window, combing out the tangled ends and trying to catch the warm breeze in an effort to dry it when my father returned.

He flung the door open and when I swung to look at him, his eyes were wide with alarm, as if he had seen something he wasn't supposed to.

'What are you doing by the window? I could see you all the way from up the lane.'

I couldn't think of an answer, simply let my hands drop to my sides and stared at him.

He disappeared into the bedroom and came back out again after a minute. I only saw a flash of the blade but I knew he had my mother's sewing scissors in his hand.

I started to run but he grabbed first my arm, then a fistful of hair. 'Stand still. I don't want to hurt you.'

My mother, who had been at the kitchen table all the while, started screaming. 'Have you gone mad? What are you doing?'

The shock of cold steel against my neck made me flinch. Then I heard the familiar, flinty clip right next to my ear, saw the first clump of hair floating to the floor before my vision blurred, everything obscured by the fog of my tears. He took care not to nick my skin and worked in silence for minutes until thick sheets of black hair lay at our feet. It looked like a dead animal, run over on the street.

What a pity, I thought. We could have sold it if he cut it all off in one straight line. My mother continued screaming. The sound of it stayed with me the entire night. Long after my father had put away the scissors. Long after he said, 'It's for your own good, you should know that.' Then, he walked away and returned the scissors to my mother's sewing basket. It was her scream which kept me up. The sound of it spoke of everything no one dared to talk about: what the soldiers were doing; young and afraid and separated from their families. It spoke of the things everyone was to keep silent about all through the three and a half years we belonged to the Japanese, and of the decades after.

The sight of my roughly cut hair unnerved my mother. She fussed with it, sitting me down at the kitchen table as soon as it was light, and trimming the back with a smaller pair of scissors to even out the ends.

After a month, she sighed and said that it was getting too late.

'We can't wait any longer. Auntie Tin needs a photo of you. We'll just make do. It looks quite nice, like this.'

At the photographer's studio, my mother and I were shown to a corner with a mirror. There was rouge paper and powder on a table next to it; she showed me how to put my lips over the paper to press the red onto my mouth while she dusted pink onto my cheeks. I couldn't stop looking into the mirror even though I didn't want to. I was used to hiding behind my hair and the loss of it revealed the unevenness of my eyes, the blunt slope of my nose, the mole beneath my left eye.

'A tear mole,' she said, when I touched it with the tip of my finger. She patted powder over it but it stood out, like a smudge someone had tried and failed to rub away.

Tears, I thought, and bad luck. But I said nothing and sat as she combed my fringe into a smooth curve above my eyes.

The photographer was a middle-aged man behind a large standing-up camera. 'Oh,' he said, seeing me for the first time. He pointed a finger to his own neck, as if flicking away his collar. 'How…modern.'

When the photos came out, my mother put them in an envelope and got my father to cycle over to Auntie Tin's. He had said nothing about the incident but smiled at me now and again as if trying to cheer me up. 'The hair makes you look young. Not bad for the matchmaker.'

There wasn't a choice this time. No one was asking me if I was ready. My father said that I would be better fed, that married couples received slightly bigger rations. 'Reason enough to get married,' he had said, trying to sound light.

We heard nothing from the matchmaker, not after two months. 'Don't worry. It's only because there are so many people looking to get married. The matchmaker has to work day and night. It might take a while but it will be no problem… No problem.'

It was the first Saturday of August when it happened. Late afternoon. My mother and I were sorting the rice for dinner, sifting broken grains and weevils from the rest when both of us looked up to a distant drone, a low whirr of activity making its way to our village. I was standing at the kitchen and an ache settled into my stomach as my father came in from the backyard. He had been digging up tapioca, tending to the plants and there was a smear of dirt on his forehead, right above his eyes, and he stood still for a moment, listening before he went to the door and looked out to where my brothers were, squatting in a circle with three other boys. Fighting crickets, I guessed, or playing with marbles, I couldn't tell.

'Meng! Yang! Come into the house,' he yelled.

By the time my brothers arrived back, panting, we could see the trucks. Two of them, the sides muddied up, as if they had driven through ditches in the rain. There were eight to ten soldiers in the back of one truck. The other was carrying nothing, making space for what they were going to take from us.

The soldiers we saw the last time had looked bedraggled and tired, as if they needed sleep and would have given anything for a shower and clean sheets. Now they peered around at us as they rolled up the lane, awake, alert, their faces peaked with something akin to hunger. Someone in the first vehicle called out and both of them sank to a stop a few houses away, close to the centre of the kampong.

The ones sitting in the back of the truck jumped out, hitching their trousers up and talking among themselves.

'Everyone, outside at once!' It was the same interpreter. I recognized his voice, unadulterated as it was without a loudspeaker.

'Don't bother hiding the rice. They'll find it anyway,' my father said to my mother as she pushed herself up from her chair, eyes wide, as though he could read her mind. 'Just let them take what they want.'

In two minutes, everyone – young, old and poorly – was standing in the dust in front of their homes. Each step my mother took was an effort so my father stayed close to her, one hand hovering near the small of her back. I had Meng's hand in mine and was looking at my feet, waiting for it to be over with when I felt him pulling away. I tugged at his fingers to get him to come closer but his chin was tilted up and he was taking little gulps of air. The men stood in a cluster by their trucks, as if waiting for a command. Then, out of the tight silence, my brother opened his mouth.

'*Konnichiwa.*'

Everyone froze. Meng was smiling, proud that he remembered the words, that he had got it right. The soldiers looked around and laughed with surprise. One of them came forward and reached into his pocket. His eyes were twinkling as he drew out a piece of candy wrapped in red and white paper and held it out in his upturned palm, in front of Meng's face.

My brother looked to my father, then my mother, for permission but their eyes were panicked. They didn't speak. After a pause, Meng shook me off to reach for the offered sweet and I watched him pick it up between thumb and forefinger. Their hands touched for a fraction of a second and the moment stretched out impossibly before Meng withdrew his hand and put the wrapped sweet in his pocket for safekeeping.

'*Ari-ga-toh goz-aiii-mas,*' he said, with an even wider smile. His front tooth was missing and it made him look even younger than he was.

The soldier ruffled Meng's hair. He was young, and like the rest, appeared to be in his twenties. He was still smiling when his eyes fell on me. His face was small, foxlike, and he was fair, unlike his compatriots, who were mostly darkened by the sun. He crooked his finger at the soldiers, who came running and they spoke for a second before the interpreter looked at me and said in Mandarin, 'Yoshida-san says he would like you to come with us.'

I shook my head and took a step backwards, right into someone's arms. Turned around to see my mother's face, tight with fear. She pulled me to her, so close that I could hear her breathe.

'You will get work, make some money for your family.'

The soldier still had his hand on my brother's head. There was a pause before he frowned and said something else. Then he lunged towards me and grabbed my wrist.

I pulled back, trying to wrench myself free and felt my mother's arms tighten around me. Then my father stepped around us, trying to put himself between us and the soldiers. His eyes were shining and his hands were stretched out in front of him. He opened his mouth wide. What came out was nothing, a croak. He spoke again and this time I heard him. 'Wait!'

'Wait, she's just a child.' He grabbed my other wrist, pulling me towards him.

The soldier closed his fingers around me, tighter, and pulled again before realizing that my father wasn't going to let go. He shouted, then flicked the blunt end of his rifle into my father's face, making him fall backwards; the skin on his eyebrow split open and blood trickled into his eye, over his cheek. The soldier rammed his rifle into my father again, this time in his stomach, making him double over. My mother finally let go of me, loosened her arms from around my body to go to my father, as the soldier stood over him, waiting, daring him to get up, his rifle in the air. As he did this, the glint of metal on his bayonet caught my eye.

Grab it, sink into it, I thought. But my limbs were stone. By the time I moved, I was too late.

Someone had appeared next to me with a length of rope, making short work of binding my wrists. There was a wooden plank leading up to the truck bed and he jabbed the bayonet at me and walked me up. I smelled alcohol on his breath as he pulled at my bonds and trussed me to the side rail. I sat there, straining at the rope, and watched as the group marched past each house, pulling girls and women away from their families. What came to mind again was the image of wild dogs, the pack of them that had burrowed its way into our coop. The pack had continued their sack of the village's coops, taking prey out of our neighbours' gardens night after night. A few each week, until the pack moved on to another village. As if they knew they were running out of luck and out of prey.

Each of the girls resisted. One of them flailed, hitting a soldier across the face. There was a wild roar and I saw her getting pushed to the ground and kicked by the men surrounding her, before being taken back into her own home by four soldiers, one at each limb. She screamed as they dragged her in. Like a pig being brought to slaughter. I heard her howls, the sound of them reaching high over the thatched roofs, cracking the languid stillness of the afternoon.

While she cried, the other soldiers picked out five more women and girls, pulling them away from their families the way they had done with me. They were mostly my age, still in school, except for one. A young mother. The wife of a young man who lived a few doors away from us. High-school sweethearts – the couple had met while they were still children, my mother had told me. It was just last week that she had come round with her baby in her arms, smiled and presented my mother with two eggs, painted red for good luck, to celebrate their son's first full month. I heard a baby's wail. Hers, I thought numbly. All the feeling had gone from my limbs and I watched as half of them were pushed in after me, and the rest into the other truck. The ones who didn't move or couldn't were hauled up, as I had been, in tears or shocked into stillness. I had to put my fingers to my face to see if I was crying. No.

There was a loud, sharp pop, then another, and then another. The four men who had pulled the woman into her hut came out. The last of them, the one who looked the youngest, was tucking his shirt tails into his trousers, his face flushed red. He could have been anyone. A friend of Yang's, sweat-soaked after a football game. Anyone. While the rest piled into the first truck, he climbed up the back and sat at the end of ours, resting the rifle across his knees.

I looked over at my family, crouching in front of our home. My mother was sitting on the ground, cradling my father's bloodied head. He wasn't moving. From where I was, I couldn't see his eyes, and I couldn't tell if he was dead or simply unconscious. I felt an urge to jump and run to him and I stood, tried to. But the length of rope tethering me to the side rails was too short even for that. I sat back down, hard, making the truck quiver.

'Ma,' I said but my voice came out in a half-whisper.

She heard it all the same. Her eyes were fixed on me, mouth open in a silent yelp. There was a rattle. I felt the truck shudder back to life, and then we were moving. Yang and several other people ran towards us, then stopped, as if held back by an invisible wall. I watched as our attap hut got smaller, watched as Meng scrambled to his feet and started running after me, while Yang tried and failed to grab him by the back of his shirt.

'Jie-jie,' he shouted.

The truck sped up. Meng pumped his arms to propel himself forward and his tiny bird's chest pushed out, filling and filling with air. He ran for a few hundred yards before tripping and falling forward in the sand. The driver took a bend in the road and I turned my head to watch as my brother pushed himself halfway up, his eyes shining, before I lost all sight of him.

It took me a while to realize that they were driving us south but until then, I could hardly see or hear from the whirr of panic in my chest, a constant whoosh in my ears which I took for the wind but was just my breath, coming in quick and much too shallow. We passed kampongs, all a blur of green and earth-brown. The wild, cheerful voices of the driver and his passenger over the grind of the engine. Then, singing. Just minutes after one of them had thrown a woman on the ground, tied her up and pushed her onto a truck like cattle. Could someone like that sing? Laugh? I thought. I was sweating, and the back of my blouse stuck to my skin. Blood on my trouser knee. Not mine. My father's. I looked up and blinked. Across from me sat the woman who had been taken away from her husband and child. She was tugging at the rope around her wrists. Don't cry, I told myself. See? She's not crying. *Don't cry and there will be nothing to cry about.* Something my mother liked to say. Mothers. The woman was still trying to twist loose of her bonds and I was reminded of a sparrow that I had seen once caught in a tangle of kite string, frantic to break free. I watched her until I felt someone's eyes on me and turned to my right. A girl. Familiar-looking. Her hair tied back into a plait. Round cheeks which dipped into a small, pointed chin, making her look elfin. Then a faint memory of my mother gushing about how pretty she was, how she would have her pick of husbands when the time came. I'd felt a stab of jealousy, fine as needle, whenever I saw her in the village after that. How foolish, I thought now, what nonsense.

'You're Auntie Ng's daughter,' she said, with a calm that made me stop and look at her full in the face. Her eyes were red, her collar ripped and flapping in the wind.

'And you...you live on the west side of the kampong.' My voice sounded odd – strained and out of place. The soldier sitting guard looked up at the sound of our voices, then turned his head to look out at the road behind the truck, unperturbed. It didn't matter, he must think, just women, talking.

Huay, I recalled. The girl's name was Huay. Her parents owned a convenience store, a tiny shop that didn't allow more than two people in it at the same time, and then their name: Seetoh, a name so unusual that they were the only Seetohs I knew of; the sound of this name conjuring up something hazily exotic each time I heard it. I had a memory of Huay's face, lit red by a paper lantern, younger siblings around her legs, tugging at her hands and clothes; Huay trying to herd them through the mid-autumn festival crush. I forced myself to smile at her. I felt I had to, and she smiled back. As if we were out on a ride, a jaunt that somebody had arranged for us. It was all just a bit of fun; it would be over in a minute. Too nervous to speak any further, I looked away, past her and returned to staring at the road, the trees.

After twenty minutes, the truck entered a wide street busy with traffic. It was lined on both sides with shops grander than the ones in Chinatown, and tall buildings with bold signs, spelling things out in English. This must be Orchard Road, I guessed. I'd passed this street a few times on the way to Chinatown. Never stopped. There was nothing for me here. It might as well have been another country. After a few minutes, the driver turned right, slipping into a residential street. More townhouses, taller, the white paint on them fresh. There were no sheltered walkways here but little gardens beyond gates, and paved walkways leading up to each front door. The truck ambled past a row of them, past a carefully made-up woman leaning out of a second-floor window, past a group of workmen hurrying boxes from the back of a van into an alley. I waited for one of the men to look up – I would wave, give a signal, I thought, and they would come to ask what was wrong and how could they help. I would arrive home that evening and tell my parents that it was alright, nothing happened, everything was okay after all. But no, the men kept their eyes on the ground. A couple of them turned their heads as if they'd smelled something rotten. Finally, the driver stopped in front of a townhouse with a signboard in front, red letters screaming something in Chinese or Japanese. All of us shrank away as the guards unlatched the tailgate, but they only chose two girls, untying the ropes from the side rails and dragging them off. My neighbour, the one with the infant, was taken off; I could see from the way she was standing, tall, her weight even on both feet, that she was readying herself to run or fight. The door opened and they were pushed in, one after the other. We drove off again.

The truck was driving east. After what seemed like hours, a deep panic set it. I couldn't understand how we could still be driving. I looked up at the sun. Wouldn't be long until it set. I wondered if they would stop at dusk. Then at the thought of night, another shot of panic. I looked around me – nothing I could recognize. How little my world was. Maybe we're never going to stop, not until we get to the edge of the island. I could already see us plunging straight into the sea, to an inevitable, watery death. Trapped and drowned the way they used to drown adulterers and fallen women. But no, no sight of water. Not a whiff of its salt and mud. Instead, more buildings and factories, all of them interspersed with swathes of grass and nothing else. Then another stop where two girls were taken off, until it was just Huay and me left.

A different neighbourhood now. The sun was ahead of us. So we're headed west, I decided, right before the truck turned left into a lane, then right again. And then we were surrounded by the thick green of tembusu trees with their low, pronged branches, like arms held wide open. The high-pitched whine of crickets. I saw a few houses far apart from each other – bungalows with black-and-white rolling curtains, and clusters of low buildings that looked like a large school or barracks. There were a few road signs in English – nothing I could make out, of course. I wanted to ask Huay but she was staring down at her knees, unseeing. If only I had gone to school, I thought. Then, another thought, bitter and fleeting: even if I could read, so what?

The sun was shining a dark orange, the curve of it almost melting into the tops of trees when the truck turned into a narrow, meandering lane. There, the canopy grew so thick that the trees blocked out much of the light and the truck snaked along in semi-darkness until it broke open into a clearing where a sentry was on duty behind the gate. He called out as he let us through and the young soldier sitting at the end of the truck called back and laughed as he untied my rope from around the side rail. Then he leaped off and jerked at the end of the rope he held in his hand until I jumped off after him, almost tipping to my knees. It was only then, standing on the warm tarmac that I realized that I was barefoot. Huay followed, hardly making a sound as she landed.

My father had talked about houses like these, houses mostly owned by the wealthy expatriate or military families from Britain. He had delivered furniture to the private residences a few times, and each time he had come home, still wide-eyed from the experience. 'You won't believe how big they are. The gardens these ang moh have,' he'd gushed. Standing there, I had a sudden image of him dismounting his bicycle, tilting his head back to stare at the two-storey bungalow, white except for the black wooden beams and window frames, and its pitched, terracotta roof. There was a perimeter of barbed wire all around it, newly raised and clean of leaf litter. Beyond that, a thick wooded area and a wall of cricket song, loud and insistent.

The same soldier marched us around the house to the back, towards a separate, single-storey building a few yards away. It was constructed in the same style, just cheaper, smaller, though it was still twice the size of my home. Compared to the bungalow, though, it looked doll-sized, unreal. A guest house fallen into ruin. Servants' quarters. The idea of the last filled me with hope, dangerous and sharp-edged. I held on to it even as another guard opened the door and I was pushed over the threshold, into the house. It smelled of rice and tea, and something bitter, medicinal. Huay stumbled in after me, scuffing her feet along the concrete floor. The front room was empty of furnishings, but for a long wooden bench lining the wall and a desk with papers and boxes on top. And then faces. Men. And a few women, dishevelled and oddly clothed, all a blur. I felt the heat of someone else's body behind me, much too close, before I was pushed by a soldier past the counter into a narrow hallway, on and on past several doors until he halted, holding on to my arm to make me stop. The soldier opened the door, then walked around to look at me. As he did so, the tip of his rifle brushed against my kneecap, making the hairs on my arms stand on end. Then he removed a knife from his belt and walked around to stand behind me. I felt him tug at my bonds and begin to cut through them. He shoved me again, harder, until I fell forward, through the doorway, onto a rattan mat. The rope loosened itself from my wrists and slipped to the ground. There was no need for it anymore.

I spun around, ready to scream but the soldier was already leaving, pulling the door shut behind him. I heard the heavy drop of the pad-lock against the wood, then footsteps as he went down the corridor.

The room was no bigger than three by four paces and separated from the ones next to it by thin plywood. At the end of it was what used to be a window, but with the glass smashed out and boarded up from the outside. Most of the space was taken up by a rattan mat. Next to it was a small rag and a dark bottle filled with clear liquid. I uncorked it and sniffed. Disinfectant. Then I sat down with my knees up, my back against the far wall. For hours, a steady stream of people went back and forth along the corridor and I froze each time the sound of footfall stopped outside. Once, I saw boot tips underneath the door and I drew myself backwards, wanting to push myself into the concrete, holding my breath until whoever it was went away.

That was how I sat the rest of the night; I couldn't sleep for the orchestra of noises outside the house. I could hear the hum coming from the woods nearby, of insect song and later, the woeful cry of the koel, which meant the sun was setting. As the scratching of crickets peaked at sundown and wound down into a high-pitched whine, the strip of daylight beneath the door receded slowly into the glow of lamplight. Eventually, someone extinguished that as well and I heard the heavy grind of a lock being turned, like a warning. Then darkness, solid and unrelenting. I sat with my back in a corner, eyes wide and staring into the tarry dark, imagining light and shapes where there were none and trying to tell time from the sounds I heard. I dropped in and out of sleep but started awake from time to time, because louder than everything else was the silence of girls like me, in rooms next to mine and rooms next to that, afraid and waiting.

Kevin

The funeral lasted three days on the ground floor of our apartment block, far away from the mailboxes so that our neighbours wouldn't have to walk past my grandmother and the tables and cheap plastic chairs laid out for the visitors every time they went to collect their post. They had covered up the open, empty space of the void deck, dressed all the walls with thick blankets coloured cobalt blue and gold and black, and curtained off the open bits that led outside. My mother said it was to let us mourn without strangers watching and so that passers-by wouldn't have to see the coffin and funeral things without meaning to. I asked her what was wrong with looking at the casket. She said some people didn't like that, some people thought it was bad luck. She once pointed out an ongoing funeral to her mother and got a smack on her head for it, she said, nodding, as if to say that's what you get for not knowing better, it was only fair.

All throughout the three days, we pretended that Ah Ma could still hear us, that she was still there. At mealtimes, we laid out a bowl of whatever we had to eat, rice or noodles, topped with curry and vegetables, and reminded her to eat. 'Ma, *chi le,*' my father called out, the way he used to when we were all sitting at the dinner table, waiting for her while she finished listening to an opera, or was done snapping the thread off a bit of sewing.

My only real job during the three days was to make sure that every visitor left with a piece of red string to ward off any bad luck from the funeral. I tied them around the wrists of my numerous cousins, all black-clothed and sombre-faced, pushed them into the hands of aunts and uncles, held the strands out to the neighbours as they got up from the tables to leave. Albert was there, with his parents and siblings. His mouth was red, as if his mother had rubbed chilli into his lips again for lying. I'd seen him once, standing outside after dinner, tears and snot running down his face. Then, for no reason at all, he turned and we locked eyes for a moment before I let the curtain drop. It was soon after that evening that he turned his attention to me and began to call me names. Now though, he held out his hand for the string. There were a few people from the market as well, a fishmonger who used to take delight in pretending to be insulted by my grandmother's haggling, and a fruit seller who kept aside perfectly ripe mangos for her, wrapped in layers of Chinese tabloids. There was no one else. No one else from her family. No siblings or cousins, no family friends.

The leftover string formed little scarlet nests in the middle of each table and I tied them around myself that first night, making the tips of my fingers bulge red and purple. When my mother noticed, she took my hands and unwound the string from my fingers, one by one. 'Nothing red for you. It's your grandmother's funeral.' As if I didn't know it already, as if I didn't know anything at all.

On the last night of the funeral, it came to me what I had to do. The knowing of it crept into my bones as the hired monk sang the final prayers with his eyes shut, as I helped my father pile the paper offerings onto a steel platform until it creaked and sagged: joss money, designer clothing, a chest full of jewellery, a chauffeured car, a villa and its two accompanying servants, all the things Ah Ma never had while she was alive. A few scraps of joss paper floated away from the pyre like butterflies lit aflame. 'Get them before we burn down the building,' my mother said. So while the money and villa and meticulously kitted-out paper Mercedes crumpled away to black and ash, I danced on the pavement and grass patches, slapping the rubber soles of my shoes against the charred runaways, knowing how foolish I looked, trying hard not to smile after days of not moving my face except to say thank you and goodbye. The effort of not smiling made my mouth crumple up and my eyes start stinging again, but it was okay. If anyone asked I would say it was from the heat of the flames, or that something had gotten in my eye. But no one asked. They were all busy staring at the fire. My parents and a few of the neighbours Ah Ma would sit with while she waited for my school bus to drop me off in the afternoon. They were just watching the whip of the smoke, the little figures in the villa and paper car twist and shrink, their painted faces vanishing into black; watching to avoid speaking, like the news was on, or a drama serial. As they did I rubbed and rubbed my eyes, wanting and not wanting someone to see me. Wondering if it was okay, at my age, to go to my mother and want to use her sleeve as a handkerchief. I would do it, go to her if she turned and looked at me. And then I would tell her about what Ah Ma had told me. My mother would know if it was okay to tell Pa or if it would be better to keep it to myself/ourselves because it would send him into his Dark Place again. There were things we kept from him because of that. The thing about Albert. About my mother taking money from her sister to 'tide us over' when my father lost his job. I watched the small crowd to see if anyone saw me rubbing my eyes.

No one did.

It was 2:00 a.m when we finished. I was falling over from sleep and my father's face had lines in it that I hadn't seen before, not just under his eyes and across his forehead but in the lower part of his face – two brackets framing his mouth, like he was going to say something loud and important. I was taking my shoes off when my mother made us stop by the front door.

'Wait, wait; wait here.' She uncovered a shallow basin of water, wide enough for me to step in. There were flower petals in it. Chrysanthemums and something smaller, pink. 'Wash your face. All up your arms as well.'

I bent over the basin and splashed. Petals stuck themselves to my cheeks.

'More, more.' Then she explained that the water was supposed to wash away anything from the funeral that might follow us home.

I cupped water with my hands and dashed my face with it, once, twice, splashing hard. My mother picked a few velvet petals off my head and gave me a towel. Then she helped my father, bringing the water to him in her palm and dropping it over his head, his arms. My father closed his eyes. When he opened them again I saw a glimmer of the Dark Place that he had gone into a few years ago. Right after he lost his job during the recession. He had disappeared for months, almost half a year. That was when I was ten. I remember because of the exams I had to take that year. My mother had yelled at him one evening because he was 'not helping'. 'Those exams will determine the rest of his life,' she had said, shout-whispering the way she did when she was really upset. 'And you're just scaring him. You're not creating a Stable Learning Environment.'

My father had cried and my grandmother tried to distract me by telling a story about her life during the war. I missed it all because I was eavesdropping on my parents and only caught her saying, '… it was so tough for so many years. I thought I was going to die just like everyone had. But everything was fine in the end. See? This is nothing. Everything is going to be okay.'

After that night, my father disappeared a little more. That was when I learned that it was possible to disappear and still be there, that it was possible to disappear even further than he had. To be emptier than empty. Blacker than black. It took him half a year to come back again and when he did, he acted as if it had never happened, just came back home one day and told us that he had found a new job working for a pool company. That they were even going to give him a company van. I smiled when I saw him smiling but I was afraid too, after that, every single day, fearful that any little thing might make him go into his Dark Place again.

I went to the bedroom, lay down on my left side (away from the other bed, from the other things that did not belong to me, did not belong to anyone now) and closed my eyes. The tape was in my bedside drawer, pushed under a few comic books. It was there and I could picture it, rattling among discarded pens and half-filled notebooks, even as I dreamed about the monk and the chanting and the wailing music.

Then I was awake again, staring at nothing. Something had woken me but I couldn't tell what. A car alarm? I thought. Maybe a neighbour, getting home late and shutting the door too loudly. Then I heard the words, soft, as if she were breathing right into my ear.

'I found you.'

I pushed myself up into sitting and put the bedside lamp on, then clicked it off at once. I didn't want to see whatever it was, if it was there.

'I found you.'

I shook my head and counted to ten, then I switched the light on again and turned to look at her half of the room. Her bed was untouched. The bedclothes were still on it, her blanket pulled up until it covered her wooden pillow, the way the nurse had pulled the hospital blanket up over Ah Ma's head so that only the top of her hair, mostly scalp, showed. The way she did it was like a curtain falling, completely. The End, the blanket was saying.

'Ah Ma?' I whispered.

No answer.

I lay back down and waited, startling when a neighbour's dog began to bark. It was no use. I sat up and put the light on again. I got out of bed, opened my drawer and took out the tape, the recorder, and a pen and some paper. Then I went to my grandmother's bedside drawer. There was a stack of tissue paper in their thin pillow cases, a pot of tiger balm, a few tubes of Po Chai Pills she kept around for her nervous stomach, and sheaves of papers and letters. When I found her flashlight (kept for emergencies, blackouts, and 'just in case of war', my grandmother had said) I rewound the tape and played it, pen in hand. Through the crackle of air between my grandmother and the recorder, this was what I heard: 'I found you. Pease don't baneme... Ifoundyou and tookyouawaay. They were dead ormowheregobemouuuuund...I...dinnnnow. Eerbuddyelsewasgoooh...and...I... waadoondydyingdohell...I...wanndeddosaveyou...Youwerejusababy, soniddle. I wannded to look forem, I did, but ondmund begamedoendend idbegame dooyears. EndnafterdatI just cuddent. I couldn't.' There was a pause here and I heard her breath, rough and dry through her throat. Then, 'Dooyouvergeefmee? I tried to look forem. Ayr reelly did. Eyydunwanyada blammee weenyfindoud. Pease forgeef me.'

Silence. And then, my own voice, 'Ah Ma...' soft and high like a child's, and another pause before I asked, 'Who? Who were you looking for?'

Her answer – 'Your parents' – made no sense to me that night and I stopped the tape right there, knowing what was going to come after and not wanting to hear it: her pleading, my deception. I wound it back and played it again, writing down what I could make out of her speech. When I looked down afterwards, this was what I had:

I found you. Please don't. I found you and took??? They were dead or more ??? I ??? Every ???? Go and I ?????? I one ???? You were just a baby??? I wanted to look for them I did but 𝍸𝍸𝍸𝍸𝍸 *And after that I just couldn't. I couldn't. Do you* 𝍸𝍸 *I tried to look?? I really did*𝍸𝍸𝍸𝍸 *...blame me* 𝍸𝍸 *Please forgive me.*

I played the tape nine times in total. The fluorescent arms on my clock were pointing to twenty past three when I finally had all the words. I remembered the way she had gripped my hand and I was relieved, now more than ever, about how I had lied to her. How I let her have that at least, even though I couldn't be sure what she was saying, I only had the faintest idea. Because this was what Ah Ma said the day she died, the last time I heard her speak:

'I found you. Please don't blame me. I found you and took you away. They were dead. Or nowhere to be found. I didn't know. Everyone else was gone and I was only trying to help. I wanted to save you. You were just a baby, so little. I wanted to look for them after the war, I did, but one month became two, and then it became a year, two years. And after that I just couldn't. I couldn't. Do you forgive me? I tried to look for them. I really did. I don't want you to blame me when you find out. Please forgive me.'

That is my grandmother/not my grandmother. That is someone else's grandmother, or no one's at all.

This was what I was thinking when the incinerator opened its metal mouth and swallowed the coffin whole. We were standing behind a thick glass window in the viewing gallery but I could imagine its hot breath, the way it might make the fine, beginning strands of hair on my arms curl if I were standing in front of it, but I felt nothing. I had seen her that morning for the last time, laid out amongst sheets of hell banknotes, a few flowers, then said goodbye along with my parents before the undertakers put her in the back of the hearse. If it hadn't been for that, I wouldn't be imagining Ah Ma now, in the fire, feeling strange that I could sense nothing of the heat; it was this strangeness that made me shiver as we watched the coffin roll in, out of sight.

Afterwards, a temple worker came to speak to my parents. 'It's going to take some time. You can come back in a few hours, or come back tomorrow. It's up to you.'

My father said we would wait, crossed his arms and sat down on a bench but my mother was already walking away, saying, 'Come, let's get some lunch.' There was a free kitchen and she corralled us towards the temple's incense-smoked dining hall, teeming with sightseers wearing large, staring cameras around their necks, and out-of-work men, their linty pockets turned out as if for proof. We had to share a table with two female tourists gripping splayed chopsticks. One of them was wearing a pink bandana on her head, both of them of an age I could only think of as simply 'younger than my mother'.

'Noodles or porridge?' my mother asked.

I shrugged. My father shrugged. She sighed and joined the queue, now past the canteen doors and trailing out onto the steps. It was some time before she came back with three large bowls swimming with vegetables and mock meat that was meant to look like char siu. She pushed one orange melamine bowl towards me. 'Eat,' she said.

The noodles, wound tight as a ball of yarn, were difficult to untangle and I spent some time coaxing each neat coil onto my spoon. I was almost finished, my stomach heavy with dark gravy and vegetables and noodles when I looked up and realized that my father was bent over his bowl, quietly weeping into his porridge. My mother had laid one still palm on his shoulder. I put down my chopsticks and spoon.

'Pa?'

In response, he put out his hand and shook his head sorry, but the more he shook his head and tried to swallow his sobs, the louder they came out, like hiccups. 'Hup, hup, hup.' His shoulders popped up and down and he pushed his porridge away, careful even in his grief not to ruin perfectly edible food. The tourist with the pink bandana dug into her backpack and pushed a packet of Kleenex, large and American blue, across the table. All around us, people were eating. The lusty suck and sip of noodles and pulpy, broken-down rice grains going into mouths and down pink-red throats. Gnashing and gulping and wiping their mouths. A lone monk came out carrying a tray laden with bowls of silky soybean curd and was immediately rushed by a tight ring of diners. 'Eat, just eat,' my father said, pressing several layers of paper tissue to his face. My mother whispered sorry and thank you to the two women as we got up and led my father away, and I did as well, though the women had turned a little away and were trying not to look.

While we passed time in Bright Hill Temple, waiting for Ah Ma's body to burn through, my father cried in the dining hall, he cried down the endless covered walkways leading from one part of the red-and-orange temple to the other, he cried sitting on a stone bench in the garden. To get away, I bought two dollars' worth of lettuce for the turtles swimming in the large pond and tried to fling the leaves as close to their mouths as I could but most of it landed on their sun-baked shells. After five minutes, there were floating clumps of green all over the pond. As I watched the turtles, trying not to breathe in the algae stink, I thought if it might be a good way of making my father stop: telling him that I didn't think it was his mother in the coffin after all, that she had said as much in the hospital the day before she passed away. I toyed with the idea, tapping him once on the arm only to gape the moment he turned towards me, his face pink and damp.

It took three hours in all. Three hours for the fire to consume everything, for the remaining fragments to be pulverized and laid out on a metal tray. When Ah Ma's ashes were finally ready, my father started weeping afresh as each of us sifted through the remains of her body, picked out nuggets of cooled, smoke-white bone and dropped them into the urn. His tears made black, domed spots in the ash. My mother and I pretended not to see.

It was only after they put the urn away in the cool darkness of the columbarium, in a numbered spot assigned just for her, that my father stopped. A bunch of joss sticks materialized and were lit. While we offered them up, I saw her photo again, pasted just off-centre on the front of her urn. Above it, her name, Lim Li San, in Chinese characters. I looked at the other passport photo faces around us. They looked like uncles and aunties, and bus drivers and drink sellers, and teachers. There were women's faces frozen in beauty shots; one looked like my mother's favourite actress, a lock of hair making a sharp-tipped curlicue on her cheek. I finished bowing and stuck the joss sticks in a tin. My hands felt gritty grey. On the way out, I put my hands behind my back while my father walked next to me, red-eyed, his trouser pockets fat with damp, balled-up tissues.

During the ride home, I inspected my hands. I couldn't see it but it was there. A layer of fine dust, straight from the fire. If it wasn't my grandmother, it was someone else's specks lingering between my fingers, hidden within my riverlike palm lines, getting under my fingernails. If it wasn't my father's mother, I thought, wasn't it possible that the real one was still alive?

Wang Di

'I've been looking for your chess partners. I tried walking past every block, past each chess table until it got late. You know, *la*. Six-thirty, seven, and everyone's gone home for dinner. I'm going to look for them again tomorrow because...' *Because who else is left? What else can I do?* '...because even though we've only spoken once, you've told me so much about them that I feel I almost know them. They must know something about you.'

For the next fifteen minutes, as she made her evening meal, Wang Di talked about the new neighbourhood. About the mall and how, instead of the smell of fish and water and earth, the market now smelled of plastic. 'But the floors are clean and dry, which is good, I suppose. Remember the time I fell near the fish stalls and my ankle went the size of a mango?' She turned and looked at his picture. 'Things have changed.'

The Old One had said those exact words as they lay in bed waiting for sleep one night. It had been on the news, the anniversary of the end of the Japanese Occupation. Wang Di found she could not sit still long enough to watch the uniformed men smile and talk about what they did during the war. Even lying down in the dark afterwards, her hands danced, fingers twisting around each other even as it sent sharp pains around her bones, up into her arms. He had put his hand over hers, a gesture so rare that it made her look over at him.

'I don't understand… No one wants to hear about the occupation anymore,' she'd said. 'They didn't back then, so why would they want to now, more than fifty years later? Besides, most of the people are dead.'

'You're not doing this for other people. You're doing this for yourself.'

She knew he was thinking about that day. When he tried to tell her about his family, what had happened during the war. How she had reacted, all the air going out of her, as if she had been punched. After that evening, he had tried a few times, but as soon as he brought up anything to do with the war, she had to leave the room. He gave up after a while. And it was only when he stopped that Wang Di realized she had wanted him to keep trying, to wear her down until she was prepared to listen. But it was much, much later before he made any mention of the war again. He had simply announced one morning, over breakfast, that he was leaving to go into the city, something about an archive, about putting away what had happened during the occupation. She had been too scared to ask him what he meant by it. Instead, she reminded him to take his walking stick along – he was in his seventies and was starting to need one on his walks. He had nodded and accompanied her to their corner – pushing the cart loaded with its folding table, the sewing machine, and bags of cloth and things. Set up shop in their usual alleyway, and left. All day, Wang Di had sat at their roadside stall, taking in the bits of sewing she could do and telling the ones who needed measuring out to return later.

'When?' they'd asked, and she had to shake her head. She feared he would never return. But he did, in the early afternoon. Went straight to work at his sewing machine, chatting with her as they waited for customers. He would do this once a week for a month, always returning in the afternoon, always sidestepping the question of what he had been doing and where. One month, that was all it took. After that, for the rest of their years together, he seldom left her alone for a few hours at a time.

'People are different now – they talk about things that we never would. You don't know until you try.' Then his voice wound lower. 'Promise me you will try. Even after.'

She wanted to chide him for saying 'after', tell him that he was crazy. He wasn't going anywhere, that she wouldn't allow it. She wanted to say she was old too, that she might go before him. That anything could happen. She wanted to say all this and every-thing else, things she should have said decades ago when they were younger. But she didn't. She barely heard herself as she told him yes, she would.

It was with this thought that she went out each morning and evening, making her collection round and filling her pushcart, all the while keeping an eye out for stone tables on the ground floor of each building, and the people sitting around them. During the day, it was mostly women; housewives and women her age waiting for their grandchildren to arrive home from school. The men came out in the evening, one by one, laying out their wooden chess pieces, waiting for someone to sit across from them and start.

She took to going up to them and asking if they had seen the brothers but they (always men, never younger than fifty) seemed to have little patience for anything else outside the square of their chessboard and would keep their eyes on their pieces as she described them: thin, average height, in their sixties, two brothers who looked like brothers.

No one knew who she was referring to.

It was only on the fourth day that someone sat up, nodded. 'Yes, yes. I think I know who you're talking about. I used to play them. They're really good, especially the –'

'Do you think they'll be here today?' Finally, Wang Di thought, finally.

'Oh, I haven't seen them for some time. A few weeks, at least.' He tilted his chin at his opponent. 'Don't they live in one of those buildings? The ones that are getting demolished?'

The opponent shrugged and hunched over the board, tapping his foot to tell Wang Di that it was time for her to go. But she stayed where she was, watching until the first man looked up again.

'Sorry *ah*, I really don't know. Maybe they moved.'

Wang Di nodded, thanked him. She felt light. As if what had been keeping her whole was being hollowed out of her. She had a sense of the familiar, and knew at once, what this was. This was what it was like to lose hope, little by little.

August 1942

'Good morning, time to get up!' I woke to see a middle-aged woman standing in the doorway, smiling. She was fine-boned, tall and it looked like someone had wrapped a length of broad cloth around her to make a dress, a sober dark blue dotted with fine white squares, the thread of which shimmered silver and gold as she moved. 'Come, follow me.' Her speech was hushed but firm, and there was a lilt in her Mandarin that I couldn't place. The skirt of her dress rustled against the doorway as she turned, and I got up to follow her down a narrow corridor and into a kitchen with a charcoal burner on a table in front of the window, a wok and two large pots next to it. There was a screen in the middle of the room and I could see someone's shadow behind it, moving calmly. Four other girls joined me in the kitchen, none of whom I'd seen before, then Huay. The woman counted heads, then smiled. 'Good morning, everyone. My name is Mrs Sato. We are your guardians now.' She turned and pointed at another woman, slightly older, in her fifties, standing next to the far wall. All of us turned to look at her but she didn't move or introduce herself. 'Now, we will need all of you to take off your clothes and shoes. Everything.'

There was a wave of movement, a gasp and shift backwards on our feet. One of the girls started weeping but the woman made a clucking sound with her tongue. 'It's just for the doctor. He's here to give everyone a quick check-up and make sure you are clean and healthy,' she said, keeping her hands close to her body while she spoke. 'Go on. The quicker you do it, the quicker you will finish.' She flashed a buoyant, maternal smile. Finish? I thought. The way she said it made me think of the market, putting what little I had left away in my basket and heading home. Maybe that's what she meant, that we could go home afterwards. And I started wondering how long it would take for me to walk back to the village, and if my family would still be there, alive, by the time I got back. *Finish*. I fixed my eyes on the cracks running through the cement floor and took my clothes off. My trousers in a heap on the ground. My blouse. Done, I gathered them up in a ball, in both my hands and held it against my body.

'Your underwear as well. Go on.'

I hesitated, frowning hard in an effort not to cry, and took them off, trying to shut out the sound of the girls. There was a noise in my head. A chattering. It took me a moment to realize that it was the sound of my teeth clattering together in my mouth. I tried to clench my jaws together but it just made the clattering louder, more violent.

I looked up to see Mrs Sato leading Huay past the screen. After five minutes, they came back and she picked out another girl and led her away.

Then it was my turn. I watched as she came closer, soundless as she walked over to me in her open-toed sandals. With one hand under my elbow, she guided me past the screen, towards a man standing next to a long wooden table.

'Could you get onto the table and lie down?' Except it wasn't a question the way she said it, had moved close, impatient to have this over with. I lifted myself up, unthinking, and slid myself back on the warm wood.

'Feet on the table, legs apart.'

It was this that made me almost spring up but Mrs Sato was close to me now. Watching. So I lay on the table, gripping the sides of it with my hands, hoping that I'd misheard. She waited for a second, then she sighed and placed her hands on my knees, forcing them wide. She stayed holding on to me and I remember thinking that her skin smelled of soap, the kind that we used to wash with before rationing was put into place. It was only when the doctor leaned forward and touched me that my eyes filled and I had to bite my lip to keep from crying out.

She started to shush me. A mother, all of a sudden, calming her own child. 'Stop crying. Nothing has happened yet.'

It was the word 'yet' that kept ringing in my ears as the doctor pushed two fingers inside me. I yelped and tried to get up but Mrs Sato's grip was stronger than her hands suggested and she held me down without much effort. With any escape made impossible, the doctor's hands were the only things I was aware of for several seconds – his skin and flesh and bone: cold, certain. The way he reached in and then paused, as if waiting, then withdrew, nodding in satisfaction at Mrs Sato before going to the sink in the corner to rinse his hands.

'Good girl. You can put your clothes back on.'

They turned away from me to confer with each other. As I felt for the floor with my feet, Mrs Sato laughed, a coquettish laugh that sounded practised, businesslike.

I don't recall walking out but I must have because the next thing I remember was being in the room I had waited in earlier with the rest of the girls. When everyone had been seen by the doctor, Mrs Sato shepherded us into the bathroom at the end of the corridor. We all had to wash between seven and eight every morning, she said, adding that there was to be no loitering, and no chit-chat – the caretaker would be close by to make sure of that. The space had a single barred window above a row of sinks and taps, showing a bit of sky, all cloud, no blue. Next to the sinks were two cubicles, both with a toilet in the floor and an earthen jar that came up to my hip. It was filled with water and there was a bucket floating on top, and in it, a bar of soap, half used. The doors had been taken off their hinges, leaving them gaping open so that the scent of soap and water wafted out freely.

Three women were standing at the sinks, finishing up. I couldn't tell where they were from but there was something different about the way they looked that went beyond place of birth or language – the way they looked their faces and moved and breathed. The way they stood. I watched as one of them dried her legs, letting the front of her robe fall open as she bent over. It reminded me of a puppet show I watched once at the market, the absolute blankness of their faces. Mrs Sato gave a dismissive wave with her hand and all three of them walked out. As they passed, the first of them looked up and gave me a little nod. This, I soon found out, was Jeomsun. She told me later on that she wanted to take our hands and lie to us, tell us that it was going to be okay. We had reminded her of herself on the first day, years ago, back at a camp in Formosa. How lost we had looked.

The older woman came in with an armful of folded cotton and handed them over to Mrs Sato. 'These are the clothes you will wear from now on,' she said, passing one to each of us.

The dress I got was blue and looked used. The weave was soft, as if it had been laundered many times over and put out to dry in the breeze. I folded mine over my arm and smoothed the worn fabric, calming myself.

It was only much later that I would admit to Huay that the dress had made me hopeful. 'I thought it could be a uniform. Hoped it was a good sign,' I told her. 'I thought we were there to be dancers, to cheer up the soldiers. Or cooks. Or servants.' Underneath this shallow assumption was a torrid wave of fear. I had an idea about why we were there, a whisper that I was trying to shut out. Listening to the whisper would have pulled me under, like an invisible current, and swept me out to sea. For now, I clung on to anything I could. Even a glint of hope as faint as this.

'But what's going to happen? When can we go home?' Huay asked. Her voice was soft, clear as a spring.

Mrs Sato's eyes flashed. It was like watching a small, silver fish dart to the surface and flicker away again into the depths. 'You're here to help serve the Japanese troops. Make them feel welcome.'

'What do you mean? What do we have to do?' someone else said.

'You'll get rewarded for good behaviour. Didn't they tell you? You can help your families by making money. I heard that everyone's hungry, aren't they? Money will help.'

All around me, there was a nervous fidgeting. A wishful twisting of shirt ends. Money, I understood. I knew Huay did as well. She nodded once, her chin dipping almost imperceptibly. Even though the house, the soldiers, the knot of apprehension in my stomach told me to think otherwise, I wanted to believe it as well and nodded along with the rest of them.

'Good, good. Now everyone needs to wash. It's going to be a long day.'

I didn't think about what she said then but the words came back to me right after, in the dark. A long day, she had said. Mentioning nothing about what we had to do.

As Mrs Sato left the bathroom, she called out in Japanese. The older woman hurried towards us and stopped just outside the door. She had a bamboo cane in her hand and leaned on it as she kept silent watch. Huay was the first to move. All of us turned away as she undressed. I felt their gaze on me as I went into the other cubicle and skimmed the surface of the water in the earthen jar. Cold. I stripped down, draping my clothes over the wall of the cubicle because there was nowhere else to put them. The patch of dried blood on my trousers had turned dark, and I found myself thinking about my father, my family, wondering if they were back inside, taking stock of what the soldiers had taken and what else they had lost. How we had spent an entire afternoon sweeping up broken glass and putting the cupboard doors back on their hinges the last time the soldiers passed through. The flash of realization – that there was nothing my parents could do now – made me start to shake, so I poured a bucketful of water over my head, washed the dirt off my feet, hands and face, and listened to the sound of water cracking as it met the floor. As I scrubbed, I focused my attention on the barred window showing a bit of sky, the sinks and taps, a convenience I wasn't used to.

This can't be too bad. It couldn't be, I told myself; a wish more than anything else.

Afterwards, I put on the dress. It was different to the ones that Mrs Sato and her assistants wore – the sleeves were short and there were two buttons on the bodice, easily fastened and undone. The fit was loose, and the skirt wide instead of slim-fitting, as was the fashion then. My things, when I looked around for them, were gone. So were my undergarments, which I had tucked within my clothes. I felt naked and started shaking again from another wave of panic. Maybe our things have been taken away to be laundered, maybe it's just the way they do things here, I told myself, pushing away the sound of Mrs Sato's voice in my head, the thin cheeriness of it when she mentioned the soldiers. We would never see our clothes again. Shoes, those who still had them, would be taken away as well. I would go barefoot for the next thirty-six months. The first shoes I got after the war were wooden clogs and I wore them until they broke, got them mended, then taped up the straps when I was too ashamed to bring them to the cobbler's anymore. But that would be years later.

'Now, don't you all look nice. Just one last thing before you go back into your rooms.' Here, she proceeded to give us our new names. Japanese names, which she said made things easier for the staff. Huay, I noted, was Kiko and mine was Fujiko. I said the words under my breath. Fujiko, the edges of it round and barbed at once, a strange fruit in my mouth.

Mrs Sato hummed a tune under her breath as she came for each of us. When it was my turn and she spun me around gently to go back up the corridor, I saw, for the first time, an armed soldier standing at the start of the entryway, watching as I was led back to the room I'd slept in. The kerosene lamp was lit and in the warm light of the single flame, it was easier to tell myself that it was going to be okay. Perhaps it wasn't what I thought it was, this place. Perhaps we were there to mend uniforms, or take care of the wounded, or prepare food in the army kitchen. It's going to be okay, I told myself, and looked around the room – the light from the flame illuminating a 'v' of brown damp spreading down from the ceiling, and, at eye-level, little dots and splashes on the walls. I went close, squinting, and saw that they were bloodstains, turned dark. Then I saw the words scratched into a corner of the plywood wall. Three characters. A name, perhaps. The name of the girl who had been in this room before. Maybe she was home now, I told myself. Maybe she had done a good job and was now home with her family.

Less than an hour later, I heard the rumble of engines as several vehicles rolled in beyond the gate and settled into the driveway, as the stamp of boots came close, closer. Then quick and unrestrained laughter, the sudden pelt of it making me start. I told myself not to panic. Reminded myself that they needed women, surely, to be nurses and cooks and cleaners.

I made myself think this until the first man came into the room that morning.

There was no mistaking it then, when the door opened and he came in. I scrambled for the exit but he only had to reach out to catch hold of my shoulder, spinning me around as the door slammed behind him. I could not help but look at him – his wide-set eyes. The shiny, wet corners of his mouth as he said something in Japanese and put his arms around me. As if we were playing a game. I kept fighting to get out of his clasp and after a moment, he stopped smiling and gave an impatient sigh before reeling back and hitting me with his open palm. I fell to the mat and he kicked me in my side, the sharp jab of it a warning more than anything else, to make sure I stayed down before he undid his trousers. Then he knelt, pushed my dress up above my waist, and put one hand around my neck as he straddled me. He kept a grip on my neck the entire time so that I couldn't move my head away from the rasp of his stubble on my cheek, his oily breath. The wet on my skin where he drooled or perspired. The sound of him as he rutted on top of me. The only thing I could do was to close my eyes and wait and wait for it to be over.

When he left, Mrs Sato rapped on the door and called through, reminding me to clean up with disinfectant. In the haze of what had just happened, her instructions were almost a comfort, a clear line of thought I could follow. Even the solidity of the bottle was comfort. It was real. My body was not. Compared to the objects in front of me, the rag, the bottle, the liquid sloshing within, I felt hollow and strangely weightless, as if I didn't exist. I wiped myself and looked down to see that the cloth had come away bloodied. The thick smear of it like something alive. It was all I could do to breathe when I thought about my mother and the way she had taught me to trim away squares of cheap cotton when I got my period for the first time. 'You're a woman now,' she had said, her voice sombre. She had not looked at me – not once – as she explained how I should replace and wash the cloths several times the first three days, fewer after. 'And keep them away from your father's things when you're doing the laundry,' she'd added at the end. I knew why without asking. We were bad luck – our things, our blood.

Then the next soldier appeared. Young and smiling. He bowed and started to take off his boots. No, no, I said out loud, I think. One, I could have lived with. Maybe. But another. I told myself to try harder, fight harder so I sat up and put my hands out when he tried to descend upon me, shoving as hard as I could. For a moment, he looked dispirited and I thought he would leave. Then he reached into his pocket and brandished a gun.

'You're a woman now,' my mother had declared. A verdict. I had said nothing, just stared at the fissures around her fingernails, shiny red, as she showed me how to fold the cloth into rectangles. How strange I had felt when I sat down to dinner with my brothers and my father a few hours later. Yang had looked at me in a way that made wonder if he sensed something had shifted in the air around us, something irreversible.

Like this. I would not be able to go back. I would not be able to look my mother or father in the eyes again.

That is what I was thinking about when the third soldier came in, the fourth and fifth. I made myself stop counting after that and kept my eyes closed all the way through each of them, their oil and dirt and rumbling, until they eased their weight off me and left the room. Until the clip of boots outside the door grew faint, and died away. A woman came in to turn down the kerosene lamp in the room. Then all was dark.

I tried to curl up into myself, on my side, but when I moved, the space between my legs felt as if it had been lit on fire so I lay still on my back and closed my eyes. That night, I heard someone crying on the other side of the wall. I was about to tap on the partition between us when someone yelled out in Japanese. The crying stopped for a second before it continued, muffled this time, as if the person had clamped her hands over her face. Even when I fell asleep, the sound of her weeping seeped into my dreams, crowding out everything else. It seemed like too soon, a minute or so, before I opened my eyes and there was light again under the door – it was dawn.

Part Two

Part Two

Kevin

It was the seventh night after Ah Ma's death and my mother was busy covering the living-room floor with talcum powder. She went from left to right and right to left, walking backwards like a sower scattering seeds. I stood watching from my doorway, and imagined Ah Ma coming in through the door with plastic bags full of groceries from the wet market and making tsk-tsk noises when she saw the silky white mess.

'Are we supposed to find her footprints in the morning? Is that a bad thing? Or a good thing?'

My mother shrugged. 'If there are footprints, it just means she came back for a visit. If they're not there in the morning, it means she didn't. Nothing good or bad about it.'

'But what will she do? If she comes back?'

'Look around, I guess. Check in on you,' she said, turning away so I couldn't tell if she was joking. She stopped for a moment at the doorway of her bedroom to say goodnight and for a moment, I saw the glow of my parents' thirteen-inch television set and my father's toes pointing straight up underneath the blanket. I hadn't told him. Hadn't had the chance, or the guts to do so. Both. I blamed him. For taking his breakfast with him in the car. For disappearing the moment he came home from work. For not sitting still long enough on the sofa in the evenings. For getting up from the dinner table the minute I had the words in my mouth and was ready to spit them out. For lying down all weekend in the bedroom with his head turned away, towards the window so I couldn't see if he was asleep. Or awake and crying.

Your mother is not... Ah Ma is not.

Dinner time was the only time I got to see him now. Dinner time was always a good time to announce important news. But it was as if he suspected that something was coming and wanted to make sure that I didn't get the chance to speak. He started eating the moment he sat down, not waiting for my mother, who had a habit of cleaning up right after cooking, soaking the dirty pans and wok and wiping down the counter. Normally, he would sit and wait, tapping the table with his chopsticks and yelling, '*Chi le!*' to my mother every ten seconds, until she appeared, drying her hands on her apron. Now he just put his head down, swallowing whole mouthfuls of rice so big I couldn't help but watch them slide down his throat, thinking he might choke, he might choke and I would have to thump it out of him quick. When he was done, he didn't linger to pick at the remnants of the fish's head or to talk about the news, the way he usually did. Now he ate and left the table so quickly the chair jumped and squawked when he stood up to go.

Your mother told me...

She is actually...

I thought about sending him a letter. Or copying the transcript of the audio recording onto a piece of paper and mailing it to him. Or sliding the tape into the car's cassette deck so it would play the moment he started it up in the morning. But I could see him throwing all of these things away without giving them another look. I could see him stopping the van and flinging the tape out of the window, not recognizing his mother's own voice because it wasn't that recognizable, actually, not after she got ill. It sounded only a little like her, like someone was trying to imitate her, close but not quite. It would just be like my father. To throw something away and not think any more of it. And besides, ambushing him like that didn't seem right or honest or brave. Or I could wait until we were all in the car, on the way to the grocery store and play it then. I wondered what would have happened, if I started playing the tape from Ah Ma's old cassette player while the van was in motion so that both of them would have to listen to it. No one could leave. No one could make it stop. I would press 'start' and just let the sound of her voice fill the little space, the tight, creaking silence, until there was no need for me to say anything. But of course, I couldn't do it.

Your mother said she…

You're actually…

You might still have…

I wanted to tell my mother that my father had gone again. Disappeared like the last time he went to his Dark Place. Except this time, the going away was literal, because instead of having to sit at home two-finger typing out his résumé and making phone calls and circling ads in the newspaper, he had a reason to be out. It was work. Even though sometimes he came home smelling of beer and sweat, as if he had dipped himself in a vat of Tiger and walked home. I thought it would be safer to ask my mother first. Just in case I went to him and the whole thing went KA-BOOM. My last attempt had gone like this:

'Ma, don't you think Pa is behaving strangely?'

'What do you mean.' A statement. Not a question.

'He's like…you know…'

She made a rolling gesture with her hands that meant keep going, keep going, which I hated.

'I mean he's not talking much. And he's not home. And he smells of Tiger beer when he comes back.'

'*Aiya, xiao hai zi*,' she said. Little child. 'Your father is just spending a bit more time at work. Anyway, these are adult issues. Don't bother yourself with them.'

'Is it about Ah Ma?' I asked, even though I knew it was, of course it was. 'Because if it is I can help. Is it about Ah Ma? And do you think I should ask him –'

'Don't ask so many questions.' She frowned at me and went back to her files and papers, all spread out on the kitchen table like a collage.

So that was that. I tried to go to sleep but the smell of talcum powder, heavy and floral, stayed in my nostrils; I couldn't help but think that any moment now, Ah Ma would walk through the living room, tracking powder into the kitchen. She would make herself a snack. A smear of margarine on white bread. A cup of hot Milo. Just a bit to eat, she always said, pinching the air with her thumb and forefinger to show just how much. *Tam po tam po*, just a little, she whispered under her breath. I imagined her sitting in her chair, facing away from the dining table as if she wanted to be able to get up and run at any moment. She had important things to do and places to go.

I had important things to do. And maybe places to go. I got out of bed and found an unused notebook in my desk drawer. Then I put the words I had transcribed onto the first page. When I was done, I looked at what I'd written and underlined the ones I thought important.

<u>I found you</u>. Please don't blame me. I found you and took you away. <u>They were dead</u>. <u>Or nowhere to be found</u>. <u>I didn't know</u>. Everyone else was gone and I was only trying to help. I wanted to save you. You were just a baby, so little. <u>I wanted to look for them after the war</u>, I did, <u>but</u> one month became two, and then it became a year, two years. And after that I just couldn't. I couldn't. Do you forgive me? I tried to look for them. I really did. I don't want you to blame me <u>when you find out</u>. Please forgive me.

I double underlined the word 'or' in the second line, then triple underlined it. On the facing page, I wrote down the questions I needed answers to:

1. Where did she find him? Where was my father left when he was a baby?

2. Who are my father's real parents? Are they still alive? Where are they?

3. Ah Ma thinks or knows my father will find out. How does she think this will happen?

These were the first questions I needed answers to. I shut my notebook and watched the curtains shift in the breeze until I fell asleep. When I opened my eyes, it was to the sound of fingers scrabbling on wood. The room was still dark, the light scanty through the drapes but it was her I saw and she was herself again; mouth un-crooked, hair off her face and wound into a bun at the back of her head. The drawers in her dresser were all yanked open, and she was kneeling in front of it surrounded by pools of fabric. She said something under her breath, like a little curse, and reached her right arm, good and mobile again, all the way into one drawer, extracting it to throw a plastic bag, then a crumpled tissue onto the floor. I rubbed my eyes and asked what she was looking for, if she wanted some help. She didn't reply, just looked in my direction and sighed as if I ought to know, as if I were foolish not to. I called out again and she told me to hush, to go back to sleep. Then she reached her other arm into the drawer, then her head. Soon she was in all the way to her torso, her waist. I blinked and she was gone. For a second, I saw the bottoms of her powdered white feet, her heels, cracked and pale, and the tips of her toes pointed out like a swimmer fighting forward. And then she was gone. Like Alice, fallen down a rabbit hole. She left nothing behind, just a sound in my head like a smothered shout.

I woke at half past seven to the sound of my parents' alarm clock. I listened to their bedroom door open and close, and drifted off again until I heard them in the kitchen; my mother pouring fresh water into plastic bottles for them to take to work and my father clinking a teaspoon in his mug. Sitting up, my body felt leaden – as if I had been running circles during the night. Even my fingers ached when I curled them, like I had been digging into stamped-down dirt. That's when I remembered: my grandmother, her reaching arms and cracked heels; a tunnel, and me following after. I rolled over until my legs dangled above the floor. Then I sat facing my grandmother's bed while I rubbed the sleep out of my eyes. I stared at her pulled-straight floral sheets and her chest of drawers (all shut up, with its contents safely tucked away inside) and wondered what I might find in it. A birth certificate with a stranger's name where my grandmother's should be. Or a picture with someone else holding my father, still a child. When they leave, I thought, that's when I'll look.

My parents were sitting at the table with half-finished coffees next to them when I walked into the kitchen. My father was pretending to read the front page of the paper, but was in fact picking up breadcrumbs on the table with his thumb and index finger, then dropping them onto his plate.

'Did you sleep okay? You were making all sorts of noises, like you were fighting someone.' She was busying herself with the breakfast things, opening the jar of strawberry jam and peeling back the metal foil that she insisted on leaving in the margarine tub even when you were scraping the plastic bottom with the butter knife. She nudged the loaf of sliced bread in my direction.

'What? No? I slept okay.' I sat down and spread a good layer of margarine on a slice of bread, then dipped it into my milky coffee. 'No dreams or anything.'

'Lunch is in the fridge. Just put it in the microwave when you get hungry. Don't use the stove. If you want eggs, I'll make you eggs tonight. And make sure to do your school work – at least two hours. If you have any questions just ask us tonight. And don't open the door to anyone, please.'

'Ma…'

'…burglaries in the neighbourhood, you know? Or go to Auntie Goh's. You can do your schoolwork with Albert. Help each other.'

I kept chewing and pictured it – Albert snatching the flag erasers out of my pencil case after he had finished copying answers from my maths worksheets, kicking me under the table as his mother handed out afternoon snacks.

'Remember, you can call me or your father if there's anything.'

'Kim, it's seven-thirty in the morning!' My father stomped out of the kitchen.

My mother and I said nothing for a few seconds. Then she flapped her hand after him. '*Aiya*, he didn't sleep well last night.'

I stirred a spoon in my coffee, round and round, trying not to touch the sides of the cup.

'Do you think he would be happier if Ah Ma hadn't died? Or if Ah Gong were still around?'

My mother's own father had died when I was little, too little to remember anything of him. The words 'Ah Gong' tasted strange in my mouth, like a foreign word, and I worked my jaw a few times to dispel the uneasiness off my tongue.

'What? What are you talking about? I have to go and get dressed,' my mother snapped. She got up to rinse the cups and plates at the sink and reminded me to wipe the surface of the table after I had my breakfast. She was just about to leave the kitchen when I remembered to ask.

'Wait… Did you find footprints?'

'What?'

'In the talcum powder. Last night. Was there anything?'

Did she come back, was what I really wanted to ask.

'Oh,' she laughed. 'No, *la*.'

I thought about the way my grandmother had looked at me last night, how she had put a finger to her lips and told me to go back to sleep, shushing me as if I were five again and resisting my afternoon nap. 'Do you think this is real, all this?'

She shook her head. 'I only did it because it's what you're supposed to do.'

I looked at her, wanting her to go on but she simply shook her head again, then swept a patch of the tiled floor with her feet. She lifted them, first her right foot then her left, and dusted the faintest cloud of white off them.

Wang Di

It was a week before she found them. Sitting at a table two blocks away from her new home. Leong was busy at a game with someone she didn't recognize, Ah Ren sitting next to his brother, so fixated on the chessboard that he didn't look up, not once. So she waited. She didn't play, but saw, from the number of pieces Leong had collected next to him that it wasn't going to take much longer.

Eventually Leong said '*Jiang*', ending the game and beaming before he spotted Wang Di. '*Ah-mhm!*' he called out. 'Grandma Chia.'

Wang Di waved. There you are, she wanted to shout, I've been looking everywhere for you. Instead, she sat down on the just-vacated seat and tried not to shake. Her mouth was dry and she had to swallow once before she continued. 'How nice to see you,' she said, wondering how to go on. How to unearth what they might know about the Old One. How to begin. 'Listen, I have something to ask you.'

She had rehearsed the words each night as she lay in bed, waiting for sleep. It came out now, stuttering and choked. As if it hurt her to say the words. While she talked, the brothers listened.

'*Ah-mhm*, I'm not sure I can help,' Leong said. The sun was setting but pinpricks of sweat were starting to collect on his lined forehead.

'Anything will do. Baker Teo told me that he used to work in town, at a shop. Maybe he told you where it was?'

'No, he didn't.' Leong looked at his brother, who had stayed silent as Wang Di spoke, simply sat on and gazed past her, to a spot just above her ear. 'Ah Ren?'

He shook his head.

'I'm sorry, *Ah-mhm*. But I'm not sure we're the right people to ask. We saw him often, but mostly we talked about chess… The only thing I can recall is that we talked about where we once lived. Which kampong, how everyone used to play outside…things like that.' He looked at his brother again before continuing. 'Our parents died during the war. Pa was working at the docks on the night of the air raid. Ma passed away a few years after that. I told him this and he said that he'd lost people too.' The man stopped here and reached into his pocket. Wang Di watched as he brought out a packet of tobacco leaves and began rolling a cigarette. 'But I don't think he said who or how. This was a long time ago, maybe a decade.'

'Oh.' It was the only thing Wang Di could manage. She was about to say thank you when Ah Ren leaned forward. He had been so quiet that she had almost forgotten that he was there at all. When he spoke, it was with a voice deeper than she imagined it would be, steadier.

'His family,' he said. 'He told us that they died during the war.'

'Do you – do you remember how? And when?'

'He didn't say. But he did tell us that they're buried in Kopi Sua cemetery. That he visits every February on their death anniversary. I remember thinking that it must mean they all died on the same day.'

'Ah Ren, don't say things you're not sure about.' To Wang Di he said, 'I'm sorry. Sometimes my brother is a little blunt.'

'I'm not making things up. I remember it well. He said February.'

The twelfth of February. This is something, at least, Wang Di thought. She was about to leave when Leong spoke up again.

'He used to talk about you. All the time. He used to tell us how good you were with the customers, how you remembered all their names and what they liked. Told us you became the breadwinner after he had to stop working on account of his age. He talked about you all the time.'

Wang Di did not notice the ache in her knees as she walked home, or the heat, still lingering even as the sky streaked red and purple. There was a quickness to her step, made buoyant by what the brothers had told her. 'Twelfth of February,' she chanted. 'Twelfth of February. Kopi Sua.'

It was only when she got home that she sank back down to earth.

If Leng had been around, she would have gone over to her apartment. Leng, who used to come over on Saturday afternoons and lean against the grill gate to chat for half an hour, an hour. She would know what to do. She had been there when the Chias moved in. She had been the one who walked her to the market that first week, who had, a few years later, helped boil the herbal concoctions from the *sinseh* when Wang Di was ill. The last time she saw Leng was late last year, in a care facility. The care worker had shrugged at Wang Di when she'd asked for Lim Poon Leng, and Wang Di had to walk the length of one floor, passing by rooms full of yelling. She had given up and was looking for the exit when she spotted Leng slumped in a wheelchair in front of a blank TV screen. At first Wang Di had tried talking, telling her about the weather, how everyone had been given notice to move out of their building, but Leng had just sat, jabbering wordlessly, making a series of noises that sounded like a toddler learning to speak. 'Hum mummm mummm mummm.' She did that for an hour. When Wang Di got back home, she told the Old One that Leng wasn't Leng anymore, and had never gone back to visit.

Now, in the new flat, she thought about her. Pictured the two of them walking through the cemetery together, Wang Di helping brace the older woman as she peered at the words on each gravestone. She hadn't been to the cemetery in years but she remembered how large it was. How it was more woodland than cemetery in parts. It always took her half an hour, twenty-five minutes if she was lucky, to arrive at her parents' graves. Much of the trek would be across uneven ground, would involve ducking past the aerial roots of banyan trees and trying to avoid treading on food offerings laid out on the ground. She had stopped visiting ever since the Old One started to need a walking stick – he would have insisted on accompanying her each time, stubborn as ever. He had never asked why she'd stopped, grateful, maybe, for the small mercy of this avoided conversation and what it implied – how old he was getting, how near the inevitable seemed. She hoped that Meng was still visiting each year. Still trimming away the grass that grew out over their parents. Still painting in their names on the dark stone.

It would be impossible, she told herself. First, there was the matter of finding out the names of Soon Wei's family members, the name of his first wife. Then there would be the graves. She had asked the brothers if they could help her look for a register, a list of people who were buried in Kopi Sua. Both of them had been apologetic when they told her that they were illiterate, that they'd left school when their father died. Wang Di had wanted to say that she understood but the brothers had gotten up then, murmuring something about returning home.

And so what, if I find them? Then what? she thought. The dead can't talk.

August 1942 – May 1943

Two days passed before I ate anything or spoke to anyone. Two full days of lying on the damp mat, being bent and held down into submission. Thumbs pushed into the sides of my mouth so I couldn't bite down. There was little reprieve, especially in the first week. One soldier would be done, would be withdrawing from me when the next man barged in, making impatient gestures while undressing himself. All of them merged to form one faceless, nameless beast – all body and inhuman noise. It was a year later, with a recent young captive amongst us that I realized that this was what they did with the new girls, that word spread so the men would queue up, the line snaking out of the door, to visit this new face and break her in like a pair of shoes. Several times during the first hours I had to put my hands up to fend off blows from several soldiers affronted by a look or any resistance on my part. One man slapped me so hard I spat out part of a tooth. I learned to play dead after that, closing my eyes and lying so still that I felt myself sinking into the floor. At night, I would see my mother before me, turning her head away in shame as I tried to sleep. Or else my own clear-eyed face looming and hissing at how pliant and easy I was. You could have killed yourself when you got the chance, or jumped from the truck, I thought; the bottle of antiseptic – there – might end things quick.

All of this until I fell into a numbing, dreamless slumber. I cannot recall getting up to wash or going to the bathroom although I must have – I remember gnashing my teeth as I squatted, the dull soreness turning so sharp it almost split me. Someone must have come for me. It was the way things went in the black-and-white house. You adhered to the schedule or they, Mrs Sato or the caretaker, dragged you along with them. At some point during the first day I noticed a bowl of rice on the floor. Left it to grow cold until it became too late. Only after insects began to swarm around it did I start to feel hungry. When it became clear that the caretaker wasn't going to give me a fresh meal before I'd finished this one, I scattered the black ants that had lined up from the wall to the bowl and scraped handfuls of rice into my mouth with my fingers. Two mouthfuls and it was gone. When the caretaker returned to pick up my empty dish in the evening, she sneered at me and I understood then that I was theirs, that I belonged to them.

'Come on, come on. Get up, lazy ones.'

The voice was close enough to wake me up from my second night of fitful sleep. A nightmare, I thought, opening my eyes. Then the door opened for someone to slide a half bowl of rice across the floor. Mrs Sato's head appeared in the gap. 'Eat. Then it's off to the bathroom with you.' Then she went on calling out instructions down the hallway. 'Make sure that all of them wear a *sakku*. If they don't have one, call out for me', and, 'don't forget to collect the tickets from each soldier!'

No, not a nightmare. I pushed myself up and was at once distracted by a jolt of pain, both sharp and dull at once, spreading from my pelvis down to my legs. I did the only thing I could. Ate. Then got up to go to the bathroom.

There were a few women in there but it was the one who'd nodded at me my first morning who came up to me then. I was washing when she came and leaned against the wall, waiting. I glanced at the exit, nervous about the caretaker but there was only her wooden cane, leaning against the doorframe. 'Don't worry,' the woman said. The trick, she told me, was to grow eyes in the back of your head. 'The caretaker has bad legs and likes to sit in the kitchen. She's supposed to watch us to make sure we don't chat in the bathroom but she gets tired. See?' She pointed at the empty doorway. 'I sometimes count up to two hundred and give up because I lose track.' She paused as if to let me take it in. 'What's your name?'

I wanted to tell her to leave me alone but I stayed silent, blinking water from my eyes. She asked again, thinking I hadn't heard and my voice cracked when I replied, 'Wang Di.'

'Jeomsun. My name is Jeomsun. You're new, aren't you? From around here?'

Without further preamble, Jeomsun told me about how she had survived the week-long transport from her hometown in Busan to Formosa, where she'd been moved from camp to camp and the women around her succumbed, one after the other, to dysentery and typhoid fever. Then she had been taken away and put on a boat to Singapore. It was luck, she said, that she was in here. 'Conditions here are better. You even have running water. The places we were in before...' There was a pause. When she spoke next her voice had lost much of its energy. 'I feel so much older now than when I started. Older than my twenty years. But you. You can't be more than sixteen, surely.'

I had to think for a moment before I replied. 'Seventeen.' I had just turned seventeen. My parents had forgotten my birthday because of the war and their frantic efforts to find me a husband. For a moment I pictured my photograph pressed between the pages of Auntie Tin's red notebook and wondered if she was still showing it to potential suitors and their parents.

Jeomsun shook her head and gave me a pitying look. 'Still… You aren't the youngest. There was a girl…before you arrived. She was twelve.'

'Where is she now? The girl?'

'She tried to run away.'

'What happened to her?'

'The soldiers caught her. They brought her back here and – the things they did to her…' She stopped there.

I wanted to ask her to go on but a change had come over her, turning her inward, her eyes hard. She looked older than her twenty years but her eyes were quick, birdlike. Her face was wide and pale, without a touch of blemish except for a faint, circular scar on her right cheek. Whenever she felt nervous or hungry, she would smooth it with the tip of a finger, as if trying to rub it away. A cigarette burn, I discovered, given to her by a soldier.

The other girls were finishing up, silent in the shells that they were already beginning to form around themselves. No one spoke. No one talked about what had happened the previous nights. As Huay passed me I saw an imprint of a hand around her upper arm but I kept my eyes on the stone floor as I went into the cubicle and flinched when I saw my reflection in the water – a bruise on my neck, my upper lip red and split with a cut. As I picked at the dried blood, I wondered what Yan Ling was doing; if she was at home in the kampong or on her way to work. If, for the first time, she felt relieved, grateful for that single deformity, the deformity her mother frequently cursed her for being born with.

In the days following, Jeomsun and I often met in the bathroom. As I washed, she would keep an eye out for the caretaker and talk, keeping her voice low so it wouldn't carry. She obsessively compared our breakfast rations, asking how many mouthfuls of rice I'd had, how many pickles; or else she complained while she washed out used condoms – as we were meant to do every morning – in the sink.

She would talk about Busan sometimes; as she did her face would change, lifting and unclouding itself as if she were being warmed by the sun. She told me about the mountains and the sprawling farmland she had grown up on, and how much she missed it. Never about her parents. All this, she communicated with a child's rudimentary Chinese, picked up during her time in Formosa, and filled in the rest with hand gestures. Whenever she was tired, she would start off in Chinese before trailing off in Korean and I leaned in to listen to her even though I understood nothing. The sound of the vowels cushioned the air around me and rolled around in my head even after we split up to go back into our rooms.

Jeomsun explained that there were two types of soldiers: officers – the ones who got as much time with us as they liked, and all the rest, who were allotted twenty minutes each, no longer. She advised me to try to please the former as much as we could, and I nodded even though I didn't know what that entailed.

'And make sure the soldiers wear a *sakku* before they do anything with you or you might get pregnant. And eat. Eat as much as you can. You never know when they will start cutting back on rations. The doctor comes every Monday to perform a health inspection so pinch your cheeks pink before you go in to see him.'

'Why?'

'You need to look healthy. Otherwise they might take you away.'

'But if we look unhealthy, they might not want us, right? And if we fall sick, they might put us in hospital, won't they? They might let us go…'

'Huh. You think they'll send you to hospital to get treated? And waste good supplies?' Jeomsun scoffed. Then she turned to face me fully, straightening herself. 'You know what happens to girls who fall sick here? Or who get pregnant?' She jerked her thumb towards the back of the house, where the rubbish bins were. Into the heap, she meant. Gone.

As much as I could that first week, I tried to avoid Huay, ignoring that pinch in my chest whenever I saw her. Her presence provided a bittersweet reminder of home – the trees, the whitewashed wood on our house, its palm-thatched roof – a familiarity that felt dangerous, untoward. I decided that I didn't want her around me – didn't want her bearing witness to everything that was happening in the house. It would not do, I thought, to have another witness to my shame. If we were ever let go, she would go back and tell everyone what had happened and I couldn't bear it. The thought of everyone knowing or suspecting anything close to this. And even if she kept quiet, I would see the regretful knowing of it in her eyes and I wanted it – all this – swept away afterwards, as if it had never happened. Except that wouldn't be possible with Huay around. If I went home and she did as well, she would be a constant reminder of what had happened, what was never supposed to happen. If not, I would be able to tell my family that I had spent the entire time working in a factory. I would lie to myself first, then to everyone else after.

It was Monday morning, after our second inspection, after the doctor nodded at Mrs Sato and she turned to nod at me as if to say *good, well done*. I remember being relieved even though I didn't know what there was to be relieved about. A little later, in the bathroom, I asked Jeomsun if we would get a visit from the doctor every week.

'No. Only for the newcomers, and then every month for the rest.'

For the rest? I thought. Jeomsun saw the look on my face. She stopped cleaning her teeth with the corner of her face cloth, took me by the shoulders and did not blink, not once, as she spoke. 'Listen. Do what helps you. If hoping helps you survive from day to day, then keep hoping that they're going to release you. The truth is, I've never seen them let anyone go. But if it helps you. I've done this for five years. Since I was fifteen. What helps me is getting through one day at a time. I don't think about what's going to happen tomorrow. I focus on being clean. Eating. Talking. If I couldn't do these things I would have died a long time ago.'

Five years. I felt myself sway on my feet.

Before I could reply, Jeomsun nodded to show that the conversation was over with and walked into the cubicle. I never found out if it was the way she had learned Mandarin, communicating as clearly as she could using the limited words that were available to her, or if this was how she was. Clear as a bell. Unmistakable. Perhaps she was exactly the same when she spoke in Korean.

I was at the sink when Huay came in. I turned and looked at her fully for the first time since we arrived. She was trying to keep her dress closed around her torso but all of the buttons on it were missing, like mine, and her left sleeve was ripped wide open, the bottom cuff dangling loose like an open jaw. The gap revealed red and purple marks all the way up her arm. When she moved, I saw more bruises blooming on the inside of her thighs. When she noticed me staring, she touched the marks on her arm, shifted her dress to cover them. When that didn't work, she let her arms fall and turned away. Someone had hung a mirror, a circle of warped plastic, above the sink and she looked into it as if she had just discovered a creature, newly born. She had never been taller than me but I saw now that she had grown smaller. Lost weight in little more than a week. How the blades of her shoulders poked through her dress like the wings of a bird.

I set about ignoring her the way I had for the past week until she turned towards me, her mouth half open to say something before dropping her eyes, no doubt discouraged by how I was standing – feet away from her, ready to leave. I was exhausted. Exhausted from the effort of keeping her away, from telling myself that I was going to be released (any day now, I just had to wait). This hope was nothing, I realized, but a vanity. Girls like Jeomsun had been enslaved for years. What made me think I might be singled out and released? Nothing. My fists were balled tight and I opened them now to splash water on my face. When I looked up again, I felt lighter, as if the effort of hoping had fallen away from my shoulders.

'Are you okay?' I whispered, keeping one eye on the door.

She shrugged and held her stomach, smoothing a hand over her pelvis. I thought, for a moment, that she was going to say what I felt as well: it hurts, here. But she didn't. Instead she shrugged again and looked down at her feet.

'Don't fall ill. Remember what Jeomsun said the other day.' I didn't know what else to say, felt my mouth hanging open, useless. Then a voice floated into my head: Have you eaten? I could picture my mother's face as she said it, and the way she said it, with a stiffness, a regret, because she couldn't manage anything else – it was the closest she came to asking *Are you well? Are you okay? I'm thinking of you.* I swallowed before saying it now, to Huay, 'Did you eat your breakfast?' Cringing at first from the briny practicality of my words, then savouring them. My mother's voice in my head echoed again, again, again.

She said yes but her eyes were distracted, flicking from my face, to the sink, to the window high up on the wall and she jumped then, at the sound of Mrs Sato's voice, ordering us to hurry. I went into the cubicle, was still thinking about my mother when Huay said, 'Do you think they're looking for us? Our parents?'

I stared at her, thinking that she had read my thoughts before realizing that my question must have reminded her of her own parents. In the water, my reflection showed a smear of darkness on my cheekbone. It was days old, I barely felt it anymore; it only made me think of my father's bleeding face. How my mother had held him as the soldier pulled me away. A bitterness gathered in my mouth and I had to spit. 'I don't know.'

'I just hope my sister is safe. She's eleven, almost twelve.'

I tried to recall if there'd been a child in the truck but couldn't. 'Did they – they didn't take her, did they?'

'Oh, no. Fortunately, no. I was watching from the truck to make sure. She'll be home right now. My parents stopped her from going to school after the invasion. I'll need to help with her schoolwork when I get back.'

I wanted to ask when she thought we would be let go but didn't. 'What's her name?'

'Rong. Xiao Rong. She's the youngest.' Over the next few months, I would find out that Huay used to carry her around when she was an infant and pretend that she was her own. That the two of them were inseparable even though they were four years apart in age. 'If being here means that Xiao Rong is safe, I would do it. Gladly.' I said nothing in reply because I couldn't imagine it – that kind of love, not yet.

The caretaker started shouting, a wordless hacking, as if she were coughing up her lungs. She rapped her cane on the floor until Mrs Sato appeared.

'Let's go, girls. Time to work,' Mrs Sato called out, long fingers reaching for us as if to stroke our arms, but just missing us. 'Remember, it goes into your wages at the end, Fujiko.' She tapped the wooden tag hung outside my door as I went into my room. In the black-and-white house, Huay was 'Kiko' and Jeomsun, 'Hinata'. But Mrs Sato and her staff were the only ones who used these names. Few of the soldiers noticed these plaques and fewer still addressed me at all, but it helped. In the morning, Fujiko was the one who pressed her lips over rouge paper to put colour into them, and then put on the clothes that were a little too big for her. Fujiko received the tickets and tucked each one under her mat before she lay down on it. At the end of the evening, I would run my thumb along the edge of the stack, measuring the thickness of it against my hand. Mrs Sato would ask for them before locking us in every night, and I would hand mine over, telling myself that it was all adding up to something, at least – a few dollars that might make its way to my parents.

These were the lies that I told myself to get from day to day. I knew, even as I sat in my windowless room, that my parents would never receive anything from Mrs Sato, that she painted this story in order to get us to comply. The involvement of money, just the very thought of it, made her captives more compliant; it made us guilty, somehow, in all that we had endured. None of us mentioned the word rape. No one had to.

Every day passed in the same way. I woke at about six-thirty to the sound of the caretaker rising from her cot in the front room and bustling about the kitchen, clinking dishes before coming to us, opening my door just wide enough to shove a bowl through. With my rising came an ache in my chest, which would grow and grow as it got closer to opening time. But I ate through it, devouring my meagre portion of rice and making the lone slice of pickled radish, just a half moon, last three bites. At seven, we would be let into the bathroom. Huay, Jeomsun and I would wait for each other, then take turns at the sink with the one toothbrush. While we cleaned up, we chatted softly, hoping not to be caught. In the meantime, Mrs Sato would arrive, filling the house with her floral perfume, the sound of her voice rising over the dash of water, our whispers.

Once the front doors opened at nine, the soldiers would begin to arrive, laughing and chattering as if they were boys making a beeline for the sweet shop after school. I would hear the clink of coins as they jangled their change in their pockets before handing them over to Mrs Sato for a ticket. Once they were in my room, they would drop the tickets – pink squares of paper – leaving me to scoop them up after for Mrs Sato. One day during my first week,

I had stood in the centre of my room and thought of the only ticker-tape parade I'd seen as a child, how the ground had looked afterwards, a mayhem of colour. Then I knelt and picked up each pink slip, counting forty-two, so I could hand them over to Mrs Sato before lights out. We would only be given another meal after the last man had left. Sometimes dinner would be withheld from me if the caretaker caught me talking to Jeomsun or Huay in the bathroom and I would have to go to sleep aching with hunger. At ten, Mrs Sato would go round to close up, locking each of us in before finally putting the bolt on the front door, leaving us with the caretaker who spoke no Chinese. Outside, she would say nothing to her driver as she climbed up into the back of the rickshaw and sat down with all her weary weight, and I would hear the wheels creaking as they went down the driveway.

I dreaded Mrs Sato's departure though I hated even more her arrival in the morning, the way a caged animal could be uneasy and hopeful around its keeper. I watched her the way I used to watch my mother, when I was five, six, wanting desperately her attention. Wanting to learn what crossed her, what would put me in her good graces. How I would look out for any warm gesture. A smile, sometimes. The way she pressed a twist of radish omelette into my bowl. I thought she was the most beautiful woman I had ever seen, the way all little girls do of their mothers no matter what they look like, until one day, they don't. The realization making their stomachs drop with disappointment.

I almost wanted Mrs Sato's favour in the same way. The way baby animals always find a parent in the unlikeliest of places, latching on out of helplessness, from having been left without a choice. Her beauty, though, was real. Even in her forties (or fifties, I couldn't tell), her skin was buffed porcelain and her hair, richly black, wound up and away from her face with a silver hairpin. Some of the girls called her Mrs Sato. Some called her 'Madam', but all of us saw her as a mother of sorts, troubling as it was. Most of us were little more than children after all, aged fourteen to twenty. I had never been away from my family, not even for a night. Mrs Sato was the closest thing I had to a guardian, whether I liked it or not. Each evening, before she left, I would take care to arrange the tickets I'd collected that day and smile as I handed them over to her. She would always smile back and touch my arm to say good job, well done.

Her absence made me nervous, as if worse could happen while she was away. The first week I had followed the sound of her departure, all the while keenly aware of how near I was to freedom, I liked to think it was simply a matter of two locks and a gate, until I remembered the men, of course. The soldiers, that large compound housing them just a minute's walk away. Their closeness as clear and present as a toothache. On each of those nights, I fell asleep hoping that I would be released the following day. I kept on hoping until it seemed like I was holding on to a shard of broken glass in my hand, and I was squeezing tight, tighter, in an effort not to let it slip away from me. After a month, I stopped. Stopped counting the days and weeks. There was a clock above the counter in the front room, which I could see if I went down the hall far enough. The clock served as my only accurate unit of time. The doctor's visit, which happened every month, served to mark the passing of four to five weeks. Each of these were small lifetimes, periods during which some of the women I slept and suffered next to would disappear and never be seen again.

'I'm never going home,' Jeomsun said. There had been another visit from the doctor. At the end of the check-up, Mrs Sato had come in with two soldiers, pointed out Quek Joo – a girl who had been brought in the same day Huay and I had – and made the soldiers bind her wrists. Then they led her out, pulling on her bonds as if she were a dog. It happened so quickly that no one had time to react.

'What do you mean you're never going home?' I said. 'You never look as happy as when you talk about Busan. Or when you talk about mountains. There are no mountains here, you know?'

'Go home to the people who sold me in the first place?'

Huay looked incredulous. 'But surely they didn't know. No one could sell their own daughter to let them be –' She stopped, refusing to use the words she knew for what we were doing, what was being done to us.

'They sold me. That's all I know. They got money from selling me then said that I was to go and work in a factory. Liars. I'm never going back to them, even if I'm let go.'

'Is that what happened? They let Quek Joo go?' She had been ill, I recalled, bleeding on and off for three weeks and soaking through countless menstrual cloths, her dress, her mat. The doctor had found her unfit. 'Contagious,' Jeomsun had overheard. Of what, we weren't sure. After she was gone, Mrs Sato had the caretaker take all her things out back to be burned.

'I don't know. Perhaps. Sometimes they move women around the different houses in one region. Sometimes they send them away to another country, like I was. Sometimes they take the sick ones to the hospital. That's what I heard. Except I don't think the Japanese are going to waste medicine on us. I've seen so many women get taken away when they were ill, both here and back in Formosa. Only a few returned.'

'Then where do you think she was taken?' Huay whispered, her voice sharp with desperation.

'Maybe she was let go. Or maybe they left her in a clearing to die. I don't know. I don't know everything.' Jeomsun got up and left.

It had been a month. One long month that felt like years. I caught my reflection in the mirror one morning and started. A stranger's face, I thought, aged and bitter, warped by the house and all that went on it in. I imagined going home and knocking on the door only to have my parents draw away from me and say 'this is not my daughter'. I could see my father shake his head, the violence in his movement making it look like shock, a spasm. They would look at me and see what had happened, what I had done. Then they would close the door in my face. I did not know anything – how we would get out of here or if we would at all – but I knew this.

Huay was still next to me and I grabbed her arm. 'Promise me something. If we do get out, we'll tell people we were working in a factory. We'll tell them that we were ill-treated, that we were fed badly but that all we did was work and put things together.' This, they might believe. Especially if it came from the two of us. Huay stared at me, and I knew I looked mad in my desperation to make her understand this. 'Do you promise?'

She nodded. A hasty, single nod. 'I promise.'

Over the course of the next few months, I learned what to do. What not to do. Mrs Sato frequently urged me to look more welcoming. 'Always so glum, Fujiko. Smile a little, smile!' And I did, especially if I was afraid. I would smile and then when the soldier was done with me, I would smile at the next one, and the one after. There was always the threat of a fist or a boot. A pistol, which I would see, tucked into his belt, out of my reach. The only thing I could do was not to resist even when the days seemed impossibly long, when it seemed that the stream of men coming through would never end. After the initial week, I served around thirty men a day. On weekends and festival days, the number went up. Forty, fifty. Both Mrs Sato and Jeomsun had told us that we were to make sure each one of them wore protection. I tried once, pushing the soldier away and pointing at the condom that he had left on the floor next to the mat. He responded by getting his knife out and pressing it against the base of my throat, leaving a shallow cut that refused to heal for weeks, then a white scar after it did. With time I found that it was easier to avoid looking at them completely. I could control nothing else but what I thought about. Not the pain, which started between my legs, fanned up to my stomach and wrapped around my lower spine. Its presence was solid, constant. The more men I'd had to work for that day, the more likely it was that I got no sleep – the ache, dull during the day, shot spikes through me when I was trying to rest. This pain, I couldn't control. But to keep alive, I made no noise, did nothing, and tried not to exist. Those were the only things I could do.

After my morning ablutions and my breakfast, I would lie down on the mat and wait. I would remain lying down much of the day except for trips to the bathroom, and mealtimes. While I was lying on the mat, I would think about how I used to hide amidst the tall grass in the field on my way back home from the market. Especially when I was finished earlier than normal. I would sit on the ground and then fall back into the soft grass. There were *lalang* with their soft white tails, and weeds sprouting white balls of fur that the wind would take away, one by one. I would lie on the mat and pretend I was there again, in the late afternoon heat, warm against the ground, watching as the clouds rolled past. I did not close my eyes. If I did, all I would hear was what was going on around me, and in the room on the other side of the thin plywood wall. So I kept them open, focusing on a water spot in the ceiling and reading shapes into it – a frog, a paper plane, the floral pattern on a blouse that I wore during the last mid-autumn festival back home.

I tried never to look at the soldiers if I could help it. The fact that most of the men seemed not to care at all, not even if I were ill or bleeding, made it easier for me to pretend that this wasn't happening. Most of them entered the room and climbed on top of me without even shedding their boots. Some came in with their trousers already balled up in their hands and left as soon as they were done.

The ones who frightened me most were the men who pretended to treat me as if I were human, at least at first, on the surface. The first time it happened, I found myself looking at someone my age – he couldn't have been more than eighteen or nineteen, with a face so nondescript, so familiar, he could have been a shopkeeper in our village or the son of a neighbour. I understood little Japanese but it was his voice, soft and reasonable, a sharp contrast to the barks and cries and spat commands, that drew me out of myself and made me look at him. He was clean-shaven and his eyes were warm, laughing. When he took his cap off, thick black hair fell forward, making him look even younger. He spoke again, and I listened this time.

'*Konbanwa.*' Good evening. He dipped his head and smiled, bringing pink into his cheeks. Then, fully clothed, he sat down on the floor, a foot away from my mat.

It felt strange to smile back. The muscles around my mouth were tight, as if withered from the lack of use. I said good evening to him and sat up.

He pointed his finger towards his chest and said, 'Takeo *desu.*'

'Fuji…' I started, before changing my mind. 'Wang Di.'

'Wang Di,' he said, trying the words out in his mouth. Then he drew something out of his pocket and put it on the mat, in front of me. A rice ball, wrapped in wax paper. I ate it in a few bites, almost choking. When I finished, I realized that he was talking. He talked for a long time, making shapes in the air with his hands and nodding at me, even though it was clear I understood none of what he said. That day, he did nothing. He was one of the few who visited and did little but try to talk to me; he didn't even try to satisfy himself on his own, as a few of them did. When his twenty minutes was up, he bowed again before rising and leaving the room, murmuring something in Japanese as he backed out. That night, I tried to guess what he might have been saying, couldn't help but hope that he would be back to visit and would take me away from this place.

'What do you mean he didn't touch you,' Huay said when I talked about Takeo the following day.

'He just sat there, with his legs crossed. Talked quite a bit. And then he left.' I referred neither to his name nor his gift of the rice ball. Any mention of food was almost worse than talking about home; provoked jealousies the way lovers might in a world outside this one.

'You be careful of him. I've heard about men like that,' Jeomsun said, 'they're always bad news.'

I made myself stop thinking about Takeo and was surprised when he appeared again in my room two weeks later. There he was, that smile again, showing his white teeth. This time, he reached forward to touch my face. I drew back out of instinct but he didn't mind. He sat back down and talked. When he leaned forward again minutes later, I hesitated only a little before letting myself be pushed back onto the mat. Nothing new, I thought, but for the first time, I looked up while he was on top of me, saw how he squeezed his eyes closed and wondered if, outside of this, back in my old world, I might have wanted to be with him. I was still thinking this, asking what this question meant of me when he finished, wiping himself with the edge of my dress. Before he left, he reached into his pocket and showed me a small white jewel – a sugar cube. I ate it quickly and was sorry when it was gone, the lingering sweetness a sharp ache on my tongue.

I thought about Takeo that night and the nights after that, blinking into the dark when I should have been asleep. I didn't want to but the thoughts came to me, as seductive and inviting as any hot meal. Perhaps I could ask him to get me out of here. Perhaps he might want me for his own. I waited. It was perhaps a month before he returned. This time, when he came in, his eyes were far away. He undressed quickly then pushed me onto the mat. I put out an arm out of surprise more than anything else. This, he took as a slight of some sort, and shoved me back, pinning me to the mat when I was down. When I reacted with a yelp, he slapped me, a tight, matter-of-fact slap. Afterwards, he put on that same smile, the smile that showed his teeth, was all politeness again when he said goodnight and left.

I would have asked what happened if I could. But the answer was clear to me: that I was as unworthy as my parents had always suggested. That I would have been better born as a boy. Everything that I had done up until my capture – helping around the house, working at the market, was all to do with righting the wrong of my birth. Now that I was here, I wasn't even nothing. Less than. It didn't matter what Takeo thought of me – he was what I deserved. Someone like that. After Takeo, the men became faceless again with a few rare exceptions: one soldier seemed to me only a boy. No older than fifteen. He had said nothing as he came into my room and I heard the familiar jangle of a belt being unbuckled, then silence. I lifted my head, looked. He was kneeling. I saw his face for just a moment – a child's face, with milk fat still on his cheeks – before he put his head in his hands and wept. He stayed kneeling as he tried to compose himself. It took him fifteen minutes. A few more and the next soldier in line would start hammering on the door. I wanted to give him a handkerchief except I didn't have one, could only sit up as he bowed again and again, whispering something that sounded apologetic. When he recovered, he dried his face on his sleeves, stood, buckled his belt and left, shutting the door quietly behind him. His ticket lay on the floor where he'd knelt. I picked it up and put it away with the rest.

Trapped within the black-and-white house during the day, my mind wandered through the walls, between the bars of the gate, over the fields in the dark. Most nights, I would dream about waking up at home from a savage nightmare, relieved that it wasn't real after all. Meng, still sleepy, would clutch my hand as I brought him to school just as light was starting to colour the sky. On my way back to the village, there would be dew on the grass, shimmering like so many glass shards floating in mid-air. I would go to feed the hens and gather their eggs, still warm from the nest, then walk to the market, savouring the electricity of the place, the heat and noise. This is where I want to live, I would think. After dinner, my mother would sit by the kerosene lamp and I would listen to the pluck and weave of her sewing. Her movements set the rhythm for the evening, quieting the boys, making my father relax into his stiff, wooden chair. And then I would go to bed with my brothers next to me, kicking each other as they drifted off. I would wake up seven hours later in the dark, slide forward until my feet touched the floor, and then it was three steps across the bedroom, then six before I got into the kitchen where my mother was. There would be porridge simmering in the pot. I would ask if I should crack a single egg in it as a treat, and she would reply yes, okay.

The first time I had this dream, I woke up thinking that I was back home. There was a wide patch of saliva on my mat and I was getting ready to inch my way off the bed when I realized I was lying on a mat, at ground level. It took a moment before I remembered, before I noticed the smell of damp in my windowless room, the sting of disinfectant, felt the chill of the cement under my hands when I reached out to touch the floor. The blow of realizing where I was took me back to my first week. I thought about drinking all the liquid in the bottle of disinfectant nearby, but I couldn't move for the weight on my body, my chest. Each time I had this dream, I minded less the moment of waking. After a while, it was all I had to look forward to – sleep.

It was just after the end of the rainy season when Mrs Sato announced that we had to give a performance in honour of the Japanese emperor on 29 April. The whole of Japan would be celebrating and this extended to all its territories – even Syonan-to, she said, using the Japanese name that had been given to Singapore. I looked around the bathroom as she talked, at the gaunt faces of the other girls and thought she must be blind or mad to ask this of us. Dengue fever had swept through the house for months, felling even the caretaker. But the caretaker received treatment and was given two weeks to recuperate elsewhere. During her convalescence, one girl – just twelve, the youngest I'd seen so far – had been found in her room, shaking and foaming at her mouth as the soldier she'd been servicing kicked at her, thinking it was all an act. Alone, Mrs Sato had seemed frayed. The soldier's loud fury, and her subsequent attempts to revive the girl had drawn each of us out of our rooms to watch on helplessly as the girl flailed on the ground and then finally stopped, her face still and white. The rest of us only suffered the milder symptoms, a few days of bone-aching fever, a rash, then a long, slow period of recovery, unaided by the fact that our rations had diminished to a third of a bowl of rice for each of our two meals, and little else. What Mrs Sato was after now: a dance, 'a bit of cheer' as she called it, seemed impossible.

'It's an important day so I need all of you to practise once a week for the next four weeks – I would give you more time if it weren't so busy here but there you are,' Mrs Sato said, her cheeks ruddy with warmth. 'Hinata,' she pointed at Jeomsun, 'you know what to do. Teach everyone a few songs, a dance. You've done this before.'

Jeomsun was no singer but she taught us the only song we needed to know: '*Aikoku No Hana*', Patriotic Flowers, which she had learned in Formosa. We practised every Monday, the quietest day after the rush of the weekend. It was only right before the emperor's birthday that Mrs Sato started talking about the stage, how it would have to be set up outside, close to the trees in case it rained. For seven days, it was all I could think about. The earth, the grass and trees. Outside.

When the day finally arrived, the six of us were led out by the caretaker and two guards towards a low, wooden platform close to the larger, main house, which was draped with Japanese flags for the occasion, the scarlet centres of them like so many blood-red suns against the white of the building. When we had got into place, one straight line in the middle of the stage, I felt – for the first time in months – the warmth on my face, arms, and legs. It had rained the night before and the air was rich with metal and earth. As we waited, the soldiers filling the rows of seats in front of us, a breeze swept through, loosening a few leaves from the rain tree above us. Green blades, small as fingernails, drifted upon the stage. One landed on Huay's head and I picked it out and held it in my sweaty hand throughout the rest of the performance. The music started without warning, and I croaked along, letting Jeomsun and the record do most of the work. It didn't matter, the soldiers were clapping before we'd even finished. We danced and sang (mouthed to) two more songs. The men sitting through it all quietly until we got to '*Aikoku No Hana*', the song making them spill over with pride so they got up, the mass of them swaying left and right. When the music was over, they roared '*banzai*' and toasted each other with the cups they held in their hands. A little way off, at the far corner of the stage, was Mrs Sato. Her face was pink and glowing, as if she'd been running laps around the compound. It might have been the heat or the smoke of the men's cigarettes, but I thought her eyes were filling, were bright with tears.

While we sang, I couldn't help but think the gate was just a short sprint away. A few hundred yards at most. How long would it take me? I wondered. And how long would it take for the men to draw their guns? The same men who had visited me in my tiny room, spat on me, kicked me and threatened me with their guns and knives. I stayed where I was between Huay and Jeomsun, filed back in the direction of the little black-and-white house. Once we were inside, the smell of the house alone – the rotted-fruit stink of crushed bed bugs; the deep, vinegary musk the men left behind – was enough to make me wish I'd run.

Celebrations for the emperor's birthday also meant time off for the men and so we worked long into the night. We were all surprised when Mrs Sato came in with extra rice balls for breakfast the next morning.

'These have sour-plum centres, my daughter's favourite. I made them myself,' she said as she handed me my portion. 'The army was kind enough to share its extra rations with me yesterday,' she added under her breath, secretive, her cheeks flushed red. She watched me take a bite, smiled, and closed the door behind her.

'Mrs Sato has been different, don't you think? A little…softer.' I asked later, in the bathroom.

I'd expected Jeomsun to pipe up with a precious nugget of infor-mation. She had been here the longest, had experience from her time in Formosa as well, but it was Huay who spoke.

'You mean yesterday? She was drunk. Most of the men were, didn't you see? I could smell it even from where we were standing. My father, he used to…' She stopped, the shame of this confession burning her cheeks.

Even Jeomsun seemed surprised by this insight. 'I know the men were drunk last night but Mrs Sato…'

That many of the soldiers got drunk on weekends was no secret; they were usually the ones who spat on me after they were done, or who worked themselves into such a rage that they spent their twenty minutes beating and cursing me. 'I thought something was different but I meant today. This morning –'

'Well, she hides it and she's not a bad drunk. Not like my father. He's sneaky as well and can turn into the devil without anyone noti-cing him take a drink. Then the next morning he would be sick. But Mrs Sato is one of those who wake up rosy-cheeked and refreshed, like nothing happened the night before.'

I couldn't picture it. Except for one time when my mother was cajoled into taking a sip from my father's glass at a wedding, I had never seen any woman take a drink of alcohol.

Jeomsun looked around her before she whispered, 'I heard she was a brothel owner back in Japan.'

'Who said that? The caretaker?' I asked.

'No, the men. Sometimes they talk. But my Japanese isn't very good. I might be mistaken. But this I know: she was married; her husband got conscripted and killed in Korea. That's why she hates me so much.' It was true. Mrs Sato never missed an opportunity to pinch her or yell at her. 'She's soft with you though,' she continued, looking at me. 'Maybe you look like someone she knew back home.'

I waved a hand at her, dismissing the thought.

Huay bit down on the side of her thumb and winced. 'Do you really think she was a brothel owner?' I knew what she was thinking: if Mrs Sato was a madam, what did this make us?

'I don't think anyone else would be able to do this. Anyone who had a normal job before the war, I mean. Don't be fooled by her. She smiles a lot but I've seen her slap a girl so hard she lost two of her teeth.'

'I didn't know that. I thought she was nice.'

'Huay, you think everyone is nice.'

'I think... I don't know. I think she's just trying to survive.'

'Oh, you two. Tell that to the parents who're never going to see their daughters again.' Jeomsun went into the cubicle, leaving us to steep in a hard silence and wish we hadn't begun the conversation.

To change the subject, Huay asked, 'What did you do? You know, back home?'

Back home. 'Nothing much. Helped out by selling eggs and vegetables at the market.'

'Oh, I remember now. I saw you at the market a few times with Yan Ling. Is that her name? Or Yan Qing?'

'Yan Ling.' Her name caught in my throat as I said it.

'I was in school. You know, I'd just decided that I would go to teacher's college straight after high school. I wanted to go back to teach in our village.'

I know the place, I wanted to tell her. 'What would you teach?'

'Chinese and maths.'

I shook my head admiringly. 'I can't even write my name.'

For a second, I had the image of Auntie Tin writing my name in her notebook, then shook my head again, quicker this time, to rid myself of the matchmaker's face, the feeling of falling that was about to overcome me, and watched as Huay leaned across me to write in the condensation on the mirror.

望弟

'*Wang*: looking forward to, wishing, looking out at. *Di*: brother,' she said. Half smiling. As if she felt sorry for me.

That was when the image formed: there I was, waiting at the door for my brothers. Except I couldn't remember what home looked like, couldn't picture anything more detailed than a house made of wood. I wondered how they were doing. Imagined them going to school, playing football afterwards in the fields, and in the evening, Yang pointing out the mistakes in Meng's Chinese homework as my father looked on, unable to help. Not for the first time, I wondered how my life would have been if I had been one of them. A boy instead of who I was. What I was now. But perhaps this was all for them – as my name suggested. My life for two of theirs.

I could almost tell myself that I had become used to it. The fact of my new life. Except that this was not my life, couldn't be anyone's – not in the sense that this was an existence I (or anyone else in the house) could have chosen for myself. A life that involved each day being divided up into twenty- to thirty-minute segments, during which my body was not my own and belonged to strangers, who seemed not to think I was human. Things were done to me that I would never speak about, could only deal with by believing that it was happening to someone else – 'Fujiko', my changeling. Unlike me, Fujiko deserved it, this other life, because she willingly pressed her lips over rouge paper to put colour into them, and wore clothes that gave the men easy access. Fujiko received the tickets and tucked each one under her mat before she lay down on the mat. She was no one, and she was me.

Throughout the months I wished for death, until that too became something that I didn't seem to deserve. I kept this thought to myself, harboured it feverishly – the way I used to dream of a better life when I was living at home with my family.

All the women in the house kept falling ill. Colds. Stomach bugs. Infections that none of us talked about because it was clear the men had passed them along to us. The three of us took care of each other in turns by saving any food we got from the soldiers and passing it along to the one who felt poorly. Other than this act of comradeship, each of us reacted to illnesses and our constant hunger in a different way. Jeomsun coped by talking about the food she would eat if she got the chance again. I coped by keeping quiet and gritting my teeth.

'Why don't you say something,' Jeomsun once begged me. 'What hurts?' And I – not knowing the proper words, only the ones used by men for cursing – could only point down.

Huay, usually the most sanguine of us, turned sombre and morbid. It seemed to be a cold, this time, though it was hard to tell. Eating little else but rice made us vulnerable to infections and stomach ailments. She had become more and more lethargic, lost all her appetite. Her forehead, when I felt it, was hot to the touch and she began to complain of aches and pains. A week after that, rashes appeared on her body – scatterings of brown spots flecking her pale skin. When I asked, she said they didn't itch, that she didn't mind them that much, not compared to everything else.

'Wang Di?' she whispered one night. Both of us had taken to pushing our mats right next to the dividing wall so we could talk sometimes. Even when we had nothing to say, hearing her breathe or mumble in her sleep gave me a small measure of comfort. 'Am I dying?'

'Don't talk like this. It's just a cold. Jeomsun had it last week and now you have it… You'll be fine.'

'I feel terrible. Maybe I should ask Mrs Sato for the doctor.'

'No, don't. You know what will happen if they get involved.'

'How do you know for sure? Maybe they were taken to hospital and let go afterwards. Did you actually see it happen?'

'I believe what Jeomsun told us.' I didn't need to add that they didn't think much of feeding us only rice and thin soup for months, much less depriving us of penicillin during the outbreak of dengue fever. I didn't dare to imagine if it might be true, what was rumoured – that they wilfully discarded girls who were too far gone to work by bringing them to a copse and shooting them, leaving their bodies to rot in the undergrowth; or else by driving them to the centre of town in broad daylight and abandoning them by the side of the road barefoot, barely dressed. Let their own people kill them with shame and loathing.

'It's okay. Maybe it's better if I'm dead. Maybe I deserve it for –'

'Stop talking and rest. You'll feel better in a day or two, you'll see.'

'I've always wanted to get married but I don't think that's going to happen, do you? I wanted three children. Two girls and a boy.'

I couldn't think of anything to say or summon up the will to lie so I stayed silent.

'Wang Di, promise me that you'll tell my family if I die in here… Tell them that I miss them. Promise me.'

'Don't talk like that. Rest. *Shh.*' If not for the wooden partition between us I would have started smoothing her hair the way my mother used to smooth mine when I was little and ill. Her fever broke the day after and she returned to herself, her smile, her quiet rectitude. It was as if she had never said any of it.

Kevin

You find things you're not ready to see when you go looking. I was nine when Ah Ma came to live with us. My mother said that she was getting old, that it was the right thing to do with my father being the only child and Ah Ma being his only parent. She found a job soon after that and I was left alone with Ah Ma in the afternoons. It was then that I started looking inside drawers, opening doors that were meant to be shut tight. Every afternoon, I sat cross-legged at the coffee table with my schoolwork and waited for her to fall asleep in front of the radio. It was the fan and the afternoon heat that did it, made her eyes flutter-flutter until they were closed. The minute I heard her making little puffing sounds in her sleep, I would get up and go to the top cupboard in the kitchen for a handful of iced gems and switch the TV on, putting a cartoon on on mute. The day I decided I was too old for daytime cartoons, I snuck into my parents' bedroom and looked into their bedside tables and the drawers in their large wardrobe filled with used and forgotten handbags, brown paper document holders, photo albums. Here is a list of things that made my heart thump when I found them:

1. A picture of my mother standing next to a man I didn't recognize; my mother is smiling in a way I haven't seen her smiling before, her lips are stretched so high up that her eyes are almost closed and

the man is looking not at the camera, but at her. I stared at the man's face in an effort to memorize it, so I would know if I ever met him.

2. My father's bank passbook. The last entry had the numbers 623.84 on it. I knew nothing and had never made a cent in my life but the first three numbers put out cold, invisible beads of sweat on my forehead. I would recall the numbers 623 several times in the next few days and each time a dull ache would open up in my stomach and I would have to close my eyes and wait for the feeling to go away before I continued reading or watching TV or trying to eat.

3. A stack of nude magazines in the drawer unlocked by a key I'd found. I flipped through them all, pages bursting fleshy-beige and pink, and put them back exactly as I found them, dog-eared, newest issue at the top.

These were things I'd never known existed. Like the way I read about this ugly, ancient fish, all spikes and jaw – how scientists thought that it was extinct but it wasn't. Except I never knew about it and learning about it made me start to wonder what else I didn't know existed. Like the thousands of books I would never finish reading (or want to), and the millions and millions of other books out there in the world that I would never even know about. And it was this not-knowing that made me sit down and want a hot drink. This not-knowing when it came to my parents; things I'd never thought about, even if they were clear as day, clear as the fact that my parents had their own parents, had their own childhoods and histories. And then one day you open a drawer and out come all the secrets that have just been sitting quietly, waiting to be found, even though you never thought about them, never suspected they existed in the first place.

It was this last thought that was pinging around my head when I went into the bedroom that day on tiptoe and crossed the invisible line that separated my side of the room from hers. As soon as I did that, I expected to hear her scold me, asking what I was doing snooping in her things. I could still feel her in the room, had to look over my shoulder twice just to make sure I wasn't being watched before I started. The top drawer was a mess and took me fifteen minutes just to sort it out into different piles of objects: hairpins, numerous and ticking like armour-shelled insects; almost five dollars' worth of loose change, which I pocketed; a bank passbook with holes punched through the front and back (meaning that the book was finished, invalid, no use to anyone anymore); palm-sized bottles of tiger balm and ointment, which stained the wood brown and red; and jumbo packs of tissue paper, some opened and half used. And then in the drawers below, her clothes, silky and static. Now and then, the fabric caught on the ragged ends of my bitten nails and when I pulled my hands away, threads hung on, stretching out a ghostly cobweb. In no time, the neat folds in her clean laundry, necklines perfectly centred and facing up, were messed up so I decided to take them all out. I removed two drawers' worth of clothing, even her cotton undergarments. Nothing. For a few seconds I sat there, surrounded by a pool of grey and blue cloth, the only colours I ever saw Ah Ma wearing, wondering how I was going to get everything back the way it was supposed to look. There was just one left. The last, bottom drawer jammed halfway so I had to reach in with my arm, making the same scrabbling sounds my grandmother had made in my dream as she felt around, like a rat locked in a wooden chest. It was here that my fingers touched cardboard and I came back out with a shoebox rustling with paper. I closed my eyes as I lifted the lid. When I opened them again, I saw a bundle of letters tied together with a length of raffia and a large, well-stuffed envelope so crumpled it looked like it had been put in the wash. I tipped the envelope upside down and shook. What fell out covered most of the tiled floor, blanketed the space in between my half of the room and what was once my grandmother's. Some of it slid away to hide under the beds and writing desk so that I had to crawl and reach for it. When I thought I had everything, I separated the contents of the envelope into two piles.

In the first pile were letter-sized rectangles of paper, with Chinese characters occupying the top three quarters of the sheet, and English words filling the rest. There were twenty-seven sheets of paper like this, all exactly like each other, all with thick black headings. '失踪!' it said, at the top of the Chinese portion, the strokes of the characters urgently whipping through the space. My eyes skipped below to the bottom.

MISSING!

My son was lost on 12 Feb 1942. Seventeen months old. Last seen in Bukit Timah. Any information, please write to 53 Chin Chew Street.

There was a name below that and I could see where the writer had paused – at the corners and beginnings and ends of each letter – where the ink had bled all the way through to the back of the paper. Some of the notices didn't have any corners, the top or the bottom or both, as if they had been ripped off a wall. Some still had the remnants of dried glue on the back, folded down so they wouldn't stick onto everything they touched. I looked through all twenty-seven of them; a few had mistakes in the English crossed out by the writer, but most were printed perfectly in the kind of handwriting that would make my teacher's face glow and fill out with satisfaction. The second pile had news clippings from years ago, torn straight from the English and Chinese language paper. There were too many for me to read through at once but the headlines stood out, thick and beetle-black. Both the clippings and the handwritten notices had the same subject. I imagined Ah Ma flipping through the paper every morning, eyes darting over the pages just in search of these words. I imagined her walking to the market, young and unrecognizable to me, tearing the handwritten notices from the wall the moment she saw them. The words '失踪' ('Missing') rang in my ears as I riffled through all the news clippings. I found only one in English.

Thousands Still Missing

The number of people who disappeared during the Japanese Occupation and remain unfound is estimated to be in the thousands. To this end, the Colony has established a department to help trace the whereabouts of those reported missing during the war. Relatives of those missing may submit an enquiry at the Missing Persons Department located within the old Supreme Court building within business hours during the week. The department is also in charge of referring cases to the police when foul play is suspected.

After reading the article, I untied the raffia bow around the letters. Counted twenty-two, all of them in small, sealed envelopes. A couple had stamps on them, but not the rest. There were no postmarks on any of them. The address, always the same, was written in Ah Ma's hand and it made me think about the first time I saw her write, how surprised I was when I saw her lined, sun-stained hands cradle the pen the way someone might cradle a fine blade, how her words curled onto the page, round and smooth. I didn't think about it. I wasn't thinking about it when I slipped out the first letter, the one at the bottom of the stack. I wasn't thinking about it when I pushed my forefinger into a gap in the seal and tore it open. No one would know, I thought. And I was right, no one could know that it wasn't already opened when it was all found out, months later. I would open just one, I told myself. Just this one. I took the letter out. It was light and almost see-through, like a single leaf pressed within the pages of a book and forgotten about for years and years. The letter was folded into thirds and it crackled under my fingers as I smoothed it out.

Wang Di

During the next few days, Wang Di fought to push thoughts of the cemetery out of her mind but it came back to her as she ate and watched TV, as she made her collection rounds. Not even the noise of rush hour, the blare of cars telling her to get off the road, was enough to drown out the voices (the brothers', Soon Wei's, her own) in her head.

At night, her dreams came with greater urgency. In some of them, she was stumbling through Kopi Sua, looking for her husband's face in the whorls of the trees. The rest were about her friends from the black-and-white house. Snatches of memory: crouching in the bathroom and letting Jeomsun plait her hair. Huay showing her a bottle of medicine the doctor had given her, tipping it from end to end so that the liquid in it sloshed musically back and forth, sending them into giggles. Children again. How they had stopped, the spell broken by the sound of male laughter outside the building. The fact of where they were. Wang Di almost welcomed these dreams but she always woke feeling as if she were the only one left in the world.

And I am. Leng could read. So could Huay. If only they were still around, they would be able to help.

So she decided. Once or twice, she tried to strike up a conversation with the neighbours as they passed each other in the corridor but she could not get beyond the initial 'hello' and 'bye-bye'. Their interaction would last two seconds and the neighbour would be gone, scuttling sideways out of the lift before the door had fully opened, slamming the mailbox shut and leaving before she could make a comment about the weather. At first Wang Di wondered if there was such a thing as being too elderly for a granny flat. Most of the people living in the building were couples, the rest were widows who had outlived their husbands and now filled their time with grandchildren and mah-jong and line-dancing in the park. But at seventy-five, she was just about the average age of the people living there.

'Maybe it's my clothes,' she said to the Old One, looking through her wardrobe of blues and greys and blacks. Everything mended and patched multiple times.

She found out just what it was upon arriving home with her collection one afternoon. There was a gathering of sorts outside a neighbour's door – a clutch of three women, two of whom were putting on their shoes, already waving as they said their goodbyes in Mandarin.

'Thank you for the *pandan* cake. It's all too much but I'm sure the grandchildren will love it.'

'No problem. Thank you for tea. It was so nice to –'

'Oh,' one of them said, spotting Wang Di and putting a hand on her friend's arm. All three glanced over, and then, just as quickly, dropped their gazes to the ground, at their hands, before looking up with stiff smiles.

'Good afternoon,' Wang Di waved.

No one responded. They went on nudging each other until the one in front, the tallest, youngest-looking of the bunch, said hello, her pasted-on smile fading as Wang Di approached with her cart. She had missed the weigh-in today, as she sometimes did, and had to return home with her gleanings – a pile of cardboard stacked as high as a table, a bagful of drink cans that she had fished out of the bins near the hawker centre. The cans were making soft *tink-tink* sounds as she negotiated the cart past the women. All six eyes glued to her and her collection.

'Excuse me,' Wang Di said, as the women pushed themselves up against the wall to make way for her.

They said nothing.

When she was in front of her door, she heard someone whisper, 'See? That's who I was talking about. Cardboard Auntie.'

She moved through the rest of the day, dimly aware that she was going through the motions. First brewing tea and forgetting it. Then making dinner and finishing it before realizing that she had no idea what she'd just eaten; the only taste in her mouth was of bitter salt.

When she opened her eyes, it was morning. For a moment, between stepping fully out of a dream and opening her eyes, she saw Huay, then Jeomsun, the scar on her cheek dark with rushed blood. She was about to say something when she felt hands, unseen, pinning her down so she could only stare up and around her, at the blank walls; the ceiling, speckled with blood, that seemed to loom endlessly above.

Wake up, wake up, wake up. Wang Di pushed herself up to sitting and looked around her. Her home. Her things. The view of the other building outside her window that she was just getting accustomed to.

She was aware of her heart, loud in her chest. As loud as it had been a few months ago when she told the Old One about what happened in the black-and-white house, the way she had to hold her hands to her chest to try to calm herself, and how, in the middle of it, she forgot and let them fall to her lap, palms up like an open book, how he caught them there.

June 1943 – November 1944

In the long months that followed, I watched as the rashes on Huay's body turned to sores, then healed to form faded marks up and down her limbs. She seemed to get better for a week or so before lapsing again into episodes of fever and sickness. This cycle repeated itself until my dismay at her illness turned to dread and a frustration that I kept to myself, the thought that she must be doing something wrong, that she wasn't trying hard enough to recover. Jeomsun and I didn't talk about it, but when her hair started falling out we took to fashioning it every morning to disguise the thinnest spots on her head. Each time her fever returned we saved what we could from our meals, or kept the morsels a few of the kinder soldiers occasionally brought so we could bring them to her in the mornings. These gifts Huay took with a gratitude that bordered on shame. When they cut our rations again (giving us soup with broken grains stirred through at night, down from a half bowl of rice) and we had to stop hoarding food for her, I wanted to apologize but left it. There was nothing to explain. Among the three of us was a silent understanding about how we should take care of each other: the three of us before the rest of the other women, and then, within that, each of us before the other.

The doctor's visits were another source of worry. I was certain Huay would be declared unfit and taken away sooner or later, but he seemed not to see or care too much. Then a small triumph. 'Did you hear them fighting? The doctor told Mrs Sato to give us more food. Said the soldiers weren't happy with the state of us. Mrs Sato said she couldn't do anything about it – she said the food was all going to the soldiers fighting overseas and that she couldn't afford to buy things from the black market. They went on and on for half an hour like that, at least.'

I thought about the bottles of saké that Mrs Sato had taken to drinking in the evening, in plain view of anyone who chanced to be in the front room. *Couldn't afford it?* 'So what happened in the end? What did they decide?'

'I don't know. They went outside to finish talking. I couldn't hear the rest.'

It became clear though, how their argument had ended – along with the soup at night, the caretaker gave each of us a half bowl of dirty rice, strewn with grit and chaff, but edible. The change was conspicuous. For the first time in months, my stomach did not grind at night and sleep came easily. I woke up still hungry, but not desperate. And though we didn't have the chance to talk, not that morning, Jeomsun and I exchanged a look as we passed each other in the hallway, what her eyes said was clear: *it's fine now – we're going to be okay.*

The act of dispensing this largesse (forced as it might have been) seemed to suffuse Mrs Sato with a looseness and cheer she didn't possess before. More and more, she would saunter in mid-morning, displacing the caretaker, who'd had to step in to count out change and dispense condoms in her absence. On these days, Mrs Sato would become rowdier as the day wore on. We all heard her. Late at night when the men had left, she would start singing to herself until the rickshaw arrived to take her away.

On New Year's Day, she brought in a record player and sang along to the songs as the men goaded her on while waiting for their turn. She stayed past the close of the doors at ten, talking to the caretaker, her speech getting slow and slurred so I knew she was drinking. Then, a few minutes of silence. I thought her gone when my door unlocked and the caretaker's face appeared, lit by the orange glow of a kerosene lamp.

'She wants you,' she said – the first words of Mandarin I'd ever heard her speak.

Rubbing my eyes, I got up and followed her down the hallway, into the kitchen. Mrs Sato was slumped over the table, a small bottle of saké in front of her. Her make-up had slid off from the heat of the day and her normally perfect up-do was slightly askew. For the first time, there was a softness in her face, the beginnings of a few lines on her forehead.

'Ah, Fujiko! Come here, sit.' She gestured to a chair next to her. Once I was seated, she reached out and I flinched, expecting a slap. But no, she put her hand over mine in a conspiratorial grip. 'How old are you? I never asked.'

Her hand was hot on mine and her thumbnail, round-tipped and pink, polished to a shine. My first instinct was to pull away but what was one more touch? Just one more, after the hundreds, thousands of others, and from a woman not much older than my mother? 'I'm eighteen,' I said.

But she had moved on. Was talking about something else. Her daughter. 'She's your age. She wanted to be a nurse but I forbade her to because that might mean they'll want to ship her off…close to a war zone. She's such a good person. Here, try this,' she said, pouring a splash of alcohol in a cup and watching as I took a cautious sip. There was a smell of sweet almonds and when I swallowed, the heat of it bit through my throat. 'Everyone should know how to drink saké, even women. Not like that. You've got to inhale it first. There you go. And then a small taste… I taught my daughter how to but she's not really one for drinking.' She poured out the last of it into her cup and set the bottle down so hard I thought it would crack.

'Ayame was supposed to get married soon but we're waiting until I get back. I want to meet the suitors myself, see what their families are like. Because you know. Men.' She stopped here and shook her head. Had she forgotten who I was or what I was doing there? There was a long pause before she continued. 'The men we see every day, they do their soldiers' duty, their shouting and killing, glorifying our country and saving others, like yours, from the white man's rule. Back home, they celebrate what their sons and fathers are doing. Even the dead go back heroes. But the women?' Here, her face turned bitter. A warped mask. 'I did my duty for a while, back home. Just like you're doing. I did it until I got the chance to leave. Help set up a place to provide some comfort to the soldiers. It drives a man wild, do you know, being so far away from home like this…'

I might have made a sound like a yes or some other noise but it didn't matter, she didn't seem to be listening.

'When this is over. When everything is as it should be, I won't go home to a hero's welcome. I am just a woman. But for now, in this place, I can save someone or I can send another away to die. I am as good as a man. Even better, sometimes I am God.'

'What happened last night? Was it you the caretaker came for? I had the fright of my life – I thought they were taking one of you away,' said Jeomsun the next morning, as she washed out a pile of condoms for reuse.

'No, it was just Mrs Sato. She wanted to… She was drunk.'

'I heard her talking. What did she say?'

I thought about repeating everything she'd said to me but in the light of day, in the filth of the bathroom and its dank closeness, none of it seemed real. Did it happen? 'She wasn't making much sense. Just rambling, mostly, about the men and war and… I don't know.'

'Was I right then? Did she own a brothel?'

I winced at the word. Brothel. 'She might have even been a… You know. A working girl. When she was young.'

It was at this moment that Huay turned around. She'd been staring at the air vent high up on the wall. I thought she'd been listening but it was clear from her face, when I saw it, that she'd been elsewhere. 'You look familiar,' she said to me. 'Maybe you can tell me when we can go home. I don't like it here. I think I'd like to go home now.'

Jeomsun laughed, more out of surprise than anything else. A coarse sound like a gasp. Huay's face stayed questioning, waiting for an answer.

She must have a fever, I thought, and put my palm on her forehead, ignoring her when she squirmed. But her skin was cool to the touch. 'What do you mean? Do you… Do you know my name?'

'Of course I do. It's…' She smiled, then faltered, flicking her eyes left and right, the fear in them clear and infectious.

I leaned into her. 'I'm Wang Di. This is Jeomsun. You're here with us, in the black-and-white house. You're not going home. Not today.' It didn't help. I could see her panic building up into wide-eyed alarm. 'It's okay, Huay. We're here now but we take care of each other. See? We're your friends.' I repeated this and nodded at her. By and by she started nodding along with me, a trusting child.

'Okay, okay.' She put her hand to her head as if it were hurting her. 'I think I'm just a little tired. I keep seeing double… Maybe my eyes are going bad.' She rubbed them, blinking like a just-woken child. But of course, at little more than seventeen, she was almost a child.

That morning, she screamed. I heard her plainly, telling someone to get off of her. There was the sound of a man's voice before Mrs Sato's voice drowned out everyone else. Then the slam of Huay's door, shutting. When the soldier in my room was done, I crept to the wall.

'Huay, don't scream. And you mustn't fight them or they'll hurt you. Do you hear me?'

There was no reply.

I heard her crying that night, the way she used to during our first nights here. She cried for a long time before I tapped on the thin wooden partition between us and asked if she was okay. No answer, then: 'How long have we been here?'

'Almost two years.'

'When can we go home? How long do we have to do this?'

'I don't know.' Then, sensing her dismay (as well as mine), 'Not much longer. We just have to be patient.'

Huay alternated between being confused or looking so worn she seemed to be sleeping on her feet in the bathroom. She complained of aches – mostly in her head and neck; pain that went away and returned, seemingly without cause. It wasn't long after the monsoon season that Mrs Sato announced the upcoming celebrations for the emperor's birthday once more. This time, the prospect of being out-doors was unmatched by my worry about what the physical exertion might do to Huay or what the lines of men would take out of all of us afterwards. I was trying to think about what we could do, how much food we could possibly spare for Huay, when Jeomsun touched my elbow and pointed at her, coming out from the shower – her rash, which we'd thought long gone, had returned and erupted in red blotches all over her back.

'I remember it now, where I saw a rash like that,' she said, pulling me away so Huay couldn't hear her. 'It's not the lack of food. We're thin and sickly too, but Huay – what she has is something else. I've seen it before, in other girls back in Formosa but never this bad…'

'I don't understand. Did they have the same illness? What is it?'

'It looks the same. Something they caught from the soldiers. The doctors don't always notice because the symptoms go away for a while before returning. It was going around in Formosa – I was one of the few who didn't get infected. At least that I know of.'

'Why didn't you say something before?'

'I wasn't sure. Thought maybe it was something else. And then it went away. I didn't want to worry anyone, least of all her.' She rubbed the scar on her cheek until she saw me watching. 'And what could we have done anyway? Ask for treatment?'

I thought about Mrs Sato, who had turned up at the usual time the day after our late-night conversation, her face a perfect mask. I had expected an acknowledgement of some sort, a nod perhaps, but she scarcely glanced up when I passed her in the hallway and seemed to avoid looking me at all if she could help it. It was as if that conversation had never taken place. It couldn't hurt to ask, I thought, and began looking to see if I could catch her on her own. But she never seemed to be alone. Especially not when the house was struggling to accommodate the increase in the number of visitors – soldiers shipped in from around the region, smelling of rain and mud and rot. We worked longer hours, sometimes seeing men past midnight. A pain that I had never thought possible lodged itself into my body so intently that I couldn't remember a time I had been without it. I started to bleed continuously, something that hadn't happened since my first week.

Then the day arrived. My limbs were heavy with dread when the caretaker escorted us outdoors. The morning passed – hot and breezeless – in a blur of song and clapping. And then it was over, and it came time for the men. The lines of them impatient and never-ending. Yet Huay seemed unaware of what was to come, even turned her face up to the sun when we were on stage. She smiled at me after the last song and I thought about saying something then, something quick to warn her but before I could, the caretaker was lining us up and pushing us into our rooms.

It was sometime in the afternoon when I heard Huay, pleading.

'Please, please. No more –' A scuffling sound, her feet on the floor. Then a wet thud and a man's shout. There was the crash of her door opening. More shouts. Words I couldn't make out. Then a soft, surprised cry before something collided into the plywood wall between us, making a crack like the sound of a tree being split apart.

'Wait! Please!' She cried. More thuds, sustained. I counted five before I realized what it was – boots meeting flesh.

When it was over, someone called out. The same male voice: '*Sato-san? Sato-san?*' Curt, bouncing off the walls in the corridor. Nothing for minutes. Only the sound of my own breath and heart in my ears. When the soldier in my room was done, I got up and peered around my door, pushing past several people to go out.

'Huay?' I nudged her door open. She was lying on her side, halfway off the tatami mat, her breaths coming shallow and quick. 'Huay?'

'Fujiko! Into your room.' Mrs Sato pulled me away from the doorway. 'At once!'

For what seemed like hours, I tried to listen out for Huay even while the men passed through, kept quiet by lying still while the men went about their business. Some time passed before I heard footsteps advancing down the corridor. The hinge whined as they opened her door and I heard a metallic click as the men talked. Then two pops, quick and deafening. I had to put my hand over my mouth to keep my heart from leaping out. Someone else in the house screamed, I couldn't tell who. When the men left, their footsteps were unhurried. The rest of the day was a blur. I was only let out after the last of the men were gone, and only to the bathroom.

The next morning, I woke to the smell of iron in the air so thick I could almost taste metal on my tongue. Then I remembered: Huay. Her door was locked when I tried it. I hadn't been sure before but the moment I saw Jeomsun at the sink, her eyes red, I knew that Huay was dead.

'They shot her?' I said, wanting to hear the words, even if they were my own. Someone had to say it. 'They shot her.'

After breakfast, Mrs Sato appeared at my door. 'Get rid of her things.' When I didn't move, she bent to look at me in the face. 'Kiko tried to attack one of the men and escape. You need to know that this is what's going to happen if you try to do the same. You still have friends here, I know, so don't try anything. No one wants to see you hurt. Kiko was foolish. Learn from her mistake.' Her eyes were soft and she lingered for a beat, as if she wanted to say something more but she rose and arranged her skirt around her legs as she walked away.

Huay. Her name is Huay, I thought to myself.

I pushed myself up to stand and stumbled into the corridor. There, on the left, was Huay's room. Her door was wide open, and I walked in. It was only then, standing there alone, that I saw that Huay had filled the little space around her tatami mat with wrappers and paper bags. All from the kitchen or from the men who went in to her, bearing gifts. Most of the bags were filled with oiled leaves and waxed paper, both used for serving or transporting food. This was all that was left of her, my last link to home. The remainders of her. A pang when I remembered how, at the beginning, I'd wanted her gone so I wouldn't have to worry about her telling if we returned home. Now I had what I wanted. Witch, I spat. My body felt heavy and I sat down then. Rifled through the odds and ends until I found I couldn't stop. I went through every one of them until I unearthed a single rice ball still wrapped in a layer of waxed paper and ate it without hesitation. In another, I found a coin which I put in my pocket. As I did this, going through and crushing all the bags and papers into a sackcloth bag, I ignored the blot in the centre of the room – a large, imperfect oval – until the caretaker came in and dropped a bucket close to me. There were a few strips of cloth in it, floating in the water like pale sea creatures. She pointed at the stain on the cement floor and left. Most of the blood had dried and it was so dark it looked like mud. The darkness had stained the mat, the black of it eating away at the rattan like a disease. I rolled up the mat, poured water on the floor and fell to my knees. My tears fell straight onto the floor as I scrubbed.

'I'm sorry,' I said. I scrubbed until most of her blood was gone. A ghost of it lingered on, as if she had seeped into the floor overnight. I worked on the patch until Mrs Sato came to get me, pulling me up by my shoulders and saying that the men were lining up, I needed to start work.

'Her poor mother. Her parents. I wonder if they will ever find out. I'm going to tell. Tell everyone what happened.' Jeomsun's voice was trembling with a cold anger that I couldn't muster up. I didn't want to talk about what had happened. Talking never helped and it certainly wouldn't help Huay now, I thought as she continued. 'I'm going to tell everyone.'

I felt tears coming up, felt myself start to shake with the effort of containing them. 'Who's going to listen? Who are you going to tell?'

'I – someone. Anyone.'

'Who's going to listen?' I repeated.

This time Jeomsun didn't reply. Her silence was unbearable and I wanted to confess about the food I had stolen from Huay's room. The coin that was hidden underneath my tatami. Instead I said, 'At least she doesn't have to be here anymore.' I bit the side of my tongue as soon as the words were out of my mouth. How scared she must have been. How desperate. I felt this same desperation rising in my chest, stewing into madness. And I let it out now, gave it voice. 'Maybe. Maybe she's just – maybe they took her away. I don't know. Maybe she's not dead. Did you see her body? I didn't. There was blood. But not a lot of it. Just a puddle. I could easily spare that amount of blood. It's just blood. Maybe she's at the hospital. Did anyone see her body? Anyone?'

I swivelled on my heels. Heaving. All the women were staring at me, mouths agape, from the other end of the bathroom. They looked so far away. Only Jeomsun was close. I felt her breath on my ear. Her lips pressing into my forehead. She said something unintelligible. Not Chinese. And then my name, 'Wang Di, Wang Di', as if trying to remind me who I was. Bringing me back to myself.

'No. Don't call me that. My name is Fujiko.' I was close to retching and bent over the sink. The cool of the porcelain. The grip of Jeomsun's hands on my shoulders. My body was light, as if the ground had been pulled from underneath me and my feet were treading air. I felt nothing much else for a long time after that.

As each month passed, the rations diminished. Dinner was once again reduced to a bowl of soup and grain, and the work I was subjected to left more and more changes on my body, each one more noticeable than the one before. The colour of my skin washed out and turned grey, scaly. This was two months after Huay's death. Patches of sores, which started out as bug bites and widened into raised welts that refused to go away. Three months. My pelvic bone jutting like the edge of a rock. Half a year. My body kept time and I watched it as if observing a strange life form. This isn't me, I thought. Even Jeomsun was starting to fade away. She spoke less and the light in her eyes – that quietly burning anger – had all but been extinguished. The same thing happened to the other girls, their colour and skin and flesh withering away into pale shadows, until they were little more than a collection of cuts and bones and bruises, badly healed. This, I thought, this is how we're going to disappear.

Many times, I dreamed about breaking away and running into the woods at night. I would hide during the day and trek at night towards the shore. There, I would be able to find someone, a fisher-man, or a raft to help bring me away from the island and onto the Malay peninsula. Or even further north of that. This was where my daydreams ended each time. I had no money to pay my way. I might end up trekking circles and dying of hunger. Even if I managed to avoid recapture and decided to remain in Singapore instead, what then? I could never go home, not anymore. With what I had done and what I was now used to. My parents would never have me back. I imagined them turning away or drowning me the way they used to drown strayed women, forcing them into pig baskets meant for taking the animals to slaughter, and then dropping them into a deep body of water. Even if I made it and arrived at a place where no one knew me, everyone would see – from the clothes that I had on, the way I looked – where I had been for the last few years. What I was.

I couldn't stop thinking about Huay, wondering what it must have been like to feel the same fear of her first day again and again. How painful her bewilderment was to Jeomsun and me, not just because of her certain, inevitable doom, but because the reminder it served us, how we had come into this place. How the months and years had chipped away our horror, and what we had to get used to to survive. I thought about the objects she had collected in her room and tried to imagine if they provided some small comfort, or a modicum of control over her life, the little life left to us in the dark of the night and early morning. Perhaps the walls – blank but for the little dashes of blood and fluid, the dark vees of water that ran down from the ceiling whenever there was a heavy storm – had simply been driving her mad. The way they were driving me mad. Eventually, like Huay, I started collecting things, things that I believed to be of value or potential use: bits of string, bottle caps; paper wrappers from candy some soldier had given me; empty tins that the cook left in a corner of the kitchen after preparing dinner; the faded thins of paper that

I coloured my lips and cheeks with, all the red rubbed out of them. I assembled them along the walls, under my mat, under the extra dress in the corner of the room. I was saving them up, for what, I didn't know. But I thought it might keep me safe somehow, that this little store of odds and ends would be useful one day – nothing would go to waste.

Kevin

I unfolded the letter and saw that it had a single handwritten line on the page. In Chinese. I folded it back up. Already, I could feel cold pinpoints of sweat beading on my forehead and under my arms. I unfolded it again and squinted at the sentence. It didn't make sense. Or it did make sense but the first word looked strange, wrong. It was a word I hadn't seen before, alien and spiky like an ugly fish with too many bones; not knowing it made the following characters meaningless. I squinted at the three words – just three on the entire page, hovering near the top like birds on the wing, ready to swoop down and land any moment on a branch – until my eyes started to water. I turned over to the other side, again and again as if expecting to find a clue, something else that I could make out. Nothing. Then I got out the Chinese dictionary from my bookcase. Except I didn't know where to start. I flipped through it front to back, back to front. I copied the word out onto a piece of paper, writing it out several times, making it larger and larger each time:

Until I couldn't see the word anymore, I could only see lines and strokes and slashes – a pile of dry twigs waiting to be lit into a bonfire. Finally, I closed my eyes and wished my grandmother were here so I could ask her what the word meant. Except I wouldn't be doing this if she were still alive, and if I were, she would probably give me a smack on the head for going through her things and reading her letters. It was no use. When I opened my eyes again, I saw that my thumb was covering the first character, so that what was left was 不起.

'Mm, 不起', I said out loud, and then, quickly, '对不起!' I jumped to my feet and waved the letter over my head, making it crackle in the air. 'I'm sorry' it read. She was apologizing to someone. But to who? And for what?

I took the second envelope and tore it open. This one was longer but not by much.

對不起, 可是我不能放棄他。他是我的一切。 求求你。。。

Again, there were a few words I had never seen before, this time, I realized what they were: traditional characters instead of the simplified characters I learned in school. I covered up the unknown words straight away, or tried to guess what they meant from what they looked like. I already had the first three words so this message was easier. All I had to do was to look up some other words in the dictionary, the ones I should know but wasn't sure about. In the end, this was what I had: *I'm sorry but I cannot give him up. He is all I have. Please...*

It came back to me then, how she had said 'please' that day at the hospital – '*qiu qiu ni*'– right before she closed her eyes. I thought about her writing these words, about the years and years she had spent, scared, waiting to be found out, until she couldn't keep it in anymore. This was what I was thinking when I opened the next envelope. This one was different, looked more like the letters we'd been taught to write in class, not just a scrap of paper with a single line dashed across it like a hastily written note. There was a date at the top – 28th December 1945 – and it was properly addressed and signed off with just two characters at the bottom. Not Ah Ma's name, I knew, because her name started with 林, Lin, just like mine, just like my father's. This consisted of just two words: 無名, the first of which I couldn't even read. I couldn't read the words at the top either, the name of the person she had written to, but the three characters looked familiar. I went back to the MISSING notices and found the same name in the Chinese version. There. There it was, the name. I reached for the recorder, pushed the button and said the three words as clear as I could.

Then I had to look up the rest of the words in my dictionary, trying and succeeding sometimes, trying and failing other times, before writing them down in English. It was fifteen minutes before I could be sure of what she'd written, before I could put down my pencil and read my translation in its entirety:

> *You don't know who I am but I am the woman who took your child.*
>
> *I'm sorry. Please forgive me.*

For the next few moments I could only hear the sound of my heart and her words 'I am the woman who took your child', ringing again and again in my ears. My hands were shaking when I drew out the next letter from the envelope and held it close in front of my face, the flutter of the page making little sighs and creaks, as if her words were coming back to life, struggling to breathe. This one was longer again, the words marching black across the page, taking up half of the white space. Too difficult, I thought, dropping it into my lap before opening the next envelope, then the next. Each one was longer than the one before. When I had unsealed the last envelope, I stopped and looked down to see my lap covered with sheets of white paper, all of them still holding the creases in them, some slithered down onto the floor around my feet as if trying to get away. All around me, pages and pages of words, pressed close to each other, as if in a hurry to get out of her pen and onto paper. There were dates on the rest of the letters and as I picked them up and set about putting them in chronological order, I realized it would take me a long time, much too long, to get them translated.

The phone rang and I had to run out of my room to pick it up.

'Boy?' It was my mother, 'Have you eaten?'

'Yes,' I lied. My stomach made a noise then, a grating, curling sound and I looked at my watch and saw that it was past one.

'Have you started on the maths worksheets yet?'

'Um –'

'Make sure you finish the pages I folded down. It looks like a lot but just do it a page at a time. Take a five-minute break when you've finished one –' she stopped and I could hear her muffle the receiver to say something to a colleague. 'So don't forget... I'll go over the worksheets with you when I get home. If you need my help, you just need to ask, okay?'

'I know, Ma.'

I hung up and went back into my room. The first two letters had already given me clues, which needed remembering. I took out my tape recorder and pressed the record button and spoke into the side of it, 'Chia Soon Wei, 53 Chin Chew Street.'

Then I went into the kitchen. From the fridge, I took out the tiffin of food my mother had prepared the night before – white rice, stir-fried choy sum, three slices of luncheon meat – and gave it a minute in the microwave. I ate standing up at the counter, with my textbook and my worksheets spread out on the table. I could not start. My mind kept going back to the letters and my mother's voice, over the phone – *if you need my help, you just need to ask*.

When she came home that evening, it looked like she had been walking through a wind tunnel. Her hair, pinned back when she left home at eight this morning, was now loose, dangling off the back of her head like a strange bird. When I said hello to her she spat tendrils of black out of her mouth before saying hello back. In her right hand she had her work things stuffed into a cotton shopping bag and in her left, two plastic bags plump with takeaway packages. Her shoulders were tilted to the left from the weight of her office bag. She looked like a broken balance scale.

'So, how was your day?' I smiled and took the food from her.

She looked at me with one eyebrow raised to say *what's wrong with you*. 'Well,' she began, in a way that sounded like *if you really want to know*, 'There was an accident at the harbour. Now all the shipments have been delayed and I have to send emails to all the clients explaining the... Anyway, my boss said I could bring work home otherwise I wouldn't be here now.'

'Oh... Where's Pa?' The letters were jammed into the back of my shorts and I was ready to show them to him. Look what I found, I would say. And then I would hang about as he started to read them.

'Parking the car. He should be up any moment.'

My father came into the room just then and my mother went to him straightaway. 'Hungry? Do you want the roast chicken or duck? I got both because I wasn't sure what you wanted. Oh, and I got an extra thing to share. Your favourite, oyster omelette.' She said all this in the voice that she had been speaking to him in ever since my grandmother died, the same voice she had used with him when he went to his Dark Place years ago. She rubbed his back and waited for a reply.

His face was more grey than human-coloured and for five seconds, he just stared straight ahead. 'Anything. I don't really feel like eating,' he said, walking into the bedroom.

I would make a note of it later, on another tape. Warning sign one: when he says he doesn't feel like eating. Warning sign two is when he gets that blank face – the face like he's wearing a mask, flattening every emotion into nothing.

'I have something to ask you. About Ah Ma.'

'Shhhh. What about Ah Ma? Keep your voice down.' She looked at the bedroom door, as if expecting my father was going to spring out any moment. I wanted to tell her not to worry. I didn't think he was in the mood to sneak about and eavesdrop on a conversation he didn't know we were having. (Warning sign three: when he starts to move incredibly slowly.)

'I wasn't shouting.'

She continued saying *shh* as she dropped her bags onto the couch and went into the kitchen.

I followed after her. 'But I just wanted to ask –'

'What? What did you want to ask about Ah Ma? Your father's not having such a good day...' She paused. 'Or week. Better not talk about something that will upset him. I'll set the table. You go and fetch him.'

I made a face. This could take forever. Just last night, it had taken my mother fifteen minutes to get him to the dining room. When we were finally seated and eating (not my father, who seemed to be chewing but not swallowing), I got the letters out, put them on my lap and looked down at them to practise my speech. *I found some letters here that I couldn't read. Hm, what could this possibly be?*

'Boy, what did I tell you about reading when we're having dinner?'

'But it's not.' I took a deep breath, then put everything on the table. Literally. Now or never, I thought, nudging the letters away from me so that my father could see it. But he had his head down, as if *he* were reading from something on his lap. 'It's not a book.'

My mother leaned over then and eyed the top page warily. 'Is that Chinese? I know I promised to help you with your homework but I haven't read Chinese in ages. It'll take me half an hour to read one tiny paragraph.' She dipped a fat oyster into chilli dipping sauce and popped it into her mouth. 'Maybe your father can help you. Right? Your Mandarin is so much better than mine.' She nudged my father's arm with her elbow.

'Huh?' My father grunted. One look at his face and I knew he hadn't been listening. A second, closer look at his glazed-over eyes told me that giving him the letters would be a bad idea. My mother was dropping pieces of food onto his plate but he didn't react. Instead, he seemed to be having a private conversation with his meal.

'It's okay,' I said. 'It can wait.'

That night, I dreamed about walking in Chinatown, through an open market. I went past a stall offering dried and salted fish, another red wooden clogs. There were rows and rows of vegetables, dewy-moist and spread out on top of a cardboard box, and rolls of cloth which a spectacled man was hawking from the back of his bicycle. I had just spotted the ice-cream man, was thinking about getting an ice-cream sandwich when I felt a hand, cold and bony, around my wrist.

'There you are. I thought I'd lost you.' It was my grandmother, except she was wearing someone else's face – her eyes were more hazel than black, and her hair was dark and cropped close to her face. 'Come on, hurry up,' she said, pulling me towards the five-foot way with one hand as she ripped posters off the pillars and walls. 'MISSING' they read. And then I saw my father's face, a stern black-and-white photo of it in the middle of each poster. 'MISSING' the posters kept screaming. But the more she tore and ripped and clawed, the more of them appeared, tiling the walls ahead of us. My grandmother kept on, until she became a whirlwind of movement, dragging me through the street so quickly that my feet lifted off the ground eventually and I was just sailing above her, watching.

'Stop, Ah Ma!' I called out. I was feeling motion sick, airsick. I called out until she slowed down and stood still.

'Here,' she said, handing me a piece of chalk. 'Now, write.' We were standing in front of my empty classroom, right in front of the blackboard. It had been scrubbed clean and was waiting to be filled with words. 'Write,' she repeated. When I didn't move, she shook her head and wrapped her hand around mine, guiding me to form the word '*wo*' in Chinese – me. We wrote and wrote, slowly cramming every square inch of the board with 我 我 我 我 我 我 我 我 我 我 我 我 我 我 我 我 我 我. We wrote until I couldn't feel my own hand any longer, until her hand, wound fast round mine, felt like my own.

'When will we be done?' I asked.

'When we finish.'

I turned my face to look at her and there she was again, just as I knew her, face dappled with age spots, lined around her eyes and mouth. 'You're back.'

'Not for long, ah boy, not for long.' She let go of my hand for a moment, leaving me to write 我 我 我 我 我 on my own while she reached over to push a button on her tape recorder. I watched the tape band roll forwards and spool around the empty reel.

'What are you doing?' I asked, still writing. I wanted to stop writing to see what would happen but I didn't dare to. 'What are you recording?'

Ah Ma kept quiet but tilted her chin to mean this, whatever, everything.

It was clear when I woke up what I had to do, who I had to ask for help, but it was three full weeks until I had to go for remedial classes. I couldn't wait that long.

The thing about wanting someone to go away is that they know it somehow, they feel it, and everything they do slows down – their speech, the time they take over breakfast, even putting on their shoes. My mother took five minutes explaining how I was supposed to heat up my food, and my father had his shoes on and was ready to go when he realized he didn't have his keys or wallet with him.

Once they were out of the door, I changed into my school uniform and packed my bag for the day – pen and paper, the recorder, and a plastic folder with all the letters tucked into it.

It was after nine when I arrived and there were rumblings within the walls. If I stood still, I could hear a high note from a flute, the tap-tap of a snare drum from the music room where the symphonic band was practising, trying to get a gold at the nationals this year. I went to the reception area, past the principal's and the administrator's station, where I had to sit and wait for my parents just a few days ago, until I got to the door labelled 'Staff Room', and knocked. When no one came to the door, I opened it and went in, walking past tables strewn with papers and stacks of exercise books. Some had photos pinned up on the low cubicle walls and a few had corners crammed with toddler-sized soft toys, half-deflated balloons, teacher's day cards signed with multi-coloured signatures from years before. There were posters on the walls with pictures of rivers and snow-capped mountains and long, steely bridges with captions below like 'BE THE BRIDGE' and 'A teacher ignites the fire that fuels a student's thirst for knowledge, curiosity and wisdom'. There were desks with heads bent over them but no one looked up when I walked past. I saw her from a distance, hunched over, a vicious red pen in hand. Unlike the others, I could see the surface of her wooden table, glass-topped and shiny. I wanted to turn and walk back out but I reminded myself of the letters in my bag.

'Lao Shi,' I said as I approached her.

She looked up, eyes owl-like behind her reading glasses. She took them off, replaced the cap on her pen and said, 'Wei Han?'

I saw her eyes alight on the blue square of cloth pinned to my left sleeve which I had to wear for another forty-one days. For Ah Ma.

'Do you have questions about the homework?'

She seemed to be in a good mood, I thought, relieved. I reminded myself to smile as I brought the letters out of my bag and held them out in front of me with both hands. An offering, a gift. 'Lao Shi, I have problems reading this,' I said, speaking in Mandarin the way we were supposed to in her class.

She put her glasses on and took the pages from me. 'What's this?'

'These are old exercise sheets I found. I'm trying to read more to improve my Chinese... Except it's written in traditional script and I can't. It's quite difficult. A lot of the words aren't even in my dictionary and I don't know where to start.'

I had rehearsed the story on the bus ride, during the walk from the bus stop to the school gate. It had sounded reasonable in my head, good even, but now that the words were out in the air, I realized it stank of nonsense from start to finish. I had to keep myself from snatching it from her hands and running out of the staff room, out of the school building, all the way back home. The seconds slowed down as I watched her leaf through what I'd given her and I felt the space that my words had taken up bubble up between us. It took up so much room that eventually, Lao Shi had to sit back in her chair. She sighed, dropped the sheaf of papers on her desk. 'This is not a story.'

My face turned red and I tried not to stammer when I said yes, it was, it was a reading exercise I found from an old exam script.

'Who are you trying to fool? I can call your mother and ask her about this, you know.'

My neck and face went hot. 'I'm sorry,' I reached for the copies. But she waved my hand away and gathered up the pages, lining up the edges and corners before putting them into a cotton tote crammed with books and files.

'You can go; I don't have time to deal with this now –'

'But, you can't –'

She turned and looked at me. The set of her face, combined with her magnified eyes made me want to laugh with fright. Then she turned back to her marking, slashing red all over someone's Chinese essay. I stood there for a few seconds, hoping she might change her mind. I didn't know what else to look at so I stared at the piece of paper she was holding. The essay started the way everyone had been taught to start a story. Good weather, bad weather. 'A piece of blue sky,' it read, 'with no cloud to be seen for miles.' When I went out into the corridor, I saw that it had started to drizzle. It began to drizzle inside my chest as well, my heart making little pitter-patters as I thought about how my mother would react when she got Lao Shi's phone call, how my father might react when she handed over the letters. It wasn't meant to happen like this. I needed to have a rewind button just like on the tape recorder so I could un-happen this and stop myself before I got the bright idea to ask Lao Shi for help. Now I had lost the letters. All of them, except the first two.

'Useless, useless,' I said to myself. The drizzle was turning into a downpour but I didn't run. The only other people around were two girls from the year above. They stared as I arrived at the bus shelter and I suddenly become aware of my washed-thin uniform, my muddied shoes. I didn't know what to do with my hands and put them in my pockets. Only then did I remember the loose change that I had brought with me, the money I had taken from Ah Ma's dresser. I counted out the coins in my hand. It was enough. Enough for the bus rides to Chinatown, and then back home.

Wang Di

'Eh, I didn't know we would have neighbours like that. People like her still exist?'

'Don't be fooled. No one goes hungry in this country. She's just one of those... You know... Not quite right, *la*.

'And did you hear her?'

'What?'

'Talking to herself!'

And here Wang Di imagined them exchanging looks, circling a finger next to their foreheads.

They were there nearly every day now. Chatting in the corridor. Using stage whispers whenever they talked about her. In response, Wang Di took to keeping her door wide open. I don't care, she wanted to shout but never did. When Wang Di wasn't outside collecting cardboard and tin cans, she folded her laundry and made her meals, sometimes humming 'Rose, Rose' as she did so she wouldn't have to hear them. Her voice rusty with disuse. Until one afternoon when 'Rose, Rose' veered into a different tune. She stopped at once when she realized what she'd been humming. The words echoing in her head. The warble of Jeomsun's off-key voice drowning out everyone else's.

Oni na rawa
Kagaya ku mi yo no
Yama sakura
Cini sati ni o-o
Kuni no hana

'*Aikoku No Hana*,' Jeomsun had explained, scoffing, as she taught the lyrics to the rest of them that first time. 'About women who honour their country.'

How the soldiers had clapped afterwards. The flowers, pink, white and orange, that they threw onto the stage. Tiny rocks that she discovered to be pieces of candy, their wrappers glittering in the sunlight. The shock of their low cheers – the unlikeliest sounds given where they were, what they had been doing for the past few months – goading them into picking everything up, crouching like children. Mrs Sato watching on like a proud mother. And then, in the days following, how she had turned her head to one side and stared at the flowers as the men moved and gasped on top of her. The blooms had lasted for days even out of water.

After that, the song kept sneaking up on her when she was least prepared for it. To drown it out, Wang Di started using the radio instead. Only sometimes. As if wearing the batteries out for only one set of ears was a waste. On weekends though, she put it on loud enough to drown out the neighbours' visiting grandchildren, their chatter over long Sunday lunches. But even that had its dangers.

The Small Reception came on one afternoon. She recognized it as the string instruments started up and clicked the radio off before it could properly begin. Then, just as quickly, she put it back on again.

If anyone asked her now, she would not be able to say what it was that made her return early the day Soon Wei blacked out at home. There were still hours to go before she was usually done with her rounds and she could have gone on, there was still space on her cart and her legs and joints were giving her no trouble. It was just past eleven in the morning and the sky was clear when she turned around and headed back. As she walked along the corridor, music from *The Small Reception* – her husband's favourite opera – reached her ears; the crash of cymbals, a high-pitched voice. She'd thought, what good luck that the Old One had it on just then, they seldom played it on the radio.

She had called out as she entered their flat, was putting away the cart when she saw the lower half of one leg stretched out from beyond the kitchen table.

When he woke up in hospital, she was ready for him. Cup and straw in hand, a napkin for any spills. He took a sip and said, 'How long was I asleep? Have you been here all day?' His words were garbled, thick with stupor.

'Not too long.'

A family – three generations of them – came in, clacking their heels and chatting among themselves a little too politely. The Old One looked up and at Wang Di, his eyes bright with the shine of a recalled memory.

'I remember when you were in hospital. You slept for hours and hours after the operation. I had to stop myself from shaking you, just to see if you would wake up. What was it? More than fifty years ago?'

She tried to imagine him sitting next to her and waiting, badgering the nurses with his questions whenever they stopped by, and felt a bittersweet sting in her chest as she smiled. She remembered little of her hospital stay, the operation. Only the years of pain and discomfort before it, and the dull, empty ache after, most of which went away in a short time. The emptiness didn't.

Back when it first began, she had tried going to the doctor, a Chinese *sinseh* in another kampong so there would be less of a chance that she might run into a neighbour. It was a few months after the end of the war and she went alone, without her mother, lied and said she was going to the market, not because she knew what it was she had but where it had come from. To her growing dismay, none of the herbal concoctions she got from the Chinese doctors helped. She put off seeing a Western doctor until she couldn't anymore. By then, she was bleeding relentlessly. The physician had been an old man who didn't blink at all when he asked about her medical history. She told him about the pregnancy and nothing else. The way the physician had looked at her then, eyes sharp as a crow's, disbelieving. The shame that crept all over her body. It was almost as bad as being back there, in that little room.

'It looks like pelvic inflammatory disease,' he had declared. 'I will give you antibiotics now but you'll need to go to the hospital for more tests.' He had given her a referral, which she crumpled up and threw away as soon as she left the clinic. She remembered how her face had burned, as if she were standing too close to a fire, how the nurse had taken her time with the antibiotics, dropping one pill at a time into the bottle. The infection went away but the pain lingered, a pain that began deep in her belly and stayed there, or shot down her spine and into her legs so she could barely stand. It came back from time to time but she said nothing about it to anyone, nothing about it to her husband after she got married. The Old One found her one evening, curled up on the bathroom floor. He'd carried her out into the living room and cradled her head while he phoned for the ambulance, wordlessly praying (to his ancestors, to any one of the many gods or spirits who might listen) as they waited.

At the hospital, the doctor quickly decided that she would have to have a hysterectomy. It took her some time before she absorbed the news, and then she had cried, refusing to look at the Old One even as he held her hands and squeezed them. After the operation, she had come to, hazy but still herself, and spoken to him through a cloud of anaesthesia. A string of apologies. 'I'm so sorry I never gave you children. That I'll never give you children. Can you forgive me?'

She said this again and again. He had stroked her hair and hushed gently until she was swept into deeper, restorative sleep. For weeks after the operation, she had the sensation of being lighter and heavier at the same time. Whenever she was alone, she rubbed circles over her stomach, around the raised, horizontal scar, thinking about what it once held, what it would never hold again.

That was the first and last time they spoke about it. A decade passed. They moved into a flat of their own, and Wang Di thought she had come to terms with it until Leng asked her if she wanted children. Leng had two of her own, a boy and a girl. Wang Di wasn't surprised by the question. They had known each other for nearly a year and the topic was bound to come up. Still, she struggled to respond.

'Maybe you can adopt. Nothing wrong with that, you know. So many people do it. There are some families with too many kids and some who want just one but cannot...' She stopped there. It was difficult to know what the problem was if the woman didn't talk.

Wang Di considered telling her everything. About her hysterectomy. About why she had needed the operation in the first place. About the child as well. The one whom she still saw from time to time – tucked into a passing pram, sitting in the lap of a woman on the bus. For years he had stayed a baby, no more than a few months old. Then, one day she looked up from her meal at the hawker centre and saw a boy who could have been a mix of her and Soon Wei and felt she must know him. That it was him. Her mind latched on to the idea of the child, fully grown, and she continued to spot him on occasion. Less frequently as the years passed. *Shen jing bing!* Madness. She wondered how Leng might react to this ghost child of hers, tried to picture the expression on her face, her usual kindness and concern wrestling with a growing alarm.

'If it's because of the money, you shouldn't worry. The further the war's behind us, the better things will get. You'll see. And besides, children don't need very much. Look at mine, growing like weeds.'

'I don't know. I guess I am worried about that. There's no room for a child in this flat, not really.' She knew this sounded weak at best but there was no way to explain this to Leng without giving every-thing away: how if she wanted to adopt, she would have to go to her husband and explain what had led to this. What had happened to her. So she changed the subject. Continued changing it each time until Leng got the message.

If not for what had happened to her, they might have had a child in his fifties now. Instead, it had just been the two of them. They had been happy. It was more than she thought she deserved.

Fifty-four years, she realized, watching him now. We've been married for fifty-four years, she wanted to say. 'The doctors said you can go home in a few days,' she told him. She ignored how poorly he looked – his hollow cheeks, the blueness of his lips, and wanted to reach out and rub the pale cast, like a fine dusting of flour, from his face.

He turned to gaze out of the window. It was raining and large drops of water were tapping on the glass, the green, metallic smell of rain filling the room. There were storms almost every day during this time of year. The kind that felled trees, stranded cars in the middle of roads, with water rising so quickly past the tops of canals and spreading into the ground floor of homes and shops and schools it seemed it would never stop. She tried to remember if she had shut the windows before leaving home. There would be a good splash of rainwater on the floor of course – the panes were old and the one highest up kept getting stuck in a permanent yawn. She wondered how she would feel if their place got flooded. If she went home to their things drowned and washed away.

The Old One turned back to look at her. 'We don't have much time left.'

'I'm not going home yet. The nurses aren't so strict with the visiting hours,' she said, even though she knew just what he meant.

'I just want to make sure that you are all right' – and here he paused to look for words that would cause her the least anguish – 'when I'm gone. You can't just keep it all inside you like you've been doing all these years. I know it's difficult. But.'

The Old One never pushed her. He seemed to know, almost from the beginning, how difficult any talk of the war was for her and had skirted the subject for years until the day at Changi beach, a few years into their marriage. She was digging her toes into the wet sand as he walked along the shoreline, bent over, collecting shells in the palm of his hand. Then he found something and straightened up. She thought it was a large mollusc or the top half of a crab until the sand and seawater fell away and revealed ivory. Human bone, a lower jaw. It was clean, and several teeth – green with algae and chipped – were still attached. Soon Wei seemed to weigh it in his hand before he pitched it into the sea. They watched as it sailed into the air and disappeared into the water with a light splash. And then it was as if it had never happened. They were just watching the light flicker and dance on the waves.

The Old One was quiet on the journey home. Over dinner, his uneasiness grew until he couldn't hold it in anymore. 'I could have brought it to the police,' he said.

Wang Di was imagining the scene, a group of blindfolded men kneeling, waist-high in the waves, while a line of Japanese soldiers got ready to fire. They had washed up over the years on beaches used as execution sites. Skulls, femurs, a hip bone.

She had wanted to tell him that it was okay, that it didn't matter, part of a jaw. But knew how wrong it sounded, how clearly untrue. That night, she dreamed about men being strung up and pushed into the rising tide. When she woke and found Soon Wei sitting at the kitchen, staring out of the window, she saw that he was thinking about it as well. She knew that it would come soon, the stories, the questions, and tried to brace herself for them.

A few days later, he turned to her while they were watching the evening soap. 'You know…' he started, 'you know I had a wife before you.'

She nodded. 'The matchmaker told me.'

'I've never told anyone how she died. How my family died during the war. It happened a few days after the invasion, before the Japanese took over. There was no warning. I don't think anyone had an idea of what was going to happen when we saw them driving into the village in their trucks –'

It was at this point that Wang Di pushed herself away from him, holding one hand to her stomach, as if stabbed. 'I'm sorry,' she said, pushing herself up from the edge of the mattress and running to the bathroom. Soon Wei followed her and waited outside, at the kitchen table just in case.

That night, he woke her from a nightmare, trying to hush her and explain that she had been thrashing and kicking. Then she felt it – a warm dampness spreading under her. Wang Di had got up and ran to the bathroom. While she was in there, he stripped the sheets, made the bed, and lay down again. When she returned, it was as if nothing had happened. All night, she kept her back turned to him, the heat of her shame keeping her awake, making her breath come quick and shallow.

He had waited for her to confide in him all that time. Fifty years. She remembered how she had fidgeted as she got ready to speak, digging her nails into her hands so that she wore the crescent scars of it in her skin for weeks after. How the words had come out that day at the hospital: 'There's something else. Something that happened in the black-and-white house.' She had almost told him everything but stopped, believing that there was still time.

The way he had assured her after she was done talking that day. She was exhausted but her eyes were still darting, as if she were a child awaiting punishment.

'You shouldn't take it with you. In the end,' he said, forgetting about himself as he'd always done.

And she had let him. Only thought about it when it was too late.

It was close to two that afternoon when Wang Di made her decision. She tucked her purse into her trouser pocket and picked up the Old One's walking stick, dusting off the smooth top of it before walking out of the apartment.

November 1944 – August 1945

Late in the year, I was woken before dawn by the first bombings since the Japanese claimed the island. The sound was distant and ghostly; it reminded me how far removed I was from my old life, how little it had to do with me now. Mrs Sato gave nothing away when she arrived that afternoon. There was no information, only hushed gossip for days about what the explosions might mean. 'Was it an air raid?' 'Maybe it was just a factory accident?'

Two weeks after the new year, there was another spate of bombings. This time, we were wide awake, gathered in the bathroom for our morning ritual – the deep boom of it was unmistakable, as was the sound of planes overhead.

'Do you know what that means?' Jeomsun's eyes were lit up, the high points in her face white and arched like the wing bones of a bird.

I shrugged. The end of the occupation, I thought, or the end of things. I was fine with either.

'Maybe when the British come, they will bring food with them. And supplies. 'I've had to use the same sanitary cloths for months now.' She filled her bucket with water, threw in her menstrual cloths and started scouring the strips with both hands. 'Do you have any clean ones to spare? Mine are so tattered they're almost useless.'

My stomach lurched. I knew where mine where – tucked in a corner of my room, untouched for weeks. My voice was barely audible when I said, 'I haven't bled in more than a month.'

Jeomsun froze. 'When were you supposed to?'

'I can't even keep track of the days anymore. How can I know –'

'Don't panic. Maybe… Maybe it's just because you're so thin,' she circled her damp fingers around my wrist to emphasize her point. 'It happened to a lot of girls when we were in China, when we were close to starving.' But she didn't sound sure; Jeomsun, who said anything she pleased and nothing at all when she didn't want to.

'Maybe I should tell…' Mrs Sato, I thought. Maybe she could do something. I thought about the way she had talked about herself and her daughter that night little more than a year ago. The way she had put her hand on mine.

'No, wait. See what happens. It could be nothing.' She gave me a stiff smile that only showed how helpless she felt, then straightened her back and turned to glare at the other girls, who were all watching, eyes agog.

'You're right. It's probably nothing.' I nodded to reassure her. A child, I thought. Impossible. Back in my room, I thought about how a Chinese doctor would deal with it – I had overheard my neighbours talking about it once, some *yatou*, little wretch, who had gotten herself into trouble. She had taken *dong quai* and a whole pineapple, cut herself slice after perfect, circular slice. I wanted to look up those neighbours and ask them if it had worked for the girl.

I saw less than ten soldiers that day. Spent most of my time thinking about my mother. How I had watched her through three pregnancies, two brothers. How one little girl had died at birth. I was six then; my task had been to boil water and keep watch over Yang as my mother screamed in the next room. I remembered the midwife's repeated urges for her to push, and how, after hours of listening to my mother groaning in the bedroom, a silence had settled, thick, unnerving, over our home. The midwife had come out with swathes of old cotton wadded together, her face glossy from exertion, the corners of her mouth set straight. She didn't look up as she passed me on the way to the kitchen. My father, who'd been waiting outside, had gone in to see my mother and left again, his face dark. 'What happened to the baby?' I'd asked, once the midwife was gone. My mother shook her head and told me not to be nosy. Then she changed her mind. 'The little girl died. Too small.' She closed her eyes and two heavy drops of tears slid down the side of her face, pooled in the seashell of her ear.

I wondered what they would have named the baby had she lived.

Names. I rested my hand on my stomach, pinched the ridges of my hip bones. No, it can't be, I thought, though I knew it was there. How clear the signs had been, looking back: small but seismic shifts in my body – the fullness of my breasts, how the rice tasted in my mouth – like something gone off. Even water was different, metallic. But I had pushed it all away, out of mind.

It wasn't supposed to happen like this. Not like this. Not the way my parents would have wanted. A man of their choosing. An auspicious date plucked out of the astrologer's book. I couldn't help trying to guess who the man might be. The other half of the child. The only face that came to mind was Takeo's but it couldn't have been – I hadn't seen him in more than a year, he could well be dead. I wondered who it was, and if the child was already formed, with eyes and ears and toes, growing.

'You. You don't know anything,' I said to myself.

Over the next few weeks, the other girls kept their distance from me as they waited for something to happen. Jeomsun was the only one who continued speaking to me, garrulous as ever, though she talked about everything else but my pregnancy: about Huay and how much she missed her, about the different things she would eat if she ever got out of here alive. There, in her words, lay a shred of hope that everything would be over before the pregnancy began to show itself. The bombing raids had begun afresh, this time in earnest. One night, I heard faint human cries carried across the island by the wind. After that came the smell of burning rubber. It was then that I thought about my family, imagined them running for shelter and crouching in a ditch. With a start, I realized that their faces were beginning to blur; all I could see was their brown legs whipping through grass, arms crossing above their heads to try and shield themselves. The faces of both boys melded into a strange composite. The wrong eyes, the wrong nose and mouth, so that I ended up picturing someone only vaguely familiar, whispering harshly for my mother to hide, quick. In the house, there was no announcement, no orders for us to get up and be ready to dash to the nearest bomb shelter situated a little away from the building. We remained in our cells while Mrs Sato gathered her people in the kitchen. I had to strain to hear the staccato sounds of their hastened speech, the rising and falling tones of anxiety. They went on like that for a few minutes before dispersing, their footsteps dusting over the concrete. Once again, soldiers ceased to come by. No one opened our cell doors except to slide food across the floor, quarter bowls of rice cooked with an increasing amount of grit.

Every night, I went to sleep hoping for the war to be over and for the baby to be gone the next day. But when I found a smear of blood in my underwear one morning, I started to cry.

'What's wrong?' Jeomsun said when she saw me.

I showed her my balled-up underwear in my hand.

'That's nothing. It happens. I know it from my mother.' She said nothing else but continued looking at me. Her eyes were steady. *Now you know what you want, at least.*

I didn't tell her that I wanted half of the baby. Nothing of whichever man had done this. I closed my eyes and tried to picture going home, walking through the door with the baby in my arms. 'Who's that?' My father might ask. And I would have to say that it was mine. He was mine. I had the image of the child all of a sudden. It would have the roundness of my face and when it smiled, I would be able to see a little of my parents, my brothers.

'They're going to find out.'

'Try to hide it for as long as you can. They might not find out. We haven't seen the doctor – not since the first bombing. Maybe he's dead. Maybe we'll be free next week. Anything could happen.' Jeomsun clasped my hands in hers and squeezed.

The air raids continued, reminding us that something was going on even if we thought the rest of the world had fallen away, given up on our little island. Both Mrs Sato and the caretaker were distracted by the lack of sleep, the diminishing rations they were receiving and their quickly emptying pantries. I kept count. Three months. Four months.

I tried to stay invisible until the bump appeared – four to five months into the pregnancy – almost overnight, as if magicked by an imp into being. I switched dresses with Jeomsun, who was almost a head taller than me. Bent double to hide my stomach as I shuffled to the bathroom each morning, keeping my eyes to the floor.

It might have worked, save for the fact that there were still soldiers coming through every single day. It was a gamble but I quickly found that few of the men cared. Some of them even rubbed the top of my belly as if for good luck before they left. My own luck lasted until one evening, when an officer came into my room. He took great care in pulling off his boots and lining them against the wall before looking at me and stopping, mid-approach, to frown. Without a word, he picked up his boots and left the room. I heard him speak – just a few short, cutting words – and Mrs Sato reply, her voice at once apologetic, coquettish, confused. Then she appeared in my doorway and pulled me up to wrench open the front of my dress. Once she saw my filled-out stomach, her businesslike manner vanished.

'How long has it been?' When I didn't reply, she grabbed hold of my arm to pull me close. 'How many months?'

'Five. Maybe six. I don't know.'

For a second she looked ready to scream, had her head reeled back, as if gathering force. Instead, she shook her head. 'Foolish girl.' The expression on her face was hard to read, seemed something like concern and tedium combined, when she nudged me back into my room. 'It's too late to do anything about it. And anyway, you'll be surprised to see how few of them mind it. Keep yourself looking well, a woman can be at her most beautiful when she is –'

'What do you care? You let Huay die. Why not have me killed as well?' *Or let me go.* The unsaid ringing out loud in the quiet after my words.

That was when I saw it – a look, as if she were seeing past or through me, at someone else entirely. 'Do you know what happens to girls like you? No family will want you back. Not like this. You don't know what they'll do to you. You don't know –' She shook her head, stopping or waking herself, both. 'If I put you out there, you'll starve on the streets or resort to doing worse things than this just to scrape by. I'm doing you a favour, trust me. I'm saving your life.' She waited for me to thank her or scream something else in reply. When I didn't, her face fell. Regret or something like it flashed on her face and she slammed the door shut.

The house saw fewer visitors as the bombings continued. Some of the soldiers walked out the minute they saw I was pregnant, some stayed to talk, perhaps pretending that I was someone else: a mother, a wife. Most of them, as Mrs Sato said, simply didn't care and did what they wanted to do with me.

I didn't tell the other girls that I was getting a little extra food, that Mrs Sato would bring me dinner on occasion: a fish head on top of the usual pitiful rations. A single tangerine. I took the food gladly but I remained the way I was – skin and bones. The baby kept growing. It seemed everything I ate went to it; it took and took from me. Every day, as my belly filled out, the other girls paled, shrank. There was more hair in the drain and less chatter in the bathroom as everyone fought to preserve any bit of energy they could gather for the day. One girl fainted in the bathroom, cracking her forehead open on the sink. Another had to be carried out of her room when an infection refused to ease. I watched from behind the half-closed door as Mrs Sato supervised her exit; a guard carrying the girl by the shoulders, the caretaker taking her feet. I never saw the girl again.

'What happened to her – the girl they took away yesterday?' I asked Jeomsun the next morning.

'She got stabbed by one of the men two weeks ago. Her wound refused to heal. I think it got infected.' She got stabbed. It wasn't the first time. It wasn't even the first time in six months. These incidents were becoming more frequent with the bombings, as if fear was chipping away at the men, the people they once were, before they left home and came here, and made monsters out of them.

'Where do you think they took her?'

Jeomsun shrugged, too weary to speculate. I wanted to tell her that it should have been me. That it was meant to be me. That I'd killed her. That I was killing everyone else in the black-and-white house. Taking up space. Eating food that could have been shared, that could save them. Each time Mrs Sato arrived with the extra morsels, my throat burned with shame even as I devoured every single crumb. I was afraid that the stink of tangerine on my dress would betray me and frequently thought about keeping something aside for Jeomsun but I never did.

I talked to myself, to the baby, as I ate sometimes. Telling it that I wished I had more to give. That I was eating for its sake. Half lies. To distract myself from my guilt, I imagined what I would do afterwards. After the child was born. I could be a washerwoman, just like my mother, raise it on my own, even put it through school. I could follow Jeomsun back to Busan, I thought. This was how I fell asleep: picturing mountains I had never seen before, grassland so wide I never saw the end of it. In my dreams at night though, I was watching the guard and caretaker carry the girl out again. Except when I looked closer, it was my face I was looking at; it was me.

The child arrived in the night. The pain started slowly, lulling me out of my sleep. At first I thought they were merely hunger pangs but the pain intensified and spread, turning my stomach tight, hard to the touch. A dampness spread under me and I turned slowly from side to side, wishing it away, until I couldn't deny it anymore – the baby was coming. I got up and paced the room. After some time, it could have been minutes or hours I couldn't tell, I sank back down again. The only position I felt better in was on all fours, knees dug into the mat. Then I felt the first of it, a pain shooting through my centre, like a vice slowly tightening around my spine, so firmly that I found it almost impossible to breathe, then releasing again. The pain built up, tightening and loosening, tightening and loosening, a little more intensely each time. I called out once or twice, sounds I'd never heard anyone make before, startling myself in the dark. Then I blacked out.

When I came to, I saw that someone had brought in oil lanterns and put them close. I felt the heat of the light, heard the faint rustle of a moth's wings. Then I saw my mother crouching next to me, getting the wordless, barking caretaker to bring in pot after pot of hot water. I was lying on my back again. Someone had put a thick wad of rolled up blankets under my head. The pain was still there – I could feel it lingering in my lower back and down my spine, gathering momentum. I closed my eyes and waited. When I opened them, my mother's face was above mine. She said something I couldn't make out – I was still making that low, animal sound and it was thick, filling my ears and head. 'I can't hear you,' I shouted, trying to be heard through the hum of noise. Someone made a shushing sound and pressed a rolled up towel to the side of my face. It felt cool against my skin and made me think of the time I was ill and in bed with a fever. The only thing that helped then was the damp towel she'd brought, changing it after it grew hot from my skin, and plunging it back into the water until it became cool again. The trill of water falling into the bucket as she wrung the water out sounded like birdcall. I remember holding my breath as she folded the cloth into a rectangle, while I waited for the shock of cold on my warm face.

I held my breath now as my mother turned away. When she turned back, I saw that it was not her after all but Mrs Sato. She was talking loudly and making faces. Then she brought both of her clenched fists up in front of her face, again and again, until I understood that I had to push. It was a long night, a long morning. Once or twice, I heard the whisper of female feet outside the door before they quickly went away again. The rest of the world went on by – trucks arriving and leaving, the sound of deep, male laughter in the front room. A series of people came to the door, and each time Mrs Sato had to get up, her face rearranging itself, forming a smile as she neared the door. I couldn't help watching as the caretaker left my room carrying bundles of dark-red cloth, heavy-looking, stinking of life and death. How did it look each time she went out like that? I thought. Then I told myself that this, in the middle of war and death and this house, was probably nothing out of the ordinary at all.

When it was over, they wrapped the baby in a clean sheet and put him in the space between my torso and my arm. He kicked feebly and made snuffling noises, like he was about to want something. The last thing I did before I passed out was to pull him to my breast and watch him latch on and feed. When I woke, it was to the sound of approaching footsteps, the clink of cutlery. Mrs Sato was holding out a bowl of rice with shreds of vegetables on top. 'Eat.'

I took the bowl from her, and she looked at me as if she wanted to say something, stood there for a while working her mouth as if trying to get the words ready. Before she could speak, there was a shout in the front room. She tiptoed out. I finished the food and drifted off again. I might have slept for minutes, an hour, but it felt like days. I only woke when I heard someone slip in, and kept still while the person hovered over me, waiting for me to open my eyes. I felt the child moving in my arms. Then I felt her bend down and pick him up, pulling him out of my reach.

'Should I take him away from you, so you can rest?'

Huay turned around. She looked just as she had when I saw her that mid-autumn festival years ago, her cheeks flush with youth. Before the war and this house and what it turned us into. She was smiling, her arm forming a perfect cradle under the baby. He was sucking her thumb, eyes bulging from the effort of trying to get something, anything out of it.

'It's okay. They said I could be with you for a few days. To help you.' There was a long pause before she added, 'You've been sleeping for more than a day now. Mrs Sato has been taking care of you herself. Did you know?'

I knew. During those moments, I saw how she might have been at home with her own people as a mother, a grandmother.

'You should have waited though. It's not a good month to have a baby.'

'What do you mean? What are you talking about?' I sat up. It only occurred to me then that I had no idea what date it was. What the baby's birthday would be.

'It's August – ghost month. Didn't you know? My mother always said it's the most inauspicious time to have a child. You really should have waited.'

I said nothing. She was still cradling him, the edges of her body fuzzy and spectral no matter how hard I tried to focus.

'Do you even want him or shall I take him away? Maybe that's a good idea. He doesn't look so well.'

No, no. I struggled to form the words but my mouth was numb. The baby started to cry. She was right. There was a yellow cast on his face and he was small. Too small. As I watched him, he pulled his thin arms out from the swaddling cloth and flailed his fists.

'No, please. He's mine,' I finally managed. 'You can go now. I can do this on my own.'

Huay made no move to suggest that she'd heard me but carried on coaxing the child. Then she looked at me. Her eyes were empty. Dark as a pond.

'Here.' She lay him down on my chest so I could pull him close. When he finally started to drink again, the room fell silent, save for the muffled plosive sounds he made as he fed.

'Have you decided on a name?'

I had, but I wasn't ready to say it yet. Too early. Naming him and saying the words aloud would be tempting fate. But I had thought of a name as soon as I saw him: Cheng Xun. A name that spelled success, ease.

I shook my head.

'You could give him away. Someone will want him. People want little boys.'

'No, I can do it. I'll bring him home.' My words echoed in the room. Home. The warmth from my baby and my exhaustion pulled me under for a second, two seconds. When I opened my eyes again, Huay was gone.

The thought of losing my child kept me awake, alert to any movement in the house so that I woke as soon I heard the caretaker rise in the morning, and squared myself in a corner of the room with him in my arms, ready to resist her, Mrs Sato, anyone. Even if it proved useless. But something was different. The house had about it an air of the abandoned. This hush, which should have been welcome, was unsettling. Fewer and fewer soldiers visited the house and the ones who did were sent to the other rooms. When I realized this, I felt guilt, then relief creeping into my bones, took to pinching the tender insides of my arms to remind myself that anything could happen, that I had to stay alert.

I saw less of Mrs Sato. Our time in the bathroom got cut short and we were watched more closely than ever by the caretaker, who seemed unnerved by the quiet suffusing the house. I refused to let Cheng Xun out of my sight and it took more than a week before Jeomsun could convince me to let her hold him while I cleaned myself.

It was one morning, as I watched Jeomsun rock Cheng Xun in her arms that I realized how little he looked. I'd refused to see it but it was clear now that he hadn't grown much in almost two weeks and was eating half of what he used to when he was just a few days old. Instead of feeding, he slept or else nuzzled blindly, pushed his fists into my chest, as if wanting to burrow himself back into the quiet.

'What's wrong with him?' I whispered to Jeomsun. The yellow of his skin was in his eyes as well, and had spread downwards, to his chest, and belly, even the soles of his feet. Jeomsun refused to look up. She had noticed it, I realized, and hadn't wanted to alarm me.

'I don't know. Has he been eating?'

'Very little. His appetite seems to be getting poorer and poorer… What should I do?'

'The doctor. Ask Mrs Sato for him.' She sounded shaky, from hunger or from fear of what she thought was to come, I couldn't tell.

I tried to get Mrs Sato's attention that day, shouting out whenever I saw her sandals pass under the door. She paused once, then went on, as if she hadn't heard me, as if I weren't there at all.

* * *

In the space of a few days came a shift in the air that seemed absolute. Instead of the caretaker's footsteps and the tap of her cane, I was woken up by the sound of engines roaring past the gates. This continued all morning. We were simply left in our rooms to wait while footsteps passed back and forth in the corridor. No breakfast. No letting us out to go to the bathroom. Only the scrabble of rummaging and the shuffle of drawers opening and closing in the kitchen and in the front room. A little later, I smelled smoke. Burning paper. This was the end, I thought. This was how I was going to die. I hammered at the door for a long time and heard the other girls' voices, their cries, until the smell of smoke faded along with the sound of boots outside.

The low whirl of activity in the house wound the air tighter, tighter. There was a roll of thunder. Then rain – a sound as familiar as my breath in my lungs. I guessed the time to be three in the afternoon.

Jeomsun shouted in Japanese, something pleading, urgent. Other voices joined in. The girl next door begged to be let out. She needed to use the bathroom, she said, and couldn't wait anymore.

No one replied.

At twilight, Mrs Sato opened my door to push a bowl of rice across the floor.

'What's going on out there? Is there any news? Please, anything.' Maybe I could push past her. I could try, at least.

She froze as if I had spat at her, then drew her arm back. The baby was in my arms and I turned away so that only the tips of her nails caught the side of my head. My ear was ringing and there was blood on my fingers when I touched my face.

'You want news? They bombed us.' Her chest was heaving. I would see Mrs Sato, decades later, whenever I came across pictures that showed the bomb's sweep of destruction, what it did – simultaneously final but lingering. A wildfire that left nothing behind. But I didn't care then. 'My home town, gone!' This last word, she screamed, slamming the door after her. The baby stirred, then stretched its mouth into a wide, red yawn.

The day it happened, the air was hot and still, waiting to break with rain. We had not heard anything for an entire morning. I was sure we were going to die like this. Forgotten and alone in our individual tombs.

Weak as she sounded, Jeomsun refused to give up. 'Is anyone out there?' she asked, in Japanese and then in Mandarin.

'Can we be let out? Please, we need water,' someone else said. No one used the words 'leave' or 'home' – as if the thoughts themselves were too painful to put into words. It was a fragile hope, one that we were afraid to bring out into the open. I said nothing; I didn't want to wake the baby. That yellow cast on his skin seemed deeper, like a stain that was refusing to wash away. He slept heavily most of the time and I found it increasingly difficult to rouse him for what little milk I could provide.

After a while, the questions stopped. I felt the others tense, their ears keening for the faintest sound: the creak of a door; a light knocking against the windows in the front room; a rustling. It was just the wind, of course, and rats going through the kitchen cupboards. The tree outside, its branch tapping on the wall.

Finally, somebody said what should have been obvious since dawn.

'They're all gone. They've left us.'

'Everyone, try your doors,' said Jeomsun. There was something in her voice I had never heard before – not from her – a desperation, a pleading.

All around me I heard the thud of door against jamb, and the other women saying, 'No, it's locked, it's no use, we're going to starve'. I tried my door as well. It was locked.

Mrs Sato kept an orderly house.

Two nights passed before someone came to us. I had gone through all the tins I had stolen from the kitchen, the saved up little wrappers and twists of paper in my room. Found half a sweet potato. A tangerine that I had kept aside and half forgotten, the flesh leathery with age.

It was morning when I heard the familiar rattle of a truck, the grind of brakes on tyres. Then, men. Speaking Japanese. I felt the usual dread settle into my stomach. The baby was still asleep; I held him tighter and shut my eyes, wishing the outside away.

Then someone unlocked all the doors and threw them wide open. I had to turn my eyes away from the light pouring in. When my eyes adjusted, I saw that there were soldiers standing in the corridor, five of them, weapons at their sides.

A man yelled, first in Japanese, then in Chinese, 'OUT! OUT! OUT!' He banged on the wooden counter to make his point. I wrapped a piece of cloth around my child, got up as slowly as I could to prevent him from stirring, and stopped at the doorway to look around before taking a few steps out, expecting any second to be seized and thrown back into the room. Jeomsun was in front of her door. Her face was pale and unreadable. I wanted to tell her it would be fine, whatever happened it would be okay. I wanted to at least mouth the words to her but the same man shouted again, and there was a surge. All of us moved into the reception area. The front door was wide open and I could see the truck, still running and churning out exhaust, and the woods beyond it.

'Go,' the man said, not shouting this time but simply saying it, gesturing towards the door.

Someone moved, I couldn't see who, my eyes were too much focused on the exit and the soldiers standing around it – their backs and shoulders tight, as if ready to spring. Someone moved and then all of us did.

'Go!' His voice cracked at the end of that single word.

I made sure my baby was held tight enough and I ran.

In a moment I was narrowing my eyes against the sun, and then opening them wide, because of the world outside the iron gates and my surprise that it was all still there. For a few seconds, there was nothing else but the scuffle and gasp of flight. Then, two gunshots, just behind. A woman's voice. One clear, unrestrained scream. For a split second I thought about Jeomsun but I didn't stop. I ran, making my way off the road and heading straight for the green instead, past the tall, wild grass, into the trees. I ran with both arms wrapped around my child, felt only then the coolness of his skin, his limp body, the shards of dry, fallen fruit embedding themselves into my feet.

Kevin

53 Chin Chew Street. I repeated the address so many times that morning – to the information lady at the bus station, to the bus driver, and then to several other people along the way, store proprietors and elderly men and women doing tai chi in a bit of green, open space, who looked like they could navigate the streets of Chinatown blindfolded, that the words started to sound strange, like a noise a baby might make when they are just learning to talk. To make sure I had remembered it correctly, I played the tape of myself saying those words, that name. Another thing I did was to cross my fingers the way Ms Pereira did sometimes in class when it threatened to rain at the end of the school day. I did it every time I passed a shop that had its doors sealed shut, rust eating away at the metal gates. There were other images that worried me – buildings with their insides out, walls cracked and torn open to reveal wires and pipes, waiting to be plastered and painted over, made into the hotels and restaurants and spas that made the older shops (traditional, Chinese-medicine clinics, one-dollar stores, clan association headquarters with their unlit, smoky interiors, eating joints with just a few tables crammed into a spartan space) look like they had stayed still for centuries.

Here it was, Chin Chew Street. I held my breath as I followed the numbers up the road, exhaling only when I got to 53. Hung above the doorway was a large black signboard with faded gold leaf within the grooves of the Chinese characters. There was a mannequin standing in the entryway, and, next to it, a wide work surface for samples to be rolled out on, examined and cut to the desired length. It was an old shop, one of those that smelled of stale jasmine rice and incense smoke and didn't seem to have working electricity; the only light seemed to come from the entrance and the picture windows at the back. The tiles on the floor were thumbnail-size and varied from shades of turquoise to peacock blue, and bales of cloth filled the shelf lengthways, threatening to spill and unfurl onto the floor. An old man was sitting in the back, hunched over a black-and-gold sewing machine. Every now and then, he made it purr, moving a long strip of cloth away from him as he did so. Then, without looking up, he raised his hand to say that he would be right with me and could I wait just a bit.

I stood with my hands hung by my sides. My palms were sweating so I wiped them on the sides of my school shorts. I wondered what to say, what to ask, how to react if this was him.

Even from where I stood, I could tell that he was quite old, in his early eighties and his back was slightly curved from bending over his sewing machine. I could see him sitting like that for decades and decades and was surprised when he stood up, at how straight his back was, how steady his stride. He stepped out from behind his sewing machine, draped a length of measuring tape around his neck, and peered at me.

'Hello, are you looking for something? Or do you want something made?'

He knows, I thought, he knows.

'Ahem. Erm. This might sound a bit strange and I hope you don't mind me asking but is your name Chia?'

The old man cocked his head to the side and leaned forward so that I looked straight into his right ear. It was large and the ear lobe dangled fatly. The kind of earlobe that, according to my grandmother, meant you were rich or were bound to get rich. 'What? Little boy, you have to SPEAK UP!' He shouted these last words as if I was the one hard of hearing, then sighed elaborately before saying, 'Some days are good, other days are bad.' He shook his head and cupped a hand behind one ear in anticipation of my speech again.

'YOUR NAME! IS YOUR NAME CHIA?'

'CHIA? NO, MY SURNAME IS TAN.'

'Oh.'

'WHICH CHIA ARE YOU LOOKING FOR?'

I thought about telling him never mind and then leaving to go to the nearest bus stop. I could get on the first bus out of here and forget about all of this. I looked around and saw that a couple was sitting outside a cafe across the street, staring and not even trying to hide it. The old man was still waiting for an answer so I took a deep breath, filling my chest.

'CHIA SOON WEI. HE USED TO LIVE HERE. AT THIS ADDRESS.'

'OH!' he said, his face and eyes bright wide and open now. 'CHIA! HE USED TO WORK FOR ME! DELIVERING CLOTH AND PACKAGES TO PEOPLE, DOING SEWING JOBS THAT I GAVE HIM. THAT WAS BEFORE THE WAR.' Then his voice softened, and he slumped a little, as if the effort of remembering tired him.

'They had a child, I remember. I never met his family then but I remember him giving out red eggs during the baby's full month celebration. But things changed when the war got closer. I had to let him go because the shop wasn't doing so well. It was a tough decision but I had to do it. To save my business. He moved out of the city and into his parents' village, I think. He came back after the war, thinner, looking older than he was, needing work and a place to stay. I gave him his old job back and let him stay here for a while' – he pointed at the door leading to the back of the shophouse – 'but he moved away after a few years. His wife was in poor health and they wanted to be somewhere quiet.'

'And the boy?'

Fingers pointing skyward, he waved his hand, meaning no more, nowhere, nothing. 'We never spoke about it… And to be honest, I was afraid to ask.' A look of regret came over his face before he glanced up in surprise, 'How did you know it was a boy?'

'I – When was this? When did they leave?'

'Oh, about forty years. Almost fifty,' he said, closing his eyes. 'So many years. Gone so fast.'

Fifty years ago. I had to swallow before I asked him the next question. 'Do you know where he is now?'

He shook his head no. I felt my feet getting heavier, sinking into the ground. This was it. A dead end. My mouth opened, as if on its own accord, and I heard a croak rising from my throat.

'Are you okay, boy?'

The old man came closer, stepping over the threshold of his shop and reaching out with his arm, as if he thought I was going to fall over. I shook my head, and put up my hand at the same time. 'Yes, yes,' I mouthed.

'Why don't you come in? You want some water? Or I could make you a cup of tea. Or Milo.'

I thought about the stories my mother had raised me on, stories about *bomohs*, witch doctors, how they gave children sweets and sugary drinks to reel them in. And strangers who would lure children into vans and then sell them across the border. I remembered her face as she said heaven knows what happened to those disappeared children. Heaven knows, she said, her eyes stretched round. Then I looked at the tailor with his tape measure, and the parting in his hair that shone brightly pink. I thought about the soft-boiled egg that my mother had put out on the table next to the bread and jam, and regretted having left home without eating anything.

The man came back with a glass of water and three chocolate biscuits on a plate, and went away again while I drank and ate. 'Here,' he said, setting down a stool so insistently that I felt compelled to sit. He perched across from me, in a chair dragged out from behind his work table. 'I really wish I had asked. It was obvious though, that he had been through something during the war.'

'Like what?'

'I don't know exactly. He never told me but it was easy to guess. Lots of things happened to lots of people during the occupation. Didn't your grandparents tell you stories?'

A wash of memories, of all the things my grandmother used to talk about, rushed through me. Nothing, not one word. I shook my head, no.

'Most people prefer not to bring it all up again. I was lucky, nothing bad happened to me or my family. Those three years and eight months weren't so bad for me, in fact. Many Japanese officers came to me regularly to get tailor-made clothing for themselves and dresses for their girlfriends. We lived quite well during the occupation. Despite everything…' He shook his head, looked as if he was about to say more, then changed his mind. 'What's that?' he said, pointing at my left hand.

I looked down to look at what he was pointing at, was surprised myself to see the dull grey machine whirring away. 'Oh, this is going to help me remember things when I can't see so well anymore.' I tapped on my glasses; the thickness of it made a dull *tik-tik* against my fingernail.

He nodded again before he asked, 'Why are you looking for Chia?'

Because he could be my grandfather, I thought. Because finding him could save my father from spiralling down into the dark. 'My grandma just passed away and I think they knew each other.

Do you think you might have their address? Or telephone number somewhere?'

'My condolences...' he said, bowing a little. 'I can ask my wife. She's the one who manages our address book but she's not here right now. It's all so long ago...'

'Oh. Okay.' I blinked and swallowed, not knowing what to say anymore. 'I guess I should –'

'This is important to you.' He fixed me with a gaze so direct that I had to look down and pretend to fuss with my hands. 'Wait,' he said, before fading away into the depths of his shop. He came back with a notepad and pen. 'Write down your name and phone number. If I find something, I'll give you a call. I can't promise you anything though.'

I nodded, letting him know that I understood. Forty years ago, fifty. He's never going to call, I thought, listening to his sewing machine stutter alive as I walked away.

I arrived home in the afternoon shouting, 'I'm back' – before remembering that no one was there, not my parents, not my grand-mother. It felt strange stepping into the quiet apartment on my own, as if I had just come back from a trip away, much longer than a single morning.

All the rest of the day, I waited by the telephone, jumping up every time it rang. My mother called in the afternoon to make sure I hadn't set fire to the apartment. Twice, I picked up the phone only to get Albert shouting abuse in my ear ('*Chao ah gua*! Retard!'). At around six, the phone rang. When I said hello there was a pause, and then the crack and shuffle of the receiver being passed from one ear to another. Albert again, I thought, and was ready to put the phone down when the old man's voice came over the phone.

'Hello? HELLO? HELLO? I'm looking for Kevin Lim.'

'Yes, I'm Kevin.'

'This is the tailor on Chin Chew Street. You came to my shop today and asked for Chia?' I could hear all sorts of noises in the background. The talk and background music of a drama serial, children squabbling.

'Yes?' I said, barely able to breathe.

'Well, my wife remembers writing his address and telephone number down... Just in case we had to send on their mail, you see. She remembers wanting to tell them that they should come by to pick up a few things they left behind but we couldn't find the number. We looked in all her address books, I promise, but we couldn't find anything...'

'Oh. It's okay. I – It was a small chance. Thank you for trying anyway.'

'Wait, don't hang up! She tried the big phone book – she's the practical one in the family – and she found one name. It might not be the person you are looking for, but you can at least call to ask. Do you have a pen with you?'

I replied yes and repeated it after him to make sure I had the correct numbers and everything:

204 Redhill Close

#09–633

2774658

I thanked him twice before hanging up and smacking my forehead with the heel of my hand. Phone books. The yellow phone directory, volumes of it, was right under the telephone, stacked high enough to function as a side table. They had been there so long that I didn't even see them anymore. I stared at the address and telephone number that I had written down, picked up the phone. Put it down. Picked up the phone. Put it down again.

Then I held my breath as I dialled, as it rang and rang and rang, only exhaling once I put the receiver back in the cradle. I tried again. No one picked up. Maybe they were out. I thought about the things my grandmother used to do in the afternoon. How she would take a walk around the neighbourhood at around five o'clock, just as the ground and air were cooling, before the sun started to set. Maybe they were out, I thought, having dinner earlier than everyone else the way elderly people do. Maybe this wasn't even the correct Chia Soon Wei and the real one was unlisted. Or didn't exist anymore. 1946 was a long time ago – anything could have happened to them between then and now. There was only one way to find out.

The story was that there used to be swordfish in the waters around the island, murderous man-eaters that terrorized the villagers who lived by the sea. It was a fishing town and the men often risked their lives to feed their families. After several men had been killed by the swordfish, the village sought help from the sultan and his army but he did nothing. Men went on dying each time they went out to sea on their wooden boats. It was at the funeral of one of these fishermen that a boy from the hilltop came up with the idea to build a barricade along the coast, using the trunks of banana trees that grew abundantly in the area. With little left to lose, the men set about building the barricade. The next day, the people stood behind the ramparts, waiting nervously as the fish swam closer and closer. One by one, the creatures hurtled towards them, only to get their bills wedged in the tree trunks. As the fish lay suffocating at low tide, villagers held the boy aloft and celebrated, calling him their saviour. These cries soon reached the ears of the jealous sultan. Paranoid that the boy would usurp his rule once he came of age, he sent his soldiers to the top of the hill to murder him. As the boy died, his blood soaked through the ground and down, down the hill. That was how it came about, the name. This was what I distracted myself with during the train ride to Red Hill.

This time, I looked up the address in the street directory, then slid a bookmark between the pages before putting it into my bag. This time, besides my recorder, I remembered to bring a small bottle of water, and a packet of biscuits. A ten-minute walk and I was standing in front of the block of flats, quite low, painted calamine-pink and pale yellow. All the way there, I thought about what I might say. These are the lines I came up with:

Hello, my name is Kevin Lim Wei Han and I found a letter that was written to you in 1946.

Hello, my name is Kevin Lim Wei Han and I think I might be related to you.

Hello, I think my grandmother might have taken my father from you during the war and raised him as her own.

Good morning, I think I might be your long-lost grandson.

I only stopped when I got into the lift, distracted by an over-whelming stench of urine. I clamped a hand over my nose and mouth, held my breath and watched the numbers ping: 1, 4, then 6. When the doors opened at the sixth floor, I lunged out onto the landing, forgetting for a moment what I was there for. When I remembered, I stood and stared into long corridors extending on both sides. Odd-unit numbers on the left, even numbers on the right. I turned left. Even though it was still light outside, the corridor was dank, shut in from all sides but the direction I was coming from. The fluorescent tubes overhead helped little, only gave a cold, greenish cast over the graffiti, the dying plants and newspapers left to curl and yellow in the heat. You could furnish a whole other flat with these things, I thought, looking at the TV consoles and wooden shelves left near someone's door. I imagined an apartment, much like ours, made up of slightly broken furniture and sunk-in sofa cushions, much too loved.

There was a man dozing in the doorway of one flat. He wore just a plaid lungi wrapped around his lower body, had stretched his legs out into the corridor. It was difficult to figure out how old he was; his skin was grooved and slack along the forehead and cheeks, but his chest looked curiously smooth. The man slept on as I approached, slowly and as soundlessly as I could. The space behind him was badly lit. It was the first time I'd seen a flat smaller than ours and I squinted to see what I could. Two single beds, pushed together at the far end of the apartment. Boxes, all yawning wide, lined up near a dull, floral-clothed sofa. I tried to make out the odds and ends sticking out the top of the boxes, then started when I realized that someone was watching me. A woman, in a housedress of a pattern similar to that of the couch she was on. I felt my face redden, and continued walking until I reached Unit 179. No one seemed to be home. The windows were shuttered, and the metal grills chained up with a heavy lock. There were no sandals or shoes outside the door where they would normally be. Instead, sticks of broken incense lay unlit, as if they'd slid out of the bundle they were sold in and never been picked up, never considered.

I hadn't thought about it. It was only when I got here that it dawned on me that they might not be home. Or they might be home but not want to speak to me, or hear my story; it was so long ago maybe they wanted to forget. Or maybe I was completely wrong. The idea of that, or of them not wanting to see me made my chest feel tight, as someone had bound it with rope and was pulling on both ends. Finally, I knocked. Nothing, not even a slight stirring of the air behind the door to hint at the rising up of old bodies, creaky legs, no voice telling me to hold on. I knocked again.

'Are you looking for the Chias?'

I turned. It was the man in the doorway, leaning out now with his upper body. I hesitated, then went to him.

'Yes. Have they gone out?'

He shook his head. 'Moved. Just moved out this week.'

'Oh,' I said. When I recovered, I asked him, 'Do you know where to?'

The man shrugged, bony shoulders pointing towards his ears. 'Don't know.'

It didn't seem like he was going to tell me more, he had closed his eyes and it was as if the conversation never happened. I was just about to leave when he said, 'I think she moved to one of those old people flats. Not too far from here… Not sure where.'

I turned back to look at him.

'She? What about him? The husband?'

He shook his head and sighed, drew out a tin of tobacco from the waistband of his lungi, and started rolling a cigarette. 'Old Chia passed away…two months ago?' He yelled over his shoulder, 'Oi, when did old Chia pass away?'

'Two, maybe three months ago.' A woman's voice, ringing clear from the dark.

I peered into the flat again, but the woman was no longer on the sofa. Then I saw her, standing in the kitchen by the window. Sunlight was streaming in, lighting up her arms as she reached past the window ledge to draw in her laundry, hung out on long bamboo poles. I watched as she balanced the bamboo between sink and dinner table, then flapped out each garment before folding it and laying it on the table. The air filled with dust motes, falling in and out of the rays of evening sun. It was only then that I realized that they had just that one window in the kitchen. That and the ventilation slats near the door, wide enough for cockroaches and lizards to slide through, nothing bigger.

'I – Thanks.'

So he's dead, I thought. He's dead.

The woman said, 'This Buddhist temple helped her with the funeral. Took care of the costs and everything. We didn't go but I heard it was alright.'

I heard a faint buzz near my ears, a mosquito, felt its body wing past the side of my face.

'Are you looking for them? What is this about?'

I couldn't think of anything to say. In the space of that silence, I saw the man keen forward. They were done giving answers, they wanted to ask questions.

'I'm, I…' I stepped back, then turned and walked to the landing.

I was just stepping into the lift when I heard the woman starting to say something else. He cut her short, yelled out that the boy was gone. He'd walked away just like that.

'He can't hear you anymore,' he said, before switching to Tamil. The rest I didn't get. The lift pinged open. I stepped inside and jabbed hard at the button to close the doors before I could hear them say anything else.

I had one thing left to do and now, now there was nothing. Nothing. I wanted to stay on the train and be driven back and forth across the country. West to East. East to West. I wanted to never get off and go back home to the empty flat. Grandmotherless. One less grandparent, and then two less. Can you lose something that you never found? I was thinking this, half dreaming, as I walked back home. My keys were in my hand when I heard something, a song that sounded like it had come from a long while away, in time and space, all the way from when Ah Ma still slept in her bed, when she would fall asleep to the Chinese opera with the song going right into her chest. One of the neighbours was playing the same song on their stereo or their radio, I thought. But the music got louder and louder as I approached our door and the little invisible hairs on my arms and the back of my neck stood up straight. I tried not to make any noise as I slid the key into the lock, the better to catch her ghost in the act. The better to ask the questions no one else could answer.

There was a clash of cymbals, the whine of an erhu just as I stepped in. There was no one around. No one. No ghost. The radio blared, making a tinny sound as the melody crested.

'Ah Ma?' I whispered.

'Hmm?'

I turned and saw my father lying down on the sofa in his work clothes, his eyes fluttering open.

'Pa?'

'Where were you? Your mother told me to come home and give you this.' He pointed at a wax-paper packet on the table. 'Chicken rice. Were you at school?'

I made a noise that sounded like yes. The takeaway package was still warm and I could feel the grease seeping through. 'Have you eaten?'

'Yes, yes.' He gave me a wan smile and pointed at the radio. 'Your grandma liked this one. When I was your age she would take me to the *getai* during the seventh month, when they performed this for free outdoors, even when it rained and they only had the ghosts watching. I didn't like it much. I only liked the fight scenes and the snacks she would buy for me on those outings. We would sit there until the mosquitoes got too much. Unless this one came on, then she would make me sit there for hours... Maybe we could go, this Hungry Ghost Festival,' he said, getting up and moving towards the door. He smelled of a mixture of chlorine and sweat and sunshine.

'Yes, sure,' I said, nodding and wondering what I had been looking for and why. I should just burn it all, I thought, the letters that I still had, the cut-outs, the notices. The tapes with their many different voices contained within.

But I didn't. What I did was this. I waited until all the lights were out that night before I crawled under my bed and the floor. I got out the shoebox and laid the recorder and the tapes in it. And the scrap of notepaper with the address and phone number of people I thought could matter, but who are really strangers, and put it back where I had found it. I buried it under layers and layers of Ah Ma's things, already smelling of mothballs now that they hadn't been worn for a week. Then I shut the drawer and tried to forget.

Wang Di

Wang Di had just arrived at Kopi Sua when it started to rain. A fine rain that seemed like nothing at first but, after ten minutes, began to form a pool on the top of her head so that rivulets of water ran down the sides of her face. Her cotton blouse was damp. Her feet making little damp sounds in her cotton shoes. She cursed herself for forgetting the umbrella. But it didn't look like rain, she argued uselessly, childishly.

The cemetery was almost deserted. At the gate, the entirety of which was bright green with moss, she had run into a middle-aged couple stepping out of a taxi. She'd decided to ask them for help and was walking towards them when the woman spoke, murmuring something in English. Then they had taken one turn, past a tree and were gone. Wang Di stared at the land before her, a craggy spread of grass and rock. There were more graves than she remembered. This meant that there was less ground for her to walk on, more spaces in which she had to negotiate every step, pardoning herself whenever she came close to stepping on a paper plate of kueh or a bowl of white rice. Brown hell notes, half burned and still folded in the shape of gold ingots clung to the bottom of her shoes so that she had to pick them off and return them to their owners.

'Sorry, sorry, sorry,' Wang Di kept saying.

When the rain finally stopped, she dried her face with her sleeve and dug the walking stick into the ground, ploughing past the graves that looked new, well kept. On the bus ride, Wang Di determined that Soon Wei had not visited in ten years. Maybe thirteen. She wished she knew what thirteen years of neglect looked like on a grave but settled on a plan to dismiss the ones that had recently been fed and tended to; then the ones that were engraved with English words instead of Chinese. The next step would be to search for those with a date between 1942 and 1946. Simple as that, she told herself. She did not want to think about what came next, what happened if she found a tombstone that met all the above criteria. It wasn't as if she would be able to read the words on it. She had an image of herself standing there until someone walked by. It might take hours. Days. That, she hadn't planned for. Shoved the thought aside when it flitted past her, light as a moth.

The search made her glad that the Old One had asked for an urn but she understood the need for this. This need for ground, for a square of space. Many times, she had to push away branches and twigs, fallen over the stones like a lock of hair. A few were unmarked, identifiable only with painted numbers. Some had photos on them, aged sepia faces peering out at her. Elderly faces and young ones. Too young. Some were flanked by red lions and guards dressed in uniform. Some were entirely crumbled, sinking into the ground like lost ships at sea. She had counted and rejected fifty-five before she realized that she was going to have to return on another day, was leaning on the walking stick, grateful for the cloud cover when she heard rustling, then a voice.

'Thigh bone.'

Rustle, rustle.

'Root.'

Wang Di saw a small object arcing through the air before landing in front of her with a sigh. She made her way over to the voice. An open grave. The smell of earth and black.

'Hello?' she called out. 'Who's there?'

Another pause. 'Hello?'

The first thing the man said when he emerged (half clothed, bandana on his forehead) was, '*Ah-mhm*, what are you doing here? It's almost six.' His face was flushed, as if embarrassed from having been caught talking to himself, or from physical exertion, Wang Di couldn't tell.

'I'm looking for a grave.'

'It's almost six. Going to get dark soon. Come, I can walk you to the bus stop.'

'Maybe you could help me. I'm looking for a grave from the years nineteen forty-two to nineteen forty-six. I don't have the names but there must be a register, right? With the dates in it?'

'Have you been looking through the cemetery like that? At the dates?'

Wang Di nodded.

'*Ah-mhm.*' He scratched his head, 'I have to tell you that some of the graves have been exhumed. You know...dug out for cremation. That's what I'm doing right now. Making sure that I have every last fragment of the body. The people you're looking for might not be here anymore.'

'But why...where do they end up?'

'Oh...in one of the columbariums. Depends on where the next of kin decides to put them.'

'And the register? There is a list of all the bodies, all the people, right?'

'Do you have a serial number?'

'No. I don't.'

'I'm sorry but without a serial number... Who are you looking for? Your relatives?'

'Yes. No. I don't know,' she said, driving the walking stick into the ground to make sure she wouldn't fall when she swung around, a hundred and eighty degrees, to go back where she came from.

She told herself she hadn't lost anything. That the thing she was looking for had already been lost when the Old One died. It was a matter of coming to terms with never having had it in the first place. The search had simply distracted her from the fact of having failed him, of never being able to recover him, his story. No, she hadn't lost anything.

The fallout occurred a few days later.

It was the way the neighbours huddled in, clucking their tongues outside her door, that did it. That, on top of everything else. She heard their tutting, lizard-like, too familiar, and she was twenty again, taking up too much space in her parents' attap hut. Feeling like she should never have returned.

It came back to her. How she had gone out onto the streets for the first time in years and how people had stared, as if they knew just from looking at her. How the neighbours found out and started treating her as if she were contagious, pulling their children away from her, turning to spit whenever they ran into her outside the public outhouse. Word spreading around like grease, getting onto everything. She had tried setting up stall at the market, against her mother's protests. And for five days, she had returned home in the afternoon with a full basket, the vegetables turned soft in the heat. So she went round to the cheap eateries that had popped up everywhere to ask if they needed help in the back, cleaning the kitchen, the toilets, anything. Even there, out of the light, she wasn't wanted. The thing they called her, that they whispered when she had her back turned: 'comfort woman'; like a slap to the face; like shutting her in a cupboard. Some of them saying that she had done it for money. That she had been looking for a husband. An easy life.

Even after her marriage, she had felt the shame of it clinging to her. The way a fishmonger never fully got the stench of scales and sea out from under his fingernails. They had walked down the street the morning after their wedding (each having stayed on their side of the bed that night, Wang Di clinging to the edge), Soon Wei showing her the neighbourhood. Chinatown. Their first home, a dingy little room smelling of tobacco and cooking oil. I'm someone's wife now, Wang Di thought, as her husband walked next to her, pointing out the indoor cinema, the best shops to get their provisions, his favourite food stalls, but Wang Di wasn't listening. Was transfixed, instead, by the appearing and disappearing faces of Huay and Jeomsun, first hiding among the market-goers, then slipping closer, until both of them were walking alongside her. *Where have you been*, she whispered, mindful of her new shoes, the clunky weight of them as she stared at their bare feet. But neither of them replied. Huay was smiling as usual and Jeomsun was holding her gaze with clear eyes that said everything and nothing. *You have to go*, she eventually said, though she was dismayed when they did, vanishing as easily as children playing hide-and-seek. She was helping Soon Wei pick out a batch of vegetables from a stall, was making an effort to smile at him when she saw Huay again, ten paces away from her. This time, Huay had something in her arms. She felt a jolt when she saw who it was, saw the furred crown of his head, his too-pale skin.

'Cheng Xun,' she said out loud, and pushed past her husband, scattering green onto the ground. By the time she got to them, they were gone again and she was left standing in the middle of the market. 'Where did you… Cheng Xun?'

She was still searching for them, was spinning around in her confusion when Soon Wei reached her, approaching slowly as if she were a wild animal one needed to be careful with. 'Are you okay?' he asked.

'I'm –' She looked up and saw that everyone was watching, backing away a little. 'It's just…'

'Don't mind them. Busybodies. Don't give them a moment's notice.' And he had given her his arm. She had slipped her hand into the crook of it. Everyone stared to show that it wasn't done, contact like that, not even between man and wife. 'Come, come,' he hushed, and they had walked off. Got the groceries for the week. The first of many Sundays.

Wang Di heard the Old One's voice now. Gravelly with age. *Don't mind them.*

'I know, I know. You're right but…'

It was the neighbours. Their whispers and looks that did it, made her habit creep back into her bones like pain from an old break. Along with it came memories of the other women. The ones she had left behind. Her friends. Huay, especially. Her bitten nails. The way she drew a perfect parting down the centre of her hair each morning, even when she was ill. All of her. Flitting through the open door of Wang Di's mind, like a bird flown into a room, trapped and panicked.

She began again with little things. Hard-boiled sweets, a kaleido-scope of colours in their cellophane wrappers. Matchboxes filched from coffee-shop tables. Plastic bags blowing in the wind which she caught with the toe of her shoe. Little things that she could fit into her pockets. She was almost proud. Felt like she could say to him, See? Nothing in my cart.

When her gleanings stopped fitting into her pockets, she started negotiating.

'I'll throw out the pile of leaflets,' she said as she returned home with a box of videotapes. A small plastic aquarium with a few stones in it in exchange for getting rid of a pair of scissors, so rusted over it wouldn't open again. A chipped vase for a pair of shoes that was missing most of one sole. She filled her new home with it, took out the news clippings he had cut and plastered them on the wall again, as if to say, See? You're the one who started it in the first place. She took the rustling of the curtains, or a sudden burst of rain, for his disapproval.

'Last time, last time. I promise.'

It was only when she woke up one morning to a flat she could hardly recognize, half filled with things from outside in place of the belongings the two of them had bought and saved up for over the decades that she thought she had to stop. Again. It was the cutlery that did it. Getting up at six and opening the drawer to find it almost empty except for a pair of chopsticks, a spoon, and a ladle. She thought she had been robbed until she remembered that she had put out a large coffee can crammed full with cutlery and utensils the day before in return for bringing home a Lego bucket. The curtains had flapped when she came in and she had put her hands up and said, *I know, I know,* gone around looking for something to trade in, finally settling for the drawer full of kitchen utensils. Things that she would never need again, she told herself. No more reunion dinners, folding a batch of pork dumplings all afternoon for the New Year's Eve meal, cooking up a pot of chicken curry that would last a week. Or savouring the look on his face as he tiptoed over to the pot to have a look at the curry bubbling and rolling over the fire.

She got to the void deck as quickly as she could but the bin had been emptied and the coffee can was nowhere to be seen. Not next to it or behind it, when she moved it around to check. She was just straightening up, shifting the bin back into place when the lift pinged and the neighbour walked out, fluorescent-yellow track shoes on her feet, a towel around her neck.

'Oh,' the neighbour said, backing away a little, as if startled by a stray cat.

'Morning.' The greeting fell out of her mouth like an apology. She didn't mean to say it. Didn't know why she did.

More for the ladies to talk about. And then, with a stab of regret: I used to have friends too, she thought. She wondered where Jeomsun was. Whether Huay's people had ever found out about her. Tried to picture what they might look like now, the two of them attritioned by the passing of fifty-five years: Huay, shrunk small and plump; Jeomsun, leaning into a walking cane with her strong arms. Wang Di tried to hold on to those images but they were quickly replaced by others more familiar to her. Two women, infinitely young. Bruises inked on their faces and bodies. Dirt and skin under their nails because they had stopped caring. A pool of water gathering in the hollow of Huay's clavicle.

Wang Di rode the lift back up, closed the door and looked around her, at the things she had brought in over the course of the last few weeks. All to obscure the white walls, the space within her empty little cage. Soon, there would be enough even to block out the windows and she wouldn't have to hear the voices of other people, sailing up with the hot air, the sound of other lives going on around her, creeping into her dreams.

To meet the silence that greeted her each day, she filled the kitchen with sounds: the kettle's sharp cry, the round splash of hot water into her tin mug, and the clinks her spoon made while she stirred in a half teaspoon of sugar. These were sounds she was used to. She poured coffee into two mugs, put pastry on two plates, same as every afternoon. Then she turned around to look at her new apartment, at how she had, in the span of mere weeks, gathered and crammed so much into the bit of space that it was starting to look exactly like her previous flat, the home she had lived in for years and years. The Old One had tried to stop it from getting out of hand in the very beginning, the first year they were married. Once he went as far as leaving the flat with a filled trash bag when it was still dark out so that he could get rid of them without her knowing. It took her a day to realize that they were gone; the things he had taken were old clothes, washed, worn and mended until they couldn't be saved anymore. Instead of discarding them, Wang Di had pushed them into the back of the wardrobe. She told herself that she couldn't live without them – the buttons that could be repurposed, the quilts she could patch together with their varying block and floral patterns of blue and pink and green. When she realized that he had disposed of the lot of them, the absence of these objects – their very potential – lurked between them like a third party in their marriage. Less than a week later, she had already begun assembling a small collection of plastic bottles, string and shopping bags in the wardrobe, beneath her trousers and under things. It took little time for them to spill over and into the sleeping area. The Old One left them alone this time.

Now, she pictured undoing all of it – pulling open the tops of the boxes in the kitchen so that their insides, a mass of red or blue plastic bags, sprang out. There were four boxes filled with these, and one with red rubber bands, all coiled into each other. Under the bed were loosely bound bales of cotton and satin, more boxes, and one suitcase falling apart but filled with cloth samples. And the dining table. That would be last. She thought about sweeping everything on it into a large bin bag. It was covered with mail that had arrived since she moved in; all of it lay unopened, unread.

What would happen if I got rid of it all? Nothing, she told herself, even as the thought sat her down, making the chair yelp. She would get rid of everything except for the large furniture and kitchen things. Except for the Old One. Except for his things.

That night, she had just closed her eyes when she heard him. A long, throaty exhale, just the kind of sound he used to make when he was falling asleep. She was so sure of it that she sat up and put the light on, even touched his pillow (his side of the bed, the sheets, which she was surprised to find were cool) to make sure that he

hadn't been there, wasn't still there, really, it was just her ears playing tricks. In the end she sat up half the night listening out for him.
Her mind wandering back to their first evening together after their
truncated wedding ceremony where the only guests had been her
parents and Meng. They had not touched each other then. Not that
first night. Nor the next. He hadn't asked for anything from her. Not
even tried to until she went to him, the end of that week because
she had wanted to. She had been nervous, going to bed. Her head
had been filled with the scent and warmth of him, gathered in her
all day. And she had moved towards him, under the thin covers, after
he settled in. Pushed her face into his chest the way she'd seen that
starlet with her beloved in the only movie she'd ever watched. Soon
Wei had taken his time. Undressing himself before asking her if it
was okay to undress her as well. Lifting her top off her, as if he was
afraid to even brush her skin with the cool cotton, and then kissing
her face. First her left cheek, then her right, before moving on to her
neck and collarbones. How different he had been. Wang Di was glad
she remembered this. The details as fine as if they'd been sketched
just yesterday. That night, as she listened out for him, she let herself
bathe in this one memory until she fell asleep again.

The next day, she sleepwalked through her collection round,
wanting to hold on to the feeling of him almost being there.

It was this that slowed her down. She was opening the door to her
apartment when she heard the phone and hobbled over just in time
to pick it up and hear a solid click, then the dial tone. Still, she held
on to the receiver and whispered, 'Hello, hello? Is that you?' before
putting it back in its cradle.

'If that was you, call me again. I needed time but now I'm ready.
Call me.' Even as she said this, she was ridiculing herself. Stupid old
woman. Crazy old woman. Like the neighbours said.

August 1945

When they found me, I was unconscious, lying at the edge of a farmer's field. They said it looked as if I had tired of working the earth at midday and decided to take a nap in the grass. That's what it looked like, if not for the abandoned huts just paces away, all of them torn wide open by a bomb years ago. All that lived in the ruins were insects and mould born from that comfortable damp, and clouds of mosquitoes hatched from ephemeral pools formed in broken bowls, a child's wooden top, crushed underfoot.

When I woke a day later, I reached out for the baby, wanting to pull him to me for his morning feed. Instead, my hand found nothing but air. That was when I remembered what I had done. How I had done it. I wanted to cry for my loss but was too tired, too hungry to do so. So I slept until the sound of birdcall, sharp and very close, jolted me awake. Mynahs, I thought, opening my eyes. The room was filled with harsh, midday light and the air stung with the smell of disinfectant.

'You're finally awake. Here…' A nurse put her arms around my shoulders and helped to sit me up. She brought me my lunch, sat next to me, and held the empty tray in her lap as I ate. She told me that a woman and her children had come across me while they were out digging for root vegetables.

'When they brought you in, we all thought you were –' She shook her head, catching herself. I continued eating, following each tiny trail of food with the spoon, scraping it clean. When I returned the bowl to her, she said, 'Oh, I almost forgot to ask. We couldn't find any papers on you so I'll need you to give me your name and address.'

I looked away and said nothing.

She tried again, repeating her question first in Malay, then faltering Hokkien, to make sure that I understood.

I shook my head.

'Do you know where your parents are?'

'No.' I paused. In that moment, I heard the other people in the ward, different voices, different languages and dialects, telling each other about who and what was left in that place they used to call home. They talked about leaving the hospital and returning to their lives as soon as they could. They talked about what they would do, afterwards.

Afterwards. I had thought about this moment for so long, swung between shame and hope so many times in the past few years, that faced with it now I felt paralysed. Shame or hope. Both. Afterwards was nothing like I thought it would be.

'I'm sure someone is looking for you.' The nurse touched my shoulder. I flinched, and wished I hadn't when she removed her warm hand. But she didn't seem to mind, continued talking, informing me that I had an infection, that they were giving me medicine for it. I let her finish. It only occurred to me to ask when she was about to leave.

'Did they find anyone else? Did they bring anyone else here?'

'Anyone else?'

'Other girls. My age. They would have worn the same clothes...' I looked down and realized only then that my dress was gone. Instead I was wearing a white cotton gown, soft from washing.

'No, I don't think so but I can ask around and let you know if there was anyone...'

I nodded and stared down at the sheets. When I looked up again again, she was gone.

I fell asleep easily but woke repeatedly in the night, convinced that I'd heard Cheng Xun whimpering. And I would find myself lying on my side, my body curled around an empty oval on the bed, the way I'd slept for the past two months. My chin just above the top of his head. Each time I remembered he was gone, I squeezed my eyes shut, wishing I hadn't been found. When I woke again, it was morning. The nurse on duty gave me my medicine and urged me to get up, get my blood flowing a little or else I was going to develop bedsores. She stripped the blanket off me and stood with her hands on her hips until I slid my feet off the bed.

I got up because what else was there to do? I made rounds on my floor, staying close to the wall in case my legs gave way. Most of the rooms I passed were filled with soldiers, mostly ang moh, who looked nothing like the proud, striding foreigners I used to see in the city. These men looked like mere clutches of twigs, skin stretched so tight over their ribcages that I could easily imagine fitting my fingers between each curved bone. Then I passed a tall window and saw the length of my own body reflected in the glass. Stopped with the shock of recognition. I looked years older. A withered stalk of a woman. Then I saw my mother's face in my own and stood staring until it became too painful to look.

When the nurse from the day before came back to check on me that afternoon, I asked for a sheet of paper and a pen. I wrote my name on it, pressing so hard that the nib went through the paper several times, marking the white bedspread. When I was finished, I handed her the paper. 'That's my name. Ng Wang Di.'

I told her my address and she repeated it back to me to make sure that she got it right.

'It won't be easy, finding them. I don't think anyone in my village has a phone.'

She nodded and said, 'I'll try my best.'

I thanked her. If she had stayed on, I might have told her that I hadn't seen my family in years. That I had been put away for a long time, and it was the time spent away that made me this way, made me speak as if each word was a cold stone in my mouth, and my thoughts rough-cut gems that I was reluctant to spit out. I might have told her I was afraid my family wouldn't want me back. That too much had happened. I would have told her, but the look in her eyes, careful and searching, suggested that she'd arrived at the truth on her own. The sun was past its peak when I fell asleep again. This time I dreamed that I was back in my little room in the comfort house. Cheng Xun was next to me and he seemed hungry for the first time in days. Relief flooded my chest and I was unbuttoning my top to feed him when I woke, blinking into the bland light of the hospital ward. My breasts were aching with milk, had made damp, dark spots in the hospital gown. It was then that I realized I wanted to be back there, in the black-and-white house with its boarded-up windows, and I wondered why I had run, why I'd left.

I woke on my fourth day in hospital to find my mother watching me. Another dream, I thought, like the dreams I kept having of my baby, and reached out. Except when I touched her arm, I felt warm skin. Dry and sun-scored, but alive.

She was smiling a terrible, painful smile when she said, '*Nu er.*' Daughter. Compounding my disorientation. *Nu er.* How many times had she called me that? Never, I was sure. I wanted to tell her, this woman, that she had the wrong person. That I was sorry, I wasn't who she thought I was.

'Don't cry, don't cry,' she said, 'or you'll make your ma cry again.' She touched my face with her hand, and it was this that finally woke me. Her hands, I knew. The hands I knew from her slaps and pinches, the yanks they dealt when she thought I was being too slow. I felt the familiar strength of them, the grip of her bones, her work-ready muscles, as she helped me up to sitting.

'Ma,' I said.

For several minutes, all we could do was stare at each other. She looked as if she had aged a decade, and as she got closer, more. The skin over her cheeks was drawn down, caved in where her molars used to be. On both sides of her mouth, deep grooves stretched and deepened as she spoke, reminding me of the wooden puppets I once saw as a child, their jaws falling open and snapping shut at the twitch of a string. I wondered if she could see what had been done to me. What I had done. And it was this last thought that made me regret not having washed that day. I would have spent the morning scrubbing myself if only I'd known. Instead, I pulled back from her and hid my hands under the sheets so she wouldn't touch them.

Twice she started speaking – 'I thought you were…' – 'Never imagined I would…' – only to choke and swallow her words each time. Eventually she managed to say, 'It's been so long.'

I nodded, wondering if I could speak again, trying to remember the things I used to say in my past life as a daughter, someone's child, but I wasn't sure there was enough of me left. For a few moments I was almost frantic, afraid that the person I was before – their unplanned-for daughter, their Wang Di – had disappeared entirely. The way a body burns and leaves nothing recognizable in its wake. Just a few shards of bone, ash. Handfuls that slip away in the wind.

I took to parroting her or giving monosyllabic answers but she did the bulk of the talking, asking few questions, making observations. 'You're so thin.' 'So are you.' 'Your father couldn't make the trip.' All the things I wanted to say filled my throat, stopped right in the middle so that I could only swallow and stare. It was all I could do not to choke on everything that I couldn't put into words.

'I brought you something – in case they aren't feeding you well here,' she said, getting out a tiffin tin filled with rice porridge, and on top, sweet-potato leaves stir-fried with chilli paste. The sharpness of the flavours made my eyes prick with tears. After a few hurried gulps, I felt the burn of the food in my stomach and made myself slow down. I knew I would be sick later but I couldn't stop. As I ate, my mother told me about my brothers: how Meng had stopped going to school ages ago, how Yang was away – the Japanese had sent him off the island to work. She didn't know where. The last she had heard of him was in 1943.

'Work? What do you mean, work? How long has he been gone?'

'For a while now. Years. After they took you –' Here she shook her head, as if to deny the memory of what had happened. 'We waited and waited for you to come back. And when you didn't… He got the idea to go to the Japanese police to try and find out where you had been taken. This was a few months afterwards…in 1943. He went with a neighbour, one of the Tan boys – he was the one who told us that the police had taken Yang, arrested him for no reason. We thought he was in prison but got a letter from him towards the end of the year – just a few lines saying that he was in Thailand. Nothing after that.'

He's dead, I thought, and looked down so I wouldn't have to see the fervid hope on my mother's face.

'Don't look so worried. I've been praying to Guan Yin for you and your brother. And see? It worked! I'm going to keep looking for Yang. When everything has settled down, he's going to turn up. Just like you did – I knew when I saw Nurse Noor that it was good news.' I pictured the nurse getting off the bus, walking the long way into the kampong while people stared from windows and doorways. I should thank her, I thought. 'Your father will be so happy to see you. He stopped working for the Japanese last November and has been looking for a job ever since. Things are so bad that it can only get better. Oh, he will be so happy to see you. You don't know how worried we all were. Three whole years.'

Two days later, my mother helped me into the trishaw that was to take us home. The journey took us through busy streets, past cars and buses and lorries, carrying people and goods meant for somewhere else; things happening that did not involve soldiers, trucks or planes. There were hawkers tending their food stalls and people bent over bowls of noodles at wooden tables, women bargaining for their groceries, people selling bundles of vegetables and sweets from a tray strapped to their necks. All of this bathed in a morning light so sharp it made my eyes water. Things had gone on. I felt my stomach churn with this realization. Once in a while though, I spotted figures, stock-still amidst all the movement and noise: an old man, mere skin over bones, squatting by a wall. Another, talking to himself. No one else seemed to see them or mind their presence, passing them as if they were walking past a tree or mailbox or a lamp.

Then I saw her. Lying in a gutter, her face half hidden behind matted hair. It looked as if she had been there for a day or two; flies were beginning to settle on her face but she made no movement to brush them away. Huay? I thought, leaning out, causing my mother to exclaim and clutch at me as if she thought I was about to leap out of the moving trishaw. But the woman's face was too sharp, and I could tell that she was older and much too tall even from where I was. *Shen jing bing*, I told myself, insane. Huay was dead. This was just another woman. Just another. I wondered where she had come from, if her family was still alive and looking for her or if they preferred her gone, like this. I thought about Jeomsun, hoping that she had left the island, gone back to her family and mountains in Korea.

My muscles tightened as we entered the village and I had to open and close my fists to get my hands to relax. There was young fruit in the trees, light green against the dark of the leaves. Stray cats on the dusty ground, showing their bellies to the sun. Home – I wouldn't have thought this possible a month ago. We passed a few houses which looked empty and others with familiar faces looking out, gawking. I wanted to disappear but Jeomsun's voice was in my ear all of a sudden, telling me to wave and ask what they were staring at. I ignored it best I could, pushed away her small, elfin anger, but wondered how my neighbours would react to my return and how much they knew.

'We're home,' my mother announced.

Home. I was just over the threshold when I froze and took a step backwards, fighting to keep acid from rising up out of my throat. I'd forgotten what it smelled like – home, a thing that used to be a bitter but steady comfort. Because underneath the scent of the kitchen, with its oils and heady sambal spices, was the smell of sun-browned skin, of male bodies and their sweat and dark, sweet breaths, all of it sharpened by the heat. It's just Ba and your brothers – no, brother, I corrected myself, act normal. Still I stayed by the door, watching my mother wait, her smile slightly fading. My father, sitting in his usual chair in the living room, had risen up, was extending his arms in welcome and walking towards me.

My body felt light. I could run, I thought. I could run now and never have to explain myself, or be around my father, my brother, both of whom I suddenly, unreasonably dreaded. It might have been this – my face, contemplating flight – that made my father stop. He dropped his hands to his side.

'You're back,' he said. Then, as if suddenly reminded of where I'd been for all these months, these three years, he looked at the floor and returned to his chair, holding on to the armrests as he sat himself down.

'Ba.'

He nodded. 'You're home now.'

I turned away, adjusting my eyes to the dim indoors and saw that my brother was crouching by the bedroom door, watching me. He was thirteen now, I realized, and a long way from when I'd last seen him. There were lines around his eyes. and below them, a darkness, as if he hadn't been sleeping.

'Meng?'

'Jie,' he replied, more out of reflex, it seemed, than anything else for even as he said it, he was getting up. I thought for a second that he was coming towards me, but he turned midway and left the house.

'Must be going out to play,' my mother said, bustling in the kitchen, not looking at me.

I went into the deserted bedroom. Everything was as it was. The spare rattan mat, which Yang used to unfurl on the floor at bedtime. That one pillow, which I always relinquished to Meng. I found my clothes stuffed deep into the bottom of the dresser, moth-eaten and much too big, and changed into them, hoping to feel like myself again. When I came out from the room, everyone was gone.

My mother went back to work that morning, hurrying in the hope that the water wouldn't be cut off before she had finished washing her basket of laundry. I offered to accompany her but she shook her head. 'You're as thin as a bamboo stick. You'll be no help.'

To make myself useful, I scooped out the sweet-potato porridge my mother had prepared before she left into bowls, filled a small dish with sambal. When everyone came back at noon to find the table laid out, there was an awkward shuffling before they sat down to eat, much too politely.

'Oh, you really didn't have to…' She made herself smile, shifting the bowls around.

'I wanted to be useful. And you, Meng, have you been going to school? Helping out?' I'd wanted to tease but the words came out shrill – sounding like a reproach.

Meng didn't look up. Instead, my mother replied for him, 'He went to school only when they were giving out milk. When they stopped doing that a year ago, he just stayed home. Helped out with the garden now and then. Isn't that right?' She moved her elbow to prod Meng into answering but stopped shy of touching him.

'Meng has grown but you look thin, both of you,' I said. Nothing. My parents darted their eyes up, then down. I realized then that I'd said something untoward and embarrassed everyone. I must have forgotten how to be myself, I thought, my old self. In the black-and white-house we'd talked about food, aches and pains, our various bodily functions. Said little else that wasn't about our bodies, survival. Three years.

My mother cleared her throat. 'We're okay. But only because we have the garden.'

They bolted their food. My brother and father got up to leave within five minutes of sitting down. Then it was my mother, murmuring about collecting the laundry. I sat there for almost half an hour, savouring every spoonful of sweet-potato porridge, looking at the damp rings their bowls had made in the wood. Wondering at the carved emptiness in my stomach even though I couldn't eat another bite. A feeling like homesickness. And I realized that it was gone: home. My idea of it. My place in it.

As I dried the bowls, I could see and smell the smoke from my father's roll-ups, hear his faint sigh as he stamped the last of it into the ground just outside the door, where he remained for most of the afternoon.

That night, the same thing happened though I said nothing. All three of them left the table within minutes of sitting down, my mother turning her back to me in order to wash the dishes at the sink, clanking and splashing as much she could to discourage me from talking.

I could be a ghost, I thought. One of those lingering souls that people just live with and skirt around, as long as it doesn't do them any harm.

At the end of my first week back, I had learned to talk about the weather, about how salty or good or bad the food was, about the neighbours. Nothing else.

Things were shifting back into place after the Japanese surrender. Schools were still shut, and my brother, left to his own devices, stayed outdoors most of the day except for lunchtime. It was a small house with little place to hide. Still, he managed to avoid almost all contact with me. When he returned, he said nothing, did not even acknowledge that I was in the same room or look up when I called out to him. I told myself to give him time, that he must still be getting used to me after not seeing me for three years. He was just a child, after all.

Dinners remained uncomfortable affairs. Afterwards, instead of sewing or doing homework and sitting by candlelight as we used to do, my parents retreated into the bedroom. Meng rolled out the mat in the sitting room and flipped through an old comic book until it got too dark.

I could hear him scuffling against the floor in his sleep as I lay awake in the bed we'd shared together when he was a child. Each time I fell asleep, I would startle awake again and reach for the baby, thinking I was in the black-and-white house. With sleep though, came dreams; I would see Huay and Jeomsun most nights, and if I was lucky, Cheng Xun as well. Then I would wake, my face damp, remembering how I'd left them like that. The relief of being back with my family and the guilt of it spilling over into each other so that I almost wished I hadn't survived. Almost.

Things will go back to normal, I told myself each day, almost believing it as I watched my family over dinner. Waiting for one of them to raise their eyes and look at me. I had been home for a week and they were still looking straight through me, half listening whenever I spoke. Meng, especially. He just needs time to get used to me again, I thought, pushing away thoughts of my baby, refusing to acknowledge that I saw him as a replacement of sorts. I told myself to be patient until I couldn't anymore. My mother had left for the public tap one day and my father was outside, smoking, when I went to my brother.

'Meng, why don't we go to the market? We can get you iced gems from the corner shop.'

His eyes flickered, tempted for a moment before he said, 'I don't want anything from you.'

'Don't be silly, you love iced gems. Come on. It's me, your –'

Leave me alone,' he spat, his voice lower, no longer a child's. 'Why did you come back?'

I was still staring, wondering the same thing when he continued, 'We thought you were dead. But they said you were living with the Japanese, those *riben guizi*. Do you know what that meant for us? For me? I lost all my friends. People talk about us. They gossip.'

It took me several beats to recover myself, before I said the first helpless thing I could think of. 'Who? What do they say?'

'Everyone. My classmates. They told me what you are. They called me a traitor, just because you're my sister.'

Before I found my tongue again, he was getting up. 'You should have just stayed with the *riben guizi*. You should have just stayed dead.'

The next morning, I followed my mother when she left for work in the morning, persisting even though she kept telling me to go back home. In the end, she let me carry the bucket and washboard as she knocked on the neighbours' doors and retrieved bags of dirty laundry from different women. No one paid me any mind. She was beginning to look more at ease when we ran into Yan Ling's mother.

'Eh! Wang Di, isn't it? Where have you been hiding her all this time? *Wah*…so skinny.' She reached forward to circle her fingers around my wrist.

I pulled away and put my hands behind my back.

My mother laughed. An empty, out-of-tune laugh. 'She was staying with family, up north in Malaya.'

Her eyes flickered. 'Oh, of course, of course… I don't know if you heard but my Yan Ling got married a few months ago. Moved to live with her husband's family.' She smiled and pointed vaguely east.

I wanted to ask her how Yan Ling was but my mother was pulling me away.

'Nice to have you back.'

People began to talk. It started quietly, with questions about where I had been, about what I had been doing during the war. My mother just smiled and murmured about having sent me to live with a relative in Malaya but it was a bald lie and her manner was too transparent. People started to sidestep us in the streets, tried not to meet our eyes even as the morning crowd at the market made it impossible for them to turn and walk in another direction. Customers stopped opening their doors when my mother came around and she lost precious work. Neighbours whom we had lived close to all our lives, whom I had known ever since I was a child, whispered among themselves whenever they saw me. Often, when they gossiped at the public outhouse, their voices carried in with the breeze, loud enough so that we caught snatches of conversation. They neither referred to me by name, nor called me 'Mrs Ng's daughter,' which they used to do. After several days I caught on. I wasn't Wang Di anymore, not to the neighbours anyway; what they called me instead was this: *wei an fu*, comfort woman.

I told myself that it could have been worse. That there were worse things to bear than this gulf between my family and me. Worse things than having to keep silent about Cheng Xun, about

Huay and Jeomsun. Years later, I heard about a girl who made her way home, only to have her parents proclaim that they had never seen her, never known her, or spoken her name in their lives. She waited outside the hut where she grew up until a storm started. Just as quickly as she had returned, she disappeared again, as if washed away by the rain and wind. And then there are those who didn't make their way home from the comfort houses; those who didn't board the ships that were meant to bring home prisoners of war and female captives from the neighbouring islands, believing – rightly or wrongly – that their families would never open their doors to them. So they stayed away. Then there are those who never got to choose, who didn't make it that far, not even close. Even Jeomsun, the most dauntless of us, had been rendered helpless in the face of this particular hope. Not of surviving, but of seeing her family again; it was the only thing that cracked her pragmatic facade – her manner becoming childlike when she talked about going home after the war, and then, a day later, almost collapsing inwards as she told me she would never be able to face her family again. I wondered if she had decided to return to Busan after all. If she'd made her way to the docks so that she could join the hordes of people clambering onto the ships sailing to Indonesia, Korea and the Philippines.

In the end, I told myself that my parents had lost too much to banish me as well. My mother clung on to the hope that my brother might return one day and though I knew Yang was gone for good, I said nothing to her. My mother's version of the truth – that her eldest son was stranded in another country, was surely making his way home – was the only one she could live with after my abduction, after the death of her parents in China.

'Such a pity that you never got to meet them, your *nai-nai* and *ye-ye*. Both of them passed away in the same week, first my mother, then my father. I only got the letters months after the fact,' she said as she chopped up sweet potatoes, tops and all, for dinner. 'I made my own funeral offerings to them with what little we had and prayed for their reincarnation. I also prayed for you and Yang, that they might help deliver both of you back home...' Here her words trailed off, as if she were still bargaining with her parents in her head – *just one more favour, one more before you move on and take the shapes of your new lives.* 'I knew that they were ill but there was nothing I could do. All they needed was some medicine, I think. If I'd had anything to spare...'

It was this. Her guilt and the thought that I would never know if I didn't ask now. 'But what about the money? Didn't you get anything? From the...the Japanese?' I could hardly say it. The words.

'What money? What are you talking about?' Then it dawned on her, what I was referring to, and she put the blade down as if making a point. Shame or anger crawled up her neck, splotching it pink. 'Don't think for a second that we got anything from the Japanese. Even if we did, we would've given it back if it meant that you could be returned to us.' Here, her eyes darted left and right. Whatever it was, the thought winged away as quickly as it'd appeared. My mother left the kitchen and I picked up the knife, a chipped, unwieldy thing, the cold metal a rude shock in my hand.

I let this fresh revelation steep in me for hours, let it gather in the pit of my stomach, believing it gone until I tried to close my eyes that night and found that I couldn't. The fact that my family had gotten nothing, that I had suffered for nothing, was less a surprise than an additional fact that I had to live with.

Years ago, my father had made a dusting motion with his hands when he mentioned how daughters were meant to be married off, how his family name would, thankfully, continue with Yang and Meng. I was, in the words of my parents during their most desperate (poorest) moments, useless. Disposable. In my little cell in the black-and-white house, I had comforted myself with the thought that my time there might give my family some relief in the way of much-needed cash for food or medicine. That there, at least, I wasn't absolutely useless. That it might make the difference between life and death for them. That was how I bore it, the rapes, the unforeseeable beatings, the humiliation of never having a choice when they told me to sit up, open wide, lie down and shut up. It was how I stayed my hand from reaching for the bottle of antiseptic and tipping the clear liquid into my throat, how I put the dress on every morning after my shower instead of ripping it, twisting the cloth until it became a pale-blue noose.

Did I do it to myself? Was it all me?

I was left to wonder what I'd been doing then. What reason I could give – if anyone asked or found out the truth – for doing what I had done in the black-and-white house if it hadn't been for my family.

This voice, my own, became another voice out of the chorus I had to listen to at night, when the quiet of the house and the village gave way to whispers, altogether as loud as a bell tower in my head, I heard over and over again – Mrs Sato's; the murmurs of the women around me, so soft they were nearly mute; the numerous men, at once faceless and distinct, and their deep laughs, thrumming through their bones and flesh and skin as they stepped into my room.

For the rest of the time I lived with my family, my mother and I spoke no more about Yang. All of them, Meng, my mother and father, avoided being alone with me, as if they were afraid any intimacy in number would encourage an outpouring on my part. I was, for most practical purposes, a person in quarantine; my sickness was without cure and kept eating away at me until I could hardly see anything of myself. All I could see when I looked at my reflection was Fujiko and it wasn't long after my return home that I broke the only mirror my family owned, a cheap plastic thing kept in the main room, which I had to step on in order to shatter. When it finally did, the little frisson of pleasure faded much too quickly and I had to put my foot down in the shards to ease the pain I couldn't reach. My father had walked in then, and looked at me as if watching one animal ravaging another. His face one of blank horror. It was then that I knew my parents might never again see me for who I was. My father said hardly anything to me at all unless it was by way of my mother; the things he did say were confined to the topic of food, either in a single directive: 'eat' or a question: 'have you eaten' or 'aren't you going to eat' when I stopped midway through dinner. He couldn't save me then, and must have felt helpless for years. Now that I was back, it seemed he was determined to make sure I could survive, albeit in the most elemental way, by bringing home food from the kitchen garden and making sure I ate. There was no malice in his demeanour, but his eyes flickered, lost, whenever they had to meet mine. There was only one way they could deal with this, one last thing they could do to secure my future.

'I think it's time to find you a match,' my mother announced one evening over dinner. 'Auntie Tin will take care of it.'

I said nothing and looked up at my father. His eyes were dull but he pulled the corners of his mouth up into what he thought was an encouraging smile. I simply nodded.

I took to going out only in the morning, before dawn. Sometimes I saw the night-soil man – stooped, old as water – carrying his full buckets from the outhouse and bringing back the empty ones. He would cross to the other side of the lane whenever he saw me and I thought at first that he was shunning me too, until he nodded one morning as I passed. Then I realized he had always done it, that people had always crossed the street to avoid him. Then another thought: that there were people who didn't know who I was, what I had done. It was during one of these walks that I stopped in front of a house with teal-blue shutters, just like ours. I knew without knowing how that it was Huay's. It seemed to be empty; there was no sign of life; no chickens roaming in the front yard, no guard dog barking. Not a sound inside either.

I went to my mother as soon as I arrived home. 'Ma, do you remember Huay? Family name Seetoh. They had a little shop. Lived in the west of the village.' The girl who had been taken along with me. The girl who did not come back.

'Yes, of course.' She didn't look at me but concentrated on tapping out spoonfuls of ground coffee into a pot. 'They bought a shop space in Ang Sua and moved there.'

'Where? Do you have an address?'

'Oh, no. I don't know. It happened very quickly. Why do you ask?' There was a grainy edge to her voice, warning me away but I made fists with my hands and watched as she lit a match and dropped it into the charcoal stove.

'The girl... She was there too. In the camp.' My face started to burn and I couldn't tell if it was from the heat of the fire or from my words. 'That's where I got to know her. Huay and another woman. Jeomsun. They were my friends. We were –'

'Auntie Tin is coming this afternoon,' my mother said, working the fire roughly, making it spit. I took a deep breath to continue but she turned around and said, 'Don't.'

'Don't tell anyone. Not me or your father or any of the neighbours. Especially not your future husband, no matter how kind you think he is. No one must know. You need to forget her, Huay, and the other girl. They didn't exist. You understand?' She reached out and I backed away, thinking she was going to strike me. But she gripped my arm and pulled me forward, as if trying to shake me awake. 'Understand? It's for your own good.'

I nodded then wiped my face, rubbing the wet between my fingers until my hand became clammy, then damp.

'Why don't you go and wash? You need to look nice for Auntie Tin.'

I nodded again but went to bed instead. Remained lying there until the matchmaker arrived, just after breakfast. My mother had to come and get me, leading me out as if I were a puppet on strings.

Auntie Tin did not smile this time. 'I'm not going to lie to you. It wasn't easy but I found someone who's interested.' She paused to look at me, knitting her brows as if to add *think before you reject him*. She was the first one to hold my gaze since I got home and I looked back defiantly, wondering if my eyes were still red and how much my face told. The gold and jade on her arms were gone, leaving her strangely naked. Her cheeks were thinner and there were a few strands of grey in her curled hair but she hadn't changed otherwise. I nodded.

'He's a bit older than you and a widower, but he's reliable. A tailor. Hardworking. I usually don't do this for the men but he had a picture and he gave it to me, to show you.' Auntie Tin brought a palm-sized, black-and-white photo showing a man in his thirties from the chest up. His face was open, and there was a dimple in the corner of his mouth, as if the cameraman had caught the beginning of a smile. He wore a pair of dark-rimmed glasses, but his eyes shone through them clearly, looking right into the camera. I didn't know anything else about him but I thought I could guess what his voice might sound like. He would have stories for me – ones that I would listen to and ones that I would not be ready for until years and years later.

I nodded at Auntie Tin. 'His name?'

'Soon Wei. Chia Soon Wei.'

Kevin

Time is a funny thing. Or time is relative, like I read somewhere. A relatively funny thing – how it speeds by when you have something to look forward to or when you need to get something done desperately (like trying to finish forgotten homework on a Sunday night by the light of a torch under your blanket, or when your Chinese-language teacher catches you in a lie and you have to see her at remedial class in three weeks). How it slows down when you have nothing to do. Especially when you have nothing to look forward to, to see how close you're getting. Like walking in a big empty field and never getting to the edge of it. When you have both of that, both wanting and not wanting for minutes to go by, time wobbles. If I squeeze my eyes shut I can almost see it, moving in front of my eyes and under my eyelids in a white wave.

This was how time went for the next two weeks: slowly, when I was alone during the day, then much too quickly once the sun had set. I wanted time to keep still, for night to stop tipping over into morning but it kept on ticking and tipping and ticking, until my two weeks were up and it was the Sunday before the start of remedial week. I acted as if it were like any other Sunday, that it wasn't the day before End Times, and accompanied my mother to the market. I was waiting for her at the aquarium stall when Albert sauntered up next to me. There was a cobalt and crimson Siamese fighting fish, with a tail longer and wider than its body. Fanned out, the fish filled up most of the space, no bigger than a coffee can. I was watching it and ignoring Albert when he started tapping on the tank, making it dart and peck at his finger each time it met the glass.

Before, I would not have said anything. Would have walked off, or pretended that I wasn't bothered by how he was taunting the creature. Instead of shrinking away though, I remembered the way Albert had sat outside his flat for hours, begging to be let back home. One night his mother had left him there as, one by one, all the lights in the building opposite went out. It was close to bedtime when Ma went over to talk to Mrs Goh. Before he went back in, Albert had looked at my mother with a mixture of gratitude and fury – as if he hated being seen like that, his face puffed and shiny from his tears. Sometimes this was who I saw. Not Albert the class bully, but Albert who was sometimes made to kneel outside, who came to school with cuts from the bamboo cane all over his arms and was sometimes made to chew a handful of bird's-eye chilli for speaking out of turn. After all that had happened last week, I saw him for who he was – no more than a child, like me, subject to the whims of the adults around us, to the world. We knew nothing.

'Stop that,' I told him now.

'Stop what?' But he did, putting his hands in his pockets. I waited for him to start shouting names at me. Instead he continued standing next to me. I saw his glance sweep the top row of goldfish, then down to the little mud-coloured ones at the bottom, meant to be dropped into the tanks of predatory fish as live feed, and I knew that he was reading the names. Arowana, kissing gourami, guppy.

After a minute he asked, 'Did you finish your homework for Lao Shi?'

It took me two seconds to get over my surprise but I said no, there was so much. I'd only done half.

'Me too... I hope she doesn't get too mad. She's scary.'

I could only nod. His mother came over then, her arms weighed down with plastic bags, two of Albert's siblings at her side. He turned to me and waved goodbye, slapping his flip-flops hard against the wet floor so that brown water splashed up around our feet.

Monday arrived. I had been up half the night dreading the alarm clock. It felt like I had just fallen asleep when it started to beep and I pressed the snooze button so many times that my mother had to come in and pull the covers from me.

When the van pulled up in front of the school gates, I had expected Lao Shi to be standing by the main entrance, arms folded and waiting for my parents to drop me off, or for her to call me out the minute she stepped into class. Neither of those things happened. She didn't even look at me. Not once. Not when we did listening exercises and dictation, not even when it was my turn to read aloud a paragraph of text. I made mistakes, tripping on words, skipping some entirely because I couldn't identify the characters, but she corrected me, calmly, quietly, as she paced back and forth in front of the room. When I sat back down, I started wondering if it had even occurred in the first place. Maybe it was all in my head – my grandmother's confession, the letters, me going to Lao Shi for help.

I had almost made it until the end of the morning, was packing my bag when it happened.

'Lim Wei Han, please stay behind after class,' she said, scribbling something in her notebook.

This is it, I thought, hoping it would be over quickly, whatever it was. A caning. Or writing *I will not lie* a thousand times. I would gladly take any punishment as long as it did not involve phoning my parents. Please, Ah Ma, I thought, do this for me and I will get you your favourite kueh every Sunday for the rest of my life. I waited for everyone to leave the room before I went up to Lao Shi with my head bowed, fingers braided behind my back. Looking sorry always helped.

A rustle. She's getting her ruler out, I thought.

'Here.'

I looked up to see her holding out a plastic folder. Flapping it in her impatience.

'Go on, take it. And close your mouth.'

I could see the lightly-yellowed paper through the clear plastic, the decades old creases in it now almost smoothed out.

I think I said thank you. I'm not sure I did.

'I don't know what you're trying to find out and I don't want to know,' she said, one foot already out of the door, 'but the national archives might be useful. They have a website and a good search engine. It's all in there.' She pointed at the folder I was clutching to my chest. Then she was gone.

The library was cool and absolutely silent. The only other people in there, besides the librarian, were two girls, sitting in front of a book about dog breeds, turning the thick pages together.

I took a seat at the other end of the reading table and got everything out of the folder. Something felt different. I turned the first page and saw that there was a sheet of foolscap tucked behind it, brand new and crisp clean. The words on it were in English, written in Lao Shi's flowing script. I flipped through the rest of it and saw that she had inserted her translations after each letter. I read all of it. All the way to the end. It was only then that I found the last page, one that I had overlooked. It had been written on the back of the original letter.

'Oh,' I said out loud, making the two girls and the librarian look up; the librarian put her index finger to her lips.

The ink on this latest letter was bright blue and new. This was the last letter Ah Ma had written. After I had read it, I went to the computer terminal and typed in the web address that Lao Shi had written down for me. In the search bracket, I typed in *Chia Soon Wei* and pressed enter. The screen blinked, then, *6 Audiovisual and Sound Recordings*. I clicked on the first link. It took me through to a page with information about the content – the date: *26/02/1983*; what it was – *audio recording*, what it was about: *Interview with Chia Soon Wei On His Experiences During the War*. Below, in the synopsis bracket: *Mr Chia Soon Wei, whose family was massacred by the Japanese during World War II, recounts his experiences during that traumatic period.*

But there was nothing I could click on to listen to it. Instead, it said, *No preview available. Contact us to request for access to the full recording.*

I clicked on all six links. None of them provided a clip that I could listen to. When I clicked on *Contact us* the screen blinked again and sent me to a page with a telephone number and an address. I copied everything down in my notebook. When I stopped and looked around me, the girls were gone and it was beginning to get dark outside. The clock showed five past four.

'It's going to rain, boy. Better leave now if you want to stay dry,' said the librarian.

I got up, shoving everything into my bag. I had to run.

28th December 1945

Chia Soon Wei,

Please forgive the abruptness of my salute. I have thought about you so much that I feel I should address you like a friend or a relative. There is no suitable word between 'Hello' and 'Dear' to address someone I've never met. 'Hello' and 'Hi' sound like we have already been in contact for a while and you were expecting to hear from me. Or it sounds like a stranger writing to ask for something and trying to cloak the request in familiarity. Which is what I am doing, really. Isn't it? The thing I'm asking of you? I'm asking you to let go. I'm asking you to forget.

Sincerely,

Anonymous

3rd January 1946

Chia Soon Wei,

This is the fifth letter that I have started. I wrote four others, read them over and over for days and then put them under my mattress. I don't want you to find me but I want to tell you how it happened that day, nearly four years ago.

I wasn't even meant to be there. None of us were, but they told us that the city wasn't safe, so we abandoned our home in the first week of December, leaving behind school and work and neighbours to move to the village. My father told us that we were moving to Bukit Timah, just to be safe, and my mother chimed in after him to say that it was only for the time being. She said it over and over again while we were packing, refusing to mention the war. Not even once. I wondered how we were all going to fit in my grandparents' attap house; my parents, and me and my five siblings, plus my oldest brother and his wife and little boy, just over a year old, but I knew not to ask. My mother said to bring only the necessities so I put together a few sets of clothing, a hairbrush, a mirror, paper and pen, two novels, and wrapped it all in a cloth bundle. Then, a few minutes before we left for the bus, I untied the bundle and added in a few more books. I even brought homework with me. On my last day of school, my Chinese teacher made me stay behind after class. She handed me a book, Dream of the Red Chamber, the cover of it worn like cloth. It was her own copy, she said, and she wanted it back when I returned to school. As I flipped through it I saw her name on the inside of the cover, the inscription someone had written in flourishing script. She told me that I needed to go back to school as early as I could to start preparing for the senior exams the following year. I was already too old, older than the other girls in class because my parents didn't have the money for the textbooks and the uniform and school fees until my oldest brother started work and could contribute to the household. We'll start preparing for the exams when this is all over, she said. When this is all over. I never started on Dream of the Red Chamber and I never saw her again. This is the first time since It happened that I've thought about Yeh Lao Shi, about Chinese classes, which I liked the most. About school and my single set of uniform, which I had to keep studiously clean throughout the week. I remember being nervous about the senior exams, how I knew I wasn't going to do well since there was never any time for me to study; my mother needed me at the stall and around the house. The book she lent me is back in the ground, burned and broken like the rest of my grandparents' home. Burned and broken like everything else in the village.

Your village. Sometimes I think about how I might have passed you on the way to the market when I lived there. We might have looked up to nod a polite hello and then walked on. Sometimes, right now, I walk past someone on the street and imagine that it might be you, that I saw the boy's smile, his eyes in the face of a passing hawker or a bus conductor. You don't know my name but if I send you this letter, you will know me as the only other adult in that village who survived. The other person who lived, and then took from you.

I want to tell you how I came to be there, and how I survived that night. And then I want to tell you how much I need to keep the child even though I think you might be his father. But I sit here and I realize that there is nothing I can say. There is nothing to explain why I cannot return him. You lost people, just as I did. I thought I had lost everything until I found the child. I found him and kept him safe when no one else could take care of him. If I do this, if I return him to you now, I will have lost everything all over again.

Sincerely,

Anonymous

17th January 1946

Chia Soon Wei,

I think about it sometimes. How we might have lived not more than twenty paces from each other. You and your wife. Me and my family. There were eleven of us crammed into my grandparents' attap hut. My grandparents were pleased to have us at first. A family reunion, my grandmother had said, clapping her hands together. But she got worn out quicker than she expected, I think. She tried to make the best of it but there were so many mouths and hands and voices that she started to hide in her bedroom during the day. Or maybe it was the air raids at night that did it, tired her out like that. Some people say they got used to it, running to their bomb shelters in the ground. We had ours in the back garden, lined with pieces of wood and sacks of dirt. One night, when the sirens started to cry, my grandmother refused to leave the house, saying that she would rather die in her own home than be found in a hole like an animal. She wept and held on to the leg of the dining table. Eventually, while the skies buzzed and trembled

288

overhead, my father and grandfather dragged her out by her armpits as she wailed, her fists held to her heart like she had been stabbed. Once she was in the shelter though, she stopped. She pulled my nephew into her lap and stroked his head until the shelling ceased and we could go back into our homes.

Not that they helped us much, the shelters, did they?

I don't know why I am alive today but I know how. I remember exactly the way I did it, hiding behind my older brother when the first shots thundered in my ears. I felt a searing pain on my leg and stepped back. No one screamed, but the circle tightened, all of us moving into each other. Then my brother stumbled, tripped over my feet and fell, taking me down with him. One by one, the others around us fell too. I closed my eyes and kept still while the soldiers came around to check, pushing their bayonets into my sister, my father. Then someone began to call out short, sharp commands. I heard the dry cracks of doors being broken down and the splintering of glass. I thought they were simply pillaging, taking food and anything else that was valuable until I smelled the char of wood and palm leaves. We're going to burn, I thought. But the wind was low that night. For hours, everything smouldered until only we remained. Us, and the trees around the village. I kept still until after they left, until nightfall. Then I got up, pulled myself out of that tangle of limbs and torsos. My clothes were damp and stained red-black but none of the blood was mine. I found a wound on my left calf, a graze, little more. I remember shivering and thinking that I had never felt cold like this before. I thought some of the others might be keeping still as well, just waiting for the soldiers to leave. It was only when I started to call out, and then to look, shifting the now-cold bodies of my youngest brother, my mother and my father, that I realized I was alone. I was the only one.

Sincerely,

      Anonymous

19th January 1946

Chia Soon Wei,

Sometimes I forget that you exist and I forget about the letters that I've written until I go to bed at night and feel them crackling and shifting under the mattress, reminding me of what I have done. What I am doing.

I have only repeated the lie once. First to myself, practising what to say if anyone questioned me. Every day, I remind myself that my name is Lim Li San. Li San. Not Mui Joo. That the child's name is Lim Yong Xiang. The Japanese had killed my entire family. This part was true. I kept the story in my mouth for weeks, perfectly rehearsed, waiting and waiting for someone to ask me whose child this was but nobody did.

The truth was I hadn't been thinking. That day, I rose up out of the pile of dead (both my parents, my brother and his wife, my baby nephew, my siblings, my grandparents). I shook each of them, begging them to wake. When that didn't work I wanted to sit there until I was dead myself, but I got up. Something made me stand up. I wanted to run. That was the first fully formed thought to come to me. I wanted to run, as if I had done it, killed them all. I remember saying it out loud, I didn't do it. I didn't do it. Like I had gone mad.

Then I heard a sound. I thought it was a cat, at first. It was a small sound, barely there. I went towards it, towards another pile of people. Dead as well. Almost strangers. Then I saw a child. It could not have been more than a year old, it was so small. I picked it up and walked out of the village.

In the first few months after That Day, no one even looked at me. Everyone had somewhere else to run to, someone to look for or after, pieces of themselves to pick up off the ground. The city was broken. With the baby in my arms, I walked past my home twice, certain that I had missed a turn. It was almost an hour before I got my bearings, and then I found myself standing in front of nothing. A blank. It reminded me of when my second brother had his teeth knocked out falling from his bicycle, how he'd walked through the door, his mouth a gash of blood and black. The houses to the left and right of ours were gone as well and I could see right into our neighbours' homes, the fronts of the buildings torn away as if they were dolls houses, made of paper. One kitchen on the ground floor remained intact, woks hung up ready for use, a scarlet 'fortune' character for Lunar New Year still stuck on the far wall. People were wading through the rubble, cutting their ankles and hands on jagged concrete. There was nothing left. Nothing.

For a long while, I just stood there, staring at the fallen apart streets, the fallen apart people, until the baby started to cry. I shouldn't have done this, I thought, starting to panic. I hugged the baby to my chest and walked back in the direction of the village. In my haze, I got lost, ending up at nightfall in a town I'd never been in before. I was turned away at every house I went to but the last. When they opened up – husband and wife both squinting into the dusk – I knew that they would offer me shelter. What I didn't know was that they would do it for more than three years. Fatimah and Sayeed were almost as old as my grandparents. Over the next few days, they told me about how they had moved to Singapore from Trengganu, up north in the Peninsula, how they had eloped after their parents, on both sides, disapproved of the match. They smiled at each other as they took turns telling me this; the pride of having chosen each other. Then, Fatimah asked me about my family. When I told her, she held my hands and said nothing for a while. When she spoke, she said that this was my home now. I could stay for as long as I needed.

It was only after the war that I realized how much they had risked their own lives in order to protect ours. Sayeed came home one day to say that he had seen men being rounded up in the city and heard stories about women being dragged away from their parents. Chinese people, he said, they're taking mostly Chinese people. The next morning, Fatimah came into my bedroom with old sarong kebayas, floral, slightly faded *with age. She smiled as she folded and pinned the excess cloth around me, as she pulled the creases out of the silky fabric. Then she wrapped a scarf around my hair, tucking in each tendril that peeked out. Ah, she said, when she was done. Can pass.*

I passed for more than three years. Twice, during the first year, a truck full of soldiers arrived in the morning, knocking on each door in the kampong. Each time, Sayeed offered up all the eggs from his chicken coop. I could only freeze, holding the baby and looking at the ground as they swept up and down the length of the house looking for things they could take. Not again, I thought, not again. But each time, they left, leaving Fatimah and Sayeed a little poorer of sugar, flour and rice. Afterwards, Fatimah would touch me gently on the shoulder to tell me it was okay again but it would take days, weeks for me to shake myself free of the need to listen out for the sound of engines, of the need to run and hide.

It was three years before it all changed, before Fatimah fell ill and passed away. Sayeed followed soon after. I felt uneasy living in their home, as if the wooden hut were a strange and unwieldy animal that I couldn't tame. So when the air raids began again, bringing with them rumours about the end of the occupation, I decided to leave.

I didn't know what I was hoping for when I left the village with the child. That things were going to go back to the way they were before the war? That I would find someone back in the city, among the broken-down remains of our home? That the past three years were just a bad dream, maybe. I don't know. Maybe I needed to see the ruins of my old home again in order to remind myself that I needed to do something. That something needed to change. It was after that, after I walked past my old home, still a shock of black and rubble, that I decided to look for a zhai tang, a vegetarian hall for women. There was one I knew of, just a few streets away. When I knocked on the door, a woman with a shaved head and a grey robe waved me in, as if she had been expecting me. We sat down at a table and she poured me tea from a clay pot and asked if I had a job. When I told her no, she nodded and said that if I wanted to stay, I would have to do all the cooking and cleaning and laundry in place of paying rent. I would have to bunk with a few other women. And the boy, she said, looking at the child sleeping in my arms, the boy would be the only male in the house, no male visitors are ever allowed, she said, looking at me hard in the eyes to make sure I wasn't thinking about it. Then she took a sip of tea and asked if I was running away from anyone. I said nothing. She waited, then asked how many people I'd lost. Twelve, I said. I counted it again in my head before I repeated myself. Twelve. The nun remained silent while we drank our tea. When I was done, she stood up and motioned for me to follow her. We walked through the single-storey house and she pointed out the altar room, the dining room and kitchen, the sleeping quarters fitted close with bunk beds.

It's been a month since I arrived. Throughout the first few weeks, no one asked. There was a story behind this, they thought, not an interesting one, not a unique one, just another story that would remind them of why they left their families (or husbands, in some cases) to live in a shared home instead. Apart from the nuns, all of the women living in the zhai tang are older, unmarried, and working in the factories and on the roads. When they come back from work in the evenings, they perch on wooden stools in the front room, one knee folded up and pressed into their torsos, like white cranes in thick-brushed paintings. They talk about their employers, about work, about food, and always want to know what I am making for dinner, even though it is never very different from one day to the next. There is a little garden in the back where I grow sweet potato and tapioca to make up for the food shortages. While I clean the plants at the sink, they hover and teach me the different ways I could use the entire plant, tip to wormlike tail, for dinner. How just a spoonful of chilli paste makes even the rough, veiny leaves taste good. When they ask me questions, they want to know how old the boy *is, how he is doing on the limited rations, little else. They call me xiao mei, little sister, bring me extra milk powder and sneak in dried fish which I hide in his porridge, so the nuns won't see.*

The most difficult thing I have to do here is to go out to run errands for everyone, getting rations, buying thread and cloth to patch up the nuns' robes. Being outside terrifies me. I have to pass patrolling policemen quite often – there are many of them around to try and quell the looting and violence. Whenever I see anyone in uniform, I freeze and try to look the other way, sure they are looking for me. I would be called in to the station and there, they would show me where I had gone wrong, the bold lie in the strokes of my pen, clear for anyone to see. Where the identification papers asked for 'name', I had put in my sister-in-law's name, hoping as I wrote, that her relatives in Shantou would never find their way here. Then I put my nephew's name where it asked for 'child or dependant'. I kept it in mind when I went to collect the remains of my family. What was left from that day. It took some time but the police eventually got around to it. I'm their daughter-in-law, I told them, I was the only family they had left.

I am not afraid anymore, not of the police anyway. The way things went during the war and in the months right after taught me that none of them knew anything. No one was in charge, not really. They were only people, with no more knowledge than you or I, trying to cross things off a list. But maybe I'm the only one foolish enough to think this.

I still have to get used to it, my new name, but as long as I am writing to you, I am no one. 無名. I haven't heard my old name in years now – it is a name that makes me think about my past life, the one I will have to forget.

Sincerely,

Anonymous

1st March 1946

Chia Soon Wei,

On 12th February, I bought a bunch of white and yellow chrysanthemums and put it on the altar, next to plates of cake and fruit and tea. I don't have any photographs of my family so I lit up a handful of joss sticks and watched them burn down to nothing. I watched until my eyes watered and then I reminded myself that I had elsewhere to be, things to do. I picked up the boy and fed him some of the leftover cake. Anything so I didn't have to think about that day.

Something has changed since I started writing these letters. As if the very act of writing has shifted the air between me and the other women. The first time I did it, it was in the evening, with the child next to me, asleep. I got out some paper and a pen that I had bought earlier that day. The other women were talking or mending their clothing, fanning themselves slowly as they drank their tea. My pen was cheap and scratchy and as I wrote, the sound of it moving across the paper got louder and louder. At least that was how it seemed. But it was just the others stopping mid-sentence, turning around to watch. They put down their sewing and their sipping and simply watched. Finally, someone said, 'Ah Mui, what are you writing?' Someone else, dissatisfied with the question, added 'Who are you writing to?' I looked up and took just a second too long. 'Family,' I replied, 'in Guangdong.'

I don't think anyone believed me. After a few seconds, when it was clear that I wasn't going to explain just who these relations were, they went back to what they were doing, but quieter, staring from time to time. I could feel my face turning red so I stopped, got up and went into my room. As though they might be able to see what I was writing just from looking at my face.

I try to be careful. Sometimes, after I finish writing these letters, I fold them away or burn them. I tell myself that someone will find and read them and realize what I have done. That I was tempting fate. Lately, one of the sisters has taken to asking whom I'm writing to. She tries to look over my shoulder as she passes by, sucking the air from between her teeth. But I know she is illiterate so I don't bother to shield the sheet of paper I'm writing on. Read it if you want, I told her once, pushing my chair back to allow her to look. She'd walked away, sucking even louder on her teeth. I should take more caution; all it takes is a letter reader and a coin or two. That's what you would do, I think, if you received this letter one day and found yourself unable to read it. Then I tell myself that I shouldn't be writing to you. I shouldn't be thinking about sending these letters but I can't stop myself. After everyone else in the room has fallen asleep – the boy in a corner of our bed and the other five women in the room – my words run wild in the dark until my voice is all I hear and I have to get up and go to the kitchen with sheets of paper and a pen. When I'm done writing, I tuck the letters under the mattress, right beneath my pillow and fall asleep the moment I close my eyes. One day I might be brave enough to send them, or to turn up on your doorstep with the boy. One day I might be ready to let him leave me.

Sincerely,

    Anonymous

                               17th June 1946

Chia Soon Wei,

    This will probably be the last letter I write to you. Or one of the last. (Sometimes I forget that I never send them anyway, or want to but never will.) It's been a few months since I wrote and a few things have changed. I'm no longer living in the zhai tang *– the same sister who tried to read my letters began to watch me and ask me questions. She started asking them in private at first, wanting to know which village I lived in before the war, where in China my parents or grandparents grew up, what happened to my husband. I told her that I lived in Bukit Timah, and that my family came from Shantou, and left it at that.*

But neither of my answers made her happy and she made that little sucking noise with her teeth again as I walked out of the room. She waited a few days before repeating the questions, this time from the other end of the dining hall with everyone seated and eating. The clink and murmur of mealtime dwindled to a low and I felt as if someone had pressed a hot cloth to the back of my neck. My answers came out stammered, and in the warm, crowded dining hall, they sounded hollow and unfinished. A silence hung at the end of my words and all around the room, dark eyes and busy mouths were waiting, waiting for me to go on. But I said nothing, I couldn't, and went back to feeding the boy his rice porridge. The sister sat back and chewed, her jaw working in a rectangle like a goat's.

I spent the next few mornings at the market, asking around about work. In the end, someone told me that a family she knew was looking for a nanny. I went that very day and got the job on the spot. The parents are wealthy, English-speaking Hakka people; they wanted a Chinese-speaking nanny for their two children. I'm picking up quite a bit of English from the children and their mother though I can't read or write it of course. My favourite part of the job is reading them Chinese-language books and then going home with the stories in my head so I can tell them to the boy. My salary allowed me to move out and rent a shared room in Chinatown. I felt bad leaving but I knew I had to. It was the only way to stop the questions that were bound to come from the rest of the women.

It's harder now, here, but easier, in a way. I live in the second-floor room of a shophouse with five other people; labourers, mostly, women who finish their day with dirt under their nails and dust on their clothes, and one amah, who wears a white-and-black uniform and sometimes brings home leftovers from her employer's rich meals. Everyone has a plaid or floral curtain covering their bunk and it is behind this curtain that I'm writing. The landlady helps to mind the children (there are three in the shophouse building, including one of her own) during the day, and in the evening everyone makes their own food. The first day I was there, I asked if they paid for cooked meals and they hushed me, told me the landlady would suck me dry. Instead, I share a paraffin stove with my room-mates and trade ikan bilis, sambal, and halves or quarters of salted duck eggs. In the evenings, when it's cool enough not to have to fan ourselves, the landlady plays her records and all of us stop what we're doing to listen to 'Rose, Rose' or 'Shangri-La'. The women talk about wanting children and tell me how lucky I am to have a little boy. 'He's going to take care of you in a few years,' they say, and I want to ask why they put their hair up, why they chose not to marry but I don't. There wasn't any need to anyway, because Poh Ju showed me the burn marks down the side of her arm. A river of shiny, stretched-out skin. 'Hot water,' she said, peering over her own shoulder, a look of mild surprise on her face as if she hadn't seen it before, or hadn't looked at it closely for a long time. 'I ran away the next day.' She told me I would hear the other stories soon enough. Everyone had a good reason to be there.

I miss nothing about the zhai tang, *except for the garden and my plants.*

I'm sure you want to know how he's doing. The boy is fine. He is healthy and finally gaining weight after years of eating rationed food and root vegetables. He doesn't speak much, even though he must be around five years old now. Sometimes he wakes up in the night to scream and no milk or food or rocking will calm him. The other women in my room don't mind. Or they don't show that they do, which is good enough for me. One of them has a little girl of her own and she says it's because of the air raids from before. That it will pass. I don't ask her where her husband is and she doesn't ask me. No one does. Whatever they (my room-mates, strangers, the hawkers I buy my groceries from every week) think, it is something charitable and I get offered extra powdered milk, and leftover cuts of meat and bone from the butcher's wife when he is in my arms.

I want to ask how you are. But since I am the only one who reads these words, maybe I could say this: You are better ever since the war ended. You are living with your parents again, perhaps in their fishing village at the shore, or helping out with their pineapple farms that are doing so well now that people are starting to have more money to spend on food. You are still young and there is a woman next door with clear, round eyes, and dimples on her cheeks. She smiles at you whenever you pass each other on the street until you get the courage to ask to visit her at home one evening, you have nothing to lose anyway. Her parents like how hard you work, leaving home at five every morning and only coming home at six, and they nod when you ask them for their daughter's hand. You set up home with her, maybe even building it with your own hands. There is a large front yard for herbs and a mango tree, and an extra bedroom for the children you will have.

This is the least I can wish for you.

Sincerely,

Anonymous

2nd January 2000

To my son,

If you've read this far, it would mean that you now know much more than I have told you in the last fifty-eight years. So much happened during the war but there are some things I have been brave enough to do, and some things that I just couldn't face doing.

When I made up my mind to keep you, or rather when I realized that I couldn't return you, I wrote these letters. I started the first few determined to send them out to Chia Soon Wei, whom I believe to be your father. And then I wrote because I couldn't not. The same as when I kept you...because I couldn't not. I didn't throw the letters away either even though the threat of you finding them was enormous, especially when you started to read and write, because I wanted to use them to explain myself to you somehow.

I thought I could do it. I told myself that I had to tell you the truth when you turned eighteen. You had every right to know. When you reached your eighteenth, I changed it to twenty-one. Twenty-one turned to twenty-five. Eventually I stopped bargaining with myself. Like I said, there were some things that I just couldn't face doing.

My only hope was that you would stumble upon this after my death and I'm glad you have now. I hope that it's not too late and that you will forgive me someday.

Your loving mother

It took me ten minutes to run all the way home. The clouds were just beginning to break – a drop here and there – when I arrived. I got the shoebox out from the chest of drawers, found the piece of paper with the telephone number on it and dialled, thinking all the while that the roar in my ears was coming from my own head, my heart. I wanted to get it out as soon as I could, so when someone finally picked up, a woman, I said it straightaway – asked if she was Mrs Chia. She didn't understand me, so I asked again, in Chinese. She said yes, so I told her who I was and who I might be to her. She gave me her address and I asked if it would be okay if I went to see her that evening. After putting the phone down, I looked out of the window and realized what it was, the noise. Just the sky. Falling open.

Part Three

Part Three

Wang Di

Sometimes you don't realize that you have been waiting for something, sitting patiently for years and years, like looking out for the postman when you are expecting an important letter. You don't know until it arrives on your doorstep and stares you in the face. There is wanting and there is a kind of waiting drenched in hope. Like Wang Di's name, 'welcoming a brother'. The wait for someone who didn't exist yet. Who might not ever exist, but was longed for.

She had been waiting for so many years that it was almost no surprise when the boy called. The coming rain had driven her home, the sureness of it in the metal of the air, in the sound of the trees, the dry ache in her bones. When she heard the phone ring she was still turning her key in the lock and it took some time for her to slip out of her shoes and reach the phone, so she fully expected to hear nothing by the time she said hello. But when she did and she heard his voice, she could tell who he was even before he told her.

'Hello? Is this Mrs Chia? The wife of Chia Soon Wei?'

'Yes, yes,' she'd breathed.

'I think – I think I might be your grandson.'

He didn't sound sure. But she knew who he was. The Old One, she thought. Or more accurately, a *form* of him. You can meet someone's aunt or nephew or cousin and wonder how these two people could be related, they were nothing like one another. And you could meet two people and see at once which parts of them were exactly the same. (Their eyes, the way they talked and walked, she told him much later.)

When they agreed that he would come and visit straight away, Wang Di didn't want to hang up for fear that the boy was just an elaborate daydream or he would get off the phone and change his mind about coming to see her. So she sat there listening to the phone go *boop boop boop* in her ear for a minute before she got to her feet, wishing that someone else could have been there to tell her if this was really happening. She stood up, sat down again, and stood up to go to the kitchen. She filled the kettle and forgot to put it on the fire. Dropped freshly laundered clothes in the washbasin before realizing that they were clean. 'Oh, stupid, stupid,' she said, rescuing an undershirt and a pair of trousers, poking a finger at a blue-and-white blouse that was darkening wet. 'I could have changed into that,' she sighed, pinching her collar to her nose to see if it smelled old, of heat and sweat. 'Stupid,' she said again.

Then she gave up and gave in. Stood by the door to keep watch. When he appeared at the far end of the corridor, squinting at the numbers on the doors, she unlocked the gate and threw it open so he could see her. And he did, walking up to her determinedly, with a bowlegged gait, stopping only to shed his flip-flops and leave his umbrella outside the door. He walked straight in. The way someone might if they were used to how it looked inside her apartment. The way the Old One had, closing one dark eye to the mess. It didn't matter. The boy didn't care. He smiled. It was only when Wang Di tried to smile back, the corners of her lips trembling with effort, that she realized how nervous she was.

Watching him standing in the middle of the apartment she realized her legs were getting noodly-soft and she wanted to pull him to her and hold him there. She wanted to laugh and weep and cover her face with her hands, or at the very least, hold on to his arm as they talked. But she did none of that.

Instead, she cleared her throat for the fifth time and said, 'My name is Wang Di.'

'My name is Kevin. Kevin Lim Wei Han.' He stuck out his hand.

She stuck out hers. A plump, warm hand and a rough, twisty-barked one met. They shook. Wang Di didn't want to let go but she did.

'Do you want something to drink? Milo?'

'Yes. Thank you.'

She ran into the kitchen, rummaging and tipping things over until she found the green Milo tin. A chocolatey malt smell filled the kitchen. Ten cardboard-tasting biscuits next to the hot mug. When she got back, he was standing up, looking at the news clippings that the Old One had cut out, that she had put up again on these pristine new walls just days ago. The woman in a traditional Korean dress stared back at them.

She could hear the Old One's voice in her head, so close that she had to open her own mouth and spit out his words. 'That,' she pointed, 'is a review of a book about comfort women. And that one is an article about how the comfort women in South Korea have been demonstrating. But they're dying, the witnesses, one by one.'

He had nodded and nodded and looked at her with eyes just like the Old One's. Like he understood everything. Right then.

They sat back down again and it was all she could do to stop herself from smoothing his hair, and later, from staring as he ate all the crackers she had laid out. Wang Di smiled just watching him eat. It was only when she quietened down, got used to the fact of the boy being in her flat that she noticed the little tape recorder in his hand. When she asked him what it was for, he looked at the gadget as if seeing it for the first time.

'I'm using it to remember things. Like a daily journal. It's not that I'm going to forget this,' he said, 'or anything that you say. It's just…a habit. Like I can't help it anymore.'

She nodded. She knew all about habits that couldn't be helped.

The boy drank the last, sweetest dregs of his Milo and swallowed. 'I'm here because my grandmother told me… She said she took my father from his parents during the war. She told me this and then she passed away.'

She bobbed and bobbed her head to make him go on.

'But she did it to save him. She thought his parents were dead.' He picked up his school bag from the floor, unzipped the top and got out a bundle of letters, spreading them out on his lap to show Wang Di. 'She wrote all of these. She wanted my father to read them after she died but I was the one who found them instead…' Here he shrugged, a gesture that made him look older than he really was. Then he took out a picture and pointed at a face in it. 'And that one. That's my father.'

Wang Di wanted to tell him that the picture looked like a facsimile of the one Auntie Tin had given her – and how much the man in the picture looked like Soon Wei when she met him for the first time. She remembered him walking into her parents' home, dipping his head out of shyness. She wanted to say all this but a thickness had filled up her throat and she found she could only smile and nod, smile and nod; the tears gathering up behind her eyes, blinding her.

Kevin waited until he was sure the tears in her eyes were gone before he took a deep breath. 'Was it – did you lose a child? During the war?'

'Yes.'

'So it's true. He's my grandfather. And you're my grandmother.'

Wang Di shook her head. 'It wasn't your father I lost. Soon Wei and I never had a child together. I was his second wife. His first wife died in the war. I – I don't know how she died. I never let him tell me.'

'Oh,' the boy said, looking unsurprised, as though he were used to things not going his way, was, at his age (ten? eleven? Wang Di guessed) already sober to the fact of disappointments, of little things never quite adding up, of questions never getting answered, and never having any control over what was going to happen.

It made him seem older beyond his years, old and young in a way that children looked sometimes, when they smiled as little as Kevin did. It had only taken her more than fifty years, she thought, and what was fifty, when the words of the people you grew up with mattered so much they formed the breadth and depth of your life, shaped the path ahead of you. All of it had begun with her waking to the world, the name she had been given. The fact of her upbringing. And then, after the horror during what was supposed to be her best years, how her mother's words, the shame foisted on her by herself, her family and everyone around her, had dictated the silence that shadowed her every move after the war. And it was this that made her try to explain it all to Kevin the way she would have in the very beginning with her husband if she'd had the courage to.

It was near evening when the boy stood up. He said he had to leave. Wang Di nodded, of course, of course. Then, 'Does your father know all this?'

'No. I did this on my own, mostly.' He stopped then, the realization and the following pride of what he had just said spreading through his chest, up to his face in a slow smile. 'I'm going to tell my father though. He will want to know. Can I – can we – come back to visit? After I tell him? I'm sure he'll want to talk…'

'Yes, of course, of course.'

Wang Di was sure she would never see him again. She stood outside, watching his back receding down the corridor. There was a ping and the boy waved one last time before stepping out of sight and letting the lift take him down with it.

Kevin

When the lift opened, I saw her right away – she was watching the corridor from behind her grill gate, and opened it as soon as she saw me. I almost fell over a pushcart, then a mountain of cardboard boxes because my glasses were all fogged up from the damp and heat of the walk. After I wiped the lenses and put them back on, I saw that the one-bedroom flat was mostly filled up with boxes and rubbish bags brimming over with random items – an empty aquarium, turned upside down, a set of children's books. I followed her as she moved through the narrow space, pushing things out of the way, nudging a box closer to the wall, kicking a bag under a table. Then she swept her hands around her in an arc to say sorry for the mess and I smiled and shook my head and smiled some more.

The old lady was small, smaller than my Ah Ma, but mostly because her back was curved, like she had bent over for years and years and there was no way for her to unbend anymore, she was stuck like that. She stood in front of me and pointed to herself. 'My name is Wang Di,' she said.

'Kevin. Kevin Lim Wei Han.'

We shook hands. It was the first time an adult had introduced herself like that to me and I had to repeat it to myself to try and keep it in my head.

'Sit, sit,' she said in Mandarin, removing a stack of fashion magazines from a chair.

Then she went into the kitchen and put a kettle under the tap, got out two melamine cups. Her teaspoon scraped the bottom of the tin, making me taste metal in my mouth and when she fanned out a handful of biscuits on a plate, her hands shook. I wondered if they always did that or if she was just nervous. As nervous as I was. Then she put everything on an upturned cardboard box and sat down opposite me. While she did all that, she kept her eyes on me, squinting and rounding them in turn.

I pretended not to see and tried not to stare at all her things scattered around me. The boxes and stacks of paper. The blue fabric wardrobe in a corner that had a cartoon print of cats and dogs on it. Her bed, the frame made of rusted metal, just an arm's stretch away. Instead, I tried to figure out how I could say the things I wanted to say.

Then she got up again, brought back a framed picture, and put it into my hands. A black-and-white photograph of a man who looked strangely familiar, but who couldn't be. He had glasses, with lenses almost as thick as my own and something else familiar. My father's eyes, I thought. His straight mouth.

The old woman touched the photograph, and then pointed towards the altar. To the lit, red candles, a plate of apples and oranges, and incense sticks in a tin, smoking away to nothing.

I wanted to tell her I knew he was dead but the only words within my reach sounded harsh, wrong. 'My grandmother, too,' I said in the end.

She nodded, her brown eyes grey at the edges of her pupils, as if the colour were bleeding out.

I dunked the biscuits in my drink and stared at the oily swirls that rose to the surface, willing the words to come. She was tapping on the side of her cup with her fingertips and it was clear that she wanted to say something as well so I looked around me to give her time.

Something on the wall caught my eye and I had to get up to go to it. Clippings, I saw, taped up, from a Chinese newspaper, and a photo of two elderly women.

'Comfort women. They want people to know what happened to them.' She said this in a mixture of Mandarin and Hokkien, the way I turned to English when I couldn't find the words in Chinese. The word she used was *wei an fu*, and I was glad I knew a little about it from the historical programmes they sometimes had on TV.

I nodded. In response, her eyes got shiny and she dropped her head. I realized then, what she meant to say, so for the rest of the time I was in her flat, I made sure not to look away from her so that she would know she didn't have anything to be ashamed about.

We sat down and I explained how I'd found her, showed her the letters that Ah Ma had written and never sent out. All this in Mandarin, and in stops and starts because I couldn't always find the right words.

Then I remembered the photo, the one my mother had cropped with a pair of kitchen scissors so she could slide it in behind the clear plastic compartment in my wallet. It was taken a few years ago at the Chinese Garden. The four of us at the foot of a bridge – me standing in front of my parents and grandmother. All of us squinting, half smiling, none of us quite ready for the camera. What the camera hadn't captured was how my parents had held hands in the garden, and how I had let my grandmother hold mine as we walked along man-made streams and trees and rocks.

'There.' I put my thumbnail right below his face, though it was obvious.

The old woman brought it close to her eyes. She peered at it for the longest time and when she looked up again, she had tears in her eyes. She blinked and rubbed at them, turning away a little. 'He looks so much like the Old One when he was young. Just without glasses.'

'I wear glasses,' I said, stupidly.

The old woman hesitated, then held her hand out. I took my glasses off and gave them to her. 'Yes,' I heard her say, 'your lenses are almost as thick as his.' Her face was a blur but I could hear the rustle of a handkerchief, make out a smudge of white being brought to her face. I let her hold on to them for a little longer so she could cry without feeling embarrassed, and to let myself ask the question I had been wanting to ask. I didn't even have to close my eyes the way I did when jumping into a pool or waiting for a doctor to plunge a needle into my arm.

'Did you…' I began, 'did you lose a child during the war?'

I waited and waited. The air slowed and turned thick hot in the flat. I heard the gasp of air as she breathed in, then, 'Yes.'

I opened my eyes. I thought about my Ah Ma taking my father, still an infant, and running through the woods. I thought about telling my father that he still had a family.

Then she said, 'But it wasn't your father I lost. You're not my grandchild. You can't be.'

'But –'

'I was the Old One's second wife. His first wife died in the war. I – I don't know how… I never let him tell me.'

Then she got up and went away, behind a wall of boxes. I heard her rummaging about, opening cupboard doors and closing them again before she came back with a tin of butter cookies. She placed it on the upturned box in front of me. The lid was so rusted over and dented in places that she had to slide her fingernails under it to wrench it open. In it were spools of coloured thread, needle cases which held needles of varying sizes. The old lady scrabbled underneath all of that and got out two things: a leaflet, which I recognized at once, and a bundle of letters bound together with pink raffia.

'Could you?' She pushed all of them towards me. My hands were shaking when I went through the small stack of letters. I flipped past two before seeing it – my grandmother's handwriting on the front of the envelope. The note inside was so short that I had little trouble reading it.

> *Chia Soon Wei,*
>
> *My name is Lim Mui Joo. I saw your posters in the city today and I felt I had to write to tell you how sorry I am. I lost my family as well. Everyone. I wish you all the best and all the luck in the world for your future.*
>
> *Lim Mui Joo*

I looked up and swallowed. My Ah Ma, I wanted to say. Mui Joo must have been her birth name. Instead, I swallowed again and took a sip from the mug in front of me. I continued staring into the mug until the old lady touched my arm and pushed the leaflet towards me.

I picked it up, cleared my throat, and read. 'My son was lost on 12 Feb 1942. Seventeen months old. Last seen in Bukit Timah.'

'This was the Old One, my husband…looking for your father,' she said, shrinking into herself even more and covering her face with her hands. Fingers ropy and twisted, the joints in her thumbs much too large. I imagined her wheeling her pushcart along, putting an arm into the mouths of public dustbins to root around for empty drink cans the way I'd seen elderly people do sometimes. I always wondered where they lived, if they had families to go home to, if they washed their own clothes – always spotless – the old way, scrubbing them in the kitchen the way Ah Ma used to until Pa threw her washboard away. It was several minutes before she moved again, before she let her hands fall from her face. 'All this time… He tried to tell me once but I wasn't ready. It was selfish of me. I could have just let him talk. But I didn't. It was always about me. Even in the last weeks of his life, his last days, it was about me. I never thought to ask him. I talked and talked and I didn't even finish. Now he's gone –'

I thought if she kept on crying like that, she would lose the colour in her eyes completely. The picture of her husband was still in her lap, and she gripped the corners of the frame now with her fingers as if she wanted to reach into it and pull him out.

'Maybe it's not too late. Maybe there's still a chance.'

My father was never one for telling stories. I remember asking him for one, when I was five or six, when my grandmother still lived on her own in a flat a few streets away. One day my kindergarten teacher asked if everyone got bedtime stories and I had looked around me to see my classmates nodding and nodding. The thought of this new thing had clung to me until it burst out that night as my father was shepherding me into bed.

'Can you tell me a story?' I said.

'A story?'

'Yes.' About dragons and seas and monsters and kings, I hoped, and lions and fairies and other worlds.

My father scratched his chin. 'I have a story about how your ma and I started going out?' he said, his voice going up at the end. He didn't wait for my reply but simply started telling me about how he had gone in to fix a shipping company's air conditioner one day and my mother, then a receptionist, had given him a mug of coffee and a biscuit, and asked if he wanted to grab a bite to eat, her lunch break was in ten minutes. 'And I said, why not?' He was up and walking away when he turned around. 'Oh, I forgot: the end.'

After that night, whenever he was in a good mood (which was not always – maybe once a week), he would sit and tell me stories about *pontianaks* and tree spirits until my mother told him to stop, they were making me cry in my sleep. Otherwise I asked questions which he would try to answer. Questions like, 'What do you remember about the war?' (Not very much, just a victory parade in which he could only see legs.) And, 'Where did you get that scar on your arm?' (He didn't know. He'd always had it.) The last question I asked was, 'What do you remember of Grandpa?' I remember the nibbling pain that I felt in my stomach when he looked away, as if he hadn't heard me. When he did turn back, after a while, his face was blank.

'Nothing,' he said, 'I've never known him.'

The following night, he had come in but we were both silent when he pulled the thin blanket up to my shoulders and left the room. I knew then, that both of us were agreeing to something, that this was as far as it would go, this short-lived ritual of ours. That it was no more.

The hour or so between my arrival home and my parents' seemed to stretch on forever. When they finally came back, I made myself sit still as my mother started on dinner in the kitchen, as my father took a long shower before sitting down in his usual seat at the corner of the sofa. The news was on when I went to him, the shoebox cradled in my arms like a stray cat I'd just brought in from the rain. 'Pa,' I said. 'I want to tell you a story.'

At first my father thought I was going to read him something from a book. One of those stories that was supposed to teach you an important lesson at the end of it. It could have been the way I started: 'You know how sometimes people aren't the people you think they are? But actually it's okay because they become the actual people they are actually pretending to be in the end?'

I had practised this but of course it sounded mad outside my head. The way things do. Like a picture I want to get down on paper but ends up looking nothing like it.

I began again. This time I went slowly and told him about Ah Ma, about what she said at the hospital. Then I stopped for a few seconds to let him absorb what I'd just said, the way the maths teacher leaves the room sometimes after explaining a mathematical rule. He would announce 'I'll leave you to absorb it a little', and then leave the classroom to come back five minutes later smelling of cigarette smoke. I'd expected my father to look surprised. To get up and leave the room. I'd expected him to protest and say that I was mistaken or that I was making things up. But he did nothing like that, just sat back in the sofa and listened.

I went on to tell him about the letters. And the newspaper clipping. Once I got there, all the words spilled out faster and faster. I talked about Lao Shi and the man in Chinatown, and how they helped me find the old lady. She was there, still living, but he wasn't anymore. I paused to take a breath and my father said, 'Who?' His first word in ten minutes.

'Gran – your father...' The moment I said that I started to think I might have been wrong. I might have made a mistake somewhere. The old lady could just be another lonely old person sitting in her flat and wanting company. But now my father's mouth was open, his eyes large. His whole face spelled out 'HOW'. So I showed him the things in the shoebox. The letters and the tape with Ah Ma's voice on it. I took everything out to convince him. But it was for myself as well.

With both hands, my father sifted through the papers, then stared, as if he didn't know where to start.

'How did you –?'

I didn't try to answer him because I knew he wasn't really asking a question. Instead, I left him alone to let him absorb everything I'd said, stopping the tape that I had been using to record what I was telling him and handing him the player so he could listen to what Ah Ma had told me, that day in the hospital. Just as I had. I left him, went into the kitchen for some water because my throat was paper dry and found my mother standing there, half hiding by the doorway like a girl playing hide-and-seek (not very well).

'Did you hear everything?'

She nodded yes.

I drank my water, holding the glass with both hands because I was shaking a little, and got ready to be scolded for having put my nose where it's not supposed to be, for having run around the island on my own like I had.

'Come here.' And what she did next was this – I went to her and she put her arms around me. The last time she did that... I couldn't remember the last time she did that. And she pushed her face into my hair and held us both there. For a while I could hear nothing except the beat of my blood in my head because she had her hands on my ears. It got too warm standing together in the kitchen like that but I didn't care.

Wang Di

As Wang Di opened the gate for the boy the second time that evening, she thought about the few times in her life she had bought a lottery ticket, about the unexpected fortune she had hoped to bring home. She'd imagined saying to the Old One, 'See? We got lucky. It could happen to anyone.' She wished he were here for this now. This windfall, she thought as she stepped back, welcoming the boy, his father and mother into her flat.

It was just as Wang Di thought it would be but quieter. The boy had called again a few hours after he'd left and passed the phone on to his father. Neither of them said much on the phone; he'd hemmed and hawed before asking if it was okay to visit that evening, if she wasn't too busy. Wang Di laughed (wincing as she heard herself – too loud, too shrill) and said please, please come. All three of them arrived just fifteen minutes later, with plastic bags of fruit and *ang ku kueh*, ruby red, in a pastry box. She tried to do everything right, to remember to offer them tea, to keep her tears in and not to let her hands shake too much. She didn't want to scare them away. And he had sat there, knees and hands together. Almost bowing as she got out the biscuit tin again and extracted the piece of paper that she had showed his son earlier. There were a few photos of the Old One from when he was in his forties and she fanned them out on the table so everyone could get a look. Then she handed the tin over to the man, Yong Xiang, and watched as he sifted through the reels of coloured thread and unfolded scraps, an IOU slip, a few receipts with the print on them entirely faded. The bottom of the tin was lined with paper and he pushed a fingernail along the edge until he got hold of the border, and lifted it right up. He knew immediately what it was; he had received a piece of paper just like it a few days ago. This one, though, was decades old, the paper leaf-thin. Under *Cause of Death* someone had typed and crossed out and typed again – war casualty. Chia Jin Lian was just twenty when she died, closer in age to Kevin than he was now. This realization made his face go still and it was a moment before he could speak again, could manage half a smile and say to his son, 'Look, Kevin. It's your…' His mouth hung open as he scrabbled for the words. Next to her, Kim looked from her son to her husband and back again.

'It's your biological grandmother. Her death certificate,' she said, the clarity of her voice shocking and soothing at the same time.

Nobody spoke for a while until Kim picked up the photo, holding the black-and-white snapshot, the one Auntie Tin had given to Wang Di so long ago, to her husband's face. 'You look like him,' she declared. Everyone else looked from the photo to Yong Xiang's face, growing pink from the heat and the tumult from all this information, and nodded sad and silent yeses.

Then Wei Han brought out the letters, the newspaper clippings, and the notices – exact replicas of the one she had just shown them.

'I found them after my grandmother passed away,' the boy said.

Wang Di held on to the sheaf of papers, turning them this way and that, and smiled. 'I can't read them. Never went to school.'

'Oh, I could read them to you if you like,' said Kim. And she did. Stopping in places to swallow a little, her throat cracked from the effort of telling. When she was done and Wang Di looked up again, she saw that Yong Xiang was standing by the window. He seemed to be looking at something far away. No one spoke for a while.

Wang Di took a deep breath and let it out. 'I can't imagine what it must have been like for them. Both of them.'

'I think she wanted to return him. But –' Kim stopped there, trying to come up with the right words.

'It can be difficult to give things up,' said Kevin. Everyone turned to look at him but he was too busy pressing buttons on the gadget in his hands to notice.

That night, Wang Di lay in bed for a long time, staring into the dark of her eyelids. Finally, she grew tired of waiting for sleep and got out of bed.

She couldn't stop thinking about what the boy had said. How it was difficult to give things up. She thought about her decades-old habit of bringing things home, things that meant nothing and had no place in her flat. She thought about how it had begun. How it had grown from squirrelling away things just to have the pretence of control over her life in that little room, to this accumulated mayhem taking over her apartment now, more than fifty years later.

The next day, Wang Di began undoing her habit the only way she knew how.

She started right where she was, in Red Hill where, years ago, her mother had said Huay's family had moved. She went to each coffee shop and headed straight for the drinks seller – always the one with all the news, all the gossip – and asked if they knew of a family who had lived in the kampong, a family named Seetoh. Then she talked to everyone around who looked above the age of seventy, sipping their morning coffee, dipping bread into a saucer of soft-boiled eggs. It helped that the name was so rare, a bright songbird in a sea of Tans and Lees. Still, she felt like giving up after fielding hours of shrugs and 'don't knows' trudging from one coffee shop to the other. Some people wanted to help, most people had something to say. Sometimes it was just, 'Sorry, auntie, I don't know anyone by that name,' or '*Ah-mhm*, were they Cantonese?' 'No,' she would answer. Hokkien. Seetoh and Hokkien, she thought, even rarer. And they would say no, no. They didn't think they were thinking about the same family at all.

'Please be lucky, please,' she said as she got within sight of the eighth coffee shop, crowded with lunch-goers.

The drinks man was pouring freshly brewed coffee into a coffee sock from high up, above his head. 'Hello, *kopi?*'

It would be her fifth of the day and her change purse was getting lighter so she went straight to the point. 'Young man, do you know anyone called Seetoh? They lived around here years ago, after the war.'

'Seetoh, Seetoh, Seetoh…' He left to go into the back kitchen. 'MA! DO YOU KNOW ANYONE CALLED SEETOH?'

When he came back, it was with a woman around her age, a little younger. She came out from behind the counter and Wang Di tried to stand up straight as she got closer. 'Are you looking for Seetoh?' the woman asked.

Wang Di nodded.

'Follow me.'

They exchanged pleasantries as they walked. 'The weather, so hot.' 'Everything is becoming more and more expensive.' 'All my children want to leave, go to Australia.' Until they were standing in front of a shop.

'Seetoh Minimart,' the woman said, pointing to the sign.

Wang Di started to thank the woman but she had already turned away, was weaving through the midday shopping crowd back to her stall. It might not be them. Even if it is them they might not want to talk. Don't be disappointed, she told herself.

A chime went ding-dong as she entered the shop. The old lady felt a little like she was entering home. The store was little, the size of her flat, and squashed tight with four narrow aisles. Boxes and boxes up the walls, along the floor. Every inch of space.

'Hello? Anyone?'

There was a shuffling, the sound of a cardboard box tumbling to the ground. 'Ow.'

'HELLO?'

'WAIT *AH*, WAIT.' The person who came out from behind the aisles was smaller than the old lady. Huay? Wang Di thought. She wanted to squint and rub her eyes. The woman was still frowning. 'Do you need help looking for something?'

When they finally sat down, squeezing their way past the boxes, into the back room, Wang Di told her that she used to live in Hougang, and stuttered a little before asking if she was part of the family who lived behind a little convenience store. The woman replied yes and shifted in her seat, as if she knew what was coming.

'I knew your sister. Huay. I'm here because I promised her, decades ago, that I would look for her family. We lived together for over two years. During the war.' Then she told the woman about the black-and-white house, said how sorry she was to have waited for so long. 'She told me all about you. She said you were her favourite, the baby in the family.'

The baby, now sixty-five, took a few deep breaths as she wiped her face with her sleeve. 'I thought she had left us. That's what they told me. She left us to get married to a Japanese officer.'

Wang Di said nothing.

'I never believed it. All those things people were saying. She would have written, at the very least.'

'Of course she would have.'

'How did she die?'

Though she had predicted the question would come, had practised answering it over and over again the night before, sitting in
front of Huay's sister made her want to change her mind. Would it
be kinder, she wondered, if she told her that Huay had not suffered
and left it at that?

'She fell ill. She was so sick that she got confused and tried to
escape. So they killed her.'

'How?'

'She was shot.'

There was a long silence. Wang Di listened as the woman ground
her teeth.

'At least it was quick.' She sighed – half relief, half sorrow. 'You
know, I was so sure that she would come back to find us gone that I
wrote a letter. Left it in the kitchen.'

'I'm sorry.'

'I remember her being taken away. I remember even though
everyone told me to forget. And I always hoped that she would come
back. But at least now I know.'

'She was always kind. She taught me to write my name.'

The woman smiled. 'Yes. She wanted to become a teacher.'

A week after their first meeting, Yong Xiang drove Kevin and Wang
Di to the national archives. It was raining and he drove slowly, knowing that Wang Di wasn't used to the movements of the van, especially
with it raining so hard that she couldn't see past the windscreen,
could only see red, mottled lights all around her. When she put a
hand to her head, he told her to press her fingers into the insides of
her wrist if she felt motion sick. It sometimes helped his wife, he said.

The downpour became a drizzle as they got closer to the city. By
the time they turned into the road that led to the national archives,
the rain had stopped. The building was modest, just four storeys high.

When they went in, Yong Xiang signed his name in a book as the receptionist chatted with someone over the phone. She smiled and nodded at him as if she'd been expecting him. Them. Wang Di said nothing, just followed them into a room filled with wide tables and low shelves stacked with files and books. It smelled of old paper and wood and must. Smells she knew and was familiar with. Kevin took the old lady by the elbow, led her to one of the computers lined up against the wall and guided her into a chair, steadying the wheels with one foot as she lowered herself into the seat.

Wang Di let them take care of everything. Yong Xiang tapping and clicking away on the computer while Kevin clamped the headset over her head. They had listened to the reel a few days ago, sat at this very table, leaned in over their elbows, and listened. Yong Xiang had gone over the recordings, all six of them, twice over.

'Okay?' he asked, giving her the thumbs up.

She said yes and held on to the headset. It was heavier than she thought it would be and she swayed her head back and forth, trying to make sure that it wouldn't fall off.

He pressed a button and a low buzz flooded her ears. Someone cleared his throat. There was a crackle of paper, then a billow of exhaled air, straight into her ear.

'Please state your name.' A man's voice, a stranger.

Another throat rattle, then, 'My name is Chia Soon Wei.'

'I was fifteen when I got my first job, considered quite late for the boys in my neighbourhood,' the Old One said. *'But my father made me stay in school. Said that he would beat me to within an inch of my life if I ever set foot in a farm, or a factory. He wanted me to do something else, learn an easier trade, or even better, become a man of letters. I could read and write, I could, but I never liked books very much. They seemed so removed from the rest of the world – the world that I knew anyway. I forget why but I decided to become an apprentice*

for a tailor, a friend of a relative. All I did for the first few months was measure out lengths of fabric that people came to buy but I thought this seemed practical. Everyone needs clothes and I could eventually have a store of my own, if I did well enough. That's what I longed for. To have a place of my own.

'I was still working at Mr Tan's shop when Japan invaded China. I remember volunteers coming around to collect money, donations for the resistance army in China, and Mr Tan saying that we had to do all we could for our people back home. I donated a little money. I didn't tell him this but I didn't think of China as home anymore. My parents had long stopped writing to the family that was left in our village. I think a lot of people came to Singapore thinking to go back once they made enough money… There was always talk about going back but as the years went by, Singapore became home. Myself, I never thought about leaving. I was only two when we left so I remember nothing about Chaozhou. Home is where you build your own family. In 1939, I was newly married to a girl from the same kampong. We had always known each other and our parents got along and approved. She moved in with me and my parents the way people did in those days. This was home. We were just starting to build a life for ourselves.

'We were just beginning. I was just beginning, in a way. About a year later, we had a child, a boy. Suddenly, there was someone else to take care of. It made me feel different, less of a person, and more. Because there was a part of me in that little boy, you see? But I was more because I had real responsibilities now. I'd helped create a human being. I felt so helpless when things started to go wrong. My son was about a year old when my employer let me go because business was being affected by the war in China.

'We never thought that the Japanese would come to Singapore. That even if they did, the British forces would see them off. Then in December, they bombed the naval base, which was in the north of the island, and the city centre. From that day on, I began stockpiling food. I think a lot of people did. We couldn't imagine it before, but after that day, people started getting scared. I mean, I was still optimistic but every day, I returned home after work with a few cans of powdered milk, pickled vegetables, sometimes a slice of salted fish wrapped *in newspaper. I didn't say this to my wife but I felt that something was going to happen. When she stumbled upon the cupboard full of tins – she was bound to because she was the one managing the kitchen – she just looked at me, as if she knew.'*

The interviewer said, *'So it was only after that first bombing in December that you realized that Singapore was going to be implicated in the war?'*

'Yes. Everyone seemed so confident. We all thought there was no way... Even after that attack, I thought – we thought – that it would pass. That the Japanese would move on. I don't know. Maybe because we were a small island. I thought, why would they want a little island like ours?

'The rest of December 1941 was relatively quiet. There were several false alarms, with the sirens going off for no reason. After a while, people started to ignore them. Life went on, as it does. People went to work and school, bought and sold things at the market. Then at the end of the month, the air raids started again. This time, we could hear the planes roaring over our heads. It continued every night for a week. Each night it woke my little boy and he would scream as my wife and I brought him to the shelter, just a little way from our home. All of us, my parents, our neighbours, about fifteen to twenty of us, would cram into that shelter. It was little more than a dugout reinforced around the sides with wooden planks and sandbags. It had a zinc roof so that when it rained, there would be such a racket, the tap-tap-tap of raindrops close to our heads. My parents would be the last to arrive because my mother had arthritic knees. She would lean on my father and he would support her even though his own legs were bad. They would be the last to arrive. Each time I saw that, I thought, that was love.

'It got worse in January. That's when they began to attack us during the day. We tried to go on with life as usual. I went to work whenever I could, doing odd jobs as a labourer. Sometimes the sirens rang all day so I couldn't even leave the house. My wife occupied herself by preparing for the Lunar New Year celebrations. She wanted to go to the market to buy a hen, she said, there was still time to fatten one up before reunion dinner on New Year's Eve. I said yes but we never got around to it... One day, I saw the planes as I ran

from a construction site I was working on to the public shelter. I only saw them for a moment but they were majestic things – sleek and gleaming in the sunlight. At first I couldn't figure out whose planes they were. When I realized that they belonged to the Japanese, I felt foolish. I thought – many of us had thought – that their planes couldn't possibly match up to the ones flown by the British army. And yet there they were, flying over us, day after day, dropping bombs, and the British army didn't – couldn't – do anything about it...

'It went on for the rest of the month, and into February. I heard that many people were killed during these raids, mostly because of flying shrapnel. Our kampong didn't suffer a hit but I'll always remember this cloud of thick, black smoke rising far away, blocking out the sun. During the next couple of weeks, we spent so much time in the shelter that my wife sometimes brought bread and kaya *along, dealing out slices whenever someone got hungry. We would take turns holding our toddler. Often he would sleep right through until we got the all clear to go back into our homes.'*

The interviewer said, *'When did you realize the Japanese were gaining the upper hand?'*

'I didn't know. The British were so optimistic on the radio. Churchill sounded strong, confident. I didn't think the island was going to fall but there were whispers about the Japanese invading part of the island; villages in the north. But I didn't pay much attention to it. Just rumours. Even if it were true, we lived close to the south of the island and I had hoped that the resistance fighters and the armies would stop them before they got any closer. A few of our neighbours packed up and left, we saw them making their way with cloth bags filled with a few supplies. I don't know where they were headed. But we stayed.

'And anyway, I couldn't think about anything else but what was in front of me – taking care of my family, putting food on the table, my job. Between running to the shelter and waiting for the shelling and bombing to come to an end, I didn't have the time or energy to think about much else. My mother and wife were also busy preparing for the Lunar New Year. It's strange to think of it now but we were excited about it – as if it were any other year. I

remember my neighbours had bought fireworks. Their children couldn't wait and set off a string of them a week before; it gave the people living close to them the fright of their lives – they thought it was gunfire or bombs or something. My wife. She was so cheerful when I returned home after work one evening and I asked why. She said she was lucky, she got the last bit of duck from the hawker. She had saved up for months for it. That was the day before...before it happened. Up until then, I felt that things would be okay if we just made it past the new year, somehow.'

The Old One sighed. There was the sound of a chair being scraped across the floor. *'It started early in the day. The sound of guns, of gunfire. I found out that the British and a local resistance army were fighting the Japs, but I only heard it through the news and word of mouth much later. That day, all we knew was that it sounded close, the fighting, so we stayed in the air-raid shelter until it stopped. I remember my boy playing with a rattan ball that a neighbour had given him for his first birthday. He had just started to walk on his own and the whole time we were in that shelter, he was stumbling around, picking the ball up and then throwing it again. He had got used to the noise the way some people got used to living near the railway and having trains roar past their homes every day.*

'There was a lull in the sound of gunfire, and for no reason at all I thought "we have to leave". Just like that. Then I told my family, said we should go back into the house to pack up. Neither my parents nor my wife protested. While my wife packed clothing for all of us, I went into the kitchen to retrieve some of the food that I had put away. It was then that I heard the sound of heavy vehicles nearby. Nothing else. Just the sound of engines. I thought it might be the British troops passing through so I carried on packing. We were almost ready to leave when I heard the crunch of tyres on sand and then footsteps coming our way.

'Someone yelled in Hokkien and Mandarin, telling us to step out of our homes. I remember walking out of the house, holding my hand out behind me to tell my family to stay put. There were soldiers, some of them carrying rifles, others with swords fastened to their belts. They looked tired and dishevelled,

as if they'd all been dragged through the forest all morning. Some of them had stains on their uniforms the colour of dark mud. Blood, I later realized. These were Japanese soldiers.

'There was one man. I remember him. He was the one who told us to come out. He was standing next to another man who kept turning to him, speaking in Japanese. He yelled again, his face so distorted by his wide-open mouth that I felt a wild urge to laugh. Until he punctuated his words by firing a pistol into the air at the end of his speech. Soon, everyone was standing outside their houses, in the sun. I felt my wife clutch the back of my shirt, heard my son cry. He sounded so far away but I turned and he was right there, in her arms.

'There was no more talking. A few of the soldiers came forward and corralled us into a circle, tighter and tighter, jabbing with their bayonets. While they did this, a few others assembled themselves in front of us, into a row, their weapons pointed. My son was still crying. So were the neighbours' children. There was nothing but the sound of them and their mothers trying to shush them. As if silence would help. One of the soldiers said something, made a joke I guess, because the others responded by laughing. The sound of their laughter cracked right through the air and for a second there was a lull in the children's cries.

'The first shots rang out. There were screams. People panicking. The bodies around me surged left and right. I could only pull my wife close, watch her curve her body around our child. Then I felt a bolt of fire in my leg and fell. So did everyone else. That was how it ended.

'When I woke up in the hospital, they told me that the surgeon had removed a bullet from my left leg. There was also a stab wound in my chest, just miss-ing my lung. The doctor said I was lucky to be alive. I asked them where my family was. They couldn't tell me. I said I had to go back to the village to look for them, they might still be there, I said. Or they could be in another hospital. The nurse just shook her head in silence before turning her face away. The painkillers carried me off to sleep for several hours. Later on, when I asked again, she finally told me that I'd been the only one they found alive.'

'*You were the only one to survive?*' the interviewer said.

There was a long silence before Soon Wei continued. '*I got discharged two weeks later and went back there. To the kampong. There was no one around. The houses were all empty and it was a while before I found my own. I could hardly distinguish it from the others – so changed it was by the absence of life and sound. The way a loved one might look different, unrecognizable, when emptied of themselves. I was using a crutch and I remember sliding over the mud because it had rained heavily that morning. Inside, anything of any value had been taken. Even the single gold pendant my in-laws had given to my wife as part of her bride price, even that, they'd found and taken. There was nothing to save. Nothing was left.*

'*After that I went to the police for help but the moment I entered the station I knew there was little hope. Something seemed to be going on. People moving in and out with boxes. Chaos. I waited all day to speak to someone before a young man took pity on me and tried to help. He was Indian and used a bit of English, a bit of dialect to tell me that he was new – they had got rid of all the Chinese police officers. I gave him my address and tried to tell him about my family but it was difficult. I was also in pain, not fully recovered from my injuries. He saw that and gave me a glass of water, then told me to return the next day.*

'*When I arrived the following morning, the man was there, waiting. He asked me to follow him outside, where he had parked his bicycle, pointed at the pillion seat at the back and told me to get on. He took me to the morgue. I – I had never seen so many bodies in one place. Laid out on tables and floors, even in the corridor. The person in charge looked like he had not slept for days but he took the time to lead me to one body after another. I found my wife, eventually. I wouldn't have recognized her if not for the little birthmark on her ankle. Then I found my parents, right next to each other, even in death. The man said he would look out for my son but that it could be difficult, with children – their bodies were small and easily carried away. He stopped himself then. I think he realized that he had said too much. He told me that he would be in contact with the police if he found anyone and advised me to* keep checking with them, and that gave me hope. I went to the station almost every day to ask about my son and put up notices looking for him. It was only a few years later, after the war, that I came to accept that he was gone. It was made real, I guess, after the Japanese surrendered the island. After things started to shift back into place.

'I visited the kampong again. Everything looked so – normal. Everyone was back on the streets, selling food, making money, trying to earn a living. I arrived home, or where it used to be, and all that was left was wreckage. Just ash and charred wood where our lives used to be. There was a big patch in front of the houses where the earth had been turned over and patted down. I lowered myself into a squat, put my hand to the ground. There was nothing left. It was as if I had dreamed it all, what happened. I was the only one who could prove it but the only evidence I had was the absence of things… Later on, I heard that the Japanese did it as revenge. The resistance army had fought back and killed many of their soldiers and what they did in our village had been payback. But I don't know. It's just something I heard.'

The interviewer said, 'The war crimes trial after the war. Did you provide the tribunal with your testimony?'

'No. I didn't know they were collecting testimonies. Only found out afterwards. I remember listening to the news on the radio and hearing about it. My wife – my new wife – switched it off. She had suffered during the war as well and she didn't want to be reminded of what had happened. To her. At the time, I thought she was right. Why dwell on the past? It was over with and I wanted to look ahead, continue with our lives. I don't know if that was the right thing to do. But I am here now. It's been many years but I remember everything. That's something I hadn't counted on. I remember everything.'

Kevin

A month after we found Wang Di *Ah Por* (different from what I call my grandmother, because I didn't want Ah Ma to think I'd replaced her), my father put down his coffee cup at breakfast and said that it was time. My eyes went to the clock on the wall but then he continued and said it was time to clear Ah Ma's things out of the room, we couldn't let it all sit there collecting dust.

'You're growing up,' he said, as if seeing me for the first time in years. 'You're going to need the space for a bigger desk and a new bookshelf. Your own room.'

When breakfast was finished, the three of us went into my bedroom and started with the little things. My mother got all of Ah Ma's clothes out of the dresser, and collected everything sitting on top of it – a comb, countless shiny, black hairpins in a chipped teacup, a tin of scented talcum powder, and various bottles of herbal oils, each for a different kind of discomfort or pain – all of them, in a box. While she did that my father stripped the bed for the last time and put her blanket and wooden pillow in a plastic bag. Once that was done, he said it would be better if we went outside, he needed the space to get the mattress out of the door. My mother and I stood at the doorway, looking at the things we had gathered and put in the living room, just a few items, really. She didn't take up much space. When you put it all together, her belongings wouldn't have weighed much more than she did. For a few minutes, we listened to my father grunting, shifting things about, until he said 'Oh' and everything went quiet.

'Xiang? You okay? Have you hurt your back again?'

My father said nothing but he came towards us, rubbing his head and holding out a square of paper. We watched as he unfolded it and read it quickly to himself, half whispering, half breathing the words out every now and then.

'It's a letter to Ma. From him...' We watched him read it again, his eyes going from left to right and down the page. He looked a little dazed when he was done, and tried to smile to let us know he was okay. Then he handed the letter over to my mother and went back to moving the mattress and dismantling the single wooden bed. While he did that, my mother and I sat on the sofa; I looked over her shoulder as she read it out for me.

When we were done putting everything into trash bags, I helped my father drag first the mattress, then the bedside table and the chest of drawers to the skip. Afterwards, when I got back home, it was like going into a stranger's room. Going in past that familiar scratched up door and finding my things in that changed space, minus a bed and the tiny bottles of ointment that Ah Ma used to scatter around the room. Minus her.

I thought it was a good time to look at what I had done and I lined up all the tapes I had, all five of them, on my bed. Each one had a different label on the front.

What it sounds like to be bullied
How to know when Pa is going into his Dark Place
What Ah Ma said
What I found out
Wang Di Ah Por

The last one was hardly used. I was putting it back in the tape recorder when my mother knocked on the door. It was the first time she did that, knocking, and it made me feel strange saying 'yes?'

'Everything okay? How's your holiday project coming along?'

'It's okay, I think. I mean, I think I know how I'm going to do the show and tell.' Then I went on to tell her about how I was going to do it, taking bits of sound from each tape I had made and putting it all into a five-minute segment. I would make it into a story. I could picture my classmates sniggering while I gave my talk. Even Ms Pereira might laugh, at least when she thought no one was looking. But I didn't care. 'You see? A sound story,' I said and waited for her to react. She didn't say anything at first but when her face cracked from her smile – that was how wide her smile was – I knew it would be okay.

We brought the letter along when we visited Wang Di Ah Por the next day. This time, it was my father who read it out. As he read, she closed her eyes to listen to him. When she heard her name being read out, her eyes flew open like someone shocked awake, but happy (the way I wake up on Saturday and Sunday mornings, much too early, before realizing that I can go back to sleep).

Lim Mui Joo,

  Thank you for writing to me and for your well wishes.

  Perhaps this sounds strange but there is something familiar about you (your name? the way you write/speak?) that makes me think we might have known each other in this life (or the last). Life has surprised me so much these past few years that I discount nothing these days. I received a few messages as a result of the notices I put up. None of them have led me to finding my family but almost all of them have led me to kindness. One of them led me to a matchmaker who introduced me to my new wife. Wang Di was also affected by the

*war. She still has nightmares and wakes up from them in the night.
I don't know how to help her and I can't as long as there are things
I have not come to terms with myself. My belief is time will help. I
can only wait.*

*I'm sorry that you've lost people too. I cannot imagine how hard it
was for you to tell me this and I wish you all the best for your future.*

Best wishes,

      Chia Soon Wei

When he was done reading, my father pressed the letter into her
hands and said that she should keep it. Ah Por could only nod and
smile.

It was that evening that Wang Di Ah Por told me she needed my
help. She said it while my father was changing a light bulb that he
saw was blown out and my mother was pretending to wash the mugs
that we'd drunk from, secretly checking to make sure that there was
enough food in her cupboards while we talked. I had been waiting for
it, I'd seen it from the way Ah Por looked – that day at the archives.
So when she came to me, I told her it was a great idea and maybe we
could have her story put along with the rest. We went to the national
archives again that week, just the two of us. When we arrived, the
person at the desk looked at us as though she thought we were lost
and needed directions to somewhere else.

'Eh, wait… I recognize you. You've been here before. Are you
looking for something?'

'We just want to ask if Ah Por, my…grandmother can come and
be interviewed. You're doing a history project, right? About the
Japanese Occupation?'

'Oh, why didn't you say so.' She was smiling as she picked up
the phone on her desk. 'But I'm not in charge of that. You'll have
to go to the other department and they will arrange for someone
to interview you. Let me just call them to see if there's a colleague

you can speak to…' And she held out a finger to mean she wanted me to stay right there.

I told all this to Ah Por and she started to shake her head no.

'Tell her not to call anyone. I don't want to speak to a stranger. Tell her I only want you to do the recording.'

I waved my hand to get the woman's attention. Her eyebrows leaped up and she put her hand over the receiver of the phone. 'No one's picking up. They must be out for lunch.'

'She doesn't want to have someone else interview her. She only wants me to do it.'

'Oh. I'm afraid that's not… I don't think they'll do that. You see, it all has to be done by a professional. Someone trained to do this type of thing. The interviews will be held in a room with specialized equipment. They can't just allow *anyone* to do it… How old are you anyway?'

I told Ah Por what the woman had just said and she shook her head no no no again, turned and started to walk out of the door. She didn't slow down until we were close to the bus stop.

It was there, sitting in that empty bus stop, with the cars whizzing past much too quickly, that we decided what we would do.

I tried to be professional, like the woman said, and spent all that evening coming up with questions to ask Wang Di Ah Por. We agreed I would visit after remedial class the following afternoon, and then every other day for the rest of the June holiday so I would have time to do my school work. It was one of the things she always asked me after, 'Have you eaten?' 'Are you working hard at school?' I would say yes and she would say it was one of the most important things to do, learn to read and write.

The first thing I did upon arriving at her flat for our first interview was to decide on where to sit. The best place, I thought, would be the dinner table, or what was supposed to be it except it was covered in everything that had nothing to do with eating. I cleared the table top, made sure to pick two chairs that we could comfortably sit in for a long time and arranged them so we would be facing each other. Then I placed the tape recorder right in the middle and asked Ah Por to sit because we were about to begin. That's when she started twisting her hands together the way she does when she gets nervous, and I got nervous too, knowing how important this was for her. The feeling went away the moment I pressed the button on the recorder. I started by asking her name and then I read the first question that I had come up with: 'What happened at the end of 1941?'

I had a whole list of them but after the initial question, I didn't need to say a word. All I had to do was show up and sit across from her and press the red button on the recorder. She had been saving her story up for so long that it was all she could do to keep from bursting with it. The first time, I got there after my remedial classes and stayed for three hours. It took quite a lot out of her, all that talking. She said some of it in Chinese and some of it in Hokkien, which I didn't always understand. These were the parts I would have to work out afterwards, at home, by playing the tapes over and asking my mother. I was just about to ask if she was okay, she looked a little pale, when she asked me the same thing.

'Of course. Of course, I'm okay.'

'I was thinking if this might be just…a little too…'

But I assured her that I was fine. It was only when I got home that I felt it, the weight of all her words sitting in my chest. The only way I could feel better again was by putting it all down on paper. That was how I spent the next few weeks, interviewing her during the day, and then writing it all out in my own words, telling her story as best as I could. I didn't think about it when I started the first chapter with the heading 'Wang Di – 1941' – but it looked right when I read it over.

So I began all the other chapters like that. With her name, because the stories belonged to her, and the year it was set in.

It was during the third session that I noticed the changes in her flat. I could tell by how much I could stretch my arms out, it was like I could grow a little each time, more and more as the boxes and things shoved up against the wall vanished from her home. I wanted to say something, the way my mother tells me 'good job!' whenever I figure out the answer to a difficult question all on my own. I thought it would be strange though, to say something like that to someone five times my own age. So what I said instead was, 'I like your rug' when I saw that she had brought home a newish-looking carpet and laid it out where the boxes used to be, in a heap. And 'your chairs are so comfortable' when she got rid of all the magazines and papers that had been occupying the seats by the dinner table. All she did when I said those things was smile and nod.

The June holidays were almost over when we got near the end. I knew it was near the end because she kept repeating it, to herself, mostly. 'Almost done,' she would say, 'almost done.' Like she was looking at a finishing line some way ahead and was walking towards it even though she was exhausted. She was telling me the part about her leaving the comfort house when she fell silent and reached out to stop the recording. She had never told this part to anyone and didn't know if she could, she said.

'All that… Everything I just told you. Everything's true.' Her eyes were wide and she looked like she had just realized this herself, or remembered it, right at that moment, that it had happened to her – the things she told me, had been telling me over the past few weeks. And I understood just then that she was reliving each moment while she spoke, while we sat at the table across from each other in her flat. She would have to go to bed alone that night and her dreams would be her only company.

I wanted to suggest a little break, to get her to eat the kueh that I'd brought. It would be easy, comforting. Instead, I sat there and waited until she was ready. Sometimes all you had to do to get someone to talk was to be silent.

Wang Di

I ran until I couldn't anymore, then I walked and walked for what seemed like hours but it could have been nothing, no more than fifteen minutes. Once or twice, I fell but I kept going because I was too terrified to stop; for as long as I kept moving, I would be getting further away from the house in the woods and I wouldn't have to look at his face – the stillness of it, his absolute quiet. 'I'm going to get you home,' I whispered. I pictured finding a hospital and leaving him there. He would be safe and he would go to someone who wanted a baby. There's always someone who wants a baby boy, I thought. But another part of me imagined arriving home with him in my arms. There, the image froze. Try as I might, I couldn't bring to mind the faces of my parents at the door, letting me in. Instead I saw myself, as easily as I saw my feet, scratched and muddied by the undergrowth, standing and waiting in front of a closed door that would never be opened to me. I was still trying to picture my parents' faces when I came upon a clearing and a wide field beyond it. There were a few huts, their roofs fallen in, walls sloping to the ground. Still I called out. No answer. Then I looked down into my arms. At his closed eyes, his eyebrows, so soft they were hardly there. His cupid's-bow lips were pale, almost blue. Cold. My legs wouldn't work anymore so I sat, leaned back against a tree and closed my eyes.

When I woke up, I was in hospital. The child was next to me. The first thing I said to the nurse was a lie: 'The child isn't mine. I found him.' The words came so easily, they must have been right. 'He belongs to someone else,' I added. I remember her face, kind, distant, unreadable. She took him away and I fell asleep again, this time for days.

That is one story.

Or, I sat for a long time in the clearing waiting for him to open his eyes, touching his face, holding my ear above his nose to try and hear him breathe. I sat there as the sun crept from east to west, as a light rain fell in the late afternoon. The crickets were starting up when I accepted that he wouldn't, that his quiet was permanent, there would be no waking him. And there I was, surrounded by different trees, choosing which one to bury him under. I chose a young angsana and broke into the ground with my fingers. The damp soil came away in my hands quite easily. I made a deep hollow in the earth, smoothed the cloth around him again to cover his face, and put him in. It took everything I had to push the soil over him, patting it firm when that was done. I sat for a long time touching my hand to his resting place. I told myself he was safe, that there was nothing he would have to fear anymore. When I woke, I was somewhere else.

Or, I called out in the clearing and an old woman, so small and bent that the grass had hidden her completely, stepped out from within the field. She had been foraging, had a little basket filled with leaves and tapioca in the crook of her arm. She asked if I was okay and if I needed help. Her hut was just ten minutes' walk away, she said. It was a tiny village – no more than eight families – and as we approached, people came out to look or stared from their doorways. She said not to mind them, and led me in. It was just her and her husband, no one else, and she made me a meal from the things she'd found. Yam and rice, the porridge tinged orange from the sweet root. While I ate, she fed the child for me, spooning the gruel into his mouth. There were a few goats in the village, she said, and if she asked she might be able to get some milk. There was a softness in her voice, and I thought about asking where the rest of her family was but I didn't, afraid of the answer. Before it got dark, her husband went out and returned with a rattan mat. They made a bed for me in the sitting room, gathered as many blankets as they could find to make it comfortable, and told me I could stay for as long as I needed to. I thanked them and waited for them to fall asleep. Before I left, I made sure the baby was warm and nestled in the middle of the blankets. The last words I said to him were: 'I told you I would find you a home.' I stumbled for half an hour in the twilight until I became too exhausted to continue and ended up back in the clearing, under a tree. I slept until I was found again.

'But,' he said, 'but which one is true?'

I said all of them were. All of them. Every one of the things I told him, with my thousands and thousands of words and sounds, every one of them was true.

'But…' he repeated. The furrows between his eyebrows getting deeper, pinched in.

So I asked him, 'Which one do you think is true?'

He took his time, and when he looked up, he was sure.

Acknowledgements

A great number of books and articles and documentaries about comfort women and the Asia-Pacific War have aided and propelled the writing of this novel, especially *The Rape of Nanking* by Iris Chang; *Omdat Wij Mooi Waren* (*Because We Were Beautiful*), a documentary by Frank van Osch.

Thank you, Nelle Andrew, for your bold guiding hand. Thank you, Marilia Savvides and the rest of the team at Peters, Fraser + Dunlop.

Thank you, Juliet Mabey, for your electric wisdom. Thanks to all at Oneworld for their support and warmth, especially Kate Bland, Anne Bihan, Alyson Coombes and Paul Nash, all of whom helped put the book together, piece by piece.

Thank you, Peter Joseph, John Glynn and Natalie Hallak at Hanover Square Press for making a safe home for Wang Di in the US.

Thanks to my parents, who generously allowed me to use our family history in this novel. (And who are still looking, sometimes, for that lost child.)

Thanks to my fellow writers, Bette Adriaanse, Erik Boman and Genevieve Hudson, for your eyes. Thanks to Cheryl Goh, for your safe pair of hands.

Thank you, Marco.

© Aline Bouma

JING-JING LEE was born and raised in Singapore. She has a master's degree in Creative Writing from the University of Oxford and has published poetry and short stories in several journals and anthologies. Jing-Jing's novella, *If I Could Tell You*, was published by Marshall Cavendish in 2013. Her debut poetry collection, *And Other Rivers*, was published by Math Paper Press in 2015. *How We Disappeared* is her first novel. She currently lives in Amsterdam.